Rhodesia's Hangover

Rhodesia's Hangover

An African dilemma

P.P.K. Walther

authorHOUSE®

AuthorHouse™
1663 Liberty Drive
Bloomington, IN 47403
www.authorhouse.com
Phone: 1-800-839-8640

First published by AuthorHouse   07/28/2011

ISBN: 978-1-4567-8485-0 (sc)
ISBN: 978-1-4567-8524-6 (ebk)

Printed in the United States of America

Any people depicted in stock imagery provided by Thinkstock are models, and such images are being used for illustrative purposes only.
Certain stock imagery © Thinkstock.

This book is printed on acid-free paper.

All events described in this book, except for those on public record, are fictional and are not real descriptions of real people, living or dead. Historical events are reported from the authors' point of view only.

Dr. Robert Fenn wishes to assert his rights as author.

Acknowledgements

The Author would like to thank all the people who have input, in some form or other, to the story in this book. Especial thanks must go to two ex Rhodesian Special Forces soldiers (Dave and Chris., one a Selous Scout and the other one Rhodesian S.A.S. squadron) who gave freely of their memories and stories. Neither wish to be named as they still fear that their war service may compromise their civilian lives *(even in South Africa Chidudu exerts a real influence!)*. One ex South African 'Reccie' (Craig, NOT the Craig in this story!) has become a good friend and a great fount of technical information.

Many books on the *Chimerunga* were read, some of those tales have been re-cycled, re-dressed and re-told.

I also owe a debt of gratitude to USS who provide support.

P.P.K.W.

'We can shrink from change, yet is there anything that can come into being without it? What does Nature hold dearer, or more proper to herself? . . . . Do you not see, then, that change in yourself is of the same order, and no less necessary to Nature?

Meditations of Marcus Aurelius, Roman Emperor & Philosopher A.D. 168

Prelude

By the end of each day he was exhausted, physically and mentally. 'Just why does everybody have to be so bleddy dumb?' he thought; why couldn't they solve the problems for themselves instead of loading him with all the day-to-day crap minor problems. He paid 'em to solve problems themselves, not run to him all the time!

He reached into the bottom desk drawer and lifted out the bottle of 'Oude Meester' and his well used glass. Looking at the glass, he saw that he could hardly see through it, 'What the hell?' he thought loudly to himself 'the brandy'll sterilise the glass, so I'll have no bother!' He poured himself a generous dop and simultaneously thought 'Whoa down there boy, you've got to drive home tonight.' He knew somewhere deep in the back of his mind that he was abusing, not using, the alcohol, but it sometimes helped him sleep at night and fight off the mental demons of his time in the Rhodesian bush.

"Stuff it", he said loudly to his empty office, "this kak'll still be waiting here for me tomorrow morning and maybe I can get a run at it and finish it first thing." With that he stood up and walked to the office door. Before he left, he looked around and still felt that small tingle of pride when he realised that all this it was all his, this second office including the problems, built by his own efforts, so worth working to keep going despite the problems.

By the time he was at his car, his thoughts were again with his family. Suzy, he knew, was loosing patience with his recent behaviour, but he was trying the best he could. He was not getting enough sleep, not nearly enough, the memory flashbacks saw to that. He wasn't relaxing nearly enough, so tightly wound that all the time the smallest thing caused him to be angry to her. It wasn't her fault, none of it was her fault, but how could he tell her that he could help himself?

Driving home to Durbanville through the streets of Brakenfells, he was aware of how the area, though wealthy, was getting that less cared for, disreputable air. There, just across the street, was old Monday with his supermarket trolley, busy picking through bins searching for something only he saw as valuable. Monday had appeared a few weeks earlier pushing the trolley, his only worldly possession, a refugee from Zims' implosion. Monday, he knew, spoke Shona first and poor English second, but what else could you expect of a rural Zimbabwe villager? Monday was proud and didn't like it acknowledged that he rummaged through bins to survive, so he didn't flash his head-lights to acknowledge him.

Turning into the drive of his house, he could see house lights and knew Suzy would be waiting inside for him. Slowly the drive gate opened, silently as far as he could hear, but he added the job of greasing the gate track to his week-end jobs. Once fully onto his drive, he thumbed the electronic garage door opener and waited for the door to open fully. Each evening, he followed the same routine, drive gate first, then garage door, then close drive gates, believing that that system gave no chance for any skellum to infiltrate his private space. He did this religiously, driven by his increasing paranoia, fear which he hardly noticed.

Once the door was three quarters open and high enough to admit the car he started forward, his mind already at home, so he didn't notice the movement in the shadows at the corner of the drive. It was only as he opened the car door and was dragged out of the driving seat ands thrown roughly to the concrete floor that he began to realise that his life had taken a considerable turn for the worse. He was wedged tightly between the car and wall, lying almost face down with his right arm trapped under him. When he turned his head to see what was happening, he saw, at uncomfortably close quarters, was the business end of an AK 47. He froze. At least two muggers were there, they shouted to each other and in all the confusion, he caught the word '*maningi*' (white man) in Shona, the language of Mashona land and he was straight back to his Rhodesian army days.

They were excited and high on adrenaline and dagga, loud and victorious. That proved to be their down fall. Suzy had seen his car lights sweep onto their drive and was waiting for him to walk into the house through the garage door. When she heard the shouting coming from the garage her first reaction was to hit the panic button and set off the external siren.

Suddenly, the whole area was drenched in an ear-piercing blast of sound so painful that the muggers automatically covered their ears and forgot about him and his car. They turned and fled back up the drive, running through the pools of darkness to get away, but not before one let off a burst of fire aimed at silencing the siren. The bullets were sprayed in a wide arc, none going near the siren, whilst two slammed into the rear wall and dropped, hot and burning, onto the bare neck of the man on the floor.

At that time, garage door muggings were unusual in Durbanville, but the trend was coming from Johannesburg, or rather that was what the ADT investigator said when he responded to the emergency. Soon a small, well organised armed ADT team were at the house before going off to scan the district for the muggers. Although shaken and with an evil red burn on his neck from a spent bullet, he could tell them very little. They soon established that the muggers were almost certainly newly arrived illegal immigrants, who had lighted on this part of Durbanville as a 'soft touch', just ripe for robbery.

When they eventually arrived, the SAP said much the same thing and seemed happy to let ADT deal with things. In the meantime, once he had hauled himself back to his feet and got into the house, he first had to concentrate on stopping his hands shaking. 'Stupid', he thought to himself, 'I should be used to confrontations with AK's after my time in the bush', but no matter how he tried to rationalise that nights' events, he knew that he had been scared. Badly scared! Mortally scared in fact, more scared than he ever had been during the whole bush war.! Suzy was calm, much calmer than he was, and soothing to his fears, but what he couldn't overcome was the sheer bloody terror and helplessness that gripped him there in the garage, his feeling of total helplessness. Even the worst times during the war had not been as bad as that, he had had been armed and able to defend himself.

When the evening had returned to normal, the police had gone, the neighbours departed and the ADT crew officially 'off premises', he tried to relax. Even after the second whisky he felt tense, certainly, less tense than earlier, but still 'tight'. Once the bedroom lights were off, he felt his body begin to tense again. Suzy, next to him in bed, was warm and soft and soon asleep, but he found himself listening to every sound, unable to sleep. Every time he closed his eyes, the first image projected on his eye lids was that of the black hole at the end of the AK barrel staring straight down into his eye.

Eventually, of course, he fell asleep, a disturbed sleep asleep full of gun flashes, Rhodesian smells and battle noises. He was restless all night tossing and turning, breaking into a sweat at frequent intervals. Suzy slept better, but she was still disturbed and woken regularly by his sudden jumpy awakenings. In the morning both were still tired and irritable. He was reluctant to leave home go to work, but eventually he forced himself out. Just driving his car away from home felt to him like leaving his security behind and that he was entering a dangerous world.

On his way to work, there was Monday scavenging in the bins again, he noticed but paid no attention. Walking into his office he found it unchanged from the previous night, all the work was waiting for him in the order in which it. He sat down at his desk pulled some files towards him, but he couldn't concentrate on the contents. Instead he spent time checking and re-checking his physical security.

'Why am I so edgy?', he kept thinking to himself. It was after lunch that he really began to make a contribution to his company's work. All through the day he couldn't concentrate like he normally did, he was distracted the whole day long. It wasn't until he left for home that the fear began to return. As he got nearer home his a level of worry increased until it was taking all his time simply to drive. Tonight, he had left work early, deliberately to get home whilst it was still light. He didn't drive straight onto his drive, instead he drove around the area looking for people out of place, strange faces that he did not know. He saw only Monday again, but he was becoming part of the scenery, so he drove back to his drive, opened the gate and drove into his garage. He realised that his hands were sweaty, gripping the steering wheel and he felt his heart was beating fast. Once a garage door was locked and he was home again he began to relax, his pulse rate came down and a feeling of security began to wash over him. He was still edgy, however, and Suzy was aware of it.

"I've never known you like this before, what happened to the big, brave soldier boy that I knew and loved?" Susie asked him.

"Don't worry, I'll get over it." he said. "Worse things happen at sea, it will pass!"

"It seems to be you who has the problem, all this is because you're not right in the head!"

"I've got worries . . . ." He began, but that was as far as he got.

"You astonish me" she replied, "You are supposed to protect us, not us protect you! We are your family, you are cracking up, so how can we be safe?"

"This has been in my mind all day, I think we have to move to a safer area."

"No! You move somewhere else until you've got everything together, then I'll decided when it's safe for you come home. You are not the man I married, you've become a whisky drinking whimp. If you want us back you will have to get your head together! You were difficult before, but now you are impossible!" Suzy told him in no uncertain terms.

Within a day, he had moved into the back room at his office. He kept the Johannesburg office working as normal, his associates could run that part, but they were not to know that he had taken up residence in the office This frantic burst of activity did not reduce the nightmares or the paranoia, but l at least, it took his mind off his current position. He phoned Suzy every night and told her what he had achieved it during the day, she was sympathetic, but wouldn't move to invite him back home until she was sure that he wasn't going mad. The new situation calmed him and he began to sleep more regularly and was not as paranoid as before, life was improving. His brandy drinking eased off, he no longer needed to be three quarters drunk to go to sleep. He was working better and even accepted an invitation to a night out with some of his ex-Intelligence pals.

The evening was going well, copious quantities of 'Castle' were being poured down parched throats, when he felt a tap on the shoulder,. Looking around, he saw a small group of his ex-Special Branch colleagues standing nearby and the ex-Inspector inclined his head to ask him to join them. Standing with this serious, quiet group in the midst of the barely contained mayhem of a military re-union was like walking into a commercial freezer. The atmosphere around the group was icy and deadly serious, so distinct from the rest of the room that every-one read the atmosphere and avoided them. As he joined the icy atmosphere his ex-Co looked at him with those sharp eyes he remembered so well and told him simply, 'Mugabe's up to his tricks again!'

Chapter I

An unwilling émigré

Craig needed a long holiday in a warmer climate than Britain could provide in mid-May 1972, of that the Doctor was sure. A year of a more gentle, relaxed life-style, initially with some help and attention and the broken neck would get as good as new quickly. Without this extra help and attention, his recovery could be complete quite naturally, but slower than possible and each extra day that that was held back would increase the chance of accidental damage further. Or at least THAT was the Doctors opinion!

Mid 1972 in the U.K. was an unhappy era of political battles, trade unions against the Conservative government, compounded with U.K.'s entry into the E.E.C. and, more unpopularity, compounded by the switch to a decimal currency. All at once, it appeared that everything in Britain was changing and not for the better! As always, when the trade unions got on their high horses and flexed their industrial muscle, their fine words about their weaker comrades were the first victims of selfishness. This time it was the nurses who were trodden underfoot by the miners' pay demands despite all the miners protestations of support for the nurses claims. As normal, the strong scooped the wages pot dry and then issued weasel words supporting the claims of the smaller and weaker unions.

Health care in Britain was an unhappy industry to be in, all the more especially should you be in need of the service. With constant electricity no longer guaranteed and power cuts in force to preserve power station coal stocks, even minimally conducive conditions to recovery of good health couldn't be predicted.

Bearing that in mind, the Doctor asked if there were any friends or family living in a warmer climate to whom Craig could go to aid his recovery. After a brief family conference, the idea of going to Aunty Doris in Cape Town was rejected. After all, South Africa was THE international pariah because of apartheid, but Doris's son and his wife were farming in the Rhodesian Highlands and they would help. Seven years before, Ian Smith had declared U.D.I., trying to establish Rhodesia as a republic, away from British control. Although the Wilson government had declared U.D. I. illegal and imposed sanctions, there was a tacit understanding of Rhodesias' action, and some sympathy for it, in the U.K.

For Craig to get there from the U.K., however, he would have to get first to Johannesburg and then fly to Rhodesia from there. Organising the trip would be little problem, but he needed confirmation that he would have an address in Rhodesia before he could leave the U.K. Money restrictions were tight, he couldn't export much sterling (he didn't have much!), what he wanted to take would be noted in his passport and examined as he entered the departure lounge at Heathrow. Craig had been assured that the South Africans would issue him with a visitors' visa on arrival and that, with an address in Rhodesia, he would get the same reception at Salisbury airport. With inter—continental air travel still so rare at that time he didn't know anyone who could either help him or verify these sparse facts. Whatever he did would be an enormous leap into the unknown, he could find no precedents or guidance from amongst his friends. Much advice was proffered, none of it supported by any actual evidence or experience. As he was going 'to Remote Parts', Craig was told that his health was his first priority; it was, that was WHY he was going, but the list of potential ailments and prophylactic injections seemed endless. His two pals, who had been talking bravely about 'going to the colonies to find a new life', looked at the list of injections and back-tracked immediately. If a new life in the Colonies demanded such extreme sacrifices, they'd happily stay in dreary old Britain! So, somewhat unsurprised Craig was back to being on his own. It would have been good to have travelled some of the way, at least, with friends, but that was not to be. HE was going to go, he was certain of that and if it had to be alone, so be it!

South Africa house were actually very friendly and helpful when he phoned them about what health concerns that he had. Their switchboard connected him to their Consulate doctor, a friendly and jovial man, who answered all Craig's questions about South Africa and Rhodesia, suggested what he need do and where he could buy the medicines. Much happier after that 'phone conversation, Craig relaxed and began to look forward to his departure.

Getting to Heathrow was comparatively easy compared to going through the formalities and to a seat in the departure lounge. At last, he was sitting there in the Formica and lino'd splendour of Heathrow Terminal 1, excited and awaiting the call to board the blue and white jumbo jet. Look, there was South Africas' vierkleur flag and the leaping Springbok on the tailplane! He had an aisle seat, but the flight wasn't full and he took the chance to try other seats. Craig just couldn't get over the sheer internal size of the body and the space and the number of seats! He had only previously flown on packed charter holiday flights, flights where lack of comfort seemed to be part of the deal and believed those conditions to be the norm. He'd expected the purgatory of twelve hours wedged in 'Sardine Class' and was delighted actually to have room. Craig celebrated by taking over a centre row of five seats and lying down to sleep for the night.

He awoke as the African sun burned its way through the cabin windows as they crossed the coast of South West Africa and the breakfast service began. Air-hostesses, he knew, were meant to be attractive and helpful, but these S.A.A girls were really special, they treated everybody as a friend and had dazzling smiles all the while. The man across the aisle from Craig began a conversation and was helpful and friendly and very concerned that Craig had no one to meet him on his arrival at Jan Smuts. Mr. Prinsloo appointed himself Craigs' guardian and helped Craig through all the formalities of entry into South Africa and even stayed with him until he boarded the Air Rhodesia flight to Salisbury. Mr. Prinsloo's last act, as he shook hands with Craig was to pass over a card with both his address and telephone number written on and tell Craig to call him when he next came to Johannesburg.

His greeting in Salisbury wasn't exactly warm and effusive. Aunty Doris's son knew about him, but seemed somehow surly and unhappy that Craig had finally arrived. Cousin Derek's attitude was cool, almost unpleasant, but Craig remembered his aunts' comment that Derek would probably feel 'slighted and a little put-on' by Craigs' appearance and Derek might view it as a slur on his competence. Much as Craig had tried to tell

Derek (through his mother) that he hadn't any intention of staying more than six months, or until he was fit and well, Derek, it seemed, saw him as something of a rival. A rival to what?, was what worried Craig, as far as he was concerned, he was there on sufferance.

Finally in the tranquillity and isolation of the farm, Zanddrift, he could appreciate why Derek considered the city hectic and crowded, though Craig thought that even Salisbury had a slow, rural feel to it. After settling in to his allocated room in the brick kaya next to the main building, he shared dinner in the main household with Derek, his wife, Mareta, and Zandra, their young daughter. No sooner had Zandra been brought into the main room than her black ouma entered and reclaimed her, swept her up into her arms and left to feed the little girl. Throughout his stay at Zanddrift Craig only saw Zandra about half a dozen times, her ouma seemed determined to isolate here from outside contacts! After supper Craig found that he had to provide his own entertainment much more so than in back home. For him, the easiest thing seemed to write a letter home so that his parents would know that he was well and that all the long range arrangements had worked. Craig was used to watching T.V. before turning into bed, but here, on a Rhodesian farm, it was the radio that played the same role. The first news item caused Derek to get agitated, a report of an attack on a farm in the north, near the newly created Zambian border. Apparently the farmer, his wife and child had been shot by 'nationalist marauders' who had melted back into the night, leaving the frightened farm labourers to raise the alarm. As they had no mechanised transport, the labourers had waited until morning and harnessed up a donkey cart before contacting the police and telling their story. Derek listened to the news report with increasing agitation. Before the news bulletin was finished he snapped the radio off and angrily exclaimed "It's started!" No further explanations were given, Craig was apparently supposed to understand Derek's cryptic comment. In answer to his questions, the only answer Craig got 'was that all must turn in early as tomorrow will be a long day.'

The following day, Derek was more taciturn than even Craig expected, the only comment that he understood was when Derek muttered something about 'that bloody man Wilson', a comment Craig believed was aimed at the British Prime Minister.

Only later could Craig understand Dereks' anger when Ian Smiths' 'kith and kin' plea at the time of U.D.I. had been so roundly condemned by the U.K. government.

Regularly both Derek and Mareta would go away from the main homestead and blast away at rough targets for hours on end. Weeks passed until Craig was asked if he preferred a revolver or a rifle? Bemused, he sputtered an answer that he had no idea about either. Derek was aghast that a man of Craig's age had no experience of guns or fire-arms in general, insisting that Craig join the regular times on the farms shooting range. Derek developed a very superior and condescending attitude to Craig about shooting, but insisted that Craig get used to carrying a gun at all times because the 'blacks' had finally started their race war against the whites.

Craig at first thought that Derek was simply being paranoid, transforming a simple farm raid into a major incident, but if he were, it seemed that most of the community shared Derek's thoughts. Daily news bulletins from the Rhodesian Broadcasting Service began to mention what the Patriotic Front said from their safe haven in Zambia. Joshua Nkomo seemed to be the leading light, but the Reverend Ndabaningi Sithole was also prominent and, from these reports, the minority Matabele seemed to be the most politically aware. Craig listened with interest, he had only ever vaguely heard about these things whilst he was in England and had had no interest, but now they seemed more immediate and real. From the tone of some of the broadcasts even Craig could catch the unspoken, but clearly articulated, worry that pervaded these news reports. Asking around the locals, on the days he went to the nearby town, got him the answer that it was all the fault of either Britain (and exclusively Harold Wilson) or 'The Communists'. Rhodesia had the right to be independent of Britain and to be able to decide its' own future, was the common belief. After all hadn't Rhodesia's commitment to Britain and the Empire been proven at times of greatest need, so why hadn't independence freely been granted to a close and loyal ally? Muted mutterings of 'perfidious Albion' occasionally surfaced in discussions, but were suppressed by the comment 'Well, we're independent NOW!'

What most of these comments sounded like to Craig was exasperation at the antics of an old, but dear, doddery maiden aunt. What was actually happening was that a 'can-do' spirit was being forged inside the small, but determined, community of the white Rhodesians. Craig's letters to his parents, although not frequent, were extensive and reflected his growing experiences and feelings about all aspects of life in a sanctioned Rhodesia.

As Craigs' health improved and he grew back to his normal strength level, he started helping in jobs around the farm. His early attempts at help were anything but helpful. He had not fully got into the Rhodesian farmers mindset, he insisted on helping in some jobs that 'it was not right for a European to do'. Once he showed himself to be more than a passable mechanic Derek was happy to leave things like that in his care, even to trusting him to go to town and have special parts made by the local engineering works. In this aspect, Craig had swiftly become a complete Rhodesian, he was happy to repair and adapt and 'make do and mend', the attitude that he had always employed in Britain. Within the local farming area Craig gained a reputation as a 'fundi' who could design and make anything in metal work. As he helped more and more people, he was feeling increasingly at home and starting to consider Rhodesia increasingly as his emotional home. This closer identification with the country and the people made him far more sensitive to their mood and he started to absorb some of the anxieties of his new friends. His visits to more outlying farms increasingly kept him away from Zanddrift for days on end. No-one there seemed unduly worried about his absences from the farm, the local bush-telegraph seemed to inform everybody quickly where he was and what he was doing.

As the days passed, Craig realised that he was happier than he had been 'at home' in the U.K. and that, unconsciously, Rhodesia was becoming his home, the tone of his reducing flow of letters home clearly reflected his changing mood. Rhodesia seemed to seep deep into him almost osmotically, he was never aware of the change in him, it just happened. Swiftly, too swiftly it seemed, his return date was advancing to meet him, the new Craig, tanned, leaner and even more self-reliant than ever before. His shock was real and profound when he opened his diary at the beginning of the week to see the thickly underscored date, four days hence, and the statement 'return flight'. For a short while Craig stood in shock and didn't know what to think. He didn't know whether to feel glad about returning to his 'old' life, but feeling glad about returning also meant that he should feel glad about leaving Rhodesia, but about that he couldn't feel that. The more he thought about leaving that beautiful land, the more he realised that he couldn't! Rhodesia had become part of him and he, part of Rhodesia, of that he was absolutely certain!

Craig didn't discuss his feelings with Derek or Mareta immediately, but sounded out some of the 'Rhodesian old hands', the post war British immigrants, who had departed a war-weary Britain for a chance of a life in the tropical sun. Their advice was unequivocal. "Throw your return ticket away and settle here, it's a great life!" was the popular opinion. Indeed, there were no dissenting European voices and Europeans were all that Craig asked. With such a positive response, Craig's bias to Rhodesia was only reinforced, but his positive manner was quite rudely shattered when he tried to confirm his ideas with both Derek and Mareta. Their attitude changed from being uninterested to become openly hostile.

"You won't be welcome to stay here any longer," said Derek "we've done what my mother promised you we would. It seems that our best efforts weren't good enough for you, you've spent more time with the neighbours than us and now you expect us to welcome you to stay as long as you want!" Craig simply stood dumbfounded at Derek's statement, not only did he not expect such vehemence, but had no thoughts of staying on at Zanddrift as a guest. In his farm travels, Craig had made friends with the district policeman, who had promised him employment with the local police force. With the police job would come accommodation of some kind for him, so Craig had never even contemplated asking to stay at the farm with Derek and Mareta.

Craig had faith in his future as a police officer in Rhodesia. He appreciated that he wouldn't make the police job a lifetime career, but in the interim, it appeared the perfect step for him to take at that time. He hurriedly drafted a letter to his parents, telling them that he had a permanent job offer and asked if they tell the Sheffield factory for whom he had worked that he wouldn't be returning to the steel works in the near future, please? So confident of this move was Craig that he included the unused return ticket in the letter, asking his mother to 'get his money back' for the unused flights home.

Once the letter was finished and everything safely sealed in the air-mail envelope ready for a visit to the local post office the next morning, Craig put the letter in his shirt pocket. He arranged to move out to the police barracks as soon as formal approval had been given to him joining the police. Dereks' attitude to him softened somewhat, although Derek's happiness that Craig was moving away from Zanddrift was painfully obvious. In record time (it seemed to Craig) his letter of appointment as trainee police officer appeared and Craig, already packed and waiting, got a lift into town to become a policeman and join the British South African Police force.

Chapter 2

Part of the BSAP

Basic training passed swiftly and pleasantly for Craig. Certainly, there were grueling tasks and physical training to be undertaken, but he was back to full fitness now and he relished the physical challenges. There were also hours spent in the class-room, most of it learning about the law and how it was applied. He had more trouble with the apparently paternalistic approach taken to the blacks, but was concerned how rapidly this paternalism turned to unforgiveness once a certain line was crossed. Being from UK, he did not appreciate where this line was; to all his trainee friends that dividing line was clear and unequivocal. Much of his training seemed predicated on the fact that it was only the natives that committed crimes. Apparently, whatever a white person did was usually regarded as a minor misdemeanor, deserving only of a few quiet words. Life, however, was good, he was doing a job that he increasingly enjoyed and he was more than happy to have left the U.K'.s weather behind.

His training progressed steadily, when it came to 'fire-arms' part, he was, initially, at the back of the course, all his course-mates having had years more experience than he. Being seen as the course 'duffer' ignited Craig's ambition and he put much more time in on the firing range. His determination was rewarded, he made a good friend of the armaments sergeant who helped him, but also noted his talent and interest in the mechanics of fire-arms. Compared to the average police trainee Craig must have fired off three or four times the amount of rounds that they did, but with each round fired his ability and confidence grew. In the long hours spent in the armaments store Craig's engineering back-ground once more proved valuable. He rapidly learned how to strip and service every type of gun in the place, but he seemed to have an uncanny appreciation of the other half of the fire-arm; the ammunition. He quickly learned to tell, by sound alone, what type of round was fired from what type of gun; he learned, almost understood naturally, the different performances possible from an ammunition change.

"Remind me not to upset you, lad", Matt, the armoury sergeant, "you can leave me standing about ammunition!"

In the final graduation tests, Craig scored well in every subject and, to his delight, was rated 'sniper' level with his rifle score. Before finally leaving training, all the new Police officers had an individual interview with the training camp commandant, who had each of their personal files to hand, on his desk. These interviews had been widely trailed and each student knew that this meeting would influence his future in the police service. Craig had no idea, or indication, as to where his service would be. He expected that he would be given a 'bush beat', a wide ranging rural beat rather than an urban or car crime role and, as he read the placements list on his last day, began to get rather worried that he couldn't find his name.

"You lucky bastard," said directly to a puzzled Craig by Piet, his training partner, caused him to shrug and ask 'Why?'

"You've only gone and landed the bleddy Army liaison job, you lucky bagger!" Piet explained. "No bleedy rough necking in the bundu for you, my pal, you'll be in barracks all the time! That and the odd extra course and no disputes to settle with angry farmers. Lucky baggar!"

"I don't see my name here," Craig answered.

"Look, blast you; you're right at the top of the sheet! Lucky sod!" Piet almost shouted at him.

Army liaison, the plum job! Craig had no idea how he had achieved such a thing. All through the course the army liaison job, fairly newly created as the terrorist threat appeared, was a blank canvas, ready for the officer to create his own role. Each new policeman had a personal talk with the base Commandant before they finally took the assigned job. It was well known that to refuse the assignment resulted in a downward move; no-one ever bucked the system and improved their job offer. As he stood to attention outside the commandants' closed door Craig could only wonder if to take the police/army liaison job would be beyond him. At the appointed time he rapped smartly twice on the Commandants polished door.

"Come" spoken loudly from behind the door greeted his knock. He entered, marching smartly to stand in front of the big boss's desk and then, from the corner of his eye, saw a khaki clad figure seated to his left. He saluted, was told to 'stand easy', then immediately to sit. Craig sat, cap in hand and waited for the Commandant to speak.

"Do you know why you're here?" the question came over his left shoulder.

"Army liaison post, sir" Craig answered.

"Do you know, or even care, what that post IS?" the reply fired directly over Craig's shoulder.

"No sir, I don't know. A new post because of the uprisings, sir?" Craig answered directly to his front. He was beginning to feel apprehensive, all this time he had been facing his Commandant who hadn't spoken but had continued to look straight forward.

"Do you want to know what this post is and why we think that you can do it?" the left shoulder questioner asked.

"Yes sir, very interested, sir" Craig confirmed directly to his Commandants face.

Now his Commandant spoke "Take seven days leave and report back to this office at 0730 on the sixteenth. Dismiss!"

Before he knew it, Craig was outside the office door and a civilian aid gave him a leave docket and suggested that he find some-one else going his direction to share a lift with. Reality began to kick in; Craig felt as if he had just woken up and wondered if the past few minutes had been real. The leave docket in his hands suggested that the experience had been real and that he could wonder about the liaison job for a week before he got any answers. Leaving the Commandants office, he walked directly to the base canteen, where the end of course booze-up was starting. He carefully folded his leave pass into his breast pocket, hung his stiff new cap on a hat-peg and dived into the noisy, throbbing bar and fought his way to the counter to buy a beer.

"Good material!" said the khaki uniformed man to the Commandant.

"He'll do a good job", replied the Commandant, "not too hide-bound by being a local boy."

"Any trouble for him, still officially being a British Citizen?" enquired the khaki man.

"Wouldn't think so, he's more Rhodesian than the rest of group!" answered the Commandant.

"Not one of those anti-imperialists then?" the khaki man mused.

"No, no, he appears to be the genuine article. Loyal to us, England no longer considered." The Commandant commented.

"Ah well, we'll find out in the next month or so" said the khaki man cryptically.

Craig's one week leave was spent mainly with Piet at his family's small farm outside of town. For the first time since arriving in Rhodesia Craig really experienced the full power of Rhodesian hospitality, something that he had not experienced in Zanddrift. Piet's mother spoiled both of them, her 'boys' as she happily called them both, readily including Craig in all the family celebrations and equal to Piet, her real son. Craig, normally an unsentimental sort of guy, at times had tears in his eyes, tears of happiness and acceptance. He was soon a part of the family, Mrs. Uys's second son in all but name. Craig had the shorter leave and so whilst Piet still had another week of lounging and being spoiled with his mothers' cooking, he had to go back to barracks. Just going back to barracks became a family event. All his newly acquired family piled into the car to take him back to barracks and wave him goodbye as he walked through the gates!

It was immediately obvious that the pace of his life had stepped up at least a gear, he had training courses booked solid for 6 weeks, some police courses, the others taught by Army personnel. What he had thought would be a fairly relaxed time proved to be anything but. What Craig hadn't appreciated was that Army liaison was more of an intelligence role than simply exchanging information over a telephone. His first two courses were basically Army Intelligence based and he rapidly learned that his role was seen as that of a link man between the military establishment and the civilian power of the police. He did have a purely police role which was to tour the outlaying farms and advise the farmers on security based on the most recent intelligence information to hand.

Craig did one course that he enjoyed very much and that was 'mines and booby traps.' He was able to utilise some of his engineering background when dealing with improvised mines and explosives and he really enjoyed the practical side of the course, too. His Army instructor said more than once that Craig must have been born sneaky, he had an ability to do unexpected things and hide mines where no right thinking soldier would dare. It was during the course that Craig demonstrated a natural sympathy with devices that go 'bang'. He seemed to know, quite automatically, how to make them, place them and set them for maximum effect, he also seemed to have X-Ray vision when deactivating booby-traps, seemingly almost to take them apart as if he knew the builder's design. When it came to 'tuning' ammunition, he also showed exceptional skill and adapted every round in his personal armoury to increase its penetrative power. Until he demonstrated his 'special' ammunitions capability by hitting a target through a large tree, his ideas were not taken seriously. The day he fired one of his modified.303 rounds from a WW2 Lee—Enfield rifle through a thick tree, which continued on to shatter a concrete building block was the day that people began to take him and his ideas on ammunition seriously. Asked why he had chosen to demonstrate his ammunition that way, Craig simply replied that 'Terrs hiding behind trees won't be safe anymore.'

Part way through his liaison course, Craig was sent to the principal military base, he thought for yet another course. This one was different where he met a select few engineers, armourers and artificers who were VERY interested in his ideas about ammunition and booby-traps. That week was one of the happiest Craig had had up to that time. It was a week of mixing with like minded explosives freaks with the whole week punctuated with deliberately planned explosions, both large and small. Rhodesia, because of the U.D.I. sanctions placed upon her, was forced to exploit every bit of talent within her borders; the result was that some truly unique (and cheap) solutions to problems were found. Along with the rest of the course members Craig was expected to let his imagination run free and to originate solutions to unusual situations. He made friends with every course member and tried to learn something from each of them. By the end of the week, Craig had a new party trick. He had been shown (and better yet, taught) how to blow a corn stalk through an inch thickness of wood, leaving the wood with a neat hole punched through it and an apparently undamaged corn stalk laying on the floor behind the wood.

If Craig had thought deeply about the incongruity of a police man being trained by many different military specialists, he might have begun to find his situation highly unusual, but he didn't as he was enjoying himself too much. At the end of the explosives course, he had almost to be physically dragged out of the Army post and returned to the police training academy.

With all his comings and goings he only saw Piet Uys briefly and then only for a short time. Piet had got the posting that he had wanted; he was going off to one of the more rural 'beats' in the country where his spoken Sindabele would be put to good use. Over a few beers in the canteen, both told the other the high-lights of their training, Piets' much briefer than Craigs'. By the end of their first drunken evening together Piet got maudlin and pressed Craig to remain in close touch with the family, 'as my mum has adopted you as the second son she always wanted' Craig again felt the lump in his throat grow, so he swallowed a large draught of beer to hide his embarrassment. Piet wouldn't be silenced until Craig gave him his gravest word, sworn to the strongest oath he could imagine. In the morning, both with extremely sore heads, were at the transport section, Piet to go off to his posting and Craig going off to a different police post in Salisbury to begin his 'Intelligence' training. This course was a scheduled one month course, run by the BSAP, but with 'significant' military 'input', Craig was informed.

What at first Craig expected to be a 'mish-mash' of a course actually turned out to be a most intriguing time of mental jig-saw building. He was taught how not to ignore the smallest shred of evidence or the most inconsequential off-hand comment. To do any intelligence task well required both patience and a logical memory; an ability to think laterally was also an assest to be prized. Small pieces of information gathered from multiple and varied sources had to be critically sifted and then re-combined to reveal the big picture. Obviously, the more information that could be unambiguously attributed to any source, then the clearer the final picture would become, BUT unambiguous sources were extremely rare. What Craig was told was that his job would be was as a mid-level 'information assembler', he would receive information direct from contacts with armed terrorists and he was to attempt to identify the terrorists' overall objectives. At that point, his job was to pass on his finding 'up the tree' for more senior Intelligence officers to assess.

The very detective aspect and analysis of intelligence work that was involved really appealed to Craig. In Intelligence work he found an unexpected part of his own character, he was fascinated by the chess-like nature of attempting to get into his opponents mind. An extra intriguing dimension to this mental game was that the opposition was so culturally different from himself, so he had to try to think as they would. Even during exercises on the course, he was brought into contact with translators from the Rhodesian African Rifles, who would politely translate and tell Craig what the words on the pieces of paper said. Although these training exercises were designed to test the student's ability to piece together random bits of information and detect a common direction, Craig was not really happy. Most exercises seemed too artificial and managed and thus did not feel real, so he took to asking his R.A.R. translator about motives, meanings and intentions from the African point of view. His appreciation that the African perspective had hidden value was not a universally popular point of view. Many of the older Rhodesia hands seemed only to focus on the white Rhodesian perspective, believing that the terrorist insurgency would have no effect on the average black Rhodesian. That white rule in Rhodesia was an undisputed good thing for everyone was not questioned in many official quarters, but Craig learned otherwise when the Africans were allowed to voice their opinions. There was certainly no general dislike of the white man, nor any love of the terrorists. There were plenty of minor 'niggles' that caused annoyance, but what Craig learned was that the average African hated and feared the insurgents much more than the worst white. By getting an African perspective Craig's intelligence jig-saw was subtly biased that way; in short he saw more shades of grey and not the 'all or nothing' picture that he was supposed to find.

It was this very slight bias that Craig built into his intelligence assessments that cost him marks. He was not pushing the official 'party line' and the more senior officers (both BSAP and Armed Forces) tried to tell him that the way to learn the 'true' translations of the writing found on odd bits of paper was to consult a native language speaking white officer. Craig could not explain his reasoning behind that decision, other than taking initiative, but somehow, it felt to him the best thing to do. After the 'office work' of attempting to assemble a viable intelligence picture from the bits of raw data that they had been fed, the next part of the course was an 'in the field' exercise to collect fresh raw data. To his astonishment Craig found that he had been allocated to the first group in the exercise, this he thought was a bit of an honour. What he later found out was that the latter exercise groups were the ones to be in, the first two groups had to work despite any negative African reaction. By the time the last groups were going out, inevitably, the locals knew and generally just stood out of the searchers' way and let them get on with the search. What Craig was also not aware of was that he was in the group being screened as potential front-line intelligence gatherers. The better he performed in this test, the more likely he was to be following immediately behind the front line Police or attack troops to gather any intelligence 'hot' in the field.

Following on immediately after the intelligence course was a more military course when even as police officers, the course members were trained in 'bush craft', alongside their military counter-parts. Despite being essentially 'a townie', Craig quickly got the hang of much of the training. He never admitted, and never would admit to any-one, just how scared he was at times, especially when rehearsing likely ambush situations. When it came to bomb clearing and armaments de-activating part, he was in his element once more and never missed a beat. All the instructors noted his overall ability and generally rated him highly and at selection conferences, his overall performance was never questioned. If Craig had been expecting, or even hoping for, a 'hands off' intelligence role, he was to be disappointed. That he was capable of coping with, and surviving, almost any situation thrust him directly into consideration for front-line intelligence work where even his 'weakness' of reading intelligence with an African perspective could be valuable. When his final posting was announced, it came as a surprise to him, as did the rank he had gained. He finished the course as a simple constable, but began his first posting as acting police lieutenant, attached operationally to the R.A.R.

Once again he spent his leave with the Uys family, enjoying being cosseted by his adopted mother, only too happy to enjoy all the idle leisure time he could find. Talking in the evenings about what he had been doing seriously interested the Mr and Mrs. Uys and at first he couldn't really understand why. Piet had been deployed out on a 'bundu' posting and was enjoying it very much, but he was reporting an undercurrent of unease in the tribal territories. This unease wasn't easy for Piet to 'read', the messages that he was getting basically said that in the tribal lands, each chief was under pressure to feed any terrorist that strayed into his tribes' area and to pass information on about the security forces. To enforce their edicts, the 'freedom fighters', whilst proclaiming freedom from white tyranny, were happy to inflict their own terror on the tribes people. Caught between two systems, the chiefs suffered serious physical abuse from the 'liberators' should any minor infraction be suspected. Piet knew what was happening, but could not get confirmation from people in the tribal lands. They met only for a short time during Craig's pre-operational posting leave, but Piet made sure that Craig was aware of the violence hidden underneath the apparently quiet rural exterior. The comments Piet made were really no surprise to Craig as the unwritten text of the intelligence course had been the infiltration of 'terrs' into the rural lands. Just listening to Piet, it was obvious to Craig just how deeply Piet was attached to the very texture of Rhodesia and saw himself as no more, nor less, a Rhodesian as the very tribes that he was protecting in his role as a BSAP constable. And his obvious pain at the goings-on (as he called them) on his beat was plain for any-one to see, Craig sympathised and those feeling prompted Craig to promise that he'd take a special interest in the region.

Chapter 3

First assignment with the R.A.R.

Returning from the post course leave was, in some ways, a re-run of the earlier time; in other ways it was totally different. He was taken to the barracks front gate by the Uys family in their overloaded old estate car but this time as he passed by the sentry, he got a respectful salute. Craig could only wonder at the aura of power transmitted by his new shoulder insignia. This time his new temporary rank gave him some power and he was very conscious not to be arbitrary in his use of it. Although his service so far was short, he had seen too many inadequate NCOs' and junior officers abusing their small portion of power to justify their superiority to the ranks. This time, also, he was given a berth in a two man room, not an eight man dormitory. Hardly had he thrown his kit bag onto the bed than there came a knock on the door.

"C.O. requests you in the operations room, sir" rapped out by the orderly corporal.

"Coming" Craig replied.

"Now, please, sir. I was told to get you there immediately!"

"Lead the way, corporal.", Craig immediately giving up his plans to settle in.

At a very brisk walk the corporal lead the way into the camps nerve centre and zig-zagged through the building until he stood outside a discrete brown door. A quick, hard rap on the door and then the corporal lead him through to stand before a desk over which a tall, slim major leaned.

Without apparently looking up, the major simply told the corporal to 'take him to the C.O.' They marched past the desk and through the open door behind it, where upon the corporal halted, stamped his feet and rapped out "Lieutenant Burgoyne, Sir!" in his best military voice, then turned on his heel and marched out quite as noisily as he had marched in.

"One of our ex-Royal Army men, a stickler for the 'right way', I'm afraid!" commented a voice behind Craig. Turning, he saw the C.O. standing with a sheaf of papers in his hand, hidden by the open door, but deeply engrossed in examining a large scale map of the country.

"I know that you are BSAP and not Army, but we're all in this together now and increasingly going to be so until we sort these terrs. out, so you may as well get used to co-operating with us" said the C.O., a rangy Lieutenant-Colonel who Craig had never seen before. "We are, officially, aiding the civilian authority the Police—your lot to maintain law and order in the tribal territories, so we have to take a policemen with us. You pulled the short straw because you seem to have some nack of getting onto the Tribals' wavelength."

"Don't know about that, Sir," answered Craig "I just listen to what they tell me."

"Good man, Good man" replied the C.O. "You've done the Intelligence course, too?"

Craig said that he had just finished the combined Military/ BSAP course as well as the advanced armourers course.

"Better and better." commented the C.O. "You were rushed through your course a bit, I'm afraid, because we needed some-one in a hurry. There will be more training to come later, by the way. Come around here and let me show you on the map what's what, so you work out what is happening!"

"We believe that Mugabes' ZANLA boys are coming in through Mozambique around Tete with FRELIMOs' help. That puts 'em straight into Rhodesia and the T.T.L.s in Manicaland where they begin to 'make converts' of the nearest Shona tribe. That's where you come in"

Looking Craig straight in the eye the Colonel briefly described how the ZANLA terrorists attacked the local tribes' people and used terror to force these people to feed and aid them.

"Pity the poor chiefs! They are the first victims of this brand of Maoist style political 'education'. This bunch are on Chiserwe Tribal Trust Land, in the Kore-Kore area, before they stuck their ugly mugs in, the tribes people was neutral-to-un co-operative with us, but have now become decidedly untrustworthy."

Craig looked startled, obviously not completely convinced by the Colonel.

"Your record says that the natives seem to trust you and tell you things that they tell few other security people."

"I just listen, and well, encourage them to continue talking" replied Craig.

"A rare talent for a white security man!" interjected the Colonel. "Well then, you MUST have heard SOMETHING, however vague from these villagers!" the Colonel said firmly.

"What I did hear, "answered Craig "was dismissed as a crude attempt to get better treatment from us. That, at least, is what the Intelligence Major said when I reported those stories."

"That's why he's still a Major!" stormed the Colonel "If I have my way, he'll soon be a Captain in the Quartermasters' branch. Can't see the wood for the bloody trees!"

"I reported anxiety and a lack of the usual co-operation amongst the tribes people, but no-one believed me, in fact I was called the kaffirboetjie" Craig replied quietly.

"This has been going on for some time and that's why the Army 'leaned' on The J. O.C. to create joint BSAP-Army intelligence operatives like you. The natives'll speak to a copper more freely than they will a soldier.

Some of your comments got through to us, thank God, and closed a few gaps.

Oh, and by the way, welcome to Operation Hurricane!"

Now Craigs' head whirled. His accelerated advancement and the special training courses were all explained!

When it was revealed, Craigs' first assignment was to go into the field near Murewa in Manicaland West as part of the R.A.R. second wave that were trying to ambush one of Mugabes' most brutal 'Liberation fighters'. He didn't feel frightened, just worried, his worries being mostly that he would be able to do his job under fire and not turn into a shivering, nervous wreck. He didn't think he would dissolve in fear, but he knew that until the firing was live and incoming he would never know.

"These bastards use barbed wire to tie up the village chief and then rape his wives and daughters in front of the rest of the village. Supposed to tell the rest of the villagers what will happen to them IF they don't feed and help the terrs.' Said the Major to Craig during the special Intelligence briefing after the troopers had been given their orders. Going in as second wave was meant to ensure that he had sufficient time to search for and examine likely artefacts. As it worked out, the Allouettes delivered the second wave almost on the heels of the first and into an active fire-fight, with the insurgents firing off magazines of AK 47 fires at any leaf that moved. As Craig ran from the helicopter, he ran by a bush only to realise that the 'slapping' sound was not rain falling on the bush, but wild, incoming AK 47 fire from the ZANLA insurgents. Realising that, Craig dived to the ground and shelter behind the nearest rock. All around him the air around the air was full of the sound of angry bees zipping over his head and pinging off other rocks. It took a few seconds for him to realise that although he was worried, he was also quite excited to be there. His training took over from there and he felt himself grow calmer.

Moving slowly and in small movements, he brought his rifle close to his body, slipped off the safety catch and brought it into a firing position. Words from his drill instructor echoed through his mind and he deliberately shuffled his toes into the earth to provide grip. He settled and brought the rifle to bear on the location from where much of the green tracer seemed to be originating. Squeezing the trigger gently, he fired his first shot of the conflict. In the general mayhem of noise it was insignificant, but to Craig it sounded loud enough for every-one to hear it and locate him. Working the bolt rapidly, he chambered a new round and followed his first shot with a second. No more green tracer was coming out, so he searched around for other targets, resisting the urge to fire round after round wildly into the bushes. Suddenly the firing stopped and an un-natural silence fell. There was the crackle of a fire somewhere, but otherwise quiet. Craig took a moment to look around and get an idea of what had just happened. R.A.R. soldiers were all around, some in bushes, some behind the few spindly trees and some, like him, behind rocks. It looked like that had triggered an ambush in their pursuit of terrorists.

One of the black R.A.R. soldiers suddenly dived to his right and rolled into a bush. Nothing happened. Craig watched as the black soldiers re-located themselves in better firing positions when he was hit on the head by a small stone. His head jerked around and he saw a black trooper signalling that he should join him. A quick roll to the left and a hasty, scrabbled step carried Craig beneath the bushes' shelter. His new friend pointed the way for Craig to crawl leftwards, which he did and found a large boulder two paces away. He prepared himself for the dash, dashed over and settled into cover behind the rock then indicated for the trooper to join him. The trooper, too, redeployed from the bush to behind the rock. They looked at each other and the trooper raised his eye-brows as if to say 'So far, so good'.

Silence still hung over the area, but it was a tense type of silence. Something was going to happen, every-one felt it, but nobody knew what the next move would be. In the distance Craig could hear the wind sighing through the bushes. As he turned his head a small movement caught his eye, he followed the movement, focussed on it and saw a fragmentation grenade come into focus. He didn't stay to look any harder, he simply knocked down the trooper and stay on top of him. He felt the explosion as much as heard it and seconds later, a rain of soil and leaves came down on him.

That explosion seemed to break the spell of silence. Both sides began hammering away at each other again. Tracer was flying out of the bush, whilst red tracer was weaving a mad pattern onto and through the bush. Craig and his companion crawled to the left edge of their rocky protection and peered around. Without a sound, Craig pulled a grenade from his belt-pack, pulled the pin and half tossed, half rolled it low down into the bush. He had no sooner got back behind the rock when his grenade exploded right at the booted feet that he had seen right in the middle of the bush. Silence did not descend again, but firing from the bush diminished considerably. Craig was pulled out on a wide swinging run to the left by the trooper who let him drop under a tree far enough away to be able to see the back of the bush and be out of direct R.A.R. fire, yet close enough to be able to pick out targets. With no further ado, the R.A.R. trooper flung himself down and began firing single shots at the people behind the bush. He was obviously a crack shot, as each bullet seemed to remove another terrorist. Craig, his rifle resting across the top of the rock, was keeping a wary eye where the terrorist group were, ready to pick off any threat to 'his' R.A.R. trooper. Once again, an absolute silence fell over the scene and for a few moments no-one stirred, then, all of a sudden the spell was broken when one of the white R.A.R officers began to edge cautiously forward into the guerrillas' position.

As he moved forward, most of the troopers began cautiously moving out of cover, with guns at the ready and towards the terrs' lair. Craig joined in the group move, he knew that he was supposed to recover any thing that could be of Intelligence interest and he needed to be there before too much was disturbed by the troopers. He moved forward slowly, looking around all the time. There were insurgents bodies scattered around behind both trees and rocks. He found the man without feet, the man that he rolled the grenade at, he looked inert, with no weapon nearby and plenty of fresh blood around. Craig ignored him after a swift glance and pushed on through the bush towards the centre of the ambush position. He had taken only one further step when a shot rang out behind him. He quickly spun around to see 'his' R.A.R. trooper with a smoking rifle pointing at the footless terr. As Craig had passed by, the 'dead' footless terrorist had pulled out a grenade with the aim of throwing it at Craig, but 'his' trooper had been covering his back, saw the insurgents' intention and shot him dead. The grenade lay peacefully on the ground, the safety pin still in place and no longer a threat to Craig. Looking, Craig saw that it was a conventional Chinese stick grenade, that gave him his first bit of intelligence that these terrs. were ZANLA. 'His' R.A.R. trooper came up to him, telling him to shot every 'dead' terr.because they played dead and would shot him in the back without compunction.

Craig continued forward, cautiously scanning the bodies on the floor. Despite the amount of blood around, Craig had learned a shocking lesson that a terrorist looking dead and being dead were two very different things, so he resolved to shoot every 'corpse' as he moved past them.

At the centre of the terrorists' camp only a few meagre things lay, but there was a map with inward infiltration routes from Mozambique clearly marked. There was no radio and only the presumed leader had a compass in a pocket of his camouflage uniform. Once all the Rhodesian troops had gathered together, he set them to look for papers, maps and anything that was unusual. It was only then that he realised that some of the troopers had been behind the terrorists, as a 'stop group' to prevent any escape. As some had fled the battle scene, the stop group had done its' job, so bodies lay scattered over a much wider area than Craig had originally thought.

Craig had to go and start examining the bodies, seeing if their pockets contained anything of value for intelligence analysis. Anything that could give indications of where they had been and when was of value. Unfortunately, as he found, Africans do not have the European habit of putting bits of paper in their pocket, so most of the information Craig found came from their personal papers. All the dead were full time ZANLA insurgents, trained by the Chinese and carrying ZANLA identification which noted their *'nom de combat'* fore the duration of the *Chimerunga*.

Good though the stop teams had been, there seemed to be one guerrilla unaccounted for, that of the leader, who, it appeared, had fled as soon as the R.A.R. got to the area. Even after careful examination of what orders Craig could identify from his intelligence haul, he could find no obvious justification for the incursion, other than to provoke the Rhodesian security forces to respond. 'And respond they did!' he thought.

As the R.A.R. trooper sat around waiting for their lorry transport back to barracks, they all were smoking and the sweet smell of dagga was in the air.

"At times like this, after a contact, we can't stop them. Most of the terrs seem to be flying on bhang as they call it. And good stuff and large amounts, so it would be unfair to waste it, wouldn't it?" one of their officers said, a happy grin on his face.

The R.A.R. may be finished here, but Craig had to find out what had happened to the tribes' people, so that he could report back fully. He went off in a Land Rover borrowed from the R.A.R. officer along with two R.A.R. troopers and a driver borrowed at the same time. They didn't have far to go before the principal Kore-Kore settlement came into sight and they were confronted by an angry crowd of Shona speakers. Craig didn't need to understand the language to know that they were not at all welcome there, the R.A.R. sergeant tried to talk to the crowd in Shona, but was shouted down and the crowd were getting uglier by the moment. Craig had the driver pull back a distance so that he could talk to sergeant and find out was happening, only to be told that 'the Liberation war has started and that ZANLA will win and that all whites and their black lackeys will be eaten up by the victorious peoples' popular army'. As the Landy turned away, the sergeant also said that they would find the body of the white mans' jackal, meaning the village head, at the cross roads where the ZANLA forces had 'questioned' him the night before. A short way away, they came to the cross-roads and found the badly beaten and burned body of the headman bound by barbed wire to a large Mopani tree. Craig suggested that they bury the body, but the troopers simply rolled their eyes and declined to interfere. Their inactions clearly illustrated the hold superstition had on them and their dread of transgressing any spiritual affairs. Recognizing that state of affairs, Craig simply ordered the driver to get back to the main body of the R.A.R. troop and sat quietly, composing his report in his mind.

His report, when it had been written, covered the basic facts sparingly, it wasn't his job to report the fight, but to analyse the intelligence found. From the sparse pickings he had, the main points that Craig could determine were that ZANLA initiated discontent in the tribal lands to see how the authorities would react. This particular incursion had been costly to the terrorists, but as Craig emphasised, they had learned a lot from it. He extrapolated his findings and declared that all the tribal lands were potentially compromised and this inward route ought to be firmly barred against further ZANLA infiltration.

Seemingly as a result of his report, Craig was given 7 days home leave, which again he spent with his adopted family on their farm 'Fairvue'. He wangled a lift to the farm on an Army Bedford which saved him having to thumb lifts with passing motorists and as individual soldiers and policemen outside built-up areas had become targets for insurgents, his journey was safer. He had taken to the soldiers' habit of having his rifle with him at all times, so that when he walked through the front door of the homestead, he didn't have a free hand to hold Mrs. Uys when she hugged him.

"Let me look at you!" She said, then stepped a step backwards. "You've changed, you're leaner and you're harder. Your eyes are a bit remote, too. My God Craig, what have you seen, where have you been?"

At that Craig found himself almost collapsing inside, it was all he could do just to remain standing there, hang his head and shake it negatively. He dropped both his tote bag and his rifle as he fought back the memories flooding into his brain. Wisely Mrs. Uys realized that there was a conflict happening in Craig's mind and switched, seamlessly back into maternal mode, bullying him to the table for food. Out in the kitchen, she passed the word around the rest of the family that Craig wasn't to be asked any questions.

"He's like Piet was the last time he was home, so give him some peace!" she told them all firmly. "He has to re-adjust to our way of life. He's got things to deal with that only he can do, so don't annoy him with questions, just like you didn't annoy Piet. He needs us now, although he might not know it yet and we've got to give him the time to come to terms with things."

Her daughter and her friend looked at Mrs Uys questioningly, only to be told quite firmly that young service men were called on to do things that they didn't want t do, but couldn't avoid. "They do these things so that YOU can sleep easy at night, young lady! Oh dear God, now both Piet and Craig are damaged goods!"

In answer to the girls' questions, all Mrs. Uys could tell them was that when her father had returned from the battles in the desert, he had had the same look in his eyes as both Piet and Craig now had.

"In battles the boys see and do things that you, young lady, don't even want to know about let alone think about. Leave Craig alone! Only he can deal with these problems! We've got to be here for him if he wants us. Give both of them time and they'll be alright, but don't push them."

Craig slept the first full day of his leave, only getting up in time for breakfast the second morning. Once he had shaved and washed, he no longer looked the wild man with far away eyes, but almost the normal Craig once again. Although he tried, and the Uyss' also tried, he could not settle down and relax, he had to be doing something all the time. Much as he wanted to enjoy being with his adopted family he was restless and felt that he should be back in the action. Things improved almost at the end of his leave when, unexpectedly, Piet arrived at the farmstead He had somehow wangled a 48 hour pass and come to see his folks, that Craig was there was a bonus for them both.

Late into the night both boys would sit on the stoep, drinking beer, smoking and talking to each other in half sentences. Both seemed completely comfortable and at ease with the situation, but neither was voluble, much of their communications were non-verbal. It seemed that each one needed the reassuring presence of the other to approach what now passed for normality in both their lives. Whilst Craig and Piet sat together, Piet's sister and her friend were solicitous to them and it was only then that Craig paid any attention to Suzanne, an attractive red-head from Pretoria. Piet, who had known Suzanne for years, always referred to her as 'Rooikop', a friendly nickname that he used all the time. Craig was rapidly and very firmly disabused of the notion that he could refer to Suzanne the same way when he received a glacial stare and an on-going cold shoulder of monumental proportions, but he was unaffected by Suzanne's reaction to his comment, it simply carried no weight at all, because he had hardly noticed her.

All too soon Piet's pass was up and Craig decided that he would return to barracks a before his pass was up too. That way, the whole group could travel into Salisbury together, making a day out of it for the civilians whilst the boys could re-enter the comfortable fold in the barracks without any painful re-adjustment.

Craig had not been back in barracks long before his bat-man had located him and brought him up to date with the news. It seemed that Craig was the last to know, but that he would be off on courses for the next two months. All Craig got was a transport docket and instructions when to be at the next posting. Reading the paperwork, he just sighed and determined to get a final good nights' sleep before his life was taken over by the military machine once more.

Chapter 4

Training to be 'not really a soldier'.

An early start and delivery to the new barracks by a Bedford 3 ton truck epitomised Craigs' entry into the new world of 'enhanced' officer training. Just why Craig was elected to complete the military version of the officers' fast track training course, he never found out; something to do with the exploding emergency situation out on the Eastern tribal territories was as close to a reason as he ever found out. Much of the course was class-room stuff and very little was doing anything exciting. He was taught the theory of command, 'leadership' (whatever THAT was!) and many other dry subjects. It was only in the intelligence based sections that he ever really found any interest.

He had never really appreciated how the dry bits of information that he and many others had collected were pieced together to make the overall picture. Doing examples of the work emphasised to him that even a small, apparently insignificant comment could unlock a complete perspective. Such small insights made him doubly careful not to miss fine details. He thought back at some of his talks with the tribal elders and realised that his approach had been far too European oriented to be of much good, in short he wasn't sufficiently sensitive to the tribal nuances to be very good. At that moment, he realised that he would have to have a few trusted native informers and that, even then, he would have to have a black constable alongside to pick up the finer cultural details. Craig was't unduly worried by that, he thought that whichever trooper he used would give him an honest and unbiased answer, but his first try out really proved his theory wrong.

Just from the tribemans' body language, Craig could tell that the answers he got to the questions were evasive, despite being assured by the black trooper, acting as 'cultural interpreter'. The report he got was that the tribes people were well disposed to the white Rhodesian regime and fearful of the 'liberation' fighters. Simply by watching the chief's eyes, Craig could see that the chief was simply mouthing the answers that Craig wanted to hear. He was upset that the trooper with him maintained the pretence that the ZANLA fighters would not be feed and provided for by members of that tribe and probably with the full blessing of the chief!

In the bar, after the days classes Craig, off the top of his head, complained about this to another course member.

"What are you thinking of doing?" was the immediate reply. After Craig's explanation that he was trying to determine how the tribes really felt about the terrs.

"They'll never tell you, a Whitey" affirmed his confidant, "And even if you did, no-one would be interested. There are plenty of old Africa hands here, you'd have to convince them first, they know it all and wouldn't be convinced by you! In short, no matter what you 'found out', you'd never get any intelligence past them."

"Don't you think this is worth a try?" Craig was almost pleading now.

The suggestion that he mount a 'guerrilla' campaign of his own trying to get this information was made half jokingly, but Craig liked it. As he mused over that suggestion, he understood that anything along these lines would have to be totally covert: to both the Tribes people AND to his bosses! He would have to try out a completely unofficially, covert surveillence-within-a-surveillance operation and only later would he be able to assess the value of any intelligence gathered. He was in for a long and secret run!

Days later, he was still musing over the practicalities of his operation within—an-operation after classes whilst sitting at the bar. Being told that he looked worried, he gave a wan smile and agreed that he had problems that he was finding difficult to overcome. Another beer and a few further questions down the road Craig said that everything hinged on the Shona speaker because whoever had that role had to thoroughly trustworthy. Previously, his information had beenruined by the bias of the translator.

Craig bemoaned his lack of Shona and the total reliance that that he had to put on his 'companion'.

'Why don't you use a white farm-boy?' was the suggestion he got. His lack of local knowledge was exposed by that reply, so he asked for an explanation, which, when it came, floored him with its' simplicity. Thinking further on that surprising answer gave him the hope of creating a realistic plan. After a little asking around, a National Service trooper, very ill at ease, reported to Craig as he was standing in a shady doorway reading the official de-briefing notes from his last exercise.

Standing in front of Craig, the trooper was very obviously anxious as to why he had been called over to the intelligence unit. A tall, gangly youth, as sunburned as the local veld and looking as if he would be comfortable roaming wild pastures, stood before Craig, a partly smoked, stubbed-out cigarette sitting on his left ear.

After asking from where the trooper originated, the second question was how much time the trooper had spent with the local tribes' people; only to be astonished when he was told that all his child hood had been spent in the local Shona kraal playing and living as one of the kraals' children. Trooper Derkson was embarrassed by that revelation, whilst Craig finally felt a pulse of hope run through him. When Derkson was asked what his mother tongue was, he hesitated and mumbled "English, I suppose", but that was not the answer he believed, Craig could read that from his body language.

"I was told that you are fluent in the local Shona dialect" Craig retorted, somewhat dismissively.

"I am, I just didn't know what answer you wanted from me." Derkson replied.

"Just an honest answer is all I want," Craig said idly. "How good are you operating in the local culture? Do you know when the village elders are telling the truth, or just saying what they think you want to hear?"

"In a local kraal, I'm at home, they don't treat me any different because I'm white."

"So they would talk in Shona and you would know what they are saying?" asked Craig.

"Yes, especially if there are no soldiers or police around and I'm not in uniform." Derkson answered.

"What if you were in uniform, could you understand what they were saying amongst themselves, enough to tell me where their replies to me were different?" Craig commented.

"No problems with that at all, I probably understand the local Shona dialect better than I do the local English accent, or yours for that matter!" Derkson answered matter-of-factly.

Dismissing trooper Derkson, Craig felt an excitement that he was possibly on an important intelligence break through. As he returned to his room, Craig was composing his thoughts and with them the report that he was going to write. What *IF* he could sort the intelligence wheat from the deliberate chaff of the tribal leaders' answers? How important would that ability be in the coming months or years? Certainly, it would allow Craig an insight into the real situation, rather than the artificial one being fed through official channels at the moment. Now *THOSE* little snippets of information would be the real Intelligence prizes gained from this initiative to allow realistic pictures of village life on the various Tribal Trust Lands. However, he would have to prove the value of his charade and that would take time and perhaps a little luck.

Talking his idea through with a freshly arrived R.A.R. captain, he found a sympathetic audience. Captain Andy Dennison, a veteran soldier, freshly back from service in the British Army and eager to get to grips with the terrs. operating in his homeland, was keen to add what he could to Craigs' basic approach. Andy was very pro the Brits and some of that favouritism he transfered to Craig, so they spent odd spare time together. It didn't take Craig long to realise that Andy was a very different type of soldier to the ones he had worked with so far. For one thing, Andy always seemed some steps ahead of the formal 'game'. Initially, Craig put this down to the rigidity of the B.S.A.P. and Army co-operation, but he swiftly realised that that idea was very wrong, for Andy's mind worked in a totally different direction. Rather than operating on the usual 'Overwhelming Force' that the Army seemed only too willing to apply, Andy seemed more at home with the specialist strikes using small, select groups. Craig realised very quickly that the small, specialist strike forces favoured by Andy would require the best and most current local information available AND intelligence gathering was all about useful information!

When they were together, Craig deferred to Andy's experience and used him as a sounding board for various ideas and approaches that he was proposing for intelligence gathering. Andy's first reaction was support, but that didn't come unqualified. Craig's idea of an operation-within-an-operation was to Andy's liking, but he made much of the problem of keeping all knowledge of this approach clear of Craig's superiors until the value could be proven. When Andy was told that trooper Derkson was going to accompany Craig on 'normal' police visits around the kraals, Andy suggested that Derkson go dressed in B.S.A.P. uniform rather than Army, although there was little difference between the two.

"Small details that you ignore could get you killed!" Andy told him. "These guys in the kraals spend all their days looking at the same scene and immediately spot something different. It's the same when we go to their kraals, they know what we look like, so minor differences stand out like beacons to them! If they suspect Derkson ISN'T Police, but Army, word will get round the local kraals faster than a veld fire and your information will dry up as fast."

Craig immediately saw the point and decided that Derkson for information gathering purposes should, unofficially, became a B.S.A.P. constable. Derksons' transformation from trooper to constable didn't take too long or too much training, but the actual changing of uniform had not to attract attention even from their own R.A.R. soldiers. Derkson, himself, provided the answer to that problem. Some of the B.S.A.P. had been detatched into nearby accommodation and were routinely picked up from their digs at the start of a mission, one of Derkson's relatives had a spare shed, so this became Derkson's 'official B.S.A.P.' lodgings. Craig had enough control of his small party to organise Derkson's collection when the group was being assembled at the start of a 'kraal intelligence group' operation.

Before the first trial run, Craig and Andy had a long talk. Returning to the barracks, Craig sent for Derkson and warned him not to look too interested in anything he overheard unless their safety was under immediate threat. Many young men in Rhodesia knew some Shona, but not so well as Derkson did, but Craig relayed Andy's warning for Derkson not to be too obviously listening to the tribesmen in case they suspected that he understood them. Having instructed Derkson to appear broadly uninterested, the next task was to select the four black R.A.R. troopers who formed the guard section that had begun to accompany Police visits to the kraals. This, as Andy had told him, was probably an unnecessary security step, but valuable to guard against accidental exposure should one of the R.A.R. troopers know of Derkson's real status. That the R.A.R.

guard detachment know Craig as a policeman would only strengthen their cover, but any accidentally revelation that Derkson was really an Army trooper could imperil all their lives. So, to ensure the body language of the R.A.R. troopers to both Derkson and Craig was consistent and natural, they could not be part of the cover, they really had to believe that Derkson was B.S.A.P. Eventually nerves apart, all delays and doubts overcome, Craig was satisfied that all his group were fully briefed and ready, so they climbed aboard the Bedford 3 tonner to go and, to begin the deception, went to collect Derkson from his lodging and then go to the local kraal.

This first exploration of clandestine intelligence gathering went very well, despite the need for both Craig and Derkson to hide their nerves and act out their roles. Back at barracks, Craig had to debrief Derkson in detail and was immediately aware of a problem. Derkson had heard and understood almost too much from the tribal attitude. One idea was immediately verified, that was that what the chiefs said was countered by their private mutterings and body language. Indeed, Derkson had learned too much from the interviews that he had witnessed and had had some difficulty retaining the desired uncomprehending attitude, but he had managed it. Their apparent welcome of the police and the protection offered was a simple sham; in that kraal, the chief welcomed the police to their face, but, when the police left, immediately went back to supporting ZANLA. Derksen had even heard tribal elders talking Shona saying that the 'boys' would be back soon and that they must be sure that food and women were waiting for them. Almost aware that they shouldn't have been talking so freely, the elders had clammed up from that point on. Craig could learn little further from trooper Derkson except that the elders' body language betrayed their discomfort at the presence of the white authorities in their kraal, even the children had been sent indoors, being kept quiet by their mothers.

As Derkson explained from the tribes' behaviour what had actually been happening in the kraal during their visit Craig thought of the gulf that existed between the real and percieved information gathered by the authorities. In his official report to his seniors Craig daren't report his experiment directly, but did make a play that he believed that official kraal inspections were not determining the true tribal feelings, the tribes simply telling the police only what they wanted to hear. If Craig thought that no-one ever bothered to read his reports, he was very rapidly disabused of that notion. Within a day of submitting the report, and whilst the rosy glow of a job well done, was still fresh Craig was ordered to his Captains' office. Still thinking that he had achieved a minor break through, he jauntily approached the office only to be regarded by the secretary-corporals' glum face and shaking head. 'Knock and go straight in.' he was told in glum tones, which should have been warning enough.

Craig rapped on the door, opened it and walked straight into a barrage of negative invective that seemed unending and of a volume that physically assaulted him. Any self congratulation he felt for a mission successfully accomplished was blown clean away before the end of the Captains' second sentence. By the end of that particular sentence, Craig's intellectual capacity, his parental status and personal abilities had all been questioned and dismissed, out of hand.

"Just what fucking game are you playing? Your job for us is simple and straight forward, or should be! Just find out what the bloody blacks are saying. Don't you ever try to analyse, or double guess, what the blacks really mean! THAT particular job is for people more senior and better trained than you'll EVER be if you carry on trying to be smart!" were some of the invective launched at him that Craig could remember after being summarily dismissed and being told that he was off operations until further notice. Just how low his star had fallen was made painfully clear when he received an order from the senior station B.S.A.P. Inspector to report to the personnel office for re-deployment.

Chapter 5

Life in the Intelligence dog-box

Life had not stopped for Craig, however much he dreamed that it had, it had one into serious reverse! He was struck dumb by what had happened to him. After all, he was just trying to do his job better and he had tried to use his initiative. His reward? Simply to be insulted and side-lined. He could have understood the humiliation had his findings been wrong,or even had it been demonstrated to him just how false his findings were, but just the simple insults from 'up high' somehow made the matter worse.

Reporting to the Station Personnel Officer simply added to the humiliation somehow; he seemed to know all about Craig's fall from grace in more detail than he himself did. Subsequent re-deployment saw Craig running a small, 2 man rural police station lost out in the Rhodesian farming areas. Only his rank saved him from being thrown back to the most menial work of plodding around isolated farmsteads. Running the small, fly blown station that he was given was hardly any better, accommodation, such as it was, was provided and took the form of two air-less rooms attached at the back of the station. His constable lived at home, Craig lived at the station, essentially on a 24 hour a day call out basis.

As a result, Craig had plenty of time to ponder the infraction that had landed him in a virtual limbo. So little actually happened that the initial routine that he had imposed on himself soon fell by the wayside. His visits to the local farms were initially treated with suspicion, the farmers only ever getting police visits after they had complained of stock theft or trespass; any form of pro-active policing was a cause of deep suspicion. By the end of his second week, the slowness of the rural life had Craig fully slept out, totally frustrated and finding anything to do to occupy his time. He now understood why the rural police officers always seemed to be so immaculately turned-out, about the only job they had to do was to polish their shoes and Sam Browns and iron their trousers!

One compensating factor was he had use of the B.S.A.P. Land Rover, a goodly supply of diesel fuel for it and apparently unlimited access to a telephone. By the time that his first month in limbo was drawing to a close, Craig had lost all inhibitions about using the Land Rover and the telephone as freely as he wanted. He kept records of sorts of their usage in an official ledger, but as he was authorising officer, the 'reasons for usage' column only carried some vague wording and his initialled approval. What he did do was to phone Mrs. Uys daily at home and talk at length abot this and that. Piet was also away from home, but was due leave shortly and would be returning to the family farm. That decided Craig! He decided to apply for a 72 hour pass, formally by letter, knowing that the local post wouldn't even have collected his letter before he came back. That would cover him, in a sort of a way, should anything happen; similarly,the additional mileage on the Land Rover could be easily hidden by unscrewing the speedometer cable from the back of the dashboard. A few jerry-cans of diesel in the back should cover almost all eventualities and if he did run short, tractor diesel was available on every farm.

So, as the weekend of Piets' leave approached he made sure that his constable would cover for him ('So whats' to cover, hey?') He started off early, having done the minimal formal stuff, mainly paperwork and was off on the road early in the dawn cool. He left behind the Uys telephone number, but why, thinking back, he couldn't understand. Any constable could pick up the station 'phone and get connected directly to the Uys's farm, by now the telephonist knew the number by heart and probably his business there as well! As the distance between himself and his 'bush' station grew Craig found his frustrations evaporating and a holiday feeling taking over. He had been warned, by Mrs. Uys, that some other people would be at the farm, all Piets' friends and all of whom Craig had met before, so there would be plenty of company during his leave. He no longer sought out solitude and close company as he had on his last leave, now he wanted to be young again and seperation from the police force.

Each wheel rotation lightened his mood and increased his anticipation of being back with his adopted family.

At that time of year, many of the roads were dusty, so the Land Rover was soon covered in a film of fine, reddish dust and indistinquishable from other farm vehicles. Dusty and thirsty, Craig decided to stop at the next bush bar he saw; O.K., it would be near the Uyss' farm, but a cool beer before arrival would certainly perk him up and help ensure that he wouldn't arrive looking like a wet rag. It was about time that he made a more dignified entrance than his more normal one wearing a disheveled, crumpled uniform. Through the dust cloud, he caught sight of a bush bar, it was actually the red metal Coca-Cola sign that he noticed, so he slowed ready to pull in. This old Landy needed plenty of prior warning when a stop was needed, so he went through the usual procedure of trying to pull the steering wheel off whilst attempting to push the brake pedal through the floor. Having asserted his authority over the car, he parked in thebare, dusty square and strode into the bar.

As he stepped through the door, the conversation stopped mid-flow, as if cut by a knife. Every head in the place turned towards him and inspected him closely. Craig was the only white in the whole place and in full, immaculate B.S.A.P. uniform, too. Despite being last in the small queue, the bar-tender came to serve him first and asked what he wanted. Despite saying to serve the other people first, the bar-keeper sold Craig the cool beer he asked for. Feeling the strained atmosphere almost at breaking point, and appreciating that his presence was causing the strain, He downed his beer too quickly and left. As he stepped through the door, the buzz of conversation re-started behind him. Taking advantage of being out of the car, he decided to stretch his legs a little and find a suitable tree against which to pee and so selected one close to his car, towards the rear of the bottle store. His attention was mainly focussed on keeping his shiny shoes clean, but was distracted when an african man carrying a washed out, green canvas sack over his shoulder darted out from a door and into the trees as fast as his legs would carry him. Craig noticed this, thought it strange, because at this time of day the heat made most people moved as slowly as possible. He was still focused on getting to the farm and his friends as soon as he could and so he simply accepted the running African as another inexplicable facet of Africa.

His arrival at the farm-house was anything but muted! So many people were there to greet Piet and himself that they streamed off the verandah. Mrs.Uys was in her element, the more people there were, the more she seemed to thrive. Craig arrived before Piet and so bore the full brunt of the enthusiastic welcome home. Asking why so many people were at the farm, Mr. Uys hinted at that special things were happening and once Piet had arrived and the group was complete everything would be revealed. Pushing through to the kitchen, Craig found a tin-bath full of ice and cold drinks and he dug out a can of beer and popped the top and started to drink. He visibly relaxed as he stood there and felt himself slow down and begin to notice the people around him. Most of the men he saw acknowledged him by tipping their beer can towards him, others came and spoke or patted his shoulder as they passed by. One of the local farmers button-holed him, complaining that the police weren't doing enough to catch the people unsettling the local tribes people. All Craig could say was that this was no longer his district and that problems like that should be taken to the nearest police station. That comment didn't really satisfy the farmer who 'Harump'd and moved on.

Piet arrived and was mobbed by the family. Craig hung back a little to give the family free reign before he stepped over and hugged Piet. As he stood talking, he noticed a striking red haired young woman, who gave him a straight, appraising look. Breaking eye contact, she moved off to talk to some-one else. Piet noticed that Craig had seen seen the red haired woman and simply said 'Meet Rooikop, the ice maiden.' Craig shrugged his shoulders and fell back to 'talking shop' with Piet. Moments later, Mr. Uys banged the tin-bath to draw attention, when the crowd noise died away, he began speaking, telling every-one the reason for the get-together, as he called it. It seemed that two of the local belles were getting married (Craig knew both only by sight) and that Suzanne (Rooikop) was returning to South Africa, probably to get married also. At that comment Craig looked around and found that Rooikop was looking directly at him. Like the rest of the group, he joined every-one else in the cheers and best wishes to the young women. Strangely, he felt a litrtle deflated to learn that Suzanne would be moving away, although at their last meeting she had cut him dead, ignoring him totally.

It was to be a long party, few people leaving before darkness fell and those that didn't remaining there until dawn. Craig knew the reason for this, increased bandit activity had made night-time travel less safe. He was still discomforted by this, feeling his home, his base, threatened. He moved out of the party late into the night and collapsed, fully dressed, asleep across his bed. When he woke up, his uniform was no longer immaculate, but he felt fresher and sharper with no hang over. A few minutes cleaning himself up, shaved, hair combed he stepped outside to catch the morning air and the glorius early morning sun. He just stood there, face to the sun, eyes closed drinking in the early morning freshness and enjoying every moment of it.

"Ja, a mooi Rhodesian morning." Surprised him and he opened his eyes slowly as he turned towards the voice. Suzanne was standing behind him and to his left, looking into the far distance.

"I love the morning freshness." he said "Makes you glad to be alive."

"I'm off this morning, back to South Africa. Will you drive me to the train station?" she asked.

Suzanne was already packed and ready to leave. She went back inside, coming out moments later with tears in her eyes having said her 'good-byes' and walked straight over to Craigs Land-Rover. Carrying her bags to the Landy Craig put them into them into the back, then climbed into the drivers' seat.

Most of the journey to the railway station was in total silence, Rooikop didn't or wouldn't make conversation. All Craig's questions were answered, but the answers were clipped to the point of being curt. He drove along in silence, beginning to feel that he had been taken advantage of, but not really minding; even this, after all, was better than being in that little police station fiddling with the paper work. At the station, Craig open Suzanne's door, helped her out and fetched the bags. He carried them onto the platform, put them down and made to leave, only to be asked to to stay with her until the train arrived. When the train arrived, she found a suitable carriage, Craig stowed her luggage, saw her seated and turned to leave. Suzanne was crying gently and quietly by this time and as he got hold of the door handle, she grabbed hold of him, kisse his cheek and said 'Thanks for everything.' At that she sat down, covering her face with her hands. Craig, taken aback, simply said 'See you again' and stepped back onto the platform and watched the train pull out. On the road back to the farm, he initially thought about what had happened, couldn't understand it and so dismissed it from his mind. He was beginning to feel that he was understanding less and less of the current world and wondered if it were him, or was the world sometimes just incomprehensible?

Back at the farm, the population had returned to its more normal size and the pace of life had slowed to near its normal heartbeat. Piets' sisters played up a little to Craig for taking Suzanne to the railway station on his own; they made it sound like some great unrequited love affair for him. He only looked askance at them, with one eyebrow raised questioningly. Mr. Uys just laughed at the girls and told Craig that Rooikop had gone back to get married and that the girls were just pulling his leg.

"You were the person Rooikop most trusted to take her to the train, because she doesn't like you that much and that would make leaving here easier." Mrs. Uys told him, quite seriously.'Oh thanks!' thought Craig to that comment and then began to think that getting Rooikop away was probably not a bad usage of his morning. Talk within the farm soon turned to the increasing problems of traveling after dusk; when the current picture had been told him, Craig was concerned by the disintegrating security situation. It was these developments that he had indicated from his now disasterous intelligence gathering expedition, that increasing low level infiltrations of 'the boys', supported by passive local support, would only continue. What impact this would have on the farmers was fairly predictable, but just what the farmers could do about the infiltrators was not clear. Here, Craig could make a positive contribution!

During his training, Craig had undertaken an amourers course which had taught him more than the basics behind anti-personnel explosive devices. Many of the simple devices could readily be manufactured on the average farm from components found around the compound, so Craig began to manufacture some simple warning explosives. All these things were mearly to scare off trespassers, so they would have to be placed very close by the routes onto the farm property. Simple trip wires, made from fishing line, set across the paths at ankle height triggered small flares or 'flash-bangs' designed to startle the intruder by betraying his position. Craig made a few very simple, low powered devices. He and Piet searched out the infiltration paths to the farm and planted a selection of flares and 'flash-bangs' as an experiment to see if the intruders could be scared off. Both being trained by the national authorities, they arranged things so that the flares on each trail were of different colours, to aid rapid location of infiltraters; the explosives all sounded the same and were designed to startle and disorientate.Before Craig had left the farm, they had their first successes with the traps. It was full night when a series of loud bangs awoke every-one in the farm-house, rushing to the windows, they saw the flares still illuminating one of the routes with vague figures visible nearby. Satisfied with their handiwork, Piet glanced across at Craig and both grinned like happy little boys. They never realised how big a mistake they had made!

At dawn both of them climbed aboard the Landy and drove over to the site of the nights' fireworks. Carefully they examined the ground to ensure that they tripped none of the remaining charges. They needn't have worried, all the trip wires had been activated by the intruders blundering about trying to get away from the flares and explosions. Scattered in the bush were various bags of food, clothing and, more importantly, grenades and weapons. Collecting the spoils of their nights' fun, both men drove back to the farm to telephone the local police, who very swiftly came in as big a mass as possible.

Examining the insergents' treasure trove caused the local police sargent to whistle through his teeth.

"First time, I've seen Chinese grenades in this province!" he affirmed. "Look, these AK parts also have Chinese markings. You must have scared those okes good last night for them to leave these weapons!"

"The weapons bag had dropped into a narrow, little gully. They needed light to find it again, but we got there first." Piet reported.

"Well, all these bits carry rewards, so I'll make you out receipt for them and I'll put a report in." commented the policeman. "I thought you two boys were on leave this weekend, not playing cops and robbers with the terrs."

"We are, but just couldn't resist doing something." Craig said. Having said that, he continued to report the incident when the man carrying a similar bag had run out of the bundu bottle store.

"Ah, that's an important lead!" commented the Sergeant, "What did you do about it?"

All Craig could say was that as he had been in a rush, he did nothing and really questioned how important his information was.

"Well, a bag like the one you saw the running guy carrying has turned up with terrorist arms in it. So maybe what you saw really WAS important. Anyway, I'll include that sighting in my report."

What ever the report said worked strongly in Piets' favour and he became a local celebraty in his station. Craig, on the other hand, was lamblasted from top to bottom by his senior officers. Playing covert surveillance operations when he had been warned off them was the generally accepted conclusion; absent-without-leave was also mentioned frequently. Back at his small bundu police station, Craig's number 2,

Drury, his only subordinate, apologized profusely, but Craig told him not to worry as it would be he, Lieutenant Burgoyne, who would get all the stick and not him, Constable Drury. On that particular point Craig was proven completely correct, for within two days he had been ordered to Salisbury for a disciplinary hearing which he was told would decide his future within the Police service. Listlessly, he set off to Salisbury, Drury drove him to the nearby railway station in the station Land-Rover and Craig settled into an oven of a railway carriage to get to Salisbury. What had started of as a simple 'bunk off due to boredom' weekend had turned into something much more serious for Craig.

With nothing more to do but wait until the train got him to Salisbury, Craig got to thinking about his recent past and tried to identify what had caused the massive over-reaction to his mild and generally inoffensive sneaky operation in his area of Mashonaland. All the trouble had come centrally, from the joint Police/Army hierarchy, nothing he had done had disturbed the tenor of tribal life there. Eventually, in an attempt to forestall more trouble, all he could think of to say was that he had been over-enthusiastic in translating his role. Although he felt that this was his best defence, even to plead that would be to admit defeat to himself and probably condemn him a life as a full-time country cop; better, perhaps, simply to offer no defence and be thrown out or resign.

Chapter 6

Pas op vir die hond!!

Back in the Salisbury barracks, the first person he met was Andy Dennison, who pulled him off to one side to get an update on the latest intelligence picture. When told of the career damage done by the prototype mild 'covert' intelligence gathering had inflicted on Craig, Andy was dumbstruck. Craig couldn't blame Andy, because he had been a willing initiator and participant in the scheme and still believed that that information was, or should be, important to operations. Andy said that he would 'talk to someone', but Craig shrugged his shoulders and said 'Too late!'

Craig's hearing was set for the morning after he arrived in barracks. 'At least', he thought, 'they're not prolonging the condemned mans' agony. Things will be over quickly and at least I'll have the rest of the day to myself.' No sooner had he marched smartly to the Commissioner's Office than he was sent in to the hearing with the words 'They're ready for you' ringing in his ears.

As he closed the door behind him, he was hit by the first question "What were you trying to do?" Taken aback by the direct question, Craig's reply was not the model crisp answer that the Authorities teach. Another member of the panel cut his answer short by asking for his opinion on the value of such information. Once more, before he could complete his answer yet another panel member spoke up. It took Craig aback again, but as the hearing progressed it was increasingly obvious that this meeting wasn't the discipliniary hearing that he had been lead to expect. Rapidly, the panel got around to the practicalities that had had to be overcome for such an operation to be mounted and succeed.

"Don't be worried, your operation DID succeed and hasn't so much as left a ripple on the surface in the tribal trust lands." said the most senior officer there, a red tabbed and much decorated General, who was acting as Presiding Officer.

"Are you capable of repeating the same operation in a different area, say Manicaland East?" another red tabbed staff officer enquired. "Or do you even want to? I understand that you caught a load of flak from" and here the officer looked directly at the Presiding Officer, "your previous management?"

At this Craig was rocked back and managed to stutter out that he had been led to believe that this meeting was to be a disciplinary hearing initiated by his first attempt at covert intelligence gathering. That comment brought smiles to all the panel members faces and the odd embarrased grin; now Craig was truly floundering. Had there been a shift in policy somewhere that he knew nothing about; had his report been re-assessed, what had created this changed atmosphere and, more importantly, WHO was the 'new management'?

"I can see that we have you at a severe disadvantage," the Officer Presiding said. "You look completely flummoxed."

"I am! What's happening?" asked Craig.

In short, clipped, sentences the Officer Presiding gave an overview of the new policies and the changes that they had wrought. Everything he said was accompanied by vigorous nods of agreement from the other panel members. In this monologue, Craig was introduced, for the first time, to the Central Intelligence Organisation, the C.I.O., and told that his initiative had been completely along the lines down the Organisation was thinking.

"Best I can say about your previous management was that they didn't know. Need to know and all that. But they shouldn't have stifled your initiative, yours was a smart move, but they probably thought you showed them up, so 'shoot the messenger'. Easy way out!" continued the Officer Presiding. "But now we are going to exploit smart thinking like your idea. We'll break for 15 minutes now, re-convene and get into the what we need to do. Lieutenant Burgoyne, you'll sit in and contribute fully, do I make myself understood?" with a sharp look at Craig.

Coffee was available in the outer office, but most of the other officers went outside for a smoke. Craig was left alone with the General, feeing somewhat nervous and exposed, he didn't know whether, or how, to make conversation with such a high ranking officer. No 'shop talk' during work breaks was a principle quickly ingrained into all Police and Army officers, so he attempted to keep himself to himself.

"Ah, some of Rhodesia's finest out there" commented the Senior Officer.

"You mean the officers?" Craig enquired.

"No, the cigarettes! One of Rhodesias' major contributions to happiness in the outside world, our tobacco is. Pity old C.J. didn't smoke, he'd have made yet another fortune out of tobacco!" opined the General.

Craig had to acknowledge the veracity of that point, most of the Mashonaland farmers that he knew were tobacco growers and extremely proud of their crop; the comment was also instructive to Craig, showing the breadth of thought applied even to simple things.

In groups of twos and threes, the other group members returned, ignoring the coffee and walking straight into the committee room (as Craig now thought it) and taking their previous chairs. Once every-one was in the room, the door was closed and the General re-convened the meeting.

"At this point, I think it best to give a brief overview of our task here today, to keep us all focussed. I hope I do't need to remind you that Lietenant Burgoyne, although a police man, is actually one of the new breed of split Police/Army officers and that status entitles him to treatment as one of us" With that, the Senior Officer gave a crisp summary of their task that day and then threw the meeting open for discussion and debate. As he did so, he reminded the meeting that it was 'a no Hats' meeting. Seeing Craigs questioning glance, he leaned towards him and said "No one wears a hat, so we're all out of uniform and rank holds no privilege, so it's a free and open discussion, anything goes."

For the remainder of that meeting, ideas were thrown up, discussed and shot down or modified with no rancour at all. Craig found the whole process very educational; here he was in one of the most hierarchical organisations in the world and there they were talking almost like a University debating society. But it worked! When the meeting was drawn to a close, the General identified a number of agreed positions and points needing to be explored further. As he turned to leave the room, the General called Craig over, reminding him that the meeting was secret and to return to his bundu station where, the General smilingly said, he wouldn't be wasting his time in the Manicaland bundu station much longer!

When Craig arrived back at his station, constable Drury made a point of very deliberately looking at the rank boards on his shoulder. Seeing that he still had the Lieutenants boards on his shoulders, Drury raised his eyebrows questioningly. Craig told him not to worry himself as his quiet life would soon be returning since he was expecting to be posted somewhere else very soon. Craig enquired had anything important happened during his absence, Drury simply shook his head; when asked had ANYTHING at all happened in the past few days, he was told that 'a few fences had been cut at Larkshill Farm and a few cattle wandered away'. In normal circumstances that would have been the end of the matter, but these were not normal times. Since the meeting, he had been primed to note extra-ordinary events. He spun around on his heel to face Drury and asked if the fence wires had been cut, or had the twisted joints pulled apart when the cattle pushed them. At the question, Constable Drury's attitude sharpened up.

"Since you ask about it, they were cut. I saw the clean cut ends and they were still shiny, so they had been cut for less than a day. I did ask the farmer and he told me that section of fence is a newish one that he hadn't had to repair. That's why he noticed." continued Drury in his best Police reporting voice.

"Who,when and where?" Craig immediately shot the question back at the constable.

Taken a little aback by such a swift response, Drury did his best to answer precisely.

"Close up the shop, we're off to work!" was how Craig instructed him.

Within minutes, both were in the station Land-Rover to visit the scene of the wire cutting. Drury had to guide Craig because of his better local knowledge and soon they approached the wire fenced area from across the farm land. When told to stop, Craig braked heavily and skidded the car to a dusty halt. Drury climbed out, looked around to get his bearings, then marched along the fence line for a few metres. He stopped at the new repair, the wire ends having been tightly twisted together and he could see the bright sharp ends of fencing wire cut clean through by cutters. He examined the ends and was in no doubt that the fence wire had been deliberately cut. He began to look around, the ground nearby would produce no spoor, too many people had trampled the area, so he began to look wider around. Drury stood by his shoulder and saw something over a hundred metres away.

"Looks like a game kill" he said.

"What does?" asked Craig.

"That pile in the shade there" he told him, pointing down the general fence direction.

"Where? I don't see anything!" said Craig again, trying to look in the direction Drury's arm was pointing.

"Veld trained eyes, you see." replied the constable. "Don't look AT the shadow, but INTO it and you'll see. An old San hunter taught me that trick when I was a boy."

Adopting the advice, Craig maybe saw something, but nothing that he could identify, so he marched off to identify close up what Drury had seen at distance. As he closed up, he began to see the rubble of a badly butchered calf. Fighting the temptation to run to the spot, he held his arms wide open to prevent Drury passing him and disturbing any remaining spoor. This cautious approach paid an immediate dividend, there were a few sparse footprints around the carcass and the wood fire ashes. No predator had had this calf, that much was immediately obvious; no predator, that is, other than man! Craig sketched a rough shape of the boot sole prints he saw in the area, thinking that the print might identify the culprit, but all Constable Drury said was that they were farm workers boots. When asked for an explanation, the constable simply said that he'd seen plenty of farm workers wearing those boots on some of the farms around Larkshill, the fashion, it seemed, had started a shortly before Craig joined the local station. That comment alarmed Craig, but he tried not to show it to Drury, simply saying that thanks to Drurys' veld trained eyes, he would have to write a full report and send it in. A few acidic comments followed about the diligence of their superior officers and Craig made it very clear to the constable that he, Drury, would have all the pleasure of dealing with the brass all by himself!

He, himself, wrote an urgent report direct into C.I.O. In it he detailed the occurrence at the nearby farm, finding the boot spoor and that a calf had been badly butchered and cooked. Almost as an afterthought, he included his sketch of the boot spoor that he had found and the apparently off-hand comment from Constable Drury that many local farm workers in that area of Manicaland were wearing similar boots. What resulted stunned Craig, what with the speed of response and the number of troops which descended on his little bundu station as if by magic. There were three distinctly different types of soldiers at his location: one type was obviously the command/intelligence group; the second that of R.L.I. troopers, young keen and very fit, whilst the third type seemed to be scruffy individuals who kept themselves very much to themselves. Both Craig and Constable Drury were interviewed by the Intelligence types immediately on their arrival and, as a result, Constable Drury drove to the Larkshill site with the stations' Land-Rover full of R.L.I. troopers and then returned empty. Meanwhile the group of scruffy individuals asked a few questions, repacked their rucksacks ('Bergens' they called them), hitched a lift to Larkshill and left. Craig was evicted from his police station room, which became the operations head-quarters, the police station became a radio-station in moments and accomodation in the form of a tent was erected in the back yard of the police station.

After all the time when nothing at this station had ever happened, these changes completely revolutionised the character of the place. From being a boring back water posting for inefficient policemen, his post had suddenly become a buzzing military base. Being far out of town and yet so remote, these changes would never be noticed by the locals, unless one happened to wander by for a chat. His station, as he soon found out, was no longer 'his' station, but was now the 'Manicaland West operations base', consequently he was beginning to feel distinctly out of place there. Drury continued to undertake the normal police routine, as though nothing extra-ordinary was happening, but the local Army command requested that Craig remain around the site and at constant availability. He was, but there was so little for him to do that each day began to drag more than the previous one. After a few days, the R.L.I. boys came walking back to the station with the news that ZANLA was big in the area. Discipline amongst the insurgents had fallen somewhat, probably as a result of their boredom, and they had become sloppy about security.

Apparently, just a day and a half's march away ZANLA was establishing the largest base in the region. Hidden amidst the local tribal territories, where the local population had been thoroughly cowed by the insurgents' brutality to the point of open support, although still unwillingly done. 'Political re-education' of wavering natives was firmly in place, ZANLA ensured that everyone knew how and why any resisters to their authority was being punished. In short, the whole of the local region was rapidly becoming subborned into a ZANLA puppet region. Apart from learning of this Craig was definately 'out of the loop' and so he had returned to the level of boredom in which he had existed before his 'hearing' and had even become used to being denied access into the station building. 'Should life get any more boring,' he was thinking 'then I'll walk over to the dam and do something interesting like skip stones across the water!' Before he could even gather the energy to walk to the dam, he became aware that the noise emanating from the 'Manicaland West operations base' had changed from the previous quiet into an excited and frenetic burble.

"Ah, there you are Burgoyne!" an Intelligence Major called out of the 'Operations centre' to Craig. "Drop everything and come in here, we are planning something and you must be involved."

It seemed that from the information brought back by the R.L.I. troopers, the 'scruffs' of the Rhodesian S.A.S. had undertaken a long term observation of the base and were now ready to direct a full scale assault on it.

"We aim this to be the classical 'stop' operation. R.L.I. troopers will go in behind the terrs and then an R.L.I. 'fireforce' team will drop in front and squeeze the insurgents backwards into the waiting 'stop' team. All sideways movement will be halted by the surprises that the S.A.S. have left behind them. They're waiting for any one who squeezes by and will deal with them."

"I know you know this type of operation, your first intelligence gathering deployment was of this type, but you were put down too soon and too close that time. This time the briefing will be tighter!" "You'll still be out to gather any intelligence that you find, but look for anything and LEARN everything before you're off site! The other groups, S.A.S. and R.L.I. will also gather what intelligence they can, but it will be your task to co-ordinate the whole lot!"

Craig had but a short time to get prepared, about the only things in surplus at the 'Manicaland Operations base' were weapons, so he selected an R 1 rifle and a big, old but reliable Webley revolver, then he sat and cleaned both guns. When he was happy with the state of his fire-arms, he started to prepare himself. The police uniform was changed for rank-less D.P. battle-dress and canvas personal kit pouches, into which he stuffed a few grenades. This time, he knew enough to take a canvas duffle bag in which any 'spoils of war' could be carried away. He was re-checking the ammunition loaded in both guns when the Major re-appeared and told him to do that on the helicopter, as he would be off in minutes in wave two of the front 'push' group.

As before, it was all adrenaline and haste. Before he even got into the Alouette, the pilot had it hovering a few centimetres off the floor and Craig was pulled in, unceremoniously, by the R.L.I. troopers. Without hesitation, the Alouette climbed up into the sky and banked towards the terrorist base. At first, the rotor noise was all encompassing, but when they dipped towars the ground, Craig heard the crackle of small arms fire getting louder the lower they went. As the landing skids brushed the ground, the R.L.I. troopers piled out at speed. Craig followed at his best speed and ran towards the sound of action.

Off to his left there was a deeper 'boom' as an explosive charge went off; seconds later above the tree line a red/black cloud ascended. He was effectively on his own, the fire-force troopers had fanned out to go about their business, so Craig had to use caution. Without prompting, Drury's comment of 'look into the shadows, look into the trees' came into his mind and he advanced with that advice in the front of his mind. Automatically, he had taken the 'safety' off his rifle as he exited the helicopter, so now he was a fully functioning soldier again. 'Hide, then run forward' he had been instructed, so he did, but looking warily around as he moved out of cover.

It was obvious that the initial fireforce assault had caught the insurgents un-prepared, the floor looked as if a large broom had swept everything one way. Forward! Small arms fire still crackled ahead, but the volume was diminishing rapidly. Craig fought back an impulse to relax and head towards the fireforce troopers ahead of him as he came up to the first curve of guard trenches for the base. At the bottom lay a body, probably dead, otherwise seriously injured. Craig simply looked at the body, drew his revolver and put a round cleanly into the head, 'better one bullet too many than one too few!' he thought as he passed beyond the trench. 'Never turn your back on an enemy until you know he's dead!', he couldn't remember who had told him that, but he accepted that bit of wisdom unquestioningly. He could see nothing of intelligence virtue initially in the trench, he would come back and be more thorough when the insurgents had been fully suppressed. For now, he continued to move forward, all the time looking into the shadows and into the trees. He was approaching the stick of troopers that he'd flown in with, still advancing steadily searching for anything that would extend the intelligence picture, then, in a bush, he saw a figure. Stopping, he concentrated looking deeper through the bush; clearly the figure was unaware that it was under observation as it continued burying something in the bushes roots. Very carefully, Craig pulled the R1 to his shoulder and sighted on the figure in the bush; slowly, slowly the digging was finished and the figure began to turn to leave the bush and move away from the gun fire. Judging that he now had as clear a shot as he'd ever have, he squeezed the trigger, the R1 kicked and the figure fell. 'But for Constable Drury's advice, I'd have missed him' thought Craig as he pushed on towards the centre of the terrorists' camp. When he got there, the fighting had finished and gun-shots further on told the story that the 'stop' group was busy doing just that, stopping the terrs departure.

Around the centre of the camp sat two R.L.I. troopers, both wounded and bandaged. Both were conscious and aware, so when Craig told them that he was going to search for intelligence artefacts, both agreed to cover his back, should the terrs return. All the accommodation were excavated holes, some having specific purposes (Kitchen, Bedrooms) whilst others seemed to be for general usage. All were hovels, poorly constructed and badly maintained, most with more than their share of detritus, so intelligence hunting wasn't pleasant. Most of the interesting stuff to Intelligence were the Chinese made and marked equipment, everything from boots to water bottles. When he managed to examine some of the armaments that had been used, again generally everything was Chinese, which simply re-confirmed that the insurgents were ZANLA. Collecting together the pieces from the camp ready to pack before he did the body searches, he suddenly remembered the one hiding in the bush that he had shot, so he returned to retrieve what had been so important that it must be buried. Pulling the corpse out of the bush wasn't easy, it had dropped into the branches which had snagged and tore into the battledress. Eventually, by pulling on one leg, the body came clear and onto the grass. A very quick look told Craig that one bullet had sufficed, in through the left temple and out taking half the right side with it. Scrambling under the bush, the soft earth was easy to find and remove by hand. What he found was a pouch full of documents, some laminated, the rest simply folded and packed. Even a brief inspection showed that in his hands he had details of all the infiltration routes and timetables and more besides, so here was real gold, the true pay-off for the operation.

When he walked further forward to search for intelligence 'goodies', he was stopped by one of the 'scruffs'.

"Let the R.L.I. boys bring in the bodies, they know where the ambushes are, you don't."

When all the bodies were back at camp, he asked if any intelligence documents had been found, but got only cheesy grins from the now smoking R.L.I. troopers. As the sweet smell of their joints rolled through the camp, he went to search the bodies, something he did swiftly and unhappily, but found nothing of value. All bodies had to be piled together to await the arrival of a three ton truck to take the bodies away for identification. Craig elected to depart with the troopers, rather than wait for the gruesome body collection; he had nothing extra to give, but there was an urgency to pass on the document pouch. Not smoking didn't prevent him from experiencing some of the pleasure of the bhang that the troopers had 'liberated' from the insurgents. At last a happy group disembarked from their transport back at 'Manicaland Operations Centre' a.k.a the bush police station to which Craig had been posted, and he wasted no time passing on the pouch for closer inspection.

He passed the documents still in the canvas pouch to another B.S.A.P. officer that, like he, was working closely with the military. Kevin Woods outranked Craig, but was younger, had longer Police service and was obviously on the Intelligence 'fast track'. They talked together for a while, discussing Intelligence gathering problems that they had in common. Kevin actually praised Craig's attempt at subtle, indirect information gathering amongst the Shona speaking tribes, but, he thought that approach went neither far enough nor radical enough. Craig admitted that he had had further ideas, but the reaction he had initially suffered meant that he forgot them, besides his 'team' (such as it had been) had been dispersed.

"You've got yourself noticed now!" Kevin told him. "Structures are changing and we need newer thinkers now. Don't worry, things will happen!"

"What does 'don't worry' mean? I was told THAT back in Salisbury a few weeks ago and sent back here!" Craig replied bitterly.

Shrugging his shoulders Kevin simply said "You'll see!"

Chapter 7

Intelligence fast tracking (Bloedhond)

Almost as soon as Kevin drove away, Craig was told to report back to Salisbury for an undisclosed course. His orders informed him that he would be reassigned afterwards, so he should bring all his kit with him. Packing was swift and enjoyable, he had little personal gear to think about, standard issue clothing was just about that all he had. Once his duffle was packed Constable Drury drove him to the railway station, once more he got a hot and airless carriage for the long rail journey westward. At Salisbury station, Craig had a feeling of *deja vu*, for what happened seemed almost a rerun of his previous visit. He was allocated the same dormitory room and bat-man as before, but, this time, had more time to acclimatise before lance-corporal Allot suggested that he go to the division office and sort out his new schedule.

When he saw his new course, it was a month long and almost all of it would be in the class-room and not 'in the field'. At the beginning of the first lecture he, and the other course members, were unequivocally told that they were to become senior intelligence analysts. From the detailed information that they would each handle they would be responsible for the fine detail planning of raids 'anywhere in the combat area.' It was clear that the target, and general direction, of the raids would be done by others, but they were to locate and determine any 'high value' targets the loss of which would have a disproportionate effect on the enemy. 'Most will be commanders and other individuals.' intoned the lecturer. He went on to detail the types and aims of the raids that he, himself, had been involved in during the Malayan crisis in the early 1950's.

"What you MUST always bear in mind is that if we can behead the enemy's' command structure by removing a senior officer, the troops left behind will be leaderless and disorganised, therefore useless as attack forces for a long time! The last world war had many examples of 'pinpoint' raids that cost almost nothing, but achieved results out of all proportions to the forces used. We HAVE to utilise the same philosophy in this war!" Major Smart emphasised.

What followed was a bit of a history lesson, where Major Smart took the group through the German airborne attack on Eban-Emael in May 1940, where the fortified Belgian border positions had been neutralised by paratroops from the Brandenburg Regiment in a few hours. Belgian defence policy had been totally predicated on the invulnerability of that fortress to prevent an invasion by German land forces through the Ardennes and Dutch border gap. Defeat of that fortress (and so quickly) kicked the back-door to France wide open for the Wehrmacht to invade. "Which they promptly did, the Belgian Army was by-passed, the French army collapsed rapidly, France immediately sued for Armistice and the British Army was forced to retreat pell-mell across the channel through Dunkirk, leaving the Germans masters of Western Europe!"

"By any measures, that single action almost won the war for Germany before the other combatant nations had woken up. We want to do the same thing here, but WIN!" Smart emphasised each point by rapping his knuckles loudly on the desk.

"Later in that war, small, elite forces from all sides made substantial contributions very cheaply. In the Malayan Emergency, the S.A.S. evolved a 'hearts and minds' campaign amongst the jungle people. As a result the Chinese insurgents fought the British Forces, but the indigenous tribes located the Chinese and then led the British to where the insurgents were. Once more, maximum results with little fighting!"

"In this war we are going to be outnumbered, so we've got to fight smarter, which means that we've got to PLAN smarter. Your jobs, gentlemen, will be to ensure we plan smart and maximise our effort!" With Major Smart's resounding statement ringing in their ears, all members of Craig's course were clearly made aware of what was expected of them. This course was to be no vague headquarters course of information hopefully useful at some future date, theirs was to be an immediate, definitive and important war contribution.

After the Majors' blood pounding speech, the remainder of the day slowed to a 'normal' course pace and was dedicated to specific intelligence gathering topics. When the talk was about reading and understanding tribesmen's attitude, Craig was called on to talk about his experiment and the use he put it to. When he commentated that he, personally, understood more fully what the tribes' true attitude to the authorities was, although the real result, for him, had been deep trouble for him from 'on high'. At that, the instructor grinned and assured Craig that this work was now fully appreciated and that everyone would be expected to evolve their own ways of gaining information. One more comment was made and that was all the course members to keep in touch with each other to exchange both intelligence findings and share any new operations procedures that they evolve.

Lecture followed lecture, day followed day. There was no field work for them to undertake and precious little practical work, either. By the end of the first week, all course members knew the insurgents command structure and principal officers and could pick them out and correctly identify every man, his *chimurenga nomme de guerre* and his role from the existing photographic records. Each insurgent leader operated in a unique geographical region and had his own command structure. That, too, was unique, as was the management style each leader employed, but it seemed to Craig that the general rule was 'the more brutal, the better!' Sitting at the head of the ZANLA forces was Robert Gabriel Mugabe, once long time prisoner in Rhodesia, who, on release, had defected first to Zambia and then to China where he became China's well armed and supported puppet. Spoken of as a shy and quiet man, it was soon very apparent that crossing Comrade Mugabe was the way to rapid extinction for the whole family. Despite his actions, his pronouncements were accepted by the British as a reliable indicator of the Zimbabwean Africans' real voice and his stock stood high with the West.

"What better target can there be than Mugabe?" asked Craig, simultaneously with the rest of the course.

"We know full well where he is, that's not the problem. The problem is getting near enough to kill him. He moves from place to place at random intervals and is always accompanied by his special few trusted followers who have access to him at all times, but prevent any others getting close." replied the Intelligence Major lecturing the group.

Discussion flowed at that point and other course members brought up the names of Special Forces groups that Craig had never heard of. Special Forces, especially small, compact units, seemed ideally designed to undertake the task of removing the chiefs of opposing forces. That point was confirmed by the Major who then told the group how the British S.A.S. had tried on three occasions to assassinate Rommel in the Western Desert, only to miss him by a whisker each time and then have to get themselves back to Allied lines.

'Now THOSE particular expeditions failed because the intelligence, although very good, wasn't good enough! In particular, those raids were not based on the freshest intelligence; the most simple changes completely screw up such operations. IF you ever get the urge to initiate such operations, keep the plan flexible and rely on the freshest intelligence, even if you have to radio last minute changes to the guys in the field. Otherwise, the operators arrive to empty houses, or walk into security cordons.' The Intelligence Major obviously felt very strongly about this.

Craig later learned that the major had been a member of a special team that had tried to get at the ZANLA command early in the war and had just got back to Rhodesia with half the Zambian army, and not an inconsiderable number of ZANLA soldiers, on his tail in hot pursuit. No wonder he urged caution and the best intelligence in such jobs! Accepting the Majors' point of view, Craig defined his unspoken desire that such pinpoint operations were re-commenced aimed at high value targets. Craig noted this to himself and made an effort to button hole the Major during the drinks break to verify if his feelings were correct, because Craig was growing excited about the possibilities of destroying the ZANLA command structure in one or two strikes.

Caution was what the Intelligence Major advised Craig to use as his rule of thumb. That and getting the best possible and most recent intelligence on the target were the basic minimums BEFORE even suggesting that such an operation be planned. Logistics were another important factor and, Rhodesia being ever short of equipment, that problem could never be taken for granted.

"Spend time realising what we've got, usually not a lot of anything not even man power. Then, as a rule of thumb, reduce your requirements to a quarter and that's what you'll be operating on!" somewhat cynically said by the Intelligence Major. "Not that Mugabe doesn't need taking out, but start on smaller fry and learn the ropes first before trying to land the big fish."

Craig nodded his understanding, his eyes still faraway as his mind examined the problems as he saw them. Later in the week the course was given detailed briefings about the Rhodesian Special Forces and their role. Once more, Craig grew excited for he could immediately identify where and how HE would employ these groups. On his note pad he began making copious notes, interlinked with bold lines and arrows with only a few question marks appearing. Such assiduous note taking did not go unnoticed or un-remarked upon by the lecturing staff, more than one mentally noted Craig's frantic note-making and decided to find out the reason behind this burst of enthusiasm. Only one did, and that was the Intelligence Major who had earlier given him the advice about caution and logistics.

At an afternoon tea break where the course broke up into temporary grouping, the Major caught Craig along side the sugar basin as he was ladling sugar into his mug.

"I understand that we have a friend in common, Captain." Said the Major.

"Do we?" replied Craig.

"Andy Dennison" the Major answered simply.

"Andy? You know Andy? Have you known him long?" Craig suddenly became attentive.

It was then that Craig learned of Andy Dennison's service history, including his most recent attachment to the British S.A.S. from which he had just returned. Craig was silenced by what he was hearing about his pal. When the Major told him tea-time was over and that the lecture was about to re-commence Craig looked disappointed, but the Major said that he would be in the mess for drinks that evening should Craig want the story to continue. Of course he did!

After the course closed for the day, Craig dined in the Mess, tense and unsettled throughout the meal awaiting the Majors' arrival in the bar. After waiting on tenter-hooks for some time, he left the bar for a moment, when he re-entered to retrieve his beer, he saw the Major leaning casually against the bar alongside his beer-glass. At that moment, the Major saw him and waved for Craig to join him. Once his beer glass was securely in his hand the Major indicated with a nod that they should walk outside. A few paces outside the door, the Major began to talk about Andy's service record and his ideas of combating an insurgency war.

"You impressed Andy with your ideas, said that you tried to do things in a straightforward, direct way and that it was probably better if you stayed as B.S.A.P., rather transferred to the Mob." Craig was told with equal directness. "Listen, please! Your ideas about direct, surgical actions against ZANLA leaders is something we've been working on, but are still secret at the moment. If I continue this conversation any further, your status will change yet again, you will be working much further up the military Intelligence tree and become subject to full military jurisdiction, whilst still apparently a policeman." all said by the Major talking very quietly, as if it were a friendly, casual conversation. "You do realise that if you signal agreement to me now that you effectively become a military intelligence operative and will be bound by the law of military secrecy?"

"I want to do something to get rid of the terrs. and help make Rhodesia a peaceful place to live. I do want to live here!" Craig answered.

"I can take it then that you want me to continue this conversation onwards and that you're happy to be part of the Military Intelligence group working on this mission?" asked the Major directly. "It is more normal for people to be given a day or two to think over their commitment to our cabal, but the big game is a-foot and time is a luxury that we don't have. Outwardly your life would not change, but you will be under increasing pressure to perform!"

"All I can say is that I'll do my best to keep the ball rolling, it IS in my interests, also!" commented Craig.

"Be at the main gate and prepared to move out by 0700 hours tomorrow. Say nothing to any-one, just be there." rather cryptically said by the Major.

Just before 7 a.m. Craig's transport arrived; he had been expecting the usual army Bedford 3 ton truck, but what arrived was an open top two seater sports car with the Intelligence Major at the wheel and dressed in civilian clothes.

"Get in, man, don't gawk! This is supposed to be covert transport. Ditty bag in the boot and you in the passengers' seat, quick as you like!" spoke the Major, to all appearances setting off on a holiday.

"The advantage is that I can brief you as we travel and no-one can overhear." said the Major as he open the throttle and pulled away with a squeal of tyres.

Craigs' briefing was frequently interrupted by his having to ask for some information to be repeated because the wind roar made accurate hearing difficult, but by the end of the journey Craig knew that he had been made aware of some highly privileged information. He also been made aware of his personal time table, which was the month that he would spend with each of Rhodesia's elite special forces groups working with them, learning about each group, their specialities and abilities. There were four elite groups classified by the High Command as 'Special Forces', so Craig's future for the next four months was organised, the up-side was that he would get a long pass out at the end of this particular adventure, but first he was to get a seven day pass so that he could make all arrangements necessary for his coming adventure.

Chapter 8

Home leave for Christmas.

All it took was one telephone call to Mrs. Uys, who nearly blew his eardrums out of his head with her screech of joy, to arrange his leave. He was assured of a home with the Uys's as he had been previously. Mrs. Uys immediately took over all the preparations for Craig's stay, not only was he welcome, but his attendance over the family's Christmas and New Year time was compulsory! The Uys family really had become HIS family, no longer did he feel 'adopted', but a true family member. All of his time in Rhodesia had been marked with declining contact with his natural family in the U.K.; contact with them had never progressed beyond minimal, so the fade away was not noticed.

All Craig had to do was to get somewhere where Pa and Ma Uys could pick him up with the old, 'go anywhere' farm station wagon. Pulling rank, he found an army lorry leaving Gwelo barracks and heading in the general direction of Salisbury, invited himself onboard and set about enjoying the long journey. 'His' lorry was a stores transport, not personnel, so the schedule was much more relaxed and leisurely. Between stops, most of them unofficial refreshment stops, he moved from sharing the cab with Mac the driver to lazing comfortably on the stores in the back, preferring the cooler draughts flowing through the canvas. It was that un-enforced leisure that saved him when the lorry was ambushed. They were still on the correct route when a blast of automatic gun fire raked the lorry from front to back, the full length of the left hand side. Had Craig been in the passenger seat, he would have probably shot in the head. As it was, the windshield was shattered and the bullets passed harmlessly through the canvas sidewalls well above his reclining body. Before the gunfire had died away, the driver had accelerated down the road to distance himself from where the ambushers had been.

Craig walked around the lorry when MacTaggart pulled to a halt some distance away from the site. As the local ranking police officer, Craig examined the truck for the report that would inevitably be required. His belief was that the gunman had initially fired from a position fine on the left side of the road and from a reasonably long range, otherwise . . . .! Apart from a few glass splinters, the driver was unharmed and it was his coolness that had certainly saved them. Casually, the driver told Craig that this was the second time that he had driven through an ambush and that he was getting used to it! Immediately Craig's Intelligence antennae activated. He had to debrief this driver to get a better idea of where and when and if there was any consistent pattern to the attacks. Within Gwelo's Transport Divisions' drivers' pool, many similar attacks had happened that the drivers were almost getting blasé about them. It seemed that these attacks were quite random, but MacTaggart had a reasonable idea.

"The way these attacks happen is almost always a lone gunman and always from the roadside and in remote tribal land. Just seems to me that as the terrs get a gun they train by shooting us up! Now they're more trouble because they're getting AK's and not bolt action rifles anymore."

Craig nodded and tucked that comment deep in his memory, saying, "Yes, sounds realistic. So the drivers believe that the terrs are using transport vehicles for target practice?"

"Costs them nothing and they might just get lucky and cost us something big" answered Mac Taggart.

"Who do you report these attacks to, do you even bother to report them?"

"All reports are given to the Q.M.S., saves us being blamed for the damage. What he does with them, I don't know" answered Mac reasonably.

"Oh well, you write it and I'll sign it off, just make sure that I get the Q.M.S.'s name, please." By now Craig was already hatching a plan.

When the lorry rolled into Salisbury, Mac simply added a few extra kilometres on to the route and took Craig to his rendez-vous with the

Uys's. Mac got him so close that Craig expected simply to unload his bags from the lorry and straight into the station wagon, but was surrounded by the family, so Mac obliged with the luggage, a brief salute and he was away. Only Mrs. Uys and the girls were there, Mr. Uys having stayed on the farm to get the work done. To Craig, that journey back was like sitting in the centre of an aviary with all the excited chattering happening in the car. He couldn't follow any of the conversations that ceaselessly flowed around. One interesting point that he caught was that Suzanne was due to arrive later with her fiancé. He was surprised that he felt a spurt of jealousy about the fiancé. Craig and Rooikop had never seemed to get on to well, but why should he now be jealous? He was sure that she didn't like him and he had never got close to her, so why the sudden spurt?

As soon as the familiar scenery on the approach to the farm came into view Craig felt a relaxation come over him; he was home for a long leave! Back in his own room, he felt settled and comfortable. After unpacking his stuff, he walked out and around the farmstead, just to get used, once more, to being his own man again. At the dinner table that evening he was brought up to date with everyones' news and closely questioned about his! Piet, it seemed, was 'out on police ops.', but would be home by the weekend, so 'the boys' could get back together. Craig casually mentioned the attack on the lorry only to be told that attacks on private vehicles were also increasing and that some farms seemed to have been specifically targeted, even to land-mines having been laid on access tracks.

Craig's relaxed attitude evaporated as he thought about the possible consequences and he realised that his new job was going to have a direct impact on all of his new family and friends. Mrs Uys picked up on this new attitude as soon as he walked back into the kitchen, the family centre of the home. At first, she thought that Craig was concerned about Suzanne coming to Fairvue with her new fiancé for Christmas. Craig's stomach gave a sudden lurch at that bit of news and he didn't know why, but Mrs. Uys said that she knew that Suzanne liked him and thought that he liked her, too. Craig was surprised by that revelation, saying that he thought that Rooikop actively disliked him and he never thought about her.

"If you will keep calling her Rooikop, no wonder she's snappy!" he was told in no uncertain terms. "Try calling her Suzanne or Suzy and you'll see a different person. They'll be leaving straight after New Year to get married, so be nice to them!"

Chastened by Mrs. Uys comments, he excused himself and walked over to the dam to sit in the sun and think. By the time he returned to the farmstead quite a crowd had gathered. All the Uys daughters were there, very excited, as was Rooikop; Oops! he mentally corrected himself, Suzy along with a tall, thin young man. As soon as he set foot through Fairvue's doorway than the Uys girls grabbed him and introduced him to Johan, Suzy's South African fiancé. Shaking his hand, he was told to call him Hans just like everybody else did and then over his right shoulder spoke Rooikop. Half turning towards her he saw her in a new light and called her Suzy, she half smiled, then made a comment about what a slow learner he was, but that it was better late than never. Immediately, the Uys girls picked up on her put down and giggled, but soon realised that the comment had stung Craig and they began to try to flatter him, but he decided that he hadn't really summed Rooikop up wrongly, just that he and she would never get on together. As far as possible, he kept as far from her for the remainder of the afternoon.

With Hans, he had no problem talking and spoke with him for a long time. At last the inevitable question arose of where they were going to live. 'Back in South Africa, probably Pretoria or Jo'burg' he was told, Hans's parents had emigrated from Germany and settled in the Transvaal because his father worked for a car manufacturer. Hans seemed uninterested in much that Craig had to say, but there was no animosity from his side.

At the early breakfast Craig spoke to Mr. Uys about the troubles that the nearby farmers were having with insurgents. Practical as ever, he advised Craig to go and talk to the farmers and get first hand information, but added darkly 'We'll solve this ourselves given time.' Deciding on a different approach, Craig went into town and went to the police station to talk to his old colleagues. In a short time he knew that some farms were more bothered than others and those regularly bothered were close to deploying claymore mines in their more troubled farm areas. Just in general, he thought, the situation was worse than he remembered it but the farmers were struggling on. Although the farmers were occasionally wounded or killed, it was the farm workers who seemed to be targeted and bore the brunt of the trouble and injuries, it was almost as if the farm workers were the main target of ZANUs' wrath.

Craig mentally logged everything that he observed and his thoughts coming from any talks with farmers are their workers, but he could only take it so far without further information. Dammitall! he thought to himself, I'm on leave and supposed to be relaxing prior to getting more deeply involved in the Intelligence game again. With that thought, he decided that being back on the farm and acting like a civilian was his best way to relax and have a good leave.

It seemed to be a logical idea to relax on the farm, but the terrorist insurgence seemed to have different ideas. Almost as soon as he had decided to 'become a civilian for a short while' the uprising thought differently and interfered, much closer to home this time!

Just up the road, the farm next to 'Fairvue' was hit one night. Even in the quiet of a Rhodesian night, it was only the large explosions that were heard. Once heard, the whole farm responded. Craig and Mr. Uys armed themselves with guns and torches whilst Mrs. Uys called through to the local police on the radio to report the attack. It was stated community policy that everyone rallied to help the victims and chase away the attackers. She reported that both of her men-folk had armed themselves and were en-route to render what help they could. In driving from 'Fairvue', Mr. Uys had passed his labourers cottages and enlisted help from some of his men. Knowing how ZANU treated farm labourers, the workers were keen to get their retaliation against ZANU in before ZANU subjected them to their particular form of political re-education by beating and terror.

Arriving at the farm house, a scene of apparent destruction faced them, but, once more, it was the storage barns and the farm workers accommodation that had taken the brunt of ZANUs' wrath. The farm-stead had been attacked, but had been defended by the inhabitants, even Mr. Saville's children had let fly at the attackers with small calibre arms. Only daylight would reveal the full devastation wrought on the farm. Whilst all the defenders were physically well, they were all terrified, but resolute. Craig went searching around in the dark to try to determine anything that he could about the attackers. Major damage was to a storage barn that had been hit by an R.P.G., but why that empty barn had been a target no-one could guess.

As the grey of dawn strengthened and the day lightened, the damage to the farm became obvious. Bullet holes pock-marked the walls of the barns and the home-stead, but the steel shutters covering the doors and most of the windows had protected the Saville's from injury. Steel netting over the roof had held the burning torches clear until they had burned out and no longer a danger. Simple, but effective, a typical Rhodesian 'do-it-yourself' solution to the protection problem! Some bullets were embedded in the walls and were easily retrieved. Craig dug himself a hand-full out and then went searching for as many spent cartridge cases as he could find. These he knew showed that the attack weapons appeared to be AK47s' and the cartridge cases would be examined to see if any weapon had been used in any attack previously. Those examinations would be undertaken centrally at the Police labs. in Salisbury and those labs were developing a long history of specific assault rifles and where they had been used. Although he didn't know the specific details, he knew that each firing pin left a different impression on the initiator cap, similar to a finger print, and because of that, the usage of any particular weapon could be identified and plotted on a map. Craig knew that 'Leopards paw' was a very specific AK 47 hammer impression that was well known and indicated that a very experienced insurgent and his weapon were around. Before Craig could send the cartridges for examination, he was called back to Centenary, his notional home base due to a rapid change in situation.

Arriving back at base, he was seen immediately by the Intelligence Major only to be told that he would now be learning 'on the job', as they had become aware of an impending three pronged attack by ZIPRA forces entering through Mozambique. "FRELIMO and ZIPRA have been in collusion, thanks to Machel who is still trying to be friendly and helpful to us and remain a black revolutionary!" the Major said drawing his fingers down a map to indicate the insertion paths. "We got wind of one group, attacked it, captured one guerrilla and turned him. His information has panned out so far. He was talking about three co-ordinated attacks by groups entering from Mozambique. We destroyed one group, but the other two groups haven't raised their heads yet!"

Craig asked how the information had been gathered, to be told that it came from a sympathiser in one of the protected villages east of Centenary, near the Mozambician border.

"We are winning this war, there are not more than 200 hard-line terrs. out there in our estimation and our sympathisers are doing a great job."

"You know my thoughts, Sir!" replied Craig "The P.V.'s are 'hearts and mind' jobs, just like Malaya was and we are skimping on their privileges."

"We're all skimping on bloody privileges because of these damned insurgents, so the P.V.'s'll have to take it just like the rest of us!"

"Sir" answered Craig.

"You can start by taking a section of R.A.R.'s and doing the rounds of the P.V.s between here and the border and try to keep the villagers happy."

"Sir"

"Try to find out if there are any undercurrents that we need to know about, so we can deflect any trouble."

Snapping out a crisp salute, Craig marched from the office and set about establishing his R.A.R. section and his 'learning on the job' mission.

One day out of barracks, during his early morning radio report he was given the news that the rail line to Mozambique had been attacked. Base seemed to believe that the rail line was a target of opportunity, but Craig couldn't be so phlegmatic about it. To him this was a disturbing new trend which seemed to hit directly at Rhodesia's fuel sanctions busting life-line to the Mozambique coast at Maputo. Craig and his group were too far away to investigate the attack usefully, so other than note that an attack happened, his group carried their mission on unaffected. Craig was being told one thing to his face, but his troopers were reporting that there was a permanent guerrilla presence was in most villages. Some tribes had been hostile to the Government forces, but more seemed to distrust and dislike their presence amongst them, just entering some villages was an uncomfortable experience. Of the 'Protected Villages' on his route, almost all oozed antipathy to, and dislike for, anything and anybody white. Departing the last one, he was certain that the 'Hearts and Minds' struggle had been lost to the insurgents and that the tribes people in the P.V.'s were actively supporting the terrorists. Whether the tribes people had been physically suborned into support for ZANU, or terrified or simply pushed away by most of the Rhodesian forces' inherent racism, he could not say; whatever the answer was he knew they were no longer neutral or on the Rhodesians' side.

"Once the tribes are NOT on our side, we face an uphill struggle. Things will be easier for the terrs. to get in and do damage and harder for us to deal with them."

"Don't worry, the K factor will take over!" the Superintendent complacently assured Craig.

"Easy route johnnies, all of 'em. They'll do nothing rather than do something." He was confidently assured by the same Superintendent.

Craig wasn't so sanguine about the situation and appreciated that with masses of the tribes' people being uncooperative the job of the security forces would be impossible.

"There will be too many potential trouble makers for our security forces to control!"

"They respect the Polices' blue uniform. You'll see how just one policeman will be able to keep the whole rabble in control, there'll be no trouble. That's what you younger men have to realise, some of us have spent years with these people. We know them and they fear us." he was assured.

"If they fear the insurgents more than they do us, then we've lost." Craig replied warningly.

ZANU insurgents were pouring into Masvingo province and were sufficiently well settled that 'Thresher' a new operational area had just been initiated. From the number of ZANU terrorists entering the country, it was obvious that FRELIMO was aiding them. These weren't Craigs' direct problems, all this was happening too far south for him to be involved, but brought to mind what he and Andy Dennison had talked about. Andy's front-line experience gave him a more incisive view of things, but he certainly brooked no nonsense could got angry very quickly if he wasn't understood or being pompous to him. He was currently laid up, having been shot in the knee during a fire-force operation; he had argued with the operation controller about an immediate follow up operation, demanding a short pause. In his helicopter, the commander could see over 20 insurgents escaping the trap and ordered Andys' stick to intercept. Andy required some time to re-organise, couldn't follow immediately and an argument broke out between the two of them. Rumour had it that they didn't need a radio to communicate, so loudly were they shouting at each other and that a shot fired from the helicopter as it passed Andy's look-out point hit him in the knee! Unfriendly Friendly fire!

Whilst Andy was inactive, re-cooperating from his injuries Craig sought him out and bounced ideas off him. It seemed that both shared a passionate belief that clandestine operations to disrupt the insurgents in their 'safe' areas. Andy was obviously highly knowledgeable and experienced in these matters, but he would only hint where he had gained his experiences. Whilst Andy was still re-cooperating, Craig was sent down to the operation Thresher area to gain experience with the highly secret Selous Scouts. Andy had hinted to him about these warriors, but had told him nothing; knowledge was only on a 'need to know' basis and his need to know had just arrived!

Chapter 9

Into the secret world

Just as he arrived back in the Thresher operational area, the shit really hit the fan! An air strike on a terrorist camp had been successful, the only problem being that the camp struck was at Pafuri. That problem was because Pafuri was 2 km inside the Mozambique border! Not only did the worlds' press turn on Rhodesia and heap opprobrium on them in unending quantities, their closest ally, South Africa, reacted immediately by withdrawing their loaned aircraft. In one simple stroke, the Rhodesian strike force was halved and not by any enemy action. South Africa reacted vigorously because it wanted to give no reason for Cuba, already with troops in Mozambique, to support FRELIMO further. More Cuban involvement would bode badly for South Africa if their liberation struggle ever started in earnest. John Vorster performed a very public and rapid 'Pontius Pilate' imitation to distance his country from their northern neighbour. Although their strike power had been reduced and, to any outside observer, the war had become almost impossible for them to win militarily, the Rhodesian armed forces did not share that opinion.

Before the month ended, a long running series of cross border strikes against ZIPRA bases began. Craig was really 'learning on the job' in a serious way. Not only did he travel in the 'pseudo' columns in FRELIMO camouflaged trucks, he went into action with the RLI Fire-Force second wave helicopters. Once more he was in the action in the front-line, generally doing his Intelligence after the action 'thing' and trying to assemble a picture of what was happening.

Sometimes he was in follow-up action two or three times a day, he knew what he felt like, but still wondered how the conscripted 'troopies' got through their service. He frequently felt like a wet rag by the end of the day and sometimes little better in the mornings. Throughout the Intelligence community of which he was a member, the general feeling was that although reliant on their own resources, Rhodesia was winning the war. Insurgents were being roundly defeated and now making less impact on the Rhodesian way of life. Confidence was flying high with the white population despite the privations they continued to suffer, all the letters from his adopted family were happy. Piet had volunteered and had been selected to join a Police Anti-Terrorism Unit because of his tracking skills and was well into his PATU training, although Mrs. Uys was certain that the war would be over before he was ever deployed. There was a joyous and optimistic mood running throughout the white civilian population. Even when the announcement was made that Ian Smith, at the behest of South Africa, was talking with Joshua Nkomo and other black political groups about the establishment of a passive black majority government of Zimbabwe-Rhodesia, white life still seemed near normal. Many whites regretted the new name, but simply shrugged that inconvenience off as a small price to pay for peace and security. Throughout the white population, as far as Craig could see, life was mildly disrupted, the insurgency was an irritation, but their way of life would survive. Bishop Muzareva was involved as the leader of UANC and the putative prime minister of the newly peaceful country, but his political association or sympathy with the South African ANC rang alarm bells in Pretoria.

Craig occasionally saw discrepancies between what he had learned from his work and what the general white populace seemed to believe. Throughout the period of the insurrection, as far as the general public were told, captured guerrillas and their supporters were processed through the criminal courts and treated under existing criminal law. Found guilty, they could be imprisoned, fined or executed, the sentence being dictated by the civil law. This attitude deliberately fostered complacency in the white population that the insurgency was solely a civil matter and that the Police, as civil power, were the principal authority, whilst in reality the military was in the driving seat countering the real war situation. How happy the situation seemed from the perspective of the farmers, everything much as normal and the police (with military help) getting on top of the situation!

Some comments were made asking why Ian Smith should even think of sitting at the negotiation table with Nkomo and, as was calmly put to Craig, 'why should we give away our position?' Never being much of a politician Craig simply reminded the farmers' wife of Harold Macmillan's statement of the late '60's' known to every Rhodesian as the 'winds of change' speech. She quickly poo-pah'd that remark, saying that whilst Rhodesia and South Africa held firm and stood together there would no winds of change blowing through this part of Africa!

Within hours of talking to the farmers' wife, Craig was back ready for war. Despite the general populations' expectations the talks collapsed swiftly and spectacularly. Outside Rhodesia, South Africa had lost the political initiative in Angola and so was forced to cut Rhodesia off aid to ensure its' own prolonged survival. Faced with 20,000 Cuban troops in Angola, South Africa was looking not to overextend its' capabilities and ensure that Mozambique wasn't dragged into any conflict with them to prevent the horror of a war on two fronts. Rhodesias' repeated excursions into Mozambique to destroy ZANLA facilities couldn't be tolerated by the Vorster government in Pretoria. Should knowledge of S.A.'s support for Rhodesia become common knowledge, then Mozambique would become the second terrorist front into South Africa.

That, at least, was how a South African Intelligence Major explained it to Craig during their briefing. South Africa would still help Rhodesia, but even more clandestinely than before and would rotate its' elite troops into and out of Rhodesia's fronts to ensure that they were at peak efficiency when their time came. Craig, who at that point seemed to be a shuttling between the Selous Scouts and the SAS as a liaison officer, got the task of providing 'legends' and cover for the rotating South African 'recce's. He was told by the South African Military Intelligence Major in no uncertain terms that 'Secret means Secret!' Unfortunately virtually all the Recces were Afrikaans speakers, their English being so heavily accented that the game could have been given away by a simple word. To Craig, this level of operational secrecy was nothing new; the Selous Scouts would soon be revealed to the Rhodesian public as the elite unit responsible for many victories over ZANLA; the SAS somehow still remained shadowy, seeming still a myth, despite the best efforts of newspaper reporters to identify the troops undertaking special missions.

Through his South African Intelligence contact, Craig was asked quietly 'to keep an eye open for the ANC', the group who the Pretoria government regarded as their principle foe. Craig's job seemed to consist of either being at the 'sharp end' where he searched for documents or later sitting and reviewing his findings, the A.N.C. task was a welcome distraction whenever he got snowed under by the documents captured on operations. Experience had shown that one of the most vital documents was the ZANLA group leaders' diary, where many of the operational details were recorded. Any leaders diaries retrieved were treated as 'gold' from the Intelligence side and were the most useful, quick intelligence record. There was no rule as to the amount of documents that they could find. In the field, there was, at best, the diary to search for; if a base camp was attacked, then there could easily be a tonne or more of documents! However many documents were found some-one had to sift them, and praise be, Craig was now above that level.

By reading a number of the diaries, he began to piece together a vague, but believable picture. Simply by extrapolating from the already intercepted terrorist groups, what he saw frightened him, because his figures told him that rather then being on top of the threat, the Rhodesian forces would soon to be swamped!

Attempting to put this analysis to 'the management' as they were deprecatingly called resulted in him being almost laughed off the base and told 'from now on, concentrate on his liaison jobs and not to worry about tactics.' Shortly after Craig resumed his liaison role, when he was in an S.A.D.F. base outside Pretoria he was given the news that ZIPRA forces had begun operations in the central area of Rhodesia.

"We knew that these guys are coming in through Zambia, but you Rhodies didn't believe us." Captain Freddy Visser (call me Fred) told him. "Your puny little forces are going to be stretched to breaking point, their infiltration routes are so open that you've no chance of stopping them! Why don't you join us and get in with the winners?"

Craig's liaison activities, he expected, would keep him shuttling between Rhodesia and Pretoria for some considerable time to come. His personal feelings were that the South Africans were to be thanked for their support, however self interested that may be and he felt no real reason not to reciprocate their help. It was a very fine line that he was treading, he knew that, but at the level he was operating with S.A. Intelligence seemed a more personal than formal arrangement.

Before he left Pretoria, the Rhodesian Airforce had begun a series of interdiction raids into Zambia to close down the ZIPRA infiltration routes and camps. Driving over the Limpopo on Beit Bridge, at the S.A. immigrations post he was met by sad faces and questions about if he was sure that he wanted to go back. His route north, he knew, took him through the central highlands and that was the new 'bandit country' where ZIPRA had just begun operations. He drove as quickly as he could and when he had to stop he went to the nearest military facility for shelter.

Finally back at base, he could only reflect on the differences he saw. Most of the attitudes he experienced were ones of complete complacency, even at high political level (or as high as he ever saw), belief seemed to be that 'the K factor' would prevail and the Africans would achieve nothing. He contrasted that opinion with the one he knew now held sway in Pretoria, that the terrs. had been well trained and, no matter how incompetent they may be or what losses they suffered, there were more than enough to overwhelm the Rhodesian forces.

The more he reflected on the situation, Fred Vissers' idea began to look increasingly inviting, so he decided to do more 'digging' on his next trip south and see what the 'slopies' could offer him.

Winter had crept up on the armies; ZIPRA had lost many of it's central bases due to the ongoing air strikes and it was only the increasing poor weather that limited air strikes. When the weather finally caused the air assaults to cease, over 40 bases had been attacked and more than 900 dead insurgents had been counted by R.L.I. follow-up forces. Craig knew that that level of operational success would yield tonnes of documents. All those tonnes of documents didn't bother him at all simply because initial Intelligence assessments were performed 'in sector' and the Midlands were not his sector! At least the weather was conducive to the boring job of intelligence sorting, no-one had any reason to be outside, the office option would suddenly seem very attractive.

In the early spring ZIPRA, in the southern region, suddenly seemed to come back to life when they attacked the Ruda security base. These new insurgent tactics, in what many believed to have been a fully suppressed area, scored a major political victory demonstrated bythe undermining of white civilian morale. Follow up operations accounted for 5 ZIPRA terrs. killed and followed up by a classical covert operation against the ZIPRA encampment at Nyandeza. 72 Selous Scouts disguised as FRELIMO soldiers, being ordered about by Portuguese speaking 'officers' penetrated to the parade ground right in the middle of the camp completely undetected. Their timing was perfect, the guerrillas were all on parade. In the ensuing massacre nearly 1100 were killed with no injury to any member of the Rhodesian forces. Then the publicity battle was fought in the international press which went badly for Rhodesia as the guerrillas propaganda was swallowed hook line and sinker by the international media and Rhodesian forces were excoriated for massacring alleged black refugees. Covert action had triumphed in the land battle, but ZIPRA won the international propaganda battle. Rhodesian civil morale slumped even further at that betrayal.

Craig was deeply involved with the planning of a series of pre-emptive strikes against ZANLA in the 'Hurricane' area, 'his' area of expertise. During the planning processes, he found himself working increasingly closely with both the 'Scouts and the SAS, so, by default, he was developing into a covert mission intelligence specialist. He was also charged with continuing his liaison duties with the South Africans, so an unofficial part of his remit was to keep an eye on the ANC cadres. From personal experience, he knew what 'overstretch' meant and felt like! Those R.L.I. Fire-force soldiers asleep when their 'chopper' landed after the third mission of the day, experienced overstretch at the sharp end. Craig's overstretch was not so dangerous to him, but could prove to be fatal to the security force guys if he made planning mistakes due to tiredness.

Once the pre-emptive raids started, effectively as a prelude to the Geneva conference to reinforce the Rhodesian Governments' hand, Craig's Intelligence work hit a temporary blank spot. Things seemed to go into a hiatus whilst attacking storms fell on ZANU positions. Rather than be in barracks and at a loose end, he volunteered to drive down to Pretoria again to continue the official liaison with the SA military and his personal one with Fred Visser and friends. His official duties went quickly and well, formally the SA military 'suggested' that he consider continuing to help them when white Rhodesia collapsed. Fred Visser merely reinforced his earlier comments and urged Craig to think about everything that was happening.

He had leave due, so having booked a few days off duty, he drove straight to the Uys farm once he crossed the border at Beit Bridge. Walking into the farmhouse was an eerie experience. There were fire-arms every where, both military and civil, hand-guns and rifles, all ready for use and obviously well maintained. He always travelled with his personal weapons, that had become second nature to him, but to see the farm looking like an armoury shocked him.

Mrs. Uys told him that EVERYONE carried their gun all the time. Craig took that statement with a pinch of salt until he went to the local farmers' market with Mrs. Uys and the girls. Even quite young children were armed. When he even saw a sub-machine gun laying next to a baby sleeping in a pram, it was proof that the white population were not easily going to roll over and welcome black majority rule. Attitudes within the civilian population had hardened after Nkomo had laughed at the massacre of the survivors of an Air Rhodesia Vanguard by his ZANLA forces. Nkomo was not to realise, but that gratuitous violence also presaged his own defeat a few years later.

Back at the farm Craig relaxed as much as he could. Mrs. Uys still treated him as a son and fed him as such. Talking over the table after supper was nor as easy as Craig expected. There was a lot that he knew but which he could not even hint at to the family, so he kept with the colourless anodyne conversation that kept the civilian poulation calm and happy. Quite 'off the top' one of the girls asked her mother if she knew what Suzanne was going to call her baby. It was obvious that this was something completely new to Craig by his totally baffled reaction.

"Oh yes, Suzanne and Hans are expecting their first child soon, didn't you know?" asked Mrs. Uys. "I'm sure I told you in one of my letters."

Craig didn't want to admit that he was working so hard that, at best, he only ever scanned his mail meaning to read them more fully later on, but rarely did.

"Mummy, didn't you tell me that Suzanne didn't want you to tell Craig, so you didn't?" the youngest daughter said.

"No I didn't! Where did you get that idea from?" Mrs. Uys chided her fiercely.

From that reaction Craig knew that he was not supposed to have been told, but that the secret had 'accidentally' slipped out. He had to work out for himself just how accidental that slip had been. His first reaction was to believe it to have been a deliberate leak to him by the daughter. He looked at her, caught her eye and winked at her in a conspiratorial sort of way. To himself he thought of the old Intelligence adage that two people can keep a secret, but only if one of them is dead. How true! So the cat was well and truly out of the bag now; what Craig couldn't understand was just why it had been such a secret.

Conversation over the table had become stilted and more prescriptive towards the girls, but Craig tried to ease the mood. In an attempt to find some more acceptable common ground, he asked about farm security and if any of his 'surprises' had been useful. Mr. Uys was well content with the security measure Craig had installed he was told, even to suggesting that he should sub-contract himself out around the other farms in the area and 'do their security, too.' Craig sat back and asked 'Why?' In reply he was told that an increasing number of local farms were being abandoned, let to go fallow and as a result trouble was increasing in the area. He must have looked surprised at that point because Mr. Uys asked him why he thought everyone always carried a gun?

"What about Piet? Can't he do anything?" Craig asked.

"We're being told around here that it's likely that we'll have to set up a farmers version of the P.A.T.U.'s as the Police seem so hard pressed at the moment. So, if you CAN help we'd all be grateful!" answered Mr. Uys.

Next morning, and for the remainder of his leave, Craig reverted to his earlier role as armourer. He found it satisfying to improvise explosives and set his devices to trap the unwary. All the local 'front-line' farms had their passive security measures 'Craig-ised' to deny free access for the terrs. to cross that land. He manufactured each device individually before installing it, he didn't make 'spares', although he had many requests to do so. He did this because he was deeply aware of the Rhodesian image of self reliance, which meant he couldn't trust that one or other farmer wouldn't try to take one of his claymores apart to copy it. When his leave expired Craig returned once more to King George VI barracks in Salisbury feeling mentally refreshed and happy that he had achieved something practical 'for his family.'

Chapter 10

War comes to the civilians.

As September morphed into October and Spring established its' grip, conscription for white male Rhodesians was extended. Compulsory National Service was extended from 6 months to 1 year, even medical exemptions became much more difficult to get. Every young man had a role to play, although they might not know or like it. Draft dodgers from the National Service group took themselves 'down South', south of the Limpopo and into South Africa from where they couldn't be removed. Older men were re-called to the standard on a 6 weeks 'on', 6 weeks 'off' basis, and having been once been trained, were hastily re-trained and sent into the field. Serious changes to the Police Service were also happening, in short order they became an extension of the Army and in this way civil authority merged into military authority. Craig initially had thought that his transferring from the Police into the military had been exceptional, but now that move had become the norm.

As Mr. Uys had predicted, local farms were now being patrolled by drafted 'Beore' P.A.T.U. groups formed by the local farmers. Despite notional rank, each farmer led the patrol on his own land and handed over to the next member as the patrol stepped off his farm. Hardly a patrol passed without one or other of the farmers being aghast at the amount of intrusion by armed cadres onto their lands. When the patrols had been initiated most farmers had believed that they knew the level of insurgent intrusion on their farm. Each farmer believed that he and his 'boys' had the situation well under control and that intrusions were pretty low anyway. Everyone received a shock, many of them terrible shocks as proof came to light that their African labour had been subverted almost under their noses and that even long term and highly trusted workers were actively supporting the insurgents. All the expected back up support that every farmer had believed his labour would supply him was shown to be under effective insurgents control. In effect, the whole farm sector owed loyalty to ZIPRA and not to the white farmer. Complacency had betrayed many farmers into relying on the fallacy that their farm labourers 'knew which side their bread was buttered on'. Long term brutal subversion in the Chinese mode had created a mass army on each farm. Few older trusted employees were around, they had been driven off at best, or cruelly killed to intimidate the remainder in classical Chinese style. Farms had suddenly moved onto the front-line and farmers become the buffer between civilians and the terrs.

Even on farms where the labourers hadn't been totally subverted, the white boss could no longer be assured of the labourers' sympathy. Every farmer knew instinctively that stock and cereal losses had increased. Many ignored the actual extent of losses, believing that their personal knowledge of the staff and their long association with them was more trustworthy than cold numbers ever could be. By the time the true situation was revealed, the subversion had robbed almost every farmer of his farm and the true size of the problem was exposed. Farms worked during the day, but once dark descended every white had to be behind locked doors for their own security. On a small number of farms the authority of the farmer was such that control had not been totally wrested away from them, but the nights were no longer as secure as hitherto.

The Uys's farm was one such semi-secure island in a sea of hostile territory and so it became the *de facto* operations base for the region. That many of the small tracks were still covered by the Craig's anti-personnel weapons aided the reputation of the farm. To many insurgents, the Uys's farm was treated with fear. Superstitious rumour abounded that each and every path was protected by hidden Tokoloshes that struck down and killed any black that Mr. Uys hadn't personally blessed. The whole family played to these black superstitions and were generally viewed as blessed beings by the labourers. Playing on the superstitious fear of the average Rhodesian black served to strike fear into black strangers and generate a healthy, if fearful, regard for all the family.

Rhodesian forces were still interdicting ZANLA cadres coming from Mozambique on established trails. FRELIMO still claimed not to be aiding ZANLA, or any insurgent group into Rhodesia, but all the evidence was that they were. Rhodesian Military Intelligence was sharing information with its South African equivalent and they were 'bleddy certain!' that FRELIMO not only knew but were actively aiding ZANLA to infiltrate. Some small, limited Special Forces interdiction raids into Mozambique produced limited success, but enough for Special Forces Intelligence to propose more, and deeper, raids into Mozambique. At this suggestion, the Politicians went into flat panic. Such incursions into Mozambique ran the risk of bringing Mozambique formally into the war against Rhodesia, that would mean that the Cubans would get involved and THAT prospect panicked Pretoria!

Every section of the Rhodesian military machine was experiencing overstretch, too much to do and too few facilities to do it with. Military Intelligence pressed for a small number of surgical pre-emptive Special Forces strikes designed to cripple the Mozambiquian economy and demonstrate the direct cost of aiding ZANLA. October saw the first tentative exploration of that policy, but the Rhodesian forces achieved nothing; indeed they were lucky to get out of Mozambique without casualties. Unless FRELIMO had been extremely lucky, their soldiers had been waiting in ambush, the Rhodesian plans had been revealed before the raid began. Not wishing to contemplate a traitor in their midst, the high echelons of the Rhodesian command structure put the defeat down to bad-luck on their part and promptly suggested another raid. This raid, too, had obviously been compromised with an increased FRELIMO presence where they had never been before.

Both failed raids had cost Rhodesian heavily in lost and irreplaceable war materiel. Craig had been involved in the planning of both raids, peripherally with the first one, but more deeply with the second. He knew what both missions had cost the country and how little it could afford such losses. Senior Intelligence officers created a closed intelligence 'bubble' partly to try to identify the traitor in their midst and partly to get back into the groove of mission success. What was planned was a covert strike into Mozambique at a largish FRELIMO base to the east of the Thresher area. Operational planning was undertaken by the troops own intelligence units and all on a need to know basis. A pre-emptive raid to destroy FRELIMO logistic stores and disrupt communications with ZANLA was selected, with the added aim of 'liberating' FRELIMO arms and ammunition as war booty to eke out Rhodesian limited stocks. S.A.S. forces, with a few South African Recces, lead the way to 'clear' the entry route, whilst the Selous Scouts took another route to ensure the exit route remained open. Craig was to 'go in' with the R.L.I. contingent, transported to war in lorries disguised in FRELIMO paintwork. A native black Portuguese speaker had been provided by the 'Scouts to help get the column through any unexpected road blocks. At each road block, the Portuguese speaking 'officer' bawled out the FRELIMO cadres and got the whole column through without a shot being fired. 'So far, so good!' Craig thought. All the R.L.I. troops were covered in 'black is beautiful' camo. cream which was slowly being washed off by rivulets of sweat, halting too long at any road block would reveal just who they really were. Craig was sitting in the back of one of the lorries amongst the R.L.I. troopers, armed like they were with AK 47's and R.P.G.'s, dressed as FRELIMO cadres, complete with authentic east european chest kit. They would easily pass a quick visual inspection and that was the intention; anyone getting too nosey wouldn't live long enough to tell the tale!

Before they entered the camp that was their objective, the column split into two unequal parts. The larger unit carried straight on to the camp centre, the smaller section (the one which contained Craig's truck) split off and went to the rear of the base. They were to be the stop group and stopped, hidden in the bushes well behind the huts. Quickly all the troopers dismounted and fanned out, selecting ambush positions which let them all fire inwards towards the camp centre and the expected direction of the fleeing real FRELIMO cadres. Explosions began near the camp centre, then AK47 firing really began in earnest. From the direction green tracer flew, he saw Craig judged that the R.L.I. were getting little return fire, but sending plenty into the FRELIMO ranks. As the firing had started, the various units of the stop group had automatically 'tuned in' and were concentrating on the job to hand. Craig's group were on the extreme right hand of the curve into which the stop group had formatted, near what they believed were the vehicle stores. When the fleeing FRELIMO cadres came into range of the stop groups they were cut down by co-ordinated, concentrated fire from the Rhodesians. FRELIMO troops scattered trying to get away from the withering fire, some running into the vehicle sheds. Some Rhodesian fired blindly into the vehicle stores through the woven palm walls. Suddenly, one of these walls exploded outwards in a deafening thunder of outgoing heavy fire power as the FRELIMO fought back using a Soviet trailer mounted three barrel 27mm anti-aircraft cannon. All Rhodesian fire within the arc covered by the cannon rapidly died away as the stop groups realised that they were out-gunned by a considerable way. The cannon didn't have a full arc of movement, although the way it pumped shells through anything in its way, it was dissolving the remains of the vehicle shed before the Rhodesians' eyes and before too long it would have a complete arc of movement.

Craig realised that even with the cannon on a fully depressed setting the shells were flying above his head, so he crawled forward as far as possible whilst still remaining under cover. When the cannon traversed away from him, he stood up and opened fire on the FRELIMO gunner and loader with his puny AK47. By this time, he was standing fully upright and holding the AK at hip height, he twisted one way and then the other to spray the area with green tracer, but then the anti-aircraft cannon, still banging out shells in bursts of three, began swinging back towards him. Just in time he noticed the movement and, with a shout of 'Down', threw himself lengthwise onto the ground. A last 27mm cracked out of the cannon, tearing apart the air where, a second before, Craig chest had been.

Silence reigned! No more triple bangs emanated from the cannon. No further loud and angry hornets zipped over the stop groups' head. For a few seconds it was as if the world had stopped, then the cracking and popping of AK 47 discharges intruded AND they were moving inexorably towards Craig and the stop group! Craig scrambled up to the anti-aircraft cannon, AK threatening the FRELIMO gunners, but he was safe, both gunner and loader were dead, well punctured by many small arms rounds. Then, to his astonishment, out-going green tracer rounds passed him by and concentrated on the FRELIMO cadres running haphazardly towards them. Now the stop group finally had its' real targets in range and from their ambush positions accurate fire chased each FRELIMO individual until, bloodied, they dropped to the floor.

There was no logical pattern to the outgoing fire from the R.L.I., each troopie simply saw a target and fired on it. Efficient and quick, but Craig was in front of both groups, the Stop group and the rapidly advancing Attack group. He didn't want to run back to his ambush position, that would present his back to the on-coming attacker, being dressed in FRELIMO combat fatigues, meant that he was indistinguishable from the fleeing Mozambiquians and so a potential target. His infantry training kicked in, he rolled off the trailer, trusting that the stop group soldiers would remember it was him and not an aggressive FRELIMO cadre, crouched behind a trailer wheel and sighted his AK towards the oncoming group. He trusted himself to distinguish between friend and foe and relied on the R.L.I. troops behind him to keep focus on their real enemy. Craig's dilemma didn't last very long, the whole action wound up very swiftly and the AK fire died down to the odd pop from many different directions.

As soon as the two R.L.I. groups had merged back into one unified team he was approached by their captain.

"Just heard what you did with the A-A gun. Well done!" Craig demurred to answer, but the Captain continued "You were a pal of Andy Dennison, weren't you?"

"Yes, Andy is pal of mine" Craig confirmed.

"Well, did you know that on his last op. Andy got himself in front of the firing line, just as you did, but he caught a round in the head and died?"

"What Andy's dead?"

"Yes, one of the R.A.R. troopers shot him in the head. We don't know if was accidental or some type of assassination or revenge, but Andy's dead all the same."

Craig went cold and could only stare at the Captain. 'Andy dead!' was all that he could think. What he wasn't prepared to admit was Andy Dennison had become something of lucky mascot to Craig, if Andy could get by, so could he; if Andy had 'caught it', so could he! His legs went weak and had to hold onto something, but a sudden shout brought him back to reality. Time was running on, the force had to get out as soon as possible, but first they had to loot the camp. Armourers went to the armoury to remove usable weapons and ammunition, drivers ran to the transport ground either to salvage or wreck whatever vehicles were there. Craig's job was to search the offices and then filter through any intelligence taken from the dead and brought for his evaluation. He filled duffle bags with pages, note books and diaries all of which were potentially a valuable source of intelligence, but there was so much that after the first quick comb-through, the chaff were to be burned. After ensuring that all the duffles had been securely loaded on a returning vehicle Craig carried armfuls of often bloodied paper to the nearest burning hut and threw it all through the open door, waiting only until he was sure that the bulk was well alight. His job here, today, was finished, all he had to do was to sit down and be transported back into Rhodesia and then, back home, his real work would begin.

Chapter II

Rhodesia takes the path to economic war.

Octobers' strike into Mozambique won them tons of military hardware, at least a million rounds of ammunition, over 100 anti-tank landmines and about 30 assorted vehicles. Intelligence captures were just as impressive, one diary alone revealed all the active ZANLA infiltration routes, the names and numbers of the insurgents who had used them recently. Militarily, Rhodesia went from being on the back foot to becoming more aggressive, the intelligence recovered from that single raid on FRELIMO laid bare the propaganda lies that Mozambique did not support ZANLA.

Although the Rhodesian/Zimbabwean propaganda tried to expose FRELIMOs blatant lies to the Western Powers sympathy seemed to lie with the 'freedom fighters' of ZANLA and ZIPRA. Revealing the truth about third party (i.e. Mozambique's active aid) involvement was ignored; the British seemed to believe the Rhodies simply weren't 'playing the game', so instead of help, they received only more criticism. Each rebuttal of even sympathy from the West (especially the U.K.) served to stiffen the resolve of the Rhodesian fighting arms.

Rhodesia had demonstrated that it could strike successfully outside its' own borders and this lesson was very quickly learned. Unwillingly, the political leaders began to grasp that their only chance of success was to demonstrate that they could severely damage the economies of both Mozambique and Angola sufficiently to cause them to withdraw their support to all the insurgents. For more than a year the Rhodesian military high command had been requesting this of the politicians, but anxious about the 'knock-on' potential to South Africa, who didn't want to give the Cubans an excuse to intervene, had refused. Nevertheless, military targets had been selected and plans for their destruction had been made simply awaiting political clearance before they were implemented.

Craig knew some of this, but suspected a lot more. He had assiduously worked on his intelligence estimates and had even been involved in deniable target selection exercises. It was his tacit understanding that most of the offensive action would involve strikes by the Rhodesian Air Force, after some target reconnaissance by a small force of Special Forces. Andy hadn't told him that in so many words, but he had hinted that he clearly expected that to happen. With Andy's death, the need to know system closed those insights, but soon after the Mozambique raid a buzz began and the buzz said that both Mozambique and Angola 'were going to get a pasting!' Confidence within the armed forces was high as was the expectation of success.

Two raids, close together in time, but well separated in space, were compromised, the first almost costing irreplaceable aircraft, the second almost caused the loss of an S.A.S. patrol. Alarm bells rang within the military high command, 'How could such a secret missions be so comprehensively compromised?'

"One can never plan for an accident. There is always that chance, of course, but on two separate missions? I think not! Once is accidental, twice is coincidence, three times is enemy action. I don't intend it to get to the stage of three lost operations!

So gentlemen, you know what that means, don't you? A rotten Apple somewhere in the system!" the Intelligence Brigadier thundered at the rows of tightly packed Intelligence specialists.

"You are all here because in some ways, ways that might not be immediately obvious to you, you had some connection with both compromised operations. You will be questioned individually before you leave this block. When you leave here, you will each go to your rooms and do nothing until ordered back to duty. AND you will say NOTHING, not one bloody word of what is happening here today! Today is a special briefing, if anyone asks!"

What could Craig do after that tirade? He was but one of twenty or so, all of whom (to judge by the looks on their faces) were as equally non-plussed as he was. A tap on the shoulder and head jerk indicated he was wanted in a small office on the back wall of the briefing room. He marched in, saluted smartly and was told to sit in the chair before the desk. Behind the desk sat two majors, one a red-cap of the military police.

"We have to start somewhere and you seemed a good candidate because you came in via the B.S.A.P., didn't you?" quietly asked the Intelligence Major.

"Sir" replied Craig.

"All your Intelligence analysis briefs seem to be more of interest to our special groups than the general soldiery. Why is this, Captain?"

"Well sir, it all results from a sneaky approach I took to getting the tribespeople to talk behind my back whilst I was with the police. It seems someone thought I had a talent for that sort of thing." Craig mumbled his reply to his questioner, the police major remaining blank faced, giving nothing away.

"You were a special friend of Captain Andre Dennison, wheren't you?" asked by the M.P. major.

"I was a friend of Andy's and I admired his record" Craig answered simply.

"You know he was ex-British S.A.S., don't you? And that he recommended you as suitable to process sensitive data for our special services?" this time the Red-Cap Major was animated.

"I knew he was ex-S.A.S., we used to speculate about the employment of Special Forces over a few beers when he was in barracks. Then I got pulled into the whole liaison thing with South Africa and their Recces. I don't know who made the recommendation that got me liaison job." Craig answered honestly.

"And you never asked?" the Red-Cap asked interrogatively.

"I was always told never to ask questions in Intelligence." was Craig's straight forward reply.

"Hump!" from the Red-Cap.

"Tell me, Captain, where do YOU think the Intelligence leak originates?" asked the Intelligence Major.

"No idea! From what I've heard, both ops were comprehensively stuffed up, so any leak must come from command level or above, no-one at lower levels knows enough specific gen. to compromise an secret op. that thoroughly." Craig answered practically.

"Valid point!" the Intelligence Major admitted. "Tell me, you were recently operational collecting intelligence in the field, weren't you, Captain?"

"Yes, a few days ago. That's when I heard that Andy had been killed. We're still processing all the data we recovered from Mozambique." he replied evenly.

Both Majors looked at each other, the Red-Cap almost imperceptibly shook his head and the Intelligence Major nodded his head just once, then said "Thank you Captain Burgoyne, you can leave now, we have no further questions for you."

Craig stood to attention, saluted the two seated Majors, about turned and walked out of the room. He went straight to his room and flopped onto his bed and thought, 'What the bloody hell was all that about?' He didn't have to wait too long before a batman summoned him to the office of his O.C., the Intelligence Colonel. His briefing from the Colonel was short and sweet, he was to go back down to Pretoria and take the latest A.N.C. Intelligence there and also reassure the South African military that their covert special forces present in Rhodesia had not been compromised either by the Intelligence leak or by the investigation into the leak.

"Why me, sir? Surely a staff officer ought to do the job." Craig opined.

"Simple! You've been cleared by the investigation and are immediately available. They start on Staff officers tomorrow and no-one knows when any of them will be cleared. Besides, you know the Boers and they know you; personal contacts count for a lot at a time like this!" the Colonel told him bluntly. "Stay down there until the slopies believe you, then hot-foot it back!"

So, Craig was going south again, this time with a very open time brief to guarantee success. At the transport pool a nondescript car awaited him. From experience, he knew that the mechanics of the car would be top notch even though the bodywork showed the hard life that the little saloon had lead. Then he noticed the licence plate. He had been issued with a car registered in the Transvaal, that clue told him that he may be a long time 'down south', a little longer than expected and that he needed to remain inconspicuous. Having inspected the car, he signed it off and so became responsible for it. He had no intention of driving all that way without weapons and was pleased that two hidden pockets were available for his personal firearms. South African customs generally didn't look too hard at a car driven by a man in uniform, but he might have to mix with civilians and that was where problems most often arose.

Tomorrow morning, very early, he would set off to take advantage of the low temperature and try to get a long way before the heat of the day became too oppressive. Although only a six hour drive to the border, it was a further two hours to Pretoria and eight hours concentrated driving was as much as he wanted to do. Tonight he could still go to the bar before turning in early in preparation for his early start tomorrow. In the base pub, the attitude was subdued, everybody knew something was wrong, but not many knew what was wrong. After just one bottle of beer Craig couldn't stand the feeling anymore, so walked back to his room and began looking through the documentation that he was taking to Pretoria. As he could be asked to explain any of them, it was wise that he knew, at least, what each contained, but he couldn't concentrate. The more he read, the more Andy's death hit him and the overwhelming sorrow he felt simply beat him down. Thinking on what the Major had told him when he was in the field awoke visions in his mind going all the way back to his early actions and he was amazed that all the details were still fresh. He could smell the smells of blood, of cordite, of the dust and hear the crackle of burning thatch, the cries of the wounded and the cries of victory.

He knew he wasn't drunk, or at least not drunk enough, so sleep wouldn't come. He hated night alone like this, no-one to talk to because only a combat soldier could understand what he had experienced. With the front-line guys talking was the therapy and when that was not particularly successful, a few more beers ensured at least a modicum of sleep, but here with the office-boys, there was no interest in 'the hard stuff'. That had been one of Andy's great virtues; he'd been there, done that, seen the sights, smelled the smells and had become something of father confessor for Craig. Now he had to face his personal demons on his own!

Piet, he thought, would feel something similar, he'd seen action with the P.A.T.U., so he resolved to write to him and try to unburden himself. As he started to write, he realised that all mail was censored and that if he said anything too specific it would be noted and he would find himself with an appointment with the trick-cyclist at Salisbury General Hospital and a suddenly stalled career. So he decided to write to Piet but to post it from Pretoria and send it to him via the family post-box. He had been out of communication with the Uys's for too long, so if he wrote to Piet he would have to write, at least, also to Mrs. Uys. Again, another task to do in Pretoria! He was relaxing and the demons were steadily being silenced as he drifted away to sleep.

He awoke to some-one shaking his shoulder. "Good morning Sir, you asked for a 4 a.m. call and that's the time now." a mess servant said through Craig's haze. How he shaved without cutting himself to ribbons was beyond his explanation and then a fried breakfast served in his room! Only the mug of thick brown tea was recognizable, but it served its' purpose and fully woke him up. He stepped out into a chilly early spring morning and saw that dew had formed on his car, so he walked around the car and wiped all the windows with his hands and then wiped his wet hands over his face finally to wake himself up. At the first twist of the key the engine started, a small condensation cloud forming at the back of the car which followed him as he drove to the sentry barrier. A smart salute from the guard and Craig turned into the deserted road and began his solo journey to Pretoria through the lightening morning.

Driving through the rising day was cool and easy. On tarred roads, he knew he was safe from the risk of land-mines planted overnight. Lands-mines were beginning to terrorise farmers and all those who had to travel any distance on dirt roads. Early morning was the worst time, insufficient light to notice fresh dark patches on the surface under which a freshly planted mine might sit. Later in the day, as the light strengthened, changes on the road surface became easier to see, so the chance of avoiding a mine became more realistic. Besides, there was always the chance that you may be the second or third car along that particular stretch of road and if the first got through without incident, then the chances were that road hadn't been mined.

Stopping at Beit Bridge to complete South African immigration requirements was a formality, his military passes ensured that paperwork was kept to an absolute minimum. A few hours later, he arrived at the S.A. Army base outside Pretoria, was escorted to a bedroom where he stowed his bags before collapsing on the bed in a dead sleep. Armies are Armies and all start the day early. Craig was woken up by a mess waiter who left him a small tray with coffee and biscuits. He was starving and wolfed down the biscuits, washing them down with the scalding coffee. After daily prayers ended with a blessing, in Afrikaans, the whole base began to move and come to life and things started to happen. Craig was escorted into an anonymous office block and into an equally anonymous office where he was asked to wait. Before he could really get comfortable on the wooden chair, the door opened and two South African officers entered. One was Fred Visser, the other was unknown to him but had the obvious stamp of Military Intelligence and his rank badges showed he was Fred's superior officer.

"Sit, Captain," the Major snapped. "Do you know why we requested you to come here?"

"No sir, I was instructed to bring our latest Intelligence captures that relate to the A.N.C., but apart from that, no idea, sir!" Craig replied cautiously.

"Tell me about the stuff-ups on the last two special forces raids." the Major requested.

"Still under investigation at King George barracks in Salisbury, sir. I was cleared early and then immediately tasked to bring the A.N.C. stuff here, sir." he answered honestly.

"Your thoughts on the whole operational security issue 'up there'?" demanded the Major.

"Usual 'need to know' basis on all operational data. What was leaked was sufficiently comprehensive that it must have come from Staff officer level, no-one below that rank would have a complete enough picture." was Craig's honest evaluation.

"Our Recces are operating alongside your Special Forces and if that fact was blown, South Africa would be embarrassed internationally. The full ramifications of such a disclosure are giving our political masters' sleepless nights. You fully understand that?" the Major shouted into Craig's face.

"Yes, sir! Speaking personally, sir, I'm certain that Rhodesia doesn't want to lose South Africa's help or friendship and that certainly means not embarrassing your country, sir!" Craig calmly replied.

"Thank you for that personal expression of loyalty, Captain, but we are more interested as to when will you have the situation fully under control and be able to identify the traitor?" a sarcastic reply from the South African.

"We're working on it urgently, Sir, and that's the limit of my knowledge." was Craigs calm reply.

"Brief Visser here about your new A.N.C. data and take your time over it. You're confined to South Africa until WE are sure thatyour operational planning is secure!" shouted at Craig once more.

With that the Major turned on his heel and marched out of the office. He carried on marching right out of the building because his footsteps could be clearly heard all the way out.

"If the politicos panic then the situation will get out of control quick-quick and the shit will fly everywhere!" said Fred. "Show me the new A.N.C. stuff, then we'll talk about what you can do."

With that Craig began to pull hand-fulls of documents out of his duffle bag and began organising them on the small corner table. Many pages had blood on them and were thus straight of the battle-field. Hesitantly Craig said that the data was still so fresh that he had no had time to analyse it fully. Fred asked where the information had come from and was told 'Mozambique', asking how old the papers were, Craig told him that he, personally had brought it all back from the raid. At that Fred's eye-brows raised and he whistled softly. It took time even to organise the piles of documents roughly. Lunch time had come and Fred took Craig to the officers' mess or food. As they left the room, Fred locked the door and pocketed the key saying the room was a secure room in a secure building on a secure SADF facility, Craig hoped that his confidence was not misplaced, but he was hungry and intent on eating. Over a very pleasing lunch, Fred became his usual affable self once more. When Craig asked when he could return 'back North' Fred shrugged his shoulders as if to say 'no idea.'

"Let's go and read some A.N.C. secrets!" said Fred rising from the table to be followed by Craig. Around the Intelligence barracks it was obviously relaxed dress code, as no-one was bothering with formal head-gear. All-in-all, the site seemed to have a relaxed, almost leisurely attitude which could easily fool the unwary visitor. Craig wasn't fooled, he knew that the relaxed appearance would vanish like smoke in the wind if an urgent problem arose. Later that afternoon Craig began to appreciate the relaxed, time to think attitude that pervaded the building. He was so used to the 'we need everything YESTERDAY' Rhodesian approach to intelligence analysis that he tried to inject some pace into their study.

"Take time! We've got plenty; you on the other hand have very little!" said Fred. "We've got time to plan a strategy and train for it, you guys have to implement things as you go, learn-on-the-job so to speak. We watch you and learn the best ways of doing the job."

"Well, we're stretched all the time. Everybody's doing more than they thought they could do." he replied.

Fred made copious notes as they read through the documents and Craig noted that some of the comments referred to the political side of the insurgents philosophy. Fred saw him take notice and reminded him that they were facing a powerful propaganda machine and though Rhodesia might win the battles, they could easily loose the propaganda war and thus be defeated! Craig could only nod in agreement and think of all the blatant lies told to the world media by ZANLA and the way the ZANLA version was always believed.

Two days drifted by. Fred amassed a large pile of written comments, most of which he didn't share with Craig who was beginning to feel uselessly employed. When he mentioned his feelings to Fred, he was told that the next step was for the S.A. Intelligence community to review all the information. Craig immediately brightened up, only to be told that he couldn't be included in the review group, but he would be required once the group had made its' decisions. Craig was nonplussed, Fred saw that immediately and told him to take the next 4 days off. Craig felt frustrated, but appreciated that there was nothing that he could do about it. Almost in desperation he phoned home, the Uys's farm in Rhodesia, and had a good moan session with Mrs. Uys. After the initial pleasantries, he learned that Piet was 'out in the bush' and Mr. Uys was still with his 'Boere' P.A.T.U. group and enjoying himself. Hearing that some-one was enjoying himself, Craig commented that he wasn't and that he was stuck in barracks in Pretoria doing nothing. Mrs. Uys reminded Craig that Suzanne and Hans were in Pretoria and that they would LOVE to see him. Before he knew what had happened, he had written their telephone number on the back of his hand and Mrs. Uys saying that she would phone them ahead and arrange everything for him!

Chapter 12

Welcome in Pretoria?

Mrs. Uys had done a good job! When he got back to his quarters he found an envelope addressed to him sitting very obviously on his desk. On opening it, he found a handwritten message, along with a sketch map to Faerie Glen and Hans and Suzanne's home. There was an un-decypherable signature at the bottom, but he could read the rank and knew that the base signaller had taken the message and drawn the map. That was reason enough for him to go to the Signals section and talk to whoever had received the message on his behalf.

Walking into the signals office caused the signals korporal to leap to his feet and snap up a superb salute. After telling the korporal to stand easy, he asked about the map. It turned out that the korporals parents lived close by Faerie Glen and had improved the detail to the map as it had been dictated to him. Happily, he explained every metre of the road from base to Hans's house, including much detail that Craig really didn't need to know, but he did indicate the likely traffic hold-ups and routes around them. Now having a very comprehensive route, he was running out of reasons why he couldn't visit the couple. Simply saying to Hans 'Each time we meet either I wind your wife up, or she does me!' sounded weak, so he faced reality and realised that he had to pay a visit. Like a visit to the dentist, Craig thought to himself, best get the pain over with early and recover afterwards.

Suzanne answered the phone and sounded positively delighted that Craig was on the phone, which made him wary! 'Yes, everything was going well with them. Hans had had a stomach problem recently and been off work for a few days, but he was well now. Yes, the baby was due soon and she still felt 'in the pink'. Mrs. Uys was 'a darling, but she always had been!' then came the implied criticism. 'You do know how much she worries about the three of you, don't you? You are more remote than Piet or Mr. Uys and she worries so much!' Craig couldn't tell her that he was often off-base and couldn't tell any-one; to do that would have sounded far too defensive and increased the chances of Rooikop criticising him. He just mumbled something inaudible and said that he'd try to do a better job of communicating from here on. Whatever he had said worked like a soothing balm, any trace of aggression vanished from Suzanne's voice, to be replaced by an almost seductive note.

"Dinner will be cooked by the time you get here tonight. Hans will be a little late, so we'll wait and all dine together." he was told quite categorically.

Not knowing what to say, but knowing that he couldn't refuse, he just said "Thanks, what time, please?"

He only had brought only military wear with him, so the decision of what to wear was simply down to cleanest shirt and as he dressed ready for the evening he got the very clear feeling that he would stick out like a sore thumb at the dinner table. 'Never mind', he rationalised to himself, 'this is a one off invitation and I can struggle through a meal, no matter what!' Finally ready he took his improved map and started his little civilian car, then drove out of the main gate and set off to find Faerie Glen. All the path markers duly arrived at the expected time and in the expected place, so much so that he was almost surprised to find himself driving down a middle-class road, looking for number 56. Automatically Craig found himself thinking that for a newly married couple Hans and Suzanne were doing well for themselves. For the first time he found himself wondering just how he would be placed in Rhodesia when the war concluded. Would he be able to afford something similar, or would it be life on the Uys's farm until something changed? If Fred Visser were correct in his predicted outcome of the Chimerunga maybe it was time for him to start thinking about his future. Was there really a role for him with the S.A.D.F? Craig resolved to talk to Fred about the future over a few beers the next evening that they were in the barrack pub together.

He registered, rather than saw, a well dressed, heavily pregnant young woman on the left side foot-path and when he looked directly at her it was Suzanne looking up and down the road. He stopped close by, climbed out of the car and waved. She saw him immediately, her face lighting up in a tremendous smile and she walked towards him. They met and Suzanne kissed him full on the lips South African style. Craig, still a little reserved about the full on kissing routine, was hesitant which Suzanne translated as shyness and chided him gently about it. In reply he gave her a small grin which Suzanne immediately translated as a further sign of his shyness.

"Bring your car right up the drive to the front door and I'll meet you there." she said.

No small driveway, this one, it ran past the neighbouring property before turning to the right and arriving at the house. Getting out of his little car, he realised that the house was effectively hidden from view of the road, his mind automatically registering the Intelligence potential for clandestine meetings. He parked the car and was walking around casting a professional eye on the house and assessing its defensive weak points when Suzanne said to him that he obviously approved of how her house as he was looking so closely at it. Her comment caught Craig short when he realised what he had been so obviously doing and his stuttered reply only served to increase Suzanne belief in his shyness.

Suzanne was glowing with home owner's pride, now even more increased by Craig's obvious approval of her house, that happiness and contentment seemed to shine in her face. Taking him inside, they walked past the kitchen and through a cloud of wonderful smells, the like of which Craig hadn't smelled for a long time. He told her that and she took it as a great compliment, but suggested that he wait to taste the food before giving a final comment. He sat around drinking a cold beer whilst Suzanne bustled around in the kitchen rattling pots and pans and waiting for Hans to arrive back from work. When eventually Hans walked through the door Suzanne almost smothered him in a big hug and enquired solicitously about how he felt. It was only when Craig stood to shake hands with Hans that he appreciated just how wasted he looked. He cast an enquiring glance at Suzanne who smiled back at him and shook her head slightly.

Dinner went off splendidly, the food tasted, if anything, better than it had smelled and Craig wasn't slow in telling her how good the food was. Throughout the meal Hans had been tiring visibly, so it was surprise to

Craig when as soon as the food was finished Hans left the table and went to bed. Once Hans had left Craig began to make excuses and prepared to go back to the barracks, but Suzanne wouldn't hear a word of it. His simple enquiry about Hans's health froze the conversation between them. Then Suzanne told him that Hans had had stomach cancer, but that chemo-therapy had cured him and he was now completely clear and on his way back to full health. He was weak from the side effects of the chemo, but daily growing stronger.

"Should he be back at work yet?" Craig asked in a concerned way

"Hans wanted to return to work as quickly as he could. If he gets too tired during the day, the company allow him either to come home early or rest in his office. He's happy doing it that way." she replied.

"Do the Uys's know about Hans?" Craig asked.

"Well, yes and no." was Suzanne's reply. "They know that Hans had stomach problems, but not what the problem was."

"You have a baby coming and a sick husband," at that comment Suzanne shot him a fierce glance, "They regard themselves as your close friends. Mrs. Uys would be down here to help you in a flash if she knew. Why haven't you told them?"

At that Suzanne dissolved into tears and said something about 'her problems being small compared to Mrs. Uys's. Craig disagreed, saying that if she left the Uys's out of the picture that would be taken as an insult. Suzanne wept even heavier at that, but promised to phone them and tell them everything.

Wiping her eyes, she asked Craig what his future plans were, did he have a girl-friend, what was he going to do? All he could reply was that he couldn't see so far ahead, he was working flat out all the time and that when the war ended, here would be enough time to take stock of his life and make the important decisions then. To the question of whether he would stay in Rhodesia once the Chimurenga finished, all he could say was that it depends on how the war ends. By this stage of the conversation, Craig was feeling definitely uneasy, so he announced is leave time was finished (it wasn't, but Suzanne was not to know that) ands that he had to return. Before he left, he got Suzanne to promise to call the Uys's soon and tell them everything, the he walked to the door to leave. As he left Suzanne gave him another full lip-to-lip kiss and, yet again, he was amazed how much that unsettled him. A short while later, he returned to the apparent security of the base, with its' uncomplicated atmosphere and certainty of direction. Parking his car, he walked to the base pub still aware of how unsettled his feelings about Suzanne were.

Chapter 13

Rhodesias' undeclared Economic War on Front-Line states.

By the following morning, it was apparent that the Politicians at the Union Buildings had come to some decision. Immediately after morning prayers Fred Visser walked into the Intelligence suite and told Craig that he would be 'going North' in a few hours time. He called in a orderly korporal and instructed him to pack and load Craig's bags in his car, to refill it and have the base transport 'boys' to look the car over and make sure that it was capable of getting back without problem.

"If there is anything wrong, I don't want to know about it, just fix it and get everything ready for 1300 hours." were Fred's instructions. "Your side have suggested a very aggressive plan of action to us. We've agreed to go along with it covertly. Now you go home and help to plan it! Keeping me, personally, in the loop is the price that Rhodesia has to pay for our continued aid."

Briefly Fred told Craig that the planning for the opening raid would be carried out by those lower level Intelligence officers already cleared in the 'mole hunt.' The idea was to plan further raids and gradually to expand the planning staff until something was betrayed which would identify the level from where the 'leak' had come.

"You're cleared. You are needed back there, don't forget to keep in touch." was Freds closing comment as he left the office.

There was nothing else to do, so Craig started his preparations for his journey back to Salisbury. Fortunately, the mess facilities in Pretoria were better resourced than King Georges', so he set off back North with sufficient padkos and drinks to allow a non-stop drive. He went to the base signaller, left him Suzannes' telephone number and a message to pass on to her any time after 1330 hours.

His car was back there and awaiting him at 1300 hours, fully refuelled, checked over and cleaned and ready to take him back to where the action was. There was nothing else needed doing. He had his orders from Salisbury and they were exactly as Fred had told him they would be, so at 1300 hours precisely he started the car and drove out of the base, heading north, back to Rhodesia and whatever the future held for him. He broke his journey at the border crossing at Beit Bridge, staying south of the Limpopo overnight before re-entering Rhodesia. This was his last chance to relax and unwind before the long and potentially dangerous journey northwards. First light was the earliest time to drive on unfrequented roads, there was a chance of spotting any disturbances on the road surface where land-mines might have been planted overnight. He was first in the queue to get through the South African side and into the neutral strip. His first question to the Rhodesian immigration officer was if there had been 'any action' overnight, short-hand to enquire if there had been any known terrorist activity within the locality the previous night. In reply he received a shake of the head and was told 'nearest last night was Bulawayo'. His route took him in that direction, but not to town, so he relaxed a little. Using his training and experience, he had defined his route to keep to tarred roads as far as possible, inevitably, sooner or later, he would have to take to dirt roads which could easily be mined. That was where he would need maximum concentration simply to stay on the tyre tracks of the previous car. Whilst it was still safe to stop, he did so and re-arranged the food and drink within easy reach; his personal fire-arms were loaded, cocked but on 'safe' and readily to hand too. Feeling as prepared as he could possibly be, he drove north on the tarred road as fast as possible.

He arrived back at Salisbury barracks without incident, but with the passenger side foot-well full of cans and food wrappers, which he left for the transport section to clear out. After signing the car back to the transport section, he carried all his luggage back to his room, only to be found by the duty corporal and told to report to his section commander immediately. Pausing only to rinse his face, Craig marched into the Major's office.

"Ah, so you're back Burgoyne!" the Major greeted him. "And how were Boers?"

"Very cagey sir, worried about our leak exposing their covert forces." answered Craig.

"We are going to plan, and execute, a series of pre-emptive strikes outside our borders and Pretoria has given us the nod. Planning begins tomorrow, first thing. You'll be fully involved in all phases. All stages will be undertaken by established Intelligence officers most of whom haven't done the job before. We're limiting all knowledge to a few, known officers, but that number will swell as more missions are planned. That way, if one goes wrong, we'll know what command level to isolate and investigate." the Major explained. "This one is OURS, our section at least! So, welcome to the party! Be in my office 0900 hours tomorrow."

At that, Craig saluted and marched out of the office, intending to head back to his room, but he diverted and found himself at the Mess bar. Automatically, he scanned the faces there, nodding to the ones he knew best. A swift beer made him feel sleepy, so he left and finally arrived back at his room.

He was 5 minutes early for the planning meeting, so he helped himself to a cup of tea whilst the others came in.

"Good morning gentlemen!" the Major spoke. "This planning meeting is now established, and I should warn all planning virgins here that once a meeting is 'established' all matters are covered by the official secrets act. From now, everything said within these four walls is NOT to be discussed outside EVEN with fellow members of this panel! Understand?"

Heads bobbed up and down in agreement, even if the faces on the heads looked unsure.

"We're in my office, so I'll start the target selection bit now." said the Major. "Feel free to chip in with comments and ideas at any time, there's no rank here during these meetings. We want the best targets, ideas and tactics, not some arse licking, half-cocked plan that upset no-one! Oh, and by the way, the overall operational name for these raids is 'Chastise'. For the historians amongst you, that was also the name used for the RAF's dams' raid in 1943. We're hoping to achieve equally spectacular results with our shows!"

Target discussion took all morning. Craig was astonished at the depth of attention paid to the political consequences of each proposed action. Valid and worthwhile targets were identified in Zambia, Angola and

Mozambique, but the debate as to which target would produce the most devastating economic blow was unresolved.

"Lunch is served outside, gentlemen. That whole room is secure, but IF you have to talk business, do it quietly!" warned the Major. "We re-convene in thirty minutes, no-one is allowed outside, of course."

Talk continued over lunch, of course, with a frank and free expression of possibilities. It was during one impromptu discussion that Craig first heard the suggestion that Zambia could be economically strangled by retarding its' copper exports. A rather bookish-looking Intelligence Lieutenant who was an economics specialist broached the subject by asking how easy would be to blow up 3 railway bridges more or less simultaneously. This apparent naivety intrigued Craig, who asked a few simple questions, then opined that the task should be relatively simple for a selected special forces group.

"Well, if you're right, we could strangle Zambias' economy easily. All their copper exports traverse three railway bridges to get into Mozambique. Cut those railway lines and Zambia gets no foreign revenue!" commented the Intelligence Lieutenant. "Only one viable route remains for food and essentials and that is through Zaire, which couldn't sustain Zambia's requirements even in peace time."

Craig was impressed by the simplicity of the idea; three bridges to go down within a few hours of each other and Zambia would effectively be side-lined until new export routes were created and THAT would take months even in peace-time! Craig took up the conversation with the Lieutenant again and threw a few more questions at him. All the answers that he received built up his enthusiasm for the Zambian strike option; this, he told the Lieutenant, could be the answer! He confirmed that he would support the idea an attack on the Zambian rail system to severe their exports. Ian, the Lieutenant, said that he'd mentioned the basic idea early in the meeting and got absolutely no support for it, but he still thought it could be useable.

When the planning meeting re-convened after lunch, the Major's opening statement was that food breaks usually brought ideas together and who had got his ideas together? No one moved, all sat rigid and immobile. After a while, the Major began to shake his head and suggest that they 'Come on!' Craig took the bit between his teeth and said that he'd discussed an attack on Zambias' economy which should render Zambia unable to support any terrorist action against Rhodesia.

"Good man" commented the Major. "The floor is yours, give us the details."

Totally unprepared to lecture the group Craig drew a rough sketch map on the board and identified the three bridges leading from Zambia into Mozambique and thence onwards to the port at Lourenco Marques. Looking towards Ian for confirmation, he began by saying that the Zambian economy rested almost exclusively on their copper exports. Stopping that source of revenue would mean that the import of Zambian basic necessities would bankrupt their economy within moths. At that, Ian found his voice and began to put hard figures on the plan. Even Craig was impressed with the potential economic damage they could inflict so readily!

"Any other suitable ideas?" the Major asked. No-one responded, so he continued "O.K. then, we'll discuss the generalities of the joint Morris/ Burgoyne plan for the rest of the day. By the end of the day, if the plan continues to remain viable, we'll start detailed requirements planning tomorrow to bring it up to operational status."

Small concerns about the plan were raised, but none were deemed insurmountable, but the lack of up-to-date information about the target bridges, especially their style of construction and state of repair, was lacking. To try to get around the problem, an Intelligence corporal was tasked to search the Air-force archives for the latest photo-reconnaissance information on the bridges. To deflect any curious questioners, he was told that his task simply a wide ranging review of potential targets. Ian Morris lead the team to search the paper files for any applicable published information on the bridges, which found that the bridges had been manufactured in the U.K., shipped to Northern Rhodesia (as it then was) in individual units and assembled on site by local labour under the control of British engineers. That was not good news, the bridges were well designed and manufactured and so would be strong and require a lot of well placed explosives to demolish them. Since independence, the Zambians had been responsible for their maintenance and no records of regular inspection, or even painting, could be found. That was a point in favour of the plan; corrosion and general wear-and-tear over 10 years would have weakened the structures, but by how much? Up-to-date information on all three bridges was increasingly becoming the major priority of the planners. To attack the bridges with insufficient explosives and not destroy them would expose their plot to the whole world with no reward, to attack with excessive explosives would need excessive man power and time to get the stores on site. On this type of operation, speed and total secrecy was mandatory, even a minor revelation would invalidate the whole approach. Should that happen, the world-wide political consequences were unimaginable, locally, South Africa would be forced to disown Rhodesia and distance its' self as far and quickly as possible.

Because the 'need to know' philosophy was in force on planning the operation no outsiders could be trusted with the truth and so only members in the planning group could be privvy to the what was real information was for. They were stuck on the horns of a major dilemma! Small group meetings eventually offered a potential solution, the S.A.S./Recce teams operated deep beyond the international borders of all front-line states on an almost permanent basis. Craig, having been a trained as an armourer and explosives technician was elected with the R.L.I. representative to accompany an S.A.S./Recce team deep into Zambia to get the information first hand. It would be impossible at the crucial time to disguise the true reason for the long range penetration mission, so the selected S.A.S./Recce team would be immediately isolated on their return to Rhodesia. Soon after that, they would be fully informed of the plan and then they would be responsible for carrying it out!

Craig and Sean, the R.L.I. Captain, were very rapidly dispatched on a special combined short explosives and covert ops. course whilst their cover story was being assembled. Orders were openly posted for Craig and Sean to attend the 'advanced explosives' course at Gwelo and both duly left Salisbury with their kit-bags and personal weapons. No return date for the pair had been stipulated, so officially they would be in the south of the country for as long as required. Any-one seeing those orders would not expect to see them back for a few weeks, so their time covered for a few weeks.

Due to the urgency attached to the plan, less than two weeks later they were deposited at a map reference jut inside Rhodesia's northern border with Zambia. As the Bedford 3 ton truck drove back to base the pair organised themselves and then map read themselves to the rendez-vous. Sean took point, Craig following a few metres behind, both carried their rifles cocked, but on safe, it was possible that they meet ZANLA insurgents, if so they would need to defend themselves. Sean became alert, his whole body showed that his attention was focussed on something off to his front right side. Craig could see nothing, but fell to the floor, dropped his rifle off 'safe' and scanned down the rifles' sight off to Sean's right. A hand signal from Sean silently told him there was no problem but to wait. Craig relaxed slightly as Sean walked off to the right, then he heard him call "Tea up!" Moments later, the 4 man special ops. team were pouring hot tea into their billies and commenting on their approach to the R.V., their general opinion being that, for general service soldiers, it was very good, but the next few days would be hard learning for them both.

"Have your tea, then we're off. We'll get through their mine field before dusk, so we can get away from our entry point before any Zambogs interfere. We've plotted their patrol lines and frequencies, so we don't need to rush, but with you two ruperts in tow we'll have time to be extra careful" said the team leader. As always on Special Operations, no-one wore rank badges and formal ranks were disregarded, each member had his own speciality, that was why he was there and when the operation moved into that phase, the specialist then became their leader. Craig certainly found that first slog hard going, the short course just hadn't prepared him for the distance and speed that they walked. Sean and he were in the middle of an extended Indian file, the leader selecting the route whilst the tail back-tracked to disguise their spoor. Once the border was reached, it was obvious that the group had prepared a route through all the prepared entanglements and so they passed into Zambia swiftly and secretly. Now, the raiding party moved into a higher sense of alertness, the Special Ops. guys seemed, somehow, just to slip into a deeper shade of concentration. There was little wasted effort in their movements, every move was fluent and natural and Craig instinctively knew that he was with a good team. The onus was on him not to foul up and compromise the mission!

In typical style, the team moved throughout the night, the point man navigating them along a memorized route by star sightings. Before dawn they found a lie-up point far away from any signs of civilisation and recent human activity. Bone tired though he was, Craig prepared his own shelter and fell into it to rest, only to be told that he would be on watch in two hours time for two hours. He was shaken from sleep before he thought that he had really had gone to sleep, the sentry simply pointed to the look-out point, held up two fingers (two hours) and put a finger on his lips. Everything was to be done in total silence. Craig took up his assigned position, ready and alert. The sounds and sights of the African bush were a revelation to him. His operational time in Rhodesia had mainly been on farm-lands, the noises mainly of cattle, but here were animals that regarded the group as intruders in their particular realm. Sun rise was spectacular, the day brightening rapidly with the whole veld came to life and animals moved to the nearby water hole. Without question he knew why they had camouflaged their positions and moved around so carefully. He was actually enjoying himself and was shocked when his watch showed that he was 30 minutes late in handing over sentry duty. False heroics were not encouraged and he knew that he must get his ration of sleep, so he shook the next man awake and went through the same silent routine. As he climbed into his 'sack, he thought he recognized Ron, the man he had just woken, but didn't reflect too long on it. As soon as he put his head down, fatigue took over and he fell asleep.

He woke up to prodding of a boot toe and the smell of fresh tea. It was afternoon and food was being prepared on a smokeless hexamine cooker and 'ready in half an hour' was whispered in his ear. A splash of water wiped around his face swerved as his morning wash, equally a brief swill of water served to freshen his mouth. When the food came, it was a mixture of rice, curry, biltong and sugar, everything had been thrown into the pot and cooked together. After spooning down the food, Craig repacked and readied his pack, the stripped and cleaned his rifle. Ready to go, he waited with the other five until the point man signalled them to move out one by one.

They were walking for three days to get to the first bridge and when they did, their first task was to observe. Craig, as explosives technician, needed to 'eyeball' the bridge's structure closely, inspecting it by binoculars wasn't enough. To make a permanent record he took some tele-photo pictures, but still he needed to measure the steel sections in the bridge. He was acutely aware that on his expertise the success of the mission stood or fell. All day their observations revealed that no-one else was around, the bridge was in no way guarded, in the whole day two trains passed over the bridge, one heavily loaded going south, the other unloaded travelling north. Early the next morning the whole group walked to the bridge base and Craig began to measure the size of the steel sections that would have to be blown down. Almost on impulse Craig suggested that he and one other climb to the top of the gorge to inspect the upper bridge structure. His initial aim was to determine if a thorough job could be achieved by destroying the bridge at high level by using less explosive. What he saw was a bridge that had never been maintained and in a bad state of repair. Having got his pictures and measurements, both men climbed to the bottom of the gorge, rejoined the others and set off for the next target bridge.

It took a further five days to see and inspect the other two bridges, both were equally unguarded and un-maintained, and like the first were constructed of generously thick beams. Two days walking brought the team back to Rhodesia's northern border and they slipped back into the country without hindrance. Once back on Rhodesian soil, the team leader sent a one word signal, received a string of numbers, plotted them on his map and lead them off towards the east and their pick-up point. Happy that they had reached the pick-up location, the troops dropped their bergans and started to make tea whilst they waited for their pick-up to arrive. Tea time was a convivial period because the pressure of operations had lifted. Craig had been increasingly convinced that, with the exception of Sean, the team members were mono-syllabic found them talking and exchanging information and opinions freely over the tea mugs.

"So, what do you think?" he was asked by Ron, the man who had looked familiar five days before.

"To blow all three will need a lot of explosives, so it will be a hard and heavy job for whoever pulls the short straw." replied Craig. "I'd like to talk to the explosives guys at Gwelo and get their opinions, too."

"So, how's this got to do with your Intelligence gathering?" Ron asked

Craig started to tell, but remembering the need to know principle, suddenly stopped, but asked "How do you know about that?"

"I was there when you tried to get your bloody head shot off by the AA gun in Moz."

"So, you're Andy's mate! I thought I recognised you!"

"Yea, on attachment to the RLI then to smarten up their survival skills, but back with this mob now." was Ron's answer.

Overhearing Ron's answer Sean asked "How did we do?"

"If you want my personal opinion, stay in a group and don't get lost," was Ron's cryptic reply. "I won't be there to get you home every time!"

A 'beep' from the radio alerted them that the helicopter was approaching. A smoke flare was initiated so that the pilot could locate them and judge the wind speed accurately. A gale of dust and leaves announced the helicopter hovering was above and slowly it settled very close by.

"Bleedy typical, man! They've sent an Alouette, only room for four inside. Who's for the long walk back home?" asked an Afrikaans voice.

"Sod walking back, we'll do it R.L.I. style. Sean and I will sit between your feet and put ours on the skids outside. Just tell the pilot not to pull too many 'G s'!" answered Ron.

Slowly, the loaded helicopter lifted off and turned towards base.

Chapter 14

Multiferious-plots come to fruition

After a meeting with the explosives and demolition guys at Gwelo, the explosive loads and positions for all three bridges were calculated. After a consultation with Political Warfare people, Special Forces planners decided that it would be wiser to deploy a two man stick to each target. To be on the safe side, Special Forces management increased the necessary explosive weight by 10%, completely unaware of the fact that the demolition team at Gwelo had already increased their initial explosive weight estimates by 10% too. Night-time HALO parachute insertion was used, with each man carrying half the necessary weight of plastic explosive to bring down their bridge. In each mans' bergen was a excessive length of det-cord (detonation fuse) to join widely spaced packages of plastic explosive and explode them simultaneously. Each man was heavily loaded as he exited the Galaxy 9 kilometers above Zambia. They free fell for a long time until the barometric parachute released their 'chutes at about 300 metres altitude, from where they became responsible for their positioning and re-grouping. On the ground, they quickly disposed of their bulky high altitude gear and parachutes, hefted their bergens and walked off towards target.

Craig had been involved peripherally in the planning, contributing known terrorist information to the Special Forces planners to help to ease the 'hot extraction' of the attackers once the bridges had been blown. Craig wasn't parachute certified and certainly not for night-time HALO operations, so he was to sit out the actual action in King George barracks. Ron, on the other hand, was parachute trained and swiftly brought up to minimum requirements for HALO so that he could take part. Only one 'stranger' was needed and an S.A. Recce quickly stepped forward to take the honour. It fell to Craig to give the man a quick back-ground briefing to bring him 'up to speed' with the other five.

As 'H' hour approached on the selected day, the anticipation in the radio room was palpable. Craig knew that each groups' plan called for them to observe their explosion from long range, to be away from immediate reprisal.After transmitting a single word radio message (meaning either success or failure) they were then to move further away and continue moving by night until they reached a prescribed R.V. When at the R.V., another one word message told base they were in position, who then transmitted them details of their pick-up.

Craig knew the operational time-lines well and knew which bridge was scheduled first, but that did not prevent mounting excitement and every ear straining to hear the radio. Nominated time for that bridge to be blown up passed, people looked quizically at each other. Were the clocks wrong? Had the time-table been varied? Had the mission succeeded? What had happened? No-one knew. A sudden burst of morse chattered from the radio and cheers erupted from some older listeners. Most younger officers continued looking dumbly, Craig being one of them. An older officer looked at him and said the bridge was down. Craig continued looking dumb, until the officer told him that he had had to learn morse code for D-Day and he still read morse signals easily.

For the next hour everything was an anti-climax, the first group wouldn't signal again for at least a day and bridge two was scheduled for demolition until two hours after the first. Bridge three was scheduled for about the same time as number two when suddenly morse erupted from the radio again.

"Number three is down!" announced the D-Day veteran. "Where the hell is number two?"

He had just asked the question when morse chattered out once more.

"They've got number two, as well!" he announced proudly. At that the whole room erupted in cheering and back slapping.

In the midst of all the bonhomie, Craig was aware that he, personally, was awaiting the 'at R.V.' signal from group 1. He was tasked with going out in their pick-up helicopter and beginning their de-brief in flight. Another days' anxious wait was his lot, at the end of which, when the signal came, would be frenetic activity! After a sleepless, anxious night Craig was jumpy and nervous. 'How come he never got this nervous when he was going on operations himself?' he wondered and then realised that he never had time to worry, just time to get ready and go. All this waiting around really tested the nerves! He decided that he preferred actual operations to planning and operational debriefing any time and wondered how common ulcers were amongst the planning staff? His thoughts were interrupted y a urst of morse coming from the radio, he looked at the radio operators who said 'Group 1 secure at R.V.' That was Craigs' 'GO' signal, everything else was forgotten as he ran to the Alouette a little behind the pilot. Scrambles were familiar to the pilot, because before Craig could climb in, the rotor started turning rather leadenly at first, then more easily. Craig was still strapping himself in as the helicopter lifted off and banked towards the lowering sun. 'In low and fast, under the radar all the way, hover half a metre above ground whilst the two men embark and back home low and fast beneath their radar', was the pilots' instructions and he was certainly taking them to heart! After a wild low level ride, one where Craig thought they below the height of the bull elephant they passed en route, the hover came as a blessed relief. Thumps and bangs from the back and the odd wobble in height showed that their passengers were boarding as briefed. He turned to talk to the operatives, but was met with an angry question.

"Which of you two bleddy boys in blue forgot to send the reception conformation signal? Thank God the Zambongos don't operate Alouettes. We'd have shot first and asked questions afterwards!" snarled the South African Recce. Craig could only hold his hand up to that error and admit his mistake, he'd been so enthralled by the result that that bit of operational procedure had completely slipped his mind. To cover his embarrasment, he began shouting questions to both operatives. His first was to confirm that the bridge had, indeed, been destroyed and that had had 'eyes on' when the explosions occurred.

"Whoever calculated the explosives loads went a bit over the top." shouted back the S.A.S. man. "That top span must have lifted 30 metres into the air! When it came down again, the stanchions were all on the ground. It's all scrap now, they won't use that again in a hurry!"

"So, target succesfully attacked?" Craig replied.

"You could say that if you wanted." shouted back to him by the S.A.S. man.

Continued de-briefing was almost impossible in the noisy Alouette, so he shouted back "Full de-brief in barracks."

One bridge down, two to go! Already, the Zambian economy would be feeling their attack with the loss of one bridge, if the other two were destroyed, then the Zambian economy would be screeching to a dead stop by now. Never the most efficient exporter, Zambia had tonnes of raw copper stockpiled at railway heads, now only that copper at port-side would be available to the hungry world market. No exports, no payment! In one, cheap strike, Rhodesia had strangled the Zambian economy for Zambias' extensive covert support for ZANLA. When the other two bridges had been destroyed, Zambia was effectively been taken out of the war and ZANLA had lost a valuable ally.

Over a further two days, the bridge attack forces returned to base. De-briefing was an exciting time. No group reported problems, indeed some team members said that training exercises were harder. It was obvious from the de-briefing reports that surprise had been complete, which showed that smaller, compact planning groups were secure. What Craig was not aware of was that the joy of success was tempered with problems for Rhodesias' High Command. Their sucess with the localy planned three bridges operation, deliberately kept away from the upper planning Echelons. Equally covertly, the South African military sent their congratulations and expressed their relief that the operations had not been compomised.

As ever, the Rhodesian media was very interested in publicising this 'victory, although they didn't appreciate the real reason behind the strike. Even the most pedestrian journalist fully appreciated the economic impact that Zambia would suffer as a consequence and it became a matter of disinformation by Rhodesian Intelligence to deflect their own press away from economic targets in other front-line states. Craig only heard about this mild dis-information campaign when he returned back from South Africa where he had been dispatched as soon as he had written the de-briefing report of the bridge attack.

Another long day time drive to cross the Limpopo and onwards to Pretoria, the political heart of Rhodesias' southern neighbour. Once more it was Fred Visser who he met and discussed the mission, planning and operational details. Fred was happy to see that events had gone off as planned, but was vocal when he talked a traitor in the Rhodesian High Command. He was more sanguine when considering how the ANC would be affected by the probable removal of Zambia's support for ZANLA. Craig could add nothing concrete to Fred's ruminations, but soundly supported them. By hitting Zambia where it hurt, not only had Rhodesia gained a valuable breathing space, but had also, indirectly, lowered the pressure on South Africa. Craig assured him that they would plan more surgical strikes against the 'front-line states', but he had had no further details when he left Salisbury.

Fred's interest lay with defeating the A.N.C., which he approached by targeting members of their alliance partners. His interest was concerned with Communist Party involvement and Craig could only help peripherally. Within ZANLA, the communist influence was Chinese, whilst within ANC it was Soviet. To the outsider that difference might not have seemed much, but both sides believed that they represented the 'purer' form of communism and could be manipulated to attack one another to gain local mastery. Craig had exposed this flaw at low level two years earlier and exploited it by feeding scraps of intelligence to an unofficial, low-key group of his BSAP officer friends and they were using it to become very skilled as 'spoilers' in the T.T.L. In some tribal territories ZANLA and ZIPRA were continually at each others throats', wasting resources, but achieving very little. Fred knew of the group and their activity, was impressed by what they were achieving and was keen to try the same disruptive approach to the ANC/SACP co-operation. Territorially, that fell in Craig's area of interest as their bases were either in Zambia or the abandoned farm lands of Rhodesia. Once again, Fred tried to get Craig to think about that mythical time *'after the war'* and what he was going to do.

"Zimbabwe won't welcome you, which ever side wins" he told Craig in all seriousness, "with whichever black government will be in charge at the end, you'll be on thin ice and your record will count against you!"

To Fred, Craig had initially been adamant that Rhodesia was his chosen home, now he was seeing the differences between what was really happening and the Governments' propaganda reports. His visits to South Africa, although on military business, had shown him that Rhodesia's chances of outright victory were slim and that a negotiated peace was more probable. With whatever Government came to power, it would not be a whites' only one and his service record would be very unhelpful to his future. Talking to Craig, Fred could see which way he was beginning to lean, so he renewed the official offer of state support if he 'came south' and used his expertise in their cause. Unwilling finally to commit himself to the South African cause whilst Rhodesia still existed, Craig equivocated by saying that he was thinking seriously of their offer. Fred told him that the offer would remain open for a long time yet and revealed that all soldiers considered Special Forces were getting similar offers!

"The deal will be a good one for you. Depends on what you want to do and hard you want to push." Fred councelled him. "Get some firm information for us and your deal will be sweeter!"

Craig now had a quandary. For the first time in a long time, he was pulled by the thought of his future, something that he had never previously considered, his job had kept him fully involved and he had little life outside his Intelligence work. Now Fred was talking about the future and what he could get from it, Craig had never considered the future, or his future, before; now for thee first time he had some long-term thinking to do and didn't that feel unfamiliar?

He wasn't needed for a day so, on impulse, he telephoned Suzanne and asked if he could go to her house to talk. She agreed with alacrity, asked when he would be arriving and would he have eaten? Craig mumbled through his answers, not able sensibly to do anything but answer her questions.

"Good, then I'll expect you in an hour or so" she answered.

Almost as if hypnotised Craig took his pool car and drove to Farie Glen as if on auto-pilot. He seemed to wake up and realise where he was only as he turned onto her drive-way. Suzanne was standing outside the door as his car stopped. She was no longer pregnant, but looked radiant and full of health, her long red hair glowing like subdued fire in the sun-shine. As if seeing her for the first time, Craig found himself thinking 'What a stunner!' He was immediately ushered inside, into the kitchen, once more full of the perfume of freshly cooked food causing him almost to drool on the spot!

Suzanne had prepared a full lunch for them both and asked Craig to lay the table whilst she attended to Randolph. She noted the puzzled look on his face, patted her flat stomach and said 'My new man!' Craig attempted a stuttered explanation, but was shushed into silence as she picked a small bundle out of a cot.

"Meet Randolph, only a few weeks old and permanently hungry!"

What Craig saw was a very small, red face peering out of thick woollen clothing. He didn't know what to do, or say, so wisely simply made some appreciative noises.

"His timing is always perfect, I could set the clock by him" commented Suzanne. "This is the time for his mid-day feed."

"Sorry to intrude" replied Craig "I'll go outside and wait."

"Don't be silly!" she answered, "this won't take long!"

As she said that, without compunction she lifted out a breast and put the nipple into Randolph's tiny mouth. He latched on immediately and sucked hungrily at his mother. Craig, the big, brave soldier that could look his enemy eye to eye simply didn't know where to look! He was entranced by the sight, but dare not look too obviously interested, so he sat down and examined his finger nails closely.

"What about nature embarrasses you so much?" she questioned him. "This is the most natural thing in the world!"

Maybe the most natural thing in the world for her, but he daren't tell her just how much of a turn-on for him it was. Fortunately, his finger nails proved a good source of distraction and Randolph eventually turned his head away from the nipple and gave a soft burp. The breast vanished inside her dress and Randolph was laid over her shoulder and patted gently on his back. A soft, contented burp signalled that Randolph was ready for sleep and within seconds his eyes had closed and he was asleep. Suzanne gently laid him in his cot and busied about serving their lunch. Sitting at the table with her caused Craig to feel that, at that moment, they were a conventional family on a normal day.

He was aware that he was seeing Suzanne in a totally new light; before he had regarded Suzanne as a spoilt, selfish, totally self absorbed silly girl, now he saw her as a capable, competent woman. During their talk, the conversation somehow came round to the point of 'after the war.' Craig found himself talking about the offer that Fred Visser had transmitted to him. Suzanne's council was both deeper and wider than his thoughts had been and he was listening intently to her points, all of which were about life, love and home.

"You always wanted to be an Engineer" Suzanne said. "Why don't you suggest that the SADF get you through Matric and then support you through a good university? That seems like a deal useful to both parties!"

Craig nodded in agreement with all the points that she was making and realised that a realistic life plan was being created for him by a mature and sensible woman, even as he listened. By the end of a wonderful lunch, he was feeling satisfied in more than one way; food and advice, but internally, he was feeling empty. He was surprised that he actually liked Suzanne, in fact he rather fancied her and that caused his conscience to ring alarm bells. Suzanne was married and the mother of a young child, thus out of reach, it didn't stop him momentarily wondering what would have resulted if they had been so compatible on their first meeting up on the farm all those years ago? It was a wrench to leave her. He had to steel himself to the task, once decided just do it and leave quickly! Which he did with all the good grace he could muster, even so part way back to barracks he was still thinking to himself 'What if?'

Chapter 15

The price of fame?

When he got back to King George barracks in Salisbury, it was to a blaze of publicity. He realised that something big had happened by the smirk on the barrier guards' face. Once back in his room, he soon found out. His table was covered with newspaper articles and telephone messages from journalists requesting interviews with him and photo opportunities. Craig read some articles and scanned the rest. He was worried about the security implications, after all intelligence work, of necessity, needed to be conducted in the shadow and shouldn't be exposed to the full light of day. That night, in the barracks pub, he had to endure some friendly ribbing, especially when some of the journalistic hyperbole was sarcastically repeated to him. Eventually, he left to go to bed accompanied by cat-calls and ironic cheers.

In the morning, his interview with the Intelligence Major was something of a prickly affair. Craig couldn't see that all the publicity would be useful to him or the intelligence work that he'd been tasked with. To the statement that the Major made to the effect that the Zambian bridge raid had been so original and successful and that the public were looking for 'heroes', Craig could only ask, 'Why me?' Smooth words followed, but none were convincing and he was beginning believe that his service was being un-subtly terminated. He was feeling somewhat paranoid, the typical paranoia that Intelligence operative always lived with, but this was different, this had been sanctioned from above!

"The public want to know all about the raids. We can't deny their success, they're public knowledge now and we have to distract attention from our next series of targets" said the Major. "Look on it this way, in intelligence terms, you are to be our smoke-screen. You will attract all the interest away from the rest of us! Really, an overt covert operation, so that the rest of us operate from within your shadow!"

"You will be involved in the planning of the next set of raids, but there is no way that you'll do any target reconnaissance, sorry! You're too well known now."

"What impact will this have on my career?" Craig asked his most important question.

"Probably only good" he was answered shortly.

"So am I'm to be a chair-bound operative from now on?"

"By no means! Once we've got this round of strikes underway, you'll probably go on to specialise in ZANLA affairs and get to know their top players well, an important promotion for you!"

No matter how he thought of it two ideas kept echoing in his head; the first was that the General Staff had effectively painted a target on his back, the second was that he had started in the police, but later transferred to the military. Often enough comments had been made about him being 'not quite a soldier', despite his deep involvement in Army affairs. Other ex-BSAP Army transfers had heard similar comments made about them, but Craig had gone further than any other ex-policeman, that attitude still persisted in some quarters, however. That attitude had ensured that he had been a suitable sacrifice to the publicity people and the Rhodesian public, in short, for some reason he was disposable.

Many people, even in the Military, had a low opinion of the terrorists' intelligence services. Not so Craig! He had seen and read enough to appreciate that they had a formidable intelligence system, although limited in scope. To add to this, their hatred of and desire for revenge against whites were well known! His face WOULD be remembered of that he was certain! There was no reason for immediate panic though, there were many more pre-emptive strikes in the planning and the financial devastation that they could effect would be incalculable, to say nothing of the political effects. Craig was aware that the new British Government was already making very discrete contacts with all parties in the conflict trying to obtain a negotiated settlement. If Rhodesia could inflict sufficient damage to the economies of the front line states that their support for ZANLA and ZIPRA would waiver, then Rhodesia would be in a more powerful negotiating position. 'Political reality' was the all encompassing catch-phrase of the Conservative Government in London. Should the front-line states removed or reduced their support for the terrorist groups, the British Government would be forced to accept that new reality in any negotiations. That shift in the political balance would seriously weaken the terrorists' bargaining position. Craig was aware that already Zambia was in the process of ejecting both ZANLA and ZIPRA cadres and 'official' missions, it's support for those groups effectively at an end. Mozambique could be hit just as quickly and effectively as Zambia had, so Craig accepted his temporary fame in Rhodesia (and likely permanent infamy in the front-line states.) He distrusted politicians; their actions frequently counteracted their spoken promises so he decided to manufacture an alternative for himself. Privately, he decided that it would be in his best interest to open negotiations with the South African Defence Force using Fred Vissers' good offices just in case! He would still work for the Rhodesian cause as he always did, but a possible escape route for him would be no bad thing. First, though, he had the Army's' publicity tour of Rhodesia to undertake, only after that could he get down to really important work again. Once he had the details of his publicity tour to hand, he phoned the farm and talked to the 'family'. Piet was home for a short R&R, knew about the tour and had told the Uys', so Craig's news was no surprise to them. Mr. Uys and Piet had swallowed the press stories hook, line and sinker and thought him a real hero! Mrs. Uys obviously believed what the press had told them and spent time warning him to be careful as 'plenty of young women would throw themselves at him!' 'Fat chance of that' Craig thought, he knew the tour timetable by heart and knew that, even if they threw themselves at him, there was no time for him to catch them! All of the family would go to the tour when it arrived in the local town, all the family was proud of him and wanted their neighbours to know it.

Organised with typical Military thoroughness his publicity tour began late on a Sunday, as the tour called for him to be in Victoria Falls early on Monday morning. Now THAT really was showing the flag! He was within easy range of a number of both ZANLA and ZIPRA major infiltration routes. The Victoria Falls hotel had recently been shelled from the Zambian side of the river, but the feelings were that the Zambians would be licking their wounds and the tourism people would be encouraged.

There was a small permanent garrison there, composed of national service men and Craig was supposed to talk encouragingly to them. The hotel had volunteered to accommodate Craig and his driver, and so arriving there on Sunday night they checked in and went to the hotel bar for a beer. That simple manoeuvre proved very useful. Inhabiting the hotel bar was a good proportion of the army camp! Craig, always easy amongst troopers, joined them and soon was chugging cold beers down with the best of them. From them he learned that earlier that year the Zambian Army had badly strafed a Rhodesian bunker from their side of the Zambezi. Unfortunately, the Zambians didn't know that a small force of armoured cars had just arrived there; they soon did as the armoured cars destroyed their permanent observation post with cannon fire! Officially nothing had happened, but every-one knew the Zambians had suffered serious causalities and withdrawn deeper inland from their river bank position. Life had been relatively peaceful after that, at least from the Zambians' side. Beer and off duty soldiers can be an explosive blend and that mix had proven to be unstable a few times, although nothing too serious or permanent had resulted.

Later on in the evening, a very attractive flame haired woman walked alone into the bar. Only Craigs' eyes swivelled to follow her progress across the floor. Unconsciously, that hair colour made him think of Suzanne as he watched her cross to the bar.

"She's a croupier in the casino on the top floor, but spoken for. Leave her alone or there'll be trouble!" said a pimply young trooper at his table.

"She reminds me of some-one I know" murmured Craig, still watching her hips swing.

"You can get close and talk to her in the casino, but not here or there'll be a riot!" answered Pimple. "She's the only unmarried civilian woman in town, but seriously attached. We can all look, but that's all."

Being on a public relations tour was enough of a disincentive for Craig to turn back to his beer. Funny that, he thought, how seeing a red-headed woman made him think of Suzanne! To himself, he rationalised it by thinking how striking that hair colour was and how attractive, too! Once the mass of troopers went upstairs to the casino to gamble away their pay, Craig deciding that discretion was the best part of valour, finished his beer and went to his room. Alone in his room, he visualised the croupier again and in his mind somehow she morphed into Suzanne. He found that a very pleasant arrangement, realised that both women were out of his reach, but still went happily to sleep.

Monday morning officially started the tour. A nervous Craig stood up and addressed a mainly civilian audience, trying hard not to use too many military terms. He was soon disabused of the notion that they wouldn't understand them, they did! Every husband and son either were doing National Service, or had just recently finished their 6 months short service. Knowing that, Craig relaxed and simply spoke as though talking to troopies, but minus the rougher terms! His allotted 30 minutes talking time ran quickly by and then the audience peppered him with questions. His answered were avidly received, at the end of which he was given a round of warm applause. It seemed that everyone in the hall wanted to pat his back as he left, including the red-haired croupier who gave him a very warm, full force smile and a peck on the cheek. 'Ah, this trip can't be too bad!' thought Craig as he climbed into his publicity tour personal transport, a Bedford 3 ton truck!

Two more days into the tour brought him close to the Uys's farm and another 30 minute talk in a church-hall. Before walking onto the stage set for him at the front of the hall, he was surrounded by the family. Mrs. Uys was in tears, Mr. Uys was so proud of his two boys that he had his arms around both Piets' and Craigs' shoulders, slapping them both proudly and grinning broadly. Both Uys girls were 'being soppy again!" and claiming Craig all their own. Being a local boy, Craig had been applauded when he walked into the hall and mobbed by people that he knew. Eventually, he climbed on the stage aware that time was running out, told the audience that he had to rush and talked to them as friends. All the who heard him talk believed that Craigs' talk had been delivered personally to them and his stock, already high with them, was raised a further notch. Looking back, as his lorry drove down the road; he was both happy and sad; happy that he had obviously pleased his friends, sad because he hadn't been there long enough. His tour was scheduled to last two weeks, a two week long Cooks Package Tour, as some-one had disparagingly referred to it, would end in Salisbury. A few days before the Salisbury date, their routing took them almost to the South African border. In the hall, he saw some faces that he recognized and took time afterwards to speak to the men. Both were Immigration officers at the border post and both knew his face.

"Not going South today, eh?" asked the older one.

"Not today! no pass-port." Craig replied.

Smiling, the older man replied "Take my advice, son, and stay down there next time you go!"

Craig looked at him quizzically and in reply was told, "This place'll go to the dogs as soon as the new government gets in place. Your skills won't be a meal ticket for you in the new Zimbabwe. I'd get out and do something else, if I were you."

He immediately thought of Freds' offer from SADF and began to wonder how far he could push them for the conditions, but what were his conditions, he hadn't thought that far? Suzanne's suggestion that he could use the S.A. Army to fund his education suddenly seemed to be more realistic. Whether financial support could be made available to him would depend upon his bargaining skills and how valuable his knowledge could be. Without really realising it, he was deciding the future direction of his life.

On his return to King George barracks at the end of the P.R. tour, the Intelligence section was throbbing with excitement and activity. A long list of potential targets in the three other front line states had been suggested. Over one hundred suggestions of viable targets had been collected, now they all had to be rated on a complex scale which should indicate the most politically valuable to Rhodesia. All hands were needed for those jobs, the cabal of proven, trustworthy junior officers lead the most important planning tasks as the presence of a traitor had not been forgotten. It was inevitable that some aspects of the planning would reach his level or service so to minimize the impact of any treachery, only the lesser value targets were to be considered by the high ups' in the chain of command.

Craig wasn't allowed to rest, he was pitched right back into planning at full pace. He seemed to have been elected as a group leader within the small circle of planners and, by default, seemingly becoming the 'Special Forces' representative. Within the planning group he had two tasks, the first one as a filter for the other planners in his group as to what was suitable for the Special Forces to undertake; the other was to prevent task overload of Special Forces. Very soon, Craig realised that none of the planning officers appreciated just how few the number of Special Forces operatives there actually were. So effective had the myth of the S.A.S. become that over tasking was becoming a real problem, the Selous Scouts likewise were expected to undertake the work of ten times their numbers.

Chapter 16

Flat out assault.

Planning went ahead with a rare speed and enthusiasm. For once, more possible targets existed than ever before. It was obvious that now 'the gloves really were off'! Having been restrained for years by the fears of the politicians, the effects of successful attack on three Zambian rail-bridges now mesmerised Rhodesias' political leaders. Now they wanted to make up for the lost years when political restraint had prevented attacks and saved the economies of the front-line states. So devastating had the raids been and yet so cheap and easy to mount! Now more were wanted. Having tied their military's' hands for so long, the mood was now to inflict massive economic destruction on the front line states.

Of the one hundred plus possible targets indicated, nearly eighty finally cleared the planners' selection criteria. Targets were divided by country, and then further sub-divided into target types. Once each potential target had been defined each was prioritised by predicted economic impact that each held. By the middle of the second week there was a clear priority list of target defined by their expected political impact that each state would suffer with their loss.

Planning began with the highest value targets coming under close scrutiny as various attack plans for each target were mooted. As always, the demand special force troopers far exceeded the number of special force trooper that existed, so powerful was the myth of their capabilities! Loading levels of all forces was problematically high because the total Rhodesian

Military was so small; a planning off-shoot was established to deal with the personnel implications and the conscription problems. By this stage of the war virtually every white male was involved and had some formal military function and all that could be done was to extend their national service period from weeks to months.

Mozambique was the next neighbouring state attacked, when power lines were selectively destroyed. Major power lines from the Cahora-Basso dam were not touched, so their hydro-electric power supplied to South Africa was not affected, but electric power throughout the whole of Mozambique suddenly became a scarce commodity. As had happened in Zambia, the Mozambiquian economy suddenly hit the buffers and stalled. Rhodesia didn't have to admit any responsibility, it was all too clear, the long restrained economic suffocation had happened. The long threatened attacks had taken place, now Mozambique had begun to pay the price for their support of ZANLA and ANC and could no longer expect help from their Soviet and Chinese 'friends'. Without electricity, all production stopped, export goods couldn't be exported and invaluable foreign currency evaporated. At this point, Rhodesia was actually winning the war for the first time rather than fighting a major incursion with tactics suited for a minor tribal uprising.

All together 86 economic targets were attacked over the last 3 months of the year, so by the New Year it was becoming increasingly obvious that ZANLA was losing all support and being strangled by logistics problems. To mount even the most simple operation inside Rhodesia, ZANLA was forced to use the longest and most inconvenient roads. ZANLAs' plans for an invasion and nationwide conventional war against the white population supported by Chinese, Russian and Cuban armed forces were still born. Self-interest made all the front-line states increasingly refuse ZANLA territory and, even worse, refuse the 'liberation forces' access to their territory.

Within Rhodesian borders, the security forces were steadily improving their 'kill rate', infiltration trails were being found or betrayed and greater numbers of would-be terrorists captured carrying all their logistics.

In the publicity, it became difficult for Craig's name to be ignored. It seemed that the publicity machine associated his name with all the cross border economic attacks, by doing so Craigs' profile was raised immeasurably. Wrong as all the publicity was, it very soon became unstoppable and too late to change. In the Rhodesian publics' opinion

Craig was 'Mr Economic Attack' and although he had had a small part to play, he was landed with the title; no matter how unwanted it was for him. Once again Craig found himself worrying about what impact his profile would have on any further intelligence work, would South Africa still want him to join them? He could have to pay a very high price for the fame. Mrs. Uys was, of course, delighted, as her 'adopted' son; Craig's actions only reflected glory on the whole family. Piet was happy to get his head down and do his police work anonymously as one of a group, but Mr. Uys wasn't so sanguine. Being involved in the 'Boer PATU' forces, Mr. Uys was aware that Craig was increasingly becoming the 'bete noir' of the insurgents, that much he had learned over a number of captures and field interrogations. All ZANLAs' troubles were being laid at Craigs' doorstep accidentally aided by a hero hungry Rhodesian press. Officially, the military tried to play down Craigs involvement in anything, the more the military did so, the more the press believed its own publicity with the result that publicity increased. Craig was anxious that he was being increasingly identified as 'the main man' not knowing that that was exactly what the military had been hoping to achieve. With all the interest being concentrated on Craig Burgoyne, all the rest of the Intelligence section seemed cast in a deeper shadow, which was exactly the outcome that the military had wanted to achieve. He was being touted as 'the Policeman turned soldier' who was beating the Army at it's own game, not appreciating that he was deliberately being exposed to become a potential future target by the Army.

Delight was the prevailing mood throughout the whole of the Army High Command. So successful had the attacks on economic targets proven that, even before half the targets had been 'attended to', the next targets had been identified. These were the political targets, the commanders of both factions of the 'Liberation struggle', ZIPRA and ZANLA. Although Joshua Nkomo and his ZIPRA cadres was hated by the whites for the shooting down of two Air Rhodesia flights and the subsequent massacres of survivors ZIPRA was held to be less of a treat than ZANLA. Harassing raids, aimed to disrupt and distract more than kill were deemed suitable for Nkhomos' commanders. ZANLA was a different matter!

Operating from 'safe houses' in southern Zambia, Mugabe and his close confidants were viewed as the more important set of targets. Covert missions were the only possible option and that meant that the SAS/Reccie teams would be employed once more on their particular types of operation. Operational planning was 'in-house' by covert teams aided by trusted contacts within Zambia. Military Intelligence did little, but to service any odd piece of materiel or intelligence that covert operatives could not. Primary targets were the ZANLA top three of Robert Mugabe, Emmerson Mnangagwa and Perence Shiri. That particular troika of thugs, all related by family ties which ensured personal loyalty to each other, operating ZANLA as their private fiefdom. Mugabe was their organiser, the leader whilst Mnagagwa and Shiri were Mugabes 'enforcers'. In the ZANLA hierarchy, Mugabe had the top job whilst his loyal relations had effective operational control. Should ZANLA ever come to power in Rhodesia, the country would be forced to bow at the knee to the troika's whims.

Target number one was Mugabe, he was well known from his time in jail and was the most dangerous of the gang. He was living openly and ostentatiously in Zambia, with a limited ZANLA guard party, so the 'hit' on him was thought relatively straight forward, but was not to prove so.

Like Hitler, Mugabe was paranoid and always moving at random intervals, never staying anywhere more than a day and seeming not to trust his security arrangement. Despite this problem, Rhodesian agents followed the movements of him and his entourage. As he had no formal, programmed meetings which he would definitely attend didn't exist, so there was no chance of preparing a murderous reception for him in advance. About the only centre Mugabe seemed to use, and then irregularly, was his Lusaka home-cum-office, so that became the focus of attentions. Despite explosive ladened cars, a 'drive-by' R.P.G attack and numerous sophisticated mines, all attacks failed for some reason or other. The car blew up spectacularly, but only killed the gardener who was moving it, the RPG attack hit the house but nowhere near Mugabe and only succeeded in blowing out the attack cars' front and rear windscreens! Some of the mines exploded, some must have been detected, some just vanished, nothing to repay all the planning and covert action.

Mugabes close lieutenants, Mnangwa and Shiri, were on the list to be attacked, but their appearances in Zambia were few and far between; they were well employed spreading ZANLA terror deep into the black Rhodesian population. All troops were aware of the bounty that the Government would pay for confirmation that either of these two had been eliminated, but however determined the troopers seemed to be, these two thugs stayed remote.

Outside, the rest of the world was beginning to take a renewed interest in the fate of Rhodesia-Zimbabwe, mostly to sympathise with the insurgents. Their colonial 'master, U.K., had recently elected a Conservative government. Hopes ran high in Rhodesia-Zimbabwe that an accommodation could be agreed whereby the current mixed government would be accepted and supported. Despite having gained ascendancy over both wings of the terrorists by denying them safe bases in the front line states by successfully destabilising their economic bases, Britain offered no aid or succour. All that the U.K. offered were talks about talks about elections. Rhodesia-Zimbabwe felt simultaneously beleaguered and betrayed. Their historic role of being first to come to the aid of the Mother Country in her times of need had been totally discounted. What was apparent was that the U.K. wished rapidly to divest itself of its' last and most troublesome African possession, yet emerge with clean hands. Politically very Right wing, the Thatcher government proved itself to be masters of hypocrisy by dealing only with the terrorist organisation. That the African groups were loosing both politically and militarily didn't seem to count for anything, all the political 'clout' that Britain could deliver backed the insurgent's causes. Loyal and tiny Rhodesia-Zimbabwe was sold up the river to enhance Thatcher's image as a leader of the free world and an international stateswoman.

It was becoming increasingly obvious to the civilian population that Rhodesia was finished; all the utterances emanating from London supported only the Black cause. Mugabe, photographed in the bush wearing tailored combat fatigues and a beret so badly placed that he had obvious never worn one before, had, apparently, been adopted as the spirit of the struggle by Westminster. Politically, the writing was now on the wall for Rhodesia-Zimbabwe, Britain clearly wished to wash its' hands of this embarrassing little colony and nothing would stop it achieving that end. It was common knowledge that 'free and fair' elections couldn't be held because of the intimidation and terrorising suffered by the black majority, but 'free and fair' was the U.K.'s government mantra, repeated at every chance and Mugabe seemed the obvious leader to back. White Rhodesia was clearly to be sold down the river to assuage the U.K.'s feeling of colonial guilt.

Civilian moral plummeted, especially amongst the whites. Craig, once the much vaunted ***policeman turned soldier, but still British*** found himself in the political firing line and didn't know what to do! Any fame that he might have had rapidly turned to ashes, he became unpopular and shunned in equal measure, being treated as the local Brit. Suspicion was rife, he was the sell-out, rumour had it that he was the traitor in their midst and had a direct line back to London. Security force successes now against the Front Line states were resulting in pressure from London and being reflected in Rhodesia/Zimbabwe by tighter sanctions. Some one was to blame!

Being on the inside and yet an outsider Craig was the natural target. As London leaned even further towards Black Nationalism Craig was isolated, even within the military machine that he had so become a part of. As British political pressure increased further on the small colony to accept Black rule, the pressure on Craig equally increased. Sending him first to Coventry and then boycotting anything that he had done, his military colleagues isolated him very effectively. He felt like the outsider that he had never before felt, treated with disdain, completely ignored, totally isolated from any meaningful contact.

Never having had time to change his nationality to Rhodesian meant that the military service laws didn't fully apply to Craig; for instance, he could, as a non-Rhodie, resign his commission and leave the armed forces at will. When most Rhodesian males were enduring increasingly more military time than civilian, the once golden boy was free to leave the service that had been his life for seven years without hindrance. Fred Visser had been contacted, partly for advice, but also to check that the offer of employment in South Africa still held. Having become the butt of all his acquaintances displeasure over the actions of the British Government, Craigs' love affair with Rhodesia had stalled.

Once free of the Rhodesian military machine Craig had nowhere to go but return to the Uys' farm, which involved travelling into what was becoming an active combat zone as a lightly armed civilian. Of the few civilian vehicles on the road, all were happy to give him lifts as far as they were able. Back in Salisbury, Craig found an open pub and went for a beer, taking advantage of the bar telephone, he phoned Mrs. Uys and told her what had happened. When he walked through the farm-house door, she was waiting. He walked in, carrying his army duffle over one shoulder and his rifle in the other hand. Covered in dust after walking down the farm tracks from the main road, he got a hug and a glass of cool home-made lemonade. That Craig was distraught was obvious, but that was due to the attitudes of his previously close colleagues which had precipitated the schism, but he still remained at a loss for what to do next. Fred Visser phoned him at the farm and after a very long conversation advised Craig to 'come South' and cross the border, then all problems could be talked through and resolved.

Mr. Uys came back late that evening, like Craig covered in the dry, red farm-road dust, having spent the whole day following terrorists spoor. He was pleased, but surprised to see Craig in the farm-house. Craig had dreaded meeting Mr. Uys, fearing that his motives for leaving 'the fight' would be misunderstood. After his initial shock, Mr. Uys revealed that the whole family was despondent as a result of the British Governments bias towards the 'black liberation' movement. They talked long, deep into the night, both listened intently to the other, but unwittingly kept a wary ear open for unusual sounds outside the farmhouse.

As the false dawn crept over the farm both Craig and Mr. Uys had reached some accommodation with the reigning political situation. Craig had had no idea just how dispirited the whole Uys clan had become, they didn't blame the British, as such, but expressed a weary resignation of the realities of their situation. Craig had found out that, unlike he had thought, the Uys's had bought their farm immediately after U.D.I., after selling their farm in The Orange Free State, believing that the Rhodesian future would be rosier than that of apartheid South Africa. An accommodation between the U.K. and Rhodesia would soon be reached, of that they had been sure. That it hadn't been achieved had not really seemed important until what they saw as THE worst political sell-out ever achieved by the British Government was to be their future. All the Uys clan were looking to return south of the Limpopo and to crossing the Beit bridge soon and for the last time.

Mr. Uys's plans were advanced, so far that he had a prospective buyer for the farm; the price was acceptable and assured the Uys clan of a secure farm that they could work. Piet was in a similar position to that in which Craig had been, a non-national, subjected to a different contract than that of a Rhodesian. He, too, could freely resign his post in the midst of war. Craig had, unwittingly, become the trail-blazer for the whole family move and was some months in advance of Mr. Uys, so they agreed that he should lead the way and go to South Africa as soon as possible. Craig would probably locate in the 'Rand', the area covering both Johannesburg and Pretoria because of his contacts with Fred Vissser and Military Intelligence.

Chapter 17

Student Daze,

True to his word, Fred had welcomed Craig and set about establishing the terms of their working relationship as had been agreed the previous year. Craig was de-briefed at the Pretoria military base over a three week period. To say that he was there to help the South Africans didn't seem to alter the suspicious attitude with which he was viewed. He had expected a 'friendly' de-briefing period, instead the Afrikaans military took an uncompromisingly aggressive approach. Although most of the intelligence that he had passed on, with Rhodesian official connivance, was in English, all interrogations were in hard, fast and colloquial Afrikaans. His de-briefing was not a pleasant time. Craig was kept within the confines of the fort complex, not even being allowed to make any outside phone calls. How different was his treatment from his last visit there!

Suddenly, one day the established pattern changed, he was no longer under interrogation, but talking to an established Intelligence officer that he had once briefly met on one of his earlier visits. This wasn't even an intelligence de-brief, more an Intelligence up-date to the S.A. Army, similar to those he had done as a representative of the Rhodesian Intelligence service. These low key discussions were 'give and take', he learned some things and the South Africans learned things from him. Politics were certainly on the menu and he was brought up to date with Rhodesia-Zimbabwe's' position in the current negotiations. As he, and all white Rhodesians, had feared, international approval leaned distinctly towards ZANLA and ZIPRA. The long suspected traitor had been revealed to be a 'high security' cleared Rhodesian Air-force officer who rather gave the game away when he switched sides to join ZANLA when the Lancaster House got underway in London. That revelation answered many, many questions in Craigs mind. When all the operational intelligence and operation planning were kept 'between friends', ZANLA, especially, was blind-sided, suffering severe losses in action. Thinking back to the 'mole' hunt in which had been involved he realised that the major victories had been when low ranking officers, vouched for by trusted partners, had undertaken the whole planning task themselves.

Fred Visser became a regular contact, as did one of the newly promoted 'Reccies' who had gained Rhodesian operations time operating with the SAS. John Vorster was known to wish to establish a similar Special Forces group south of the Limpopo to defend the Republic once their northern bulwark of Rhodesia fell to Black nationalists. Craigs' specialist knowledge of the Intelligence requirements for Special Force operations and his knowledge of the African Insurgency groups would soon be needed in Pretoria. Those particular details, plus his extensive experience were his only bargaining chips, so he had to extract maximum value for them, that he knew.

He was 'released' from close attention' as Fred told, but to Craig it felt almost like being released from custody, but now he was more free to plan his life in his new homeland. One of the rewards that he had negotiated for taking his knowledge and expertise into South Africa was a new life here and, to help establish him, a fully paid studentship to university, plus accepted immigrant status. Craig was more than happy with the flat that he had been given, although not the most modern, it was one in a fully serviced block on the northern side of Johannesburg, complete with a daily maid service. He suspected that the flat was, or had been a 'safe' house previously and had somehow been compromised. Now no longer secure for their nefarious purposes it had been given to him. He had some fights about the University that he was expected to attend. Initially the Government had suggested Rand Afrikaans University, their new prestige university in Johannesburg and were non-plussed when Craig declined their offer. His heart was set on Wits, the University of the Witwatersrand, English speaking and with an international reputation. Anger grew as it began to appear that Craig was rejecting everything Afrikaans, but the truth was much simpler, Craig believed that his Afrikaans wasn't good enough to study in that language; his only real alternative was to attend an English language institution. Whatever the reason, many of the people on his case felt that he was deliberately snubbing them. Only later would their actions from that period become important.

In London, the Lancaster House talks were in full swing and the duplicity of the Thatcher Government was daily being revealed to the world, to the worry of Rhodesia and the fear of South Africa. Craig had the feeling that the Rhodesians Special Forces, especially the SAS, would be planning some kind of action before the final 'sell out' could occur, but he knew nothing specifically. One day, when he drove back to his apartment there were two men waiting for him. He didn't know them personally, but he knew their type, they were B.O.S.S. operatives. As he approached his flat one spoke to him in a heavy Afrikaans accent.

"We need to talk to you inside" the heavy set one said. "Now !"

"Let me past and we can go in" Craig replied and pushed between the two of them.

As the door opened, he felt himself hustled inside, but didn't object or resist, and found he was being inexorably pushed through the hall into the lounge. By this time a plan had formulated in his mind and he was quite prepared to fight both men off.

"Don't, that would be bleddy stupid and dangerous!" rapt the bigger BOSS agent. "We here to ask a few questions about London, is all."

Facing both of them, his hostility so obvious and bristling with dislike, Craig said "Ask!"

"There's been a bomb plot uncovered aimed at Mugabe, but would have taken out half the delegates, if it had gone off. What do you know about it?" Big BOSS man said.

"You're joking!" was Craig's response. "I've been under wraps here for so long . . ."

"That's what we expected you to say. Tell us what you suspect."

"Dissatisfied SAS, maybe with some help from pals in Britain, would be my guess. Doesn't sound like an official plan."

"Why not official?"

"Because if it had been an officially job, Mugabe would be dead by now!"

"Renegade S.A.S. operatives?"

To which Craig answered, "These guys have international friendships, retired comrades, sympathetic pals, good buddies with ultimate trust in each other, that's how they work. These operators are used to helping each other, call it a brotherhood within a brotherhood if you like, they'll move together and covertly and be difficult to find."

"What did you have to do with the anti-Mugabe plan?" big BOSS-man asked.

"Me? Nothing! You lot know what I was doing in Rhodesia against Mugabe, but I'm out of all that now."

"How dangerous is this 'brotherhood within a brotherhood"?

"Don't worry, they see you as being on the side of the angels, so you're safe until you sell them out!"

""How dangerous are they"?

"Dangerous! But rational. And loyal to their own, however you define that! Good friends but bad enemies!"

With that, big BOSS-man looked at his junior partner, tipped his head towards the door and both left as swiftly as they had entered. Craig had been around secret policemen enough before to know that they had whatever they came for. Whatever IT had been, he didn't know, but he had obviously told them. His course at Wits was due to start in about a week, so he had enough on his plate to worry about without thinking any further about the paranoia of South Africa's security apparatus.

Registration and Freshers' week took Craig by surprise. He was used to doing things himself and getting himself to wherever he needed to be at whatever time. That the students were accompanied by *PARENTS* and obviously cosseted by both the University and Student Union simply dumbfounded him. He was quick enough to appreciate that one of his cherished ideas about students needed to be modified and quickly! Being older and much more mature than the average student Craig felt a bit remote from the younger people, their forced drinking, assumed *bonhomie* and frenetic dancing. He was almost feeling too old and 'out of it', standing watching the young boys (he could only think of them as boys) trying become the *alpha male* to impress the girls when a female voice came over his shoulder.

"Is your son or daughter here?" asked silky smooth South African-English voice.

"No, I'm the student!" Craig replied and saw small creases appear between his questioner eyes.

"Really?"

"Yes, I've just left the Rhodesian Army to come here to study."

"Why? If that's not a rude question?"

"Something that I always wanted to do, but couldn't afford before."

"So now you're chasing your dreams, eh?"

"Yes, something like that." Craig replied, already feeling comfortable in her company, she appeared kind and non-threatening.

"My daughter's here, she's called Liza. Her father was killed on operations in South-West and the Army pays for her education."

"Sorry to hear that. My name is Craig Burgoyne."

"Elizabeth Swartz" she replied, extending her hand. Very formally, they shook hands and continued their conversation. Equally formally, Craig replied to her as Mrs. Swartz, only to be told, very firmly, to call her Liz, but not Lizzie! Within a few minutes Craig had established that Liz's husband had been a lieutenant and killed by a land-mine two years before. Craig muttered the usual condolences and made as though to move away.

"Please don't go. You're the first man that I've met since his death that is actually sympathetic. All the others seem to think that I'm searching for another man."

'Damn!' Craig thought to himself, but actually said "I've had to write too many letters to wives and I know how unpleasant it all is."

"Let's leave the kids to it and get a drink! You DO drink don't you?" asked Liz hurriedly.

"Sure! Want to go somewhere in Braamfontein? Sorry but I don't know this place well enough to name any specific place"

"Anywhere where the students aren't ! I've seen enough of them tonight."

With that Liz and Craig walked off campus and into Braamfontein to search out a quiet, pleasant bar. They found a quiet bar in the Qurinale Hotel, a bit of a tatty dive, but mercifully free of boisterous students. Looking around during their conversation made Craig suspect that a more suitable name ought to be the 'Queer an' all' for the place! Still, it provided quiet time and calm site to get to know Liz better.

Small talk ensured, Liz was concerned about how Liza would be able to deal with student life and to ensure that she would actually work rather than party. Craig said nothing, thinking that Liz obviously thought Liza immature and in need of parental oversight.

"You've got that same self contained, confident atmosphere that my husband had. Must be the Army that gave it you" Liz commented suddenly.

"Well, you soon learn to look after yourself, life can be rough otherwise" was Craig's rejoinder.

"Yes, young, fit and confident. You'll have all the girls falling at your feet soon enough."

"No, not really. These young girls are all too immature for me. I prefer my women older and wiser than these girls. More like their mothers for instance!" Craig philosophised.

"Well, that's a new pick up line, I must say!" retorted Liz. Craig looked momentarily dumbfounded before stumbling out that he wasn't referring to Liz at all, just that the students all appeared as little girls to him.

"Hmm, I wonder if I should believe you?" Liz commented. Craig's stammered reply shown that he could be rattled and that his confident image breached. Craig was now on the defensive but had long since accepted the maxim 'that when you're in a hole stop digging!' In obedience to that rule, he suggested that he'd walk Liz back to her car as he had to go home and didn't want to leave her in the bar. Liz was a little stunned at the rapid about turn that their conversation had taken and how Craig's attitude to her had suddenly become more stiff and formal. She had to decide, and pretty rapidly, what approach to adopt. Would she become remote, as Craig had, or would she try to lighten the atmosphere between them. 'Actually, I'm getting to like this guy and his attitudes' she thought to herself and those thoughts created a dichotomy in her.

"No need to end tonight just now, we've got much more time, so relax and loosen up a bit." Not quite gabbled by Liz, but spoken very rapidly. Craig was taken a little aback at Liz's apparent *volte-face* and was now totally unsure of what to do or how to react. Instinctively, he fell back on his military training, remembering the maxim about how no battle plan survives first contact with the enemy unscathed. All his experience told him to be reactive and equally to be aware of Liz's responses. How he felt his lack of real experience in social situations, he had lived almost exclusively in the closed military world with its defined formalities and now he was really out of his depth!

"With all the hang-over that will be around tomorrow morning, I don't think they'll miss me if I'm late to lectures" said Craig in what he hoped was a conciliatory tone.

"My round, I think. Same again?" asked Liz, somewhat relieved. She caught the waiters' eye and he came to the table to take their order. Liz ordered a glass of wine, whilst Craig hesitated before deciding on a Windhoek lager. Liz looked at him questioningly, so he told her he had been thinking about a coffee as he wasn't really a big drinker although he was a student!

"Ah, that military control still shows through on you" commented Liz, "Just like with Hennie."

"Hennie?" Craig asked swiftly.

"My husband," at which point Craig physically took a backward step, "or should I say, my dead husband, the late Lieutenant Hennie Swartz."

"Liza's father?" asked Craig, to which Liz nodded her head curtly.

"I can see that you can be as tight and self controlled as he was." commented Liz.

"Didn't realise that I was being tight, just surprised, that's all."

"I still haven't really got used to Hennie not being around. I miss him still." Liz replied sadly.

Having opened up that far to Craig Liz visibly relaxed and said that she'd forgotten what it was like to be on her own again. That having been said both felt happier and more at ease with each other. They didn't stay in the bar much longer and left at Liz's suggestion. Walking her back to her car, Craig decided to ask if he could get her phone number and take her out some time. Feeling privately delighted, Liz acquiesced and gave him her home phone number. As they reached her car Craig suddenly remembered about Liza and asked how she'd get home only to be told that she was in 'Res.' and could walk back the hundred meters or so from the party.

On reaching Liz's car Craig waited until she had unlocked it before opening the driver's door for her.

"Where's your car?" Liz asked. Craig said it was further up the road only to be told to 'get in' and let her drive him to his car. Once in her car Liz followed his directions to his car, stopped and asked where his flat was. Having been told that it was only a few kilo-meters away up the M1 Liz asked if it were that close 'could she invite herself for coffee to sober up, please?' Thinking that he would like both the coffee and the company, Craig demurred and suggested that she follow his car, even to parking within his complex's secure parking. Liz's reply was a brief nod and then Craig was driving away.

As Craig turned into his parking area, he remotely opened the gate and waited until Liz overtook him and then followed her inside. Craig drove into his garage and invited Liz to enter his apartment via the enclosed stair way. On entering, they walked a little way along the central hall between the bed-room and lounge then into the kitchen. Coffee took no time at all, but whilst Craig was pre-occupied with coffee, Liz wandered around inspecting his apartment. They sat in the kitchen drinking their coffees in a comfortable atmosphere, speaking occasionally and generally in muted tones.

"I know you don't have lectures tomorrow. No one does in Freshers week. That was a pretty poor excuse you tried on me Craig!" said Liz with a smile. "If you want, I can stay with you tonight. We both might enjoy it."

Nothing more needed to be said, they were both adults and it WAS getting late!

Chapter 18

Independence (finally)

Week-ends with Liz were becoming the regular feature in his newly formatting world. He still struggled with differences between his 'old' life and student life as practiced at Wits. He had fully expected that the student would all be 'liberals', but was shocked to find that some were less 'liberal' than he. As far as he could determine, student politics seemed dictated more by degree subject than by a generally liberal conscience. In his school, Engineering, the prevailing political attitude was much more conservative than amongst the humanities students, who were *'avant garde'* liberals almost to a fault. Craig kept well away from the frequent on campus clashes between both student groups.

One Thursday evening as he arrived back at his flat, he got 'hustle-treatment' once more. Again two archetypal BOSS representatives confronted him. All they wanted was to remind him, once again, to find out who the leaders of the Wits 'liberal' faction. Basically, it was a warning for him to keep his distance from the campus demonstrations but to keep his eyes open and note who the leaders were. As a requirement, that proved easily fulfilled, most demonstrations seemed to be planned to be just outside the Engineering school! For added convenience, political rallies NEVER occurred at week-ends, those days were too precious to use an anything other than relaxation and hedonism! Which meant Craig could easily fulfil his formal requirements to both the University and the State with minimal upset generally simply just by looking out of any window.

Liza was happy, she was well ensconced in her student Res. and never gave her mother too much thought. Liz, too, was happy, she had become free to live her life without having Liza permanently on her mind. Craig was the grateful recipient of Liz's new found freedom especially over the week-ends. Being new to the Transvaal region, Craig had a lot to learn and his weekends with Liz were mainly dedicated to finding new places to enjoy. Liz put her foot down, very firmly, when Craig wanted to spend a third week-end at the war museum at Zoo Lake. She thought this interest too compulsive and had decided to break him of his obsessive interest in things military. Craig didn't object too strongly, a week-end spent picnicking at Hartebeespoort Dam was acceptable to him, especially as Lizs' enjoyment was all too readily expressed.

Up north in Rhodesia-Zimbabwe, the British sponsored elections had been completed, declared free and fair with Mugabe as the clear winner and Independence Day had been set for April 18th. Reading the results, Craig felt a dreadful prescience of dread and evil emanating from the newly formed republic of Zimbabwe. As the independence celebrations drew closer, the Wits students prepared to party by demonstrating in support of the new Zimbabwe government. As far as Craig was concerned, the students were selling his generation out and simultaneously cutting the ground from under their own feet. He tried to explain his feeling to Liz, but never having every fully told her of his involvement in Rhodesia, she couldn't understand his attitude. For Craig, the RSR (Republic of Southern Rhodesia) national sticker on his cars rear bumper was still an emotional thing, to Liz it was a sad joke.

April 18th came, the Union flag was lowered for the last time and the new flag of Zimbabwe raised in it's place. Most of the celebrating students seemed to think that South Africa had rid itself of a liability and enhanced its own security, so life for them could only get better.

Even before Independence Day, hordes of white Rhodesians were flooding into South Africa via Beit Bridge, not too keen to trust the new 'democratic' government of Zimbabwe. Well prior to Independence, the Uyss' had left and bought a farm in Natal and within a few days there foresight was proven correct when the government limited the amount of wealth that emigrants could take out of the country. Many families were effectively destituted by that law, but still preferred to risk emigration as paupers to life under Mugabes' regime. Many members of the various Special Forces units, all marked men because of their war-time service, also took the road South. Some stopped briefly with Craig before passing on to their own final destination. Their first priority was to get out of the new Zimbabwe before the regime began settling debts with them and Craig, known and trusted, provided a friendly stop over to allow them to catch their breath and decide on their next move. Craig knew that all these passing visitors would be noted by BOSS, but he believed that he could describe his visitors as 'intelligence assets'.

At Wits, the end of his first year was approaching with rapidity. Exams threatened and it was common knowledge that at least 50% were expected to fail, so hard work couldn't be avoided. Craig increasingly kept his head in his books as exam day drew nearer much to Liz's displeasure. According to Liz, Liza would sail through her exams without breaking sweat, so why was Craig making such a meal of it? Craig knew why he was making such a meal of it; he HAD to pass, there was no fall back option of a forgiving family for him! Craig continued his work load but took the odd half day off to be with Liz, but he was distracted, his mind permanently on his work. This attitude didn't go down well with Liz who wasn't used to getting only minimum attention and becoming increasingly unhappy. Eventually the last exam was over and term ended, only the exam results now were needed! Craig drove to Liz's home straight from the exam room and was anxious to talk about holiday plans, only to find Liz in an uncompromising mood. He eventually calmed her down enough to get her to suggest where they should go to. Liz started talking about months on holiday, Craig questioned the time length only to be told that he didn't have to be back for three months, so why didn't they spend all his vacation touring South Africa together? Craig's curt answer of 'Money!' didn't mollify Liz in the slightest, she had given Craig all the time he wanted to swot for his exams and now she expected all his time in return. Matters went swiftly from bad to worse. Liz was in an uncompromising mood, a mood that only darkened when Craig intimated that the more money he earned, the better life they would be able to have together. If Liz deliberately misunderstood him or not, Craig would never know. Within seconds of the fateful words leaving his mouth, Liz exploded spectacularly and physically pushed him out of her home. Stunned, all Craig could do was to drive disconsolately back to his flat to sleep in his cold bed.

Laying awake, staring up at the darkened ceiling, Craig had plenty of time to try to understand Liz's fierce reactions, but he couldn't. Hadn't he implied that he saw them with a future together? Wasn't that the point at which Liz had simply gone berserk? Was it worth seeing her again and trying to patch things up? So many questions to contemplate and all the lonely night to do it! Whatever he tried, Liz somehow managed to frustrate him, her phone rang and rang, but was never answered. She didn't appear to be at home, neither was Liza. Craig knew that Liz's maid only worked there two days a week and even when he talked to the maid, but whatever she knew, she wouldn't tell. Liz had very effectively vanished as far as Craig was concerned.

Despite still wanting to find and talk to Liz, he was due to start working with a local engineering company. At the beginning of his course, he had sorted out work assignments to cover his vacation; there was an unspoken agreement that if he performed well this arrangement would be carried through into the next two years. This vacation work was part of Craig's master-plan. Not only would the experience aid him in his course, but the time would count towards his gaining professional status soon after graduation. Liz had been aware of his plan and had seemingly accepted them, but baulked when his experience programme was to start. Craig was thrown back onto his own resources. There was only one thing to do, he reasoned, and that was to commit himself whole heartedly to his training and try to catch up later. He had negotiated himself two weeks holiday at the end of January and assured himself that he would spend that time trying to re-connect with Liz.

Arriving at the company's main offices in Alberton, he spent the first day filling in forms, meeting various team leaders and having complex aspects of various projects explained to him. Patiently, Craig listened to the information pouring forth to him, silently thinking just how similar the company's system was to the Army's. He was familiar with the Army method, so was happy with the company's method; he wouldn't feel lost at all, but very much at home! Day 2 saw Craig, overnight bag packed, waiting to be taken 'to site' some distance away from Alberton. After about an hours drive, he was deposited outside a solitary 'Holiday Inn' hotel in the centre what appeared to be a gypsy city of caravans surrounding one vast building site. Checking into the hotel, he found the company had booked him in for full two weeks, but were providing him with a rental car to do his job. He spent the afternoon establishing his security credentials to get him into the site all of which were completed in time to return to the Holiday Inn for dinner.

His first task, after food, was to hightail it back to Johannesburg to pick up enough clothes to get him through the week, *en route* he could also try to see Liz again, having a very valid excuse to limit any time with her. He got back to his flat very quickly, a long, but easy enough drive, packed more clothes and left heading towards Liz's home. As he walked up her drive, he saw a curtain twitch and knew that he'd been observed; that gave him hope that he might be able to talk to her. When the door opened, it did so only a few centimetres, the security chain was still engaged. Hiding behind the door Liza asked him what his business was. Asking to talk to her mother produced only the comment 'Go away!' Stunned as he was by that answer, Craig repeated that he only wanted to talk to Liz only to be told to go away once more, but this time followed by the comment 'or I'll call the Police.' Suspecting that the Police could view him as a trespasser, which would provoke a bad reaction, he returned silently to his car. On the drive back to his hotel in Secunda, he was depressed by Liza's answer and therefore critical of the car, the radio station, the road, in fact everything that he interacted with that evening. He wasn't happy! Over 80 k.p.h., the car's steering began shaking, gently at first, but worsening as speed increased. 'Out of balance' wheels Craig rapidly diagnosed it as, but decided that he wasn't going to drive the car as it was for two weeks, the hire company would have to sort things out for him!

Craig put in a full day within the security complex that was becoming SASOL 2. He was to learn and give guidance on Quality Assurance issues. At first this seemed to be little more than collecting together vast wads of suppliers' conformance forms and checking them. 'Back to the Intelligence game again', he thought, 'checking loads of paperwork against a list for something that may not be there!' Craig went into his old 'Intelligence' screening mode and did the cross checking needed. By the end of his first week, he had the system under control, so much so that he began searching around for non-conforming stock. On his own initiative, he established a locked quarantine area where unproven pieces were removed from the production process and clearly identified. This action caused some problems, when some workers tried to obtain the quarantined stock to build into the plant. Simple blandishments didn't phase Craig, he had a mission, knew what was required of him and wasn't about to be deflected from his task by verbal abuse and threats.

Walking into the hotel at the work days' end, he diverted into the car hire agency to complain about his ratty little Corolla, if he was staying, at least he wanted a good driving car as one compensation. Even before he had set foot over the boundary into Nationwide's premises, the manageress was heading in his direction and he felt his heart sink. 'More problems I don't need today', he thought, but put on his most charming smile and awaited the onslaught.

"Are you driving?" the Ice Queen asked him standing close, directly in front of him.

Craig must have looked dumbfounded and said "What?"

"You have been told about the hotel staff trip to Swaziland this weekend, haven't you?"

"I was told about it, but not invited" he answered.

"Well, you should have been! We need you to make up the numbers. Are you coming?"

Craig, taken a little aback, muttered something neutral, only for the Ice Queen to put on her best sales demeanour to invite him formally. Craig admitted that he had planned nothing for the weekend. (Nothing? If going back to Jo'burg and trying to talk to Liz was nothing, then he had nothing planned!)

"Good, then you're coming with us! Do you mind driving the minibus? Have you got your pass-port?" staccato questions rapped at him from Ice Queen. Tired as he was, he was happy that all he had to do was shower and then dinner. He was glad that he didn't need a long drive tonight to pick up his passport, 'not in that crappy little Toyota!' he thought.

Thanks to Craig, control over the once chaotic Quality Assurance system was rapidly had regained. Within the plant, managers had noticed that control and were quietly pleased for it. What Craig didn't appreciate was that his actions had marked him as the 'ideal Quality Man' and that he had accidentally just defined the rest of his summer vacation! Plans to re-deploy Craig to another sector to extend his experience were swiftly forgotten, he was too valuable in QA to move away. Consequently late on Friday, he was asked to report to the company site manager for what he thought would be a painful meeting. He was surprised by the outcome of the meeting, gratified and frustrated at the same time; he had been told that his work in the QA unit was so valuable that he was asked to stay there all summer. Very large hints were dropped that 'they' were impressed by his work and that the company was keen to have him back for all his further vacation periods. 'Great' thought Craig, 'that makes things easier, but all summer here. BORING!'

This week-end shouldn't be boring, though, he would be somewhere different and with different people and with no problems hounding him. He left the site and returned early enough to clean up and pack and be the first of the group waiting in the hotel foyer. Within seconds, the Ice Queen was walking towards him, actually looking quite attractive out of uniform and then she was speaking to him and holding out her hand.

"Here, go and bring the mini-bus to the front" she said as she proffered Craig the key. Craig did the Queens' bidding and drove the mini-bus in front of the hotels doors. He had no chance to get out, one of the travel party brought out his bags and stowed them away and then climbed into the back of the bus. He was followed by the rest of the party, who distributed themselves throughout the bus, each one partnering up with another. Suddenly, the passenger door open and the Ice Queen climbed in, arms full of maps and papers, a quick look around and then she gave Craig the first of many directions that weekend.

It was a jolly drive with plenty of good cheer emanating from the seats behind. Although no-one offered to share the driving with him, Craig was relaxed and feeling happy; he was doing something new and novel, what better way to take his mind off Liz and her behaviour. This was different, new friends and new attitudes. At the Swaziland border every-one had to get out and be 'processed' through immigration where Craig's U.K. passport attracted some positive attention. Without too much delay, the minibus was en route again heading for Ezelwini and their hotel. As various places passed, the navigator gave the whole bus verbal descriptions of the delights awaiting them. Some of her descriptions were hilarious, all were simply humorous, Craig relaxed even further, it sounded as if an enjoyable week-end was ahead.

Chapter 19

Week-ends worth working for!

Soon they drew up outside the Ezelwini Holiday Inn. Friendly hotel staff, actually personal friends of the Secunda staff, were awaiting them. As they descended from the mini-bus each was given a room key and a cold bottle of South African Champagne. As Craig stood, feeling happy, but slightly baffled, the Swazi 'Nationwide' manageress passed him a message to meet the rest of the Secunda group in the 'If Not, Why Not?' lounge at 6.30 that evening. It was inferred that when the whole group was together, the evening would be jointly planned. By this time, Craig was the only person still standing outside, there was no-one else to ask, so he found his way to his allotted room.

Changed, showered and freshly shaven, he got to the 'If Not, Why Not?' lounge a few minutes early and found it heaving, full of black and white, men and women. Standing, Craig scanned the crowd hoping to see members of the Secunda group, but to no avail. Fighting his way to the long mahogany bar he ordered a cold Hansa and put it on his room tab. Showing his room key to the barman got him a toothy grin and a conspiratorial wink, to which Craig happily grinned back. Moments later he was literally fighting off long legged, lithe Swazi women, all of whom wanted to sit on his knee and flow around him. Initially Craig was flattered, but later became increasingly nervous and embarrassed. No other members of the Secunda group had appeared and Craig was by now wondering what had been planned for him. He had reached his record of four women climbing all over him when the first friendly face appeared. Grinning, Helena the Nationwide Secunda deputy manageress came to him and shoo'ed away the Swazi women.

"Thanks for that!" Craig said, the relief palpable in his voice.

"Moira arranged that!" Helena said, "She wanted to see how you handled the temptations here."

"Good having friends." Craig replied archly.

"She's in room 317 if you want to say anything to her." Craig DID! His relaxed and easy going mood of earlier had evaporated; he was determined to recapture some of it and have a good weekend. Buy this time, more of the Secunda group had converged in the lounge and, unsurprisingly, every-one bar him seemed to know of the 'joke'. With anger covering his embarrassment, Craig left the lounge to find out direct from Moira why he had been 'set-up'.

Stepping out of the lift, he turned right and walked towards room 317, growing more determined with each step he took. Outside the door, he saw it was not fully closed, but knocked on it and waited.

"Who is it?" Moira's voice was clear.

"Craig, the fool" he replied.

"Come in." So he did and was presented by an empty room. Looking around, his first thoughts were that Moira's room was much bigger and better equipped than his, but he still could not see Moira.

"I'm in the bath-room, be a love and open my Champagne and bring it in, please." Having been told where she was, it was obvious to Craig, so he opened the Champagne which opened with a loud 'pop.'

"Fetch two glasses, as well" he was ordered.

Picking up the bottle and two long Champagne flutes, he walked to the bathroom door, it was part opened, so he leaned gently on the door and walked in. Moira was there, in the bath, completely naked and obviously waiting for him.

"Well, pour two glasses before it goes flat!" he was commanded. Trying to remain cool and sophisticated and also play Moira back at her game, he sat on the edge of the bath and filled the first glass. Without comment, he passed it to Moira and then filled his own.

"Cheers!" he said lifting the glass to salute Moira.

"Cheers" was her reply.

When both glasses had been drained Moira commanded Craig to bring the towel. He did, unfolding the bath sheet to its full size and holding it so it hung to the floor. Unconcerned Moira stepped out of the bath and towards Craig, requesting that he dry her. He did, it gave him an unparalleled chance to run his hands over her bodily contours without guilt.

"Make sure that you dry all the nooks and crannies." he was told, which gave him free rein to explore a little further. When Moira pronounced herself dry enough, she dropped the bath sheet, took his hand and walked into the bed-room to dress. Not bothering with underwear, she pulled on jeans and a floppy Tee shirt and then slid her feet into high heeled, strapless sandals; the type called 'fuck me' sandals by men world wide. Hair combing and make-up took about the three paces it took to get to the door and, as she pulled Craig outside, pouted to even out her lipstick. Craig was still tingling from the drying episode and wondering to himself who had ever told him that South African women were *verkrampt*? Liz hadn't been and Moira certainly wasn't! Knowing Moira would be the perfect antidote to his mooning over Liz.

They walked into the 'If not, why not?' hand in hand to join the other four Secunda pairs where Moira told them that the only rule was to be ready to leave by 4p.m. on Sunday and have money ready to settle the bills. Having delivered her organisers speech, she said to Craig directly "I'm hungry, I need to eat" and proceeded to lead him towards the closest hotel restaurant. It was a happy meal, neither of them spoke of later, but both knew what the evening held. Automatically they both went to Moira's room where they spent a long and active night. On waking, Moira ordered a room service breakfast for them both before pulling on her long sleeping Tee shirt, the first item to have hit the floor last night.

Over breakfast, they discussed the plans for the rest of the weekend. Moira was happy to lead Craig around this part of Swaziland and had their remaining time already planned. For Craig, it became a magical day, he saw a part of the world that he had never even suspected existed. They visited wood-carvers, candle makers, even a sheepskin slipper manufacturer; Moira was an open, friendly and enthusiastic guide both interested and interesting. Over a picnic lunch on the edge of the 'cuddle puddle', Craig learned that of the very careful set-up that Moira had planned for him.

"When your car was reserved, the site manager kept asking every day, 'Is Captain Burgoynes' car reserved?' He got so annoying that I nearly cancelled your car! He kept going on and on, this for Captain Burgoyne, that for Captain Burgoyne! In the office we were visualising you as an old man with a moustache and walking stick, then YOU walk in! A very nice surprise for us, I pulled rank on Anny to claim first date with you. Well, she's married and got a man, I'm divorced, so my need is greater than hers!" Craig also found out that in Secunda, available women were at a premium, but Moira would have nothing to do with married men. 'Divorce does that to you.' So his lack of a wedding ring was immediately spotted and that sealed his fate! Craig found himself thinking that he could have gainfully employed such acute observers for Intelligence gathering!

Moira, it turned out, separated her professional and social life very severely. Anything that could reflect negatively on her job in any way was kept far away "And that means you Captain! When we're back at the Holiday Inn, we'll both be professionals doing our own jobs, not soppy little kids mooning around. No-one in the hotel must have any suspicions about us!" Craig had been told!

It was an idyllic afternoon, pic-nicing by the edge of the 'Cuddle-Puddle', the warm water coming from a natural spring, dappled shade from overhanging trees and a gentle breeze to cool the African sun.

"Let's drift back to the hotel and get more cold Champagne and beach towels, then come back after dusk." Moira murmured. Intrigued, Craig demurred and began packing things away. She seemed to know every-one in the hotel and exercise as much indirect power over them as she did in Secunda; she merely had to suggest something for it to be provided! When they departed later, both freshly showered (alone to Craig's intense disappointment!) as they walked past Reception two bottles of Champagne in cold packs awaited them.

"The towels are already in your car, we'll put the cool packs in now" said the receptionist and waved a porter over to carry everything to their car. Craig was impressed, but Moira seemed to regard it as her due and simply smiled at the receptionist. Dusk was falling at the normal African speed when they reached the 'Puddle' and the old guard was about to lock the gate. Unfazed by this Moira walked up to him and slipped him a 5 Rand note and a secret smile. Pocketing the money, he just asked that they close the gate and snap the lock closed when they left, he even helped to carry everything into the grounds. Small gas lights had been lit and, as dusk deepened, the whole 'Cuddle Puddle' area became more intimate. Craig opened one of the Champagne bottles and, not having glasses, they drank straight from the bottle. In no time at all they were both feeling the effects and getting giggly.

"I feel like a swim" announced Moira and stripped off, walking naked into the warm water. "Mmmmm, lovely and warm. Come on in, but open that last bottle first." Needing no second invitation Craig did just as invited and was soon bobbing neck deep in body warm water. He had placed the second bottle at arms length from the pool to keep it cool for as long as possible. Lounging and loving in that warm pool was an electric experience for Craig and they happily lost track of time.

Sometime late in the night, the air above the pool growing crisply cool, they decided that bed was a better place to be. Moira simply climbed out of the pool and wrapped herself in an enormous towel and collected her clothes in her arms. Craig dried himself, more or less, before pulling on his shorts, grabbing his clothes and walking to the car. He waited until Moira passed through the gate then closed it and snapped the lock closed.

Back in their hotel once more they used Moira's room, it seemed far more convenient to do that, ordering room service breakfasts early on Sunday morning. Craig was 'shoo'd' out of her room to his own quite early in the morning 'Can't have the church goers see you come out of my room!' They had lunch together overlooking the lawn at the rear of the hotel and then it was time to depart. Moira switched back into her professional mode once more; the Ice Queen returned.

Before getting into the minibus to return to Secunda, Moira presented everyone with their individual bill. This was the bit that Craig had been dreading, he had drawn (he hoped!) enough money for the week-end, but had fallen easily for the hedonistic life style. He opened the bill and couldn't believe the cost! In total, the bill was less than he would have spent on a decent meal for himself! Looking closely, he saw that everything carried a very hefty 'staff' discount, he wasn't staff, but he didn't argue and happily paid the amount shown.

Once more he was the driver, the route back being a mirror image of the inbound route until he pulled up outside the Secunda Holiday Inn once more. He was commanded, by the Ice Queen, to park the minibus appropriately before he went to his room. By the time that he got into the hotel everyone had gone their own separate ways, he was alone with his week-end bag in his hand in the empty foyer of a near deserted hotel. What a come down after such a week-end! Walking to his room brought a whiff of burned metal from the restaurant; was it the green carpet and walls, or what? He had a sudden flash of being back in the Rhodesian bush, a member of a 'stop' group pushing towards burning huts. A momentary panic and then it was gone, but it left him leaning on one of the walls, shaking his head to clear his vision. His heart was still racing, the adrenalin still pumped, but he was safe in the hotel, what could have happened? In his room, he sat quietly for a while until he was calm, then walked to the bar for a drink. Walking down the same corridor didn't cause any return of symptoms, but the beer certainly eased his mind!

At breakfast the next morning, he was surprised to see Moira in full company uniform and Ice Queen attitude sitting at a table drinking coffee. He went towards her, but got such a look as to steer away to a nearby table. By the end of the week Craig was ready for the weekend. He asked for his room key and it was given him, along with a sealed envelope, carrying the car hire company's logo. Not knowing what to make of this event, he leaned against the reception and slit open the envelope; the note was to confirm the request for an extended hire period for his car and a hand written addendum suggesting that he come in person to the office to discuss any details. He glanced at their office door, it looked ajar. Best get things over with, he thought, and walked straight in. Only Anny was there, Craig was actually relieved to see, so he flashed the note and asked if there was any problem, only to be told that he would have to confirm any changes with Moira the following morning.

Moira was sitting in the breakfast room the next morning and Craig, feeling that he had a business reason to talk to her, waved the note as he approached. Without speaking, Moira poured him a coffee and indicated that he sit opposite her.

"You have to return your car to the office tonight" he was told.

"But I'm staying here for a few more weeks."

"Stock control. We see the cars at the end of the initial rental period, even if it's been extended." was the formal reply.

"When can I get the car back?"

"You can't! It has a complaint against it and so it has to go back to the work-shop to be fixed. You'll be allocated another one." Craig was told.

"When?"

"By the end of today, or tomorrow morning latest" he was told curtly.

With that comment, Craig nodded and moved to a nearby table to eat his breakfast. Waiting for food, he stared deep into his coffee cup, thinking about Moira. How could she be so impersonal in public and so intensely personal in private? He decided that Moira perfectly defined an enigma, a fascinating one, but one he was beginning to think was beyond his powers of understanding or patience.

Any plans for the week-end had to be flexible. Would he have a car to go somewhere? If so; where and with whom? Liz was totally out of the question now, he wasn't going to ask her again and risk another snub. Moira? No Chance! He could only contact her through her office and knew that any contact there would have to be formal. The Uys's then? No, too far away! What a boring weekend in prospect, he expected to be on foot at least from Friday evening until Saturday afternoon, maybe even Monday morning, by which time they would HAVE to provide him with a car! A car-less weekend in Secunda confined him to the hotel, the bar and SABC television for entertainment.

Better grasp the nettle and turn his car in and be prepared! Walking into the car-hire office, he slid the keys across the counter to Anny and said "One crappy Corolla returned for fixing and left in your parking area. Any news on a replacement, yet?"

"We have to get all the 'end of contracts' in before we can allocate you anything, sorry!" she said. "Moira always does the re-allocation and extended contract organization. I'll let you know as soon as things have been decided, just hope that all cars are returned on time, sometimes they don't come back until the end of the weekend and that complicates things!"

"Oh, so better prepare for a weekend in the hotel?" Craig commented sarcastically.

"Moira will see you alright for a car, don't worry." commented Anny.

He had little confidence in that last comment and headed back to his room. Passing the open bar door he decided to start his lonely week-end with a beer. One seat at the bar remained free, so he took it and ordered what was becoming his usual drink, an ice cold Windhoek lager, to begin his boring, lonely weekend. As he lifted the beer to his lips he thought 'The weekend begins here!' and then drank half of the glass in one long swallow. Having nothing to do immediately, so he lingered a while over his beer until the restaurant opening time came around. He had decided his next two moves even before the empty beer glass touched to the bar; food followed by a shower, then he would see what the night offered.

Chapter 20

Long term comfort without commitment

Saturday morning was well advanced when Craig sauntered in for breakfast. Service, so late on a week-end, was haphazard so to begin his *ontbyt*, he picked up a full coffee pot and walked over to a table. Table service was slow, but the coffee kept him sitting at his table until the chef finally gave up trying to outwait him and cooked his order. En route to the Nationwide office, he passed reception; knowing the receptionist from last week-ends jaunt he asked 'You still here too?' A glum nod was the only answer he received and Craig knew exactly how he felt! Traffic cops completely filled the small office, overflowing through the door. There was muted conversation there; Craig thought that he could hear Moira's voice and at least two male Afrikaaners, too. Deciding that this would be the wrong time to press about his car, he walked outside and stood by the front entrance. It was then that he appreciated just how air-conditioned the hotel was! Saturday morning was well advanced, the temperature had climbed well into the thirties and the day would only get hotter still. A typical 'High Veld' summers' day, so hot that even the flies were too lazy to fly and were walking, mangy dogs lay panting in the dust under any scrap of shade that they could find. Rhodesia had rarely been has hot as this, Craig could feel himself dehydrate as he just stood there.

Back in the air-conditioned comfort of the hotel, the police conference still continued, but beyond it he saw the bar door open. Muzak filled the lobby as he walked to the bar to re-hydrate with a cold beer whilst he tried to consider his options for the remainder of the day. Eat, Sleep or Drink were the immediately available ones and none of them appealed, he desperately needed to DO something, rather than waste time doing nothing and getting bored. As he walked, he even considered calling Liz, but that thought brought him up short. 'Am I really THAT desperate?' He happened to be passing the open door of the book-shop, entering he checked out the meagre stock of paperbacks on sale. Only one title took his eye, 'Dracula' by Bram Stoker, who, according to the cover blurb, was the original author. 'Might be worth a read' Craig thought, so driven by boredom he bought the book and sauntered back to his room. Indeed, the book was captivating, he just got to the stage where Dracula was trying to inveigle his way into Lucy's home through an open door, there was a knock on his door! Craig felt his heart rate surge and the book fell from his hands.

"Yes?" asked Craig.

"Nationwide! Your contract is ready, the car is down-stairs" answered Moira formally.

"Come in, please." requested Craig.

"It's not company policy to enter clients' room. We can sort everything out out here."

Instead, the walked down to reception and completed the formalities at the reception desk. After checking through the paperwork Moira suggested that they go and check out the car 'It is part of the job, after all.' Walking outside was still like walking up to a furnace; the flies were still walking and dogs were still panting in scrappy shade, there was almost an electric tingle in the scorching, dry air. Quickly, they walked around the corner, into the shade, still hot, but not so brain fryingly hot as at the front.

"Here's your car! Not the most popular car on my books, but you can have it for the price of a Corolla." Moira said theatrically. Craig saw only a new B.M.W. 520i and asked, incredulously why this car was not popular? Moira simply shrugged and confirmed that it had been almost impossible to rent whilst on her books.

"Here's the key, try it out, see if you like it. We are supposed to give our clients a verbal briefing about each car, so I'll climb in and give you the run through!" she said unhesitatingly.

Just sitting in the car was a pleasure for Craig and when he started the engine his pleasure only increased. Driving down the main road his smile just got wider and wider. Moira chose that time to explain things to him. It was that she was divorced and had two daughters to support was why she acted remote, she couldn't risk her job in any way. Her ex-husband was supposed to have the girls one week-end in two, in reality it was more like one in four and gave her no maintenance.

"Don't think that last week-end wasn't great for me. It was! I'd like to do it again, but I can't risk getting too personal with any men in public, so that's the reason." Moira confessed. "What are you doing tomorrow?"

"I've got nothing planned, didn't know if I'd have a car" answered Craig.

"Fancy a braai?" Moira asked coquettishly.

"Sure, where?" was his immediate reply.

"My place in Ermelo! The girls want to meet you anyway." was Moira's response. By the time they had returned back to the Holiday Inn Craig had a map to get to Moira's home and had pronounced himself completely happy with the car. As she got out of the car, Moira leaned very close to him and whispered 'til tomorrow, then' in his ear before quickly kissing his ear; the car door thumped closed and she was gone. Once more Craig was caught by the enigma that was Moira!

Sunday afternoon arrived in Ermelo, as did Craig. He had bought a bunch of flowers from a street seller and presented them as soon as he arrived, the girls were interested in him, but even keener to exploit his mechanical ability! Their field motor-bike had stopped suddenly some days ago and could he get it running again? Looking around the 'bike, Craig saw that the air-filter was solidly blocked with dirt, so that was the first thing taken off to be cleaned, which then showed that the carburettor was also dirty, that was attended to next. About an hour after he arrived, with the 'bike running after a fashion, he walked into the house and straight into Moira's arms. A long, slow kiss and then a giggle "You've made a pair of fans there!" she said.

Braais are always long, slow boozy affairs, as this one was. After food, both girls went to ride their bike and left Moira and him alone. What a relaxing experience that afternoon became, with a woman who had told him that all she wanted was friendship without commitment. He found himself in full agreement with Moira's view, they could be friends without commitments no matter how deeply their 'friendship' developed!

Going back to Secunda later that evening at his own, relaxed pace Craig felt good. He wouldn't tear his heart out about Liz any more, he had no need too. Moira's attitude was that they were close friends and likely to remain so for as long as they both wanted to be, but no other pressures were involved. Craig appreciated that he had just been presented with the perfect opportunity to do well in his studies and he resolved to take full opportunity of this unique chance! Over the next few weeks it was this knowledge that kept him sane as his work-load seemed to grow exponentially. Moira's ex-husband wouldn't look after the girls at week-ends, so these generally became bachelor times and were used for catching up with the paperwork.

Year 2 was due to commence in a week's time. Craig's last Secunda week was spent getting all the paperwork together and leaving instructions for his successor. M & R were overjoyed by his achievements and were happy to guarantee that he would have work with them over the next vacation, but what work and where they had no clue. Craig really wasn't worried, it was the experience that he was after, it would all count towards his eventual Professional Engineer status and ensure that he would find a well paying job at the end of his University days.

Year 2 commenced at a much steadier pace than year 1 had done. This class was less than half the size of his freshman year; these were the ones that had proven themselves. At least once a month, he left early on Friday to dive to Secunda and Moira for the weekend. Life was heading towards idyllic for him, when one weekend he arrived to find Moira almost back in her Ice Queen mode. Nationwide, impressed by her performance running the Secunda branch had offered her a promotion along with a substantial pay rise, but to run their office near Richards' Bay in northern Natal. Despite her hard-nosed approach to Craig about being 'just good friends', Moira had a terrible conflict to resolve. Craig recognized her dilemma and tried to help her resolve it but Moira was deliberately being obtuse, she had believed that Craig 'wouldn't get under her skin' but he had.

By the time Craig left for Jo'burg, they had decided that Moira would take the Natal job, it was close enough to the Uys's for Craig to visit both families and Craig would try to get sent to the Richards' Bay project for his work placement. Craig had made much of what he had been told by the company and had assured Moira that he would be sent to Natal. Now all he had to do was to sell the idea to M & R! They proved very receptive to this idea, simply because the Uys's were Craig's registered next-of-kin, so all was established with no need to mention Moira.

History seemed to be in the course of repeating itself once M.K. began a terrorist bombing campaign throughout South Africa. Being very close to the business centre of South Africa's economic hub, Wits would be an obvious target. A Government education programme began and throughout the University, in all meeting areas, plastic signs showing what land mines, hand grenades, explosives charges looked like. Soon after these large signs were posted, time was found for government talks to all staff and students. Most of these lecturers were policemen and the odd soldier. Craig immediately recognized their type; anti-terrorist officers. He didn't know them personally, but he knew their type, after all he had been one of them, although in Rhodesia, not South Africa and was still associated with them. One of the highlights of these talks was when inert devices were passed throughout the audience. Most students hadn't done any National Service and so, were thrilled to get their hands on the 'real' thing. When the anti-tank land mine came to him, Craig had to fight the impulse to unscrew the detonator. Just feeling the weight of the mine told him that it was only an empty casing, merely a demonstrator to teach people what to recognize, should they be unfortunate enough to find one. Next the lecturer held up an ordinary Coke can and told everyone to remember this thing because the latest anti-personnel mines were made from these cans packed with explosives. "If you see a Coke can just laying about somewhere don't kick it, don't even touch it, keep clear! Look under your car, if you see a Coke can underneath, call the Police or the Army and we'll defuse it! One of these will easily destroy you and your car." At that comment, the audience was struck dumb; obviously every-one was familiar with Coke cans and the fact that now these could disguise terrorist anti-personnel mines shocked the audience. Once more, the advice was to leave untouched and call for the police bomb disposal squad. From the description of the Coke can bombs, Craig could see that they were very crude and simple devices, probably almost as dangerous to the bomb setter as the intended victim. Once the Coke can bomb had circulated the audience, firearms were next to be displayed. Craig's immediate thought was of the 'AK47' assault rifle, the infamous 'banana gun' so beloved of terrorists, it wasn't until the distinctive 'slick-slack' sound of an AK being cocked echoed around the hall that Craig had any misgivings. Before he knew what he was doing, he was on his feet and struggling with the sergeant carrying the gun; for those few moments, he was back in the Rhodesian bush and fighting for his life.

Craig came to his senses outside the hall, where he had been dragged by a group of S.A.P. officers, the adrenaline rush was subsiding, he felt the cool evening air for the first time and came back to Wits surprised and disoriented. It was not the first time that the police had seen combat veterans behave thus, they told him of one ex-soldier who reacted that way to the odour of Russian gun oil; he literally couldn't stand the smell of an AK47! That tang of Russian gun oil immediately placed him back into the bush war and he reacted to defend himself; together, that smell and the metallic clunk of the cocking action had been all it had taken. Craig was mortified by what had just happened, but the Police Officer in charge had managed, somehow, to blend the struggle for the assault rifle into his presentation and viewed the incident in a positive light.

Exam time was rapidly approaching again and time to put his head down and work. He and Moira kept in touch by regular phone calls, maintaining their personal involvement, but without any distraction. By dint of his hard work Craig flew through his exams and so was soon able to plan for his summer. First to be told his results and congratulated by the Prof. was Craig who also told that great things were expected of him. When he reported at head-office on the day his work period started Craig thought that he would be sent to Natal immediately, but it wasn't to be so. His first meeting of the day was with his technical manager, who told him that he would be working between contracting company sites and the erection site in Natal. Contractual problems and misunderstanding were blamed and the growing delays at the erection site, so Craig was to remain mainly around Johannesburg and the Rand, with weekly visits to the Natal site. His next comment shocked Craig, he was asked directly how good he was with a handgun! Stuttering an answer, he replied that he had been pretty useful, but why? It seemed that there would be an element of danger travelling long distance by car in that part of Natal as dagga growers had been known to hijack cars to use on their drug runs around the country. Company policy was to ensure that anyone driving on that route had to carry a personal firearm and be trained in its' use. Craig therefore spent his first working week around the Johannesburg area visiting contractors and practicing with his newly acquired pistol on the company firing range. His choice was an ex-SAP Walther 9mm. automatic pistol, with which he very soon demonstrated his proficiency. Each day, he stripped, cleaned and oiled the gun as he had been taught; he spent the last full day working at his old 'trade' of weapons artificer and modified 50 rounds of 9mm.ammunition into explosive bullets. All but two of these 'specials' went into his stock, two were fired into solid targets and provided satisfactorily large exit holes when the bullet head exploded. His gun had a twelve round magazine and Craig always ensured that there was one held in the breech and that the safety catch was on.

His second work week commenced by shuttling between supply companies in Germiston and Alberton, mainly on a 'get to know you and find out what your problems are' basis. All were medium sized companies, some had over committed themselves by chasing work for the prestigious Richards Bay project, others' had been swamped by the size of orders, whilst others were working well but experiencing steel supply problems. One of the biggest hold-ups was coming from a family run company that had an excellent quality reputation; it seemed that Craigs' QA reputation had preceded him. He was given the usual lightening tour around the offices and was impressed by their systems, but why their problems? This company, Durability, was an important provider to the current stage of the Richards Bay project and they were falling behind their delivery dates sufficiently to threaten one whole area of the programme. When he discussed his work schedule for the coming week his manager urged him to focus on Durability and sort out their problems as a priority, but warned him to stay out of company politics.

Duly warned, Craig arrived on the Monday morning, met the Managing Director and was allocated a small office and temporary secretarial help. No sooner had he laid his paperwork on the desk than the door flew open and as tall, conservatively dressed blond woman walked in.

"Who are you? What are you doing here? I don't know you." She demanded.

"I'm from M & R to help get our contracts back on time." Craig answered honestly, totally unaware that this was the wrong answer.

"I'm Mrs. Gunther, the Production Director, why don't I know about you?"

"My manager arranged everything with your husband, Mr. Gunther, last week."

"He isn't my husband now! Why didn't you report to me?" was the fierce question thrown at him.

Sensing that the true answer was that he had no knowledge of her, Craig hesitated and didn't speak, not wanting to get on her wrong side. Taking Craig's silence as his being totally intimidated by her, she simply said 'humph!', spun on her heel and left. Craig was left sitting at the desk in shell-shocked silence. A short while later his temporary secretary Janice came in carrying a cup of coffee for him.

"Just met the dragon, then?" she asked. "She's told M & R to move you somewhere else, quick, quick. Its civil war between the Gunthers, what he does, she undoes, what she wants to do, he blocks! You 're just caught in the middle."

Sure enough, less than an hour later, Janice came back and told him that he was to report back to M & R head-office for reassignment.

As he walked out of the Durabilty office door, a voice behind him demanded "What are you doing?"

Half turning, Craig replied quite curtly, "Back to M & R for reassignment."

"Who says?" the Dragon demanded.

"My boss" was all Craig could bring himself to say, carrying on walking without breaking step.

"We'll see", followed him to his car.

Back at headquarters, Craig didn't even manage to enter the building before he was intercepted and told to return to Durability. In the rapid discussion that followed, the value of Durability's contribution to the work was re-emphasised and Craig was urged to go back as 'all was now sorted out'. Back at Durability Craig asked the receptionist to inform Mrs. Gunther that he has been sent back by M & R and would be in the office allocated to him. Getting to his office, he went to ask Janice about the office gossip, but her room was cleared and empty.

"Mrs.Gunther has just dismissed Janice for talking to you." said Mickey, the estimate clerk. "Now THAT is dangerous for you, she thinks she controls you!" Mickey didn't see the face that Craig pulled, but he did see Craig shaking his head as he walked to his desk. For a few days his work went smoothly, the only Durability employee that he talked to was the tea man, who also fetched all the lunch time sandwiches. Following his paper trail, it was startlingly clear to Craig that the system in use at Durability was a good system that was being disrupted by the Gunthers' civil war. Decisions made by one were routinely reversed by the other and the whole of the work-force was gradually being polarized into one camp or the other. For much of the first month, he remained above the silent battle because both camps regarded him as belonging to the other. In the meantime, the actions of Mr. Gunther showed his increasing paranoia whilst those of his ex-wife became more megalomaniac. One day, just before lunch, one of the office managers ran into his room and told him to go to Mrs. Gunthers office and quieten her down.

"Why me?" Craig asked

"She's had a breakdown and is ranting in her office. You've not sided with either group yet, so you're a neutral and you are big enough to hold her down if she gets frantic. Her doctor is on his way, but she'll have to be quietened down before he gets here."

Unwillingly, Craig went to the Production Director office to find Mrs. Gunther prowling the floor like a caged lioness and ranting about how she'd been betrayed by everyone. By the time her doctor arrived, Craig had managed to calm her enough so that she was sitting down, but still angry. Obviously used to this scenario, the doctor spoke quietly to her and injected her with a pink liquid.

"She'll be calmer now. Take her home and the ambulance will soon be there." He told Craig, who had to ask where her house was. He led Mrs. Gunther by the arm from the office block to his car, made sure that she was securely strapped in then drove her home. As the car passed the dorp boundary, Mrs. Gunther shouted 'Stop', he did, her window wound down and her arm went through the open window with her small calibre automatic pistol in her hand. There was one road sign that she seemed to have a particular hatred for, for she emptied the entire magazine at the sign. When her gun was empty she threw it venomously into the car footwell and started on about that street sign again. Ever the gentleman, Craig passed her his automatic which she snatched from his hand and fired at the sign once more. This time was more successful, she must have hit the steel post behind the sign, for with a sharp crack the post was beheaded by the explosive round. Mrs. Gunther just sat there and stared, she had become totally passive, her arm still protruding from the car window.

"Can I have the gun back, please?" Craig asked and it was quietly and calmly returned to him. Mrs. Gunther remained seated and unmoving as they arrived at her home. Both maids had obviously been warned, they lead her into the house to await the ambulance, Craig simply drove home.

With one side of problem out of the way and hospitalised for an unknown time, Craig took advantage to get Durability back on programme, which took remarkably little time. Once he was satisfied that the company was going the right way, he drove to Richards Bay to get acquainted with the project and re-acquainted with Moira.

Chapter 21

Final year; Final tears

His summer of driving between Johannesburg and Richards Bay taught Craig much about his adopted country' history, both recent and older. Some week-ends he spent time with Moira, often staying over with her in her flat at the Greater St. Lucia wet lands reserve. On others, he drove south to Durban and on further to the Uys's farms to spend time with the family. Piet was happily married now and so pleased being back on a farm that life was ecstatic for him. Piet could not envisage anything better, although he still talked longingly about the old farm in Rhodesia and the good times that he'd had there. Very occasionally, he mentioned isolated bits of trouble happening in the Natal farming district and that the police made sure that the local farmers were protected. Sometimes in their talks, Piet couldn't help himself but to mention his hopes that Natal wouldn't go the way of Rhodesia. Mr. Uys was still out on his farm, working as farmers always do, from dawn to dusk, as he always had, but Mrs. Uys was quietly worried about him. Craig could understand her worries; Mr. Uys, still vigorous and apparently hale and hearty was, somehow, slowing down. According to his wife, any problems that he had stemmed from the familys' re-location in South Africa and the strain he had been under establishing the new farms. Craig knew her concerns, he himself could see that Mr. Uys was somehow different, but just how, he could not tell. Much as it had been good to see 'the family' so frequently his course at Wits pulled him back to Johannesburg.

Year 3 was the year that hard work really began to pay off. His work routine was such a firmly established behaviour pattern that things only felt abnormal if he varied from the daily grind. By no means was he an unsociable guy, but socialisation came very firmly after his academic work load, NOT before; he was focussed on a target and meant to achieve it. During his final year, three exceptional things happened, first soon after re-establishing himself back in his flat his car was stolen from the flats' locked parking area. Moira helped here by using her contacts to introduce him to Nationwides' car sales people in Jo'burg. Her influence got him an unbeatable deal on a one year old 520i B.M.W.

Second, he 'acquired' an evening parking place in Wits's underground parking area. Walking back to his car one evening, arms laden with books, he saw something under his car. Getting nearer, he saw it was an upright Coke can, just inside the right rear wheel and directly beneath the fuel tank. He slowed and began to scan the scene. It was the end of evening class time and people were pouring out of lectures to their cars to drive home. Now Craig was behaving warily and examining the back of his car, other people saw his hesitation and caught the mood. Most people turned around and went back outside, one man remembered the safety lecture ran off and found a security man. Craig walked to the car, dumped his books onto the car boot-lid and then knelt down to have a closer look under his car. By this time, word had got around and he was the only person there. Close visual examination didn't reveal any fine trip wires connected to the can, so he reached his arms slowly towards the can, held it firmly in place with one hand whilst he quickly, but gently felt the can for any detonating mechanism. There was nothing there, further the can felt empty and not stuffed full of anything, much less explosives, so he began carefully to withdraw the Coke can from under the car. By the time the security man arrived Craig was leaning against the drivers' door, books all loaded away and the Coke can sitting on the car roof. After a few minutes, the security man left with the Coke can in his possession and Craig drove home, back to his flat; 'that' thought Craig 'made a boring evening exciting!'

Finally, the third exceptional event was after the annual exams and when he got his marks. Top student of the year and immediate acceptance onto the honours year! So, his long held plans and dreams were still on track and running forward. M & R were still happy to employ him and allow him to sit his Honours and, just maybe, his Masters year later, but that would depend on his performance in the Honours year. Summer vacations were taken in Natal, as usual. Part of the vacation was spent with the family on the farm, part with Moira, They booked a holiday together just south of Durban and had a glorious two weeks of doing exactly as they pleased, answering to no-one only their bodily desires.

Refreshed, Craig returned to Jo'burg, back to the last few weeks at M&R before Wits called him back into his honours year. Up on the high veld there was a summer 'flu raging. Sickness rates were high and, once off work, it was usually 10 to 14 days before the victim returned to work pale and shaky. M&R, like every other employer was hard hit, their training division was only peopled by empty desks and work was piling up to a dangerous level. In desperation, Craig was asked to 'hold the fort' fore a while and try to keep the department functioning after a fashion.

Walking into a totally deserted suite of offices just emphasised the back-log with which Craig would have to deal. His first action was to get all the overdue messages in some sort of order, from the range of message topics, he could get a first idea of the departmental priorities. Just as he finished, one of the typing pool secretaries entered and announced that she had been seconded to him for as long as he needed her and that she was Jackie. Quickly Craig divided the pile of telephone messages into two and briefed Jackie as to what to say, then he went off, found a telephone and started phoning. By the end of the working day, they had got rid of the message back-log and Craig had some idea of the departments' priorities. Taking the bull by the horns was Craig's typical approach to paperwork, so he started by first prioritising the topics and then working through them. At one point, he was talking to the finance office at Wits. about his upcoming course, he had to hand the formal letters from M&R and the SA Government about his course costs and also the power to vary the costs distribution between them! Craig restrained any feelings to increase his funding unduly, but he managed to get an order number for all his text books and so charged to the state! That was the high spot of his two weeks in charge of training, of the rest of his time there, he simply stuck his head down and with Jackie help moved a veritable mountain of paperwork.

Richards' Bay was in need of technical help again, but time was running out for him to go, but then he got a call from Moira and decided to spend the last week of his vacation in northern Natal. Nationwide had once again noticed Moira's performance in their Richards' Bay office and were offering her the George office at a considerably higher salary. Truth be told, Moira was not the hard boiled divorcee that she painted herself, both the Natal scenery and the ready availability of Craig had softened her. Her daughters had settled at school after some initial discomfort and now Nationwide wanted her to uproot and head down to the south coast! Her two girls had almost become used to moves at short notice, but Moira had become strangely reluctant to move away once again. Craig and Moira spent a long weekend in the St. Lucia bird sanctuary, talking about their future plans, at the end of which Moira had decided to take the George job whilst Craig was at University, but that he would fly down at holiday to be with them.

For the first few months of the new academic year, Moira was too pushed establishing the new office to invite Craig to visit; he, too, had to work hard at the University. M&R had small pieces of work for him to do in his 'free' time, most were not onerous and were generally inconsequential, being mainly chasing around suppliers and just being there 'as M&R's representative'. Despite these distractions, his academic work was going well. As the course work got increasingly intense, so Craig rose to the challenge and easily showed his mastery. After the Easter vacation, the main concern for the course members was what research programme they selected for their practical work. Craig, being Craig, immediately spurned those projects of the review type; he wanted to do something and to find things out for himself. In short order, he chose a very practical project and one that was on the outside of his course. His reasoning was that this route would test him and, in doing so, would give him better learning opportunities. M&R agreed, giving its' blessing and offering to help by giving introductions to consultants in that field on M&R's' list.

His project work was a delightful time for Craig, he enjoyed the work and showed a natural talent for the subject. So impressive was his research project performance, that the company decided that that was where he should be placed in their organisation. Naturally, when the subject of his Masters year arose M&R were fully in favour of it and more than happy to support him. Craig was happy to accept their offer, his guaranteed funding from the SA government would expire with the completion of his 'honours' year and any further funding from the Government would only come if and when he undertook any odd jobs for them. His study books funding, which he had arranged himself when covering for M&Rs' training manger a year before, was still active, Craig having covered himself there by giving a very open finishing date! His contacts with Moira were re-instated after his graduation ceremony, he had plenty of time, a little money and contacts within Nationwide. It was easy to organise a job to drive new vehicles from their Johannesburg garage to George and return, some days later, with a vehicle for repair all at Nationwide's expense!

Work once more took priority once his Masters year commenced. Craig knew most of his course fellows and they were very quick to re-install Craigs' nickname of 'Doctor Swot'. This year, the research programme was much more important and was given a much higher standing and a greater time allocation. Craig elected to work again with Dr. van Eick, the same academic as last year; this time his research topic was deeper and more searching and was very well known in his field, having a wide circle of contacts, many of whom Craig got to know. Van Eick had very good contacts with C.S.I.R. in Pretoria and it was to there that they went to be given the initial work brief. With his insider knowledge of C.S.I.R.'s physical lay-out, van Eick lead Craig through various divisions and departments at high speed until they reached a closed pale blue door. On the door, the name board read Dr. M. Fellows, Section Director. Outside of his office there was a desk, but no secretary, so 'Doc' van Eick rapped forcefully once on the door, opened it and marched in.

It was obvious that both men knew the other well, the exchange of pleasantries lasted but a few seconds. Craig was introduced, shown to a chair and then bombarded with research reports pertinent to his research project. When the information whirl-wind diminished Mike Fellows (call me 'Mike') asked if Craig had any questions. He hadn't, only a bare, basic knowledge of the project, which hadn't been increased at all in the last few minutes.

"Here's my card, my direct line phone number is there and the other is for my secretary. Read that lot and then phone me to set up a meeting so we can get together to discuss where I see you starting." said Mike.

Craig had been taken aback by the speed that the reports were given to him, each one accompanied with about one line's worth of comment. His head was still whirling as he gathered all the reports together and he realised that his evening would be spent simply re-organising this massive information pile into a comprehensible sequence. After about a week Craig felt confident enough to phone Mike and initiate a serious discussion, or at least one that he had a chance of not making a fool of himself. Mike seemed impressed by his approach to the problem and allowed him virtually a free reign to come and go at C.S.I.R. as he pleased, so between the University and the Research Establishment Craig had as many facilities as he ever needed to do make an excellent job of his research project and, taking advantage of the publications facilities at C.S.I.R., had his report professionally typed, illustrated and bound, faster and cheaper than he could have done at the University. He also made many friends amongst the publications people, some of them secretaries of his age, so he never lacked for friendship.

Finally, the big day came! With all the rest of his class-mates, Craig had to attend a meeting with the external examiner, whose reputation was that of a very well qualified, but very self opinionated, researcher. Craig was first in to see the man, who seemed anxious only to denigrate the people at Wits and C.S.I.R., the whole performance left him slightly stunned. When he left, the External asked him to tell the next candidate to enter; as they passed each other on the office threshold, all Craig could do was to shrug his shoulders in doubt to his class-mate. This charade continued for two hours until the final candidate had been put 'through the mill' by the examiner, when finally a 'pass' list was taped onto the waiting room door. Immediately, there was a rush to see their final degree gradings. Expecting the worst, Craig started reading at the bottom and worked upwards. There was his name, Craig Burgoyne, with 'sumo com laude' along side it. His relief was almost orgasmic; his route to Professional Engineer status was now almost guaranteed. M&R would confirm his job offer and he wouldn't miss his dependence on Government funds and the sometimes dubious small tasks that he had been called on to do.

Chapter 22

Two masters to please.

Craig never quite got the job that he had been expecting. M&R seemed quite happy to share his employment with C.S.I.R. undertaking work for M&R and their client companies at the C.S.I.R. premises in Pretoria. For the first month, Craig seemed only to do very minor, low key studies, things that were well below his level, but they all helped him to settle in and establish himself. After about a month, he was called over to M&R's main offices to discuss what would be his next years' solid work programme in Pretoria. Because of his background, getting the security clearances needed to go on site was a formality, but during the year he would need to visit many military areas, frequently at short notice. Craig was not dismayed by that idea, he had no-one to answer to on a day to day basis, so he could come and go without let or hindrance.

Just as the meeting broke up, the senior secretary approached him, and, taking him by the arm, led him into a free office.

"I've just had a phone call. Mr. Uys died unexpectedly this morning and the family asked if you would go to farm and help them?"

Craig was stunned, he had seen the family not too long ago and, although Mr. Uys was showing signs of 'wear and tear', he had seemed well enough. With tears in his eyes, he found Mike Fellows office, told him what had happened and was told to 'clear off to Natal for a week or so and sort everything out."

Back in the main farm-house the family was gathering, each sad and damp-eyed. Marie had been the first there. She'd dropped everything on her farm in southern Natal and left her husband a note; he'd be up a soon as he could get there. Annjia had followed her younger sister into the house, arriving only minutes behind, and had taken charge of the whole situation. Her husband was inland negotiating with the Government purchasing agency about their next crop. He, too, would follow as soon as possible. Piet was there, too, but being a pragmatic farmer like his father had been was tending the crops and doing 'the necessary' in the rising heat of the early summer. Mrs. Uys had been all bustle and activity as usual until Marie had walked through the door, at which point she had promptly collapsed and been sedated by the local doctor. Despite the reason for the family reunion, there was some very subdued joy that they were all together again. Much had already been done by the time that Craig got there. Mr. Uys, as was his wish, was to be interred on the farm near the homestead; the local Dominee had organised all matters that he could help with, so little remained to be done. One last task to be done was to dig the grave where Mr. Uys had chosen. Piet knew where that was and, after dusk, Craig and Piet left the farm-house together to excavate the burrow, as was the family tradition. Neither could stem the tears rolling down their cheeks and cutting clean lines down their dust covered cheeks; neither tried to hide from the other their sense of loss although neither man spoke openly of their feelings. Being there, doing that in the gathering gloom was enough for each of them to feel the others despair.

Early the next morning the Dominee arrived followed by what few mourners who knew the details. Piet and Craig were ready, they carried the coffin outside and lowered it reverently into the soft, red earth and then stood by the earth mound ready complete the internment. Once the service ended, Mrs. Uys was helped back to the house by the Dominee and as the last of the guests turned around the corner of the house Piet and Craig began respectfully filling in the grave, both burdened by his own private memories of the man they had just interred. Family tradition, begun in the time of the Groot-Trek, when the first Uys family had moved into the interior, had been continued; that direct connection with family history was re-affirmed that day over the latest Uys grave. A day after the burial, the family dispersal began when family members returned to their own lives. Marie was staying with her mother for some, as yet undefined longer time, Annajie had her own home and husband to attend to, Piet had his farm to control, Craig was due back in Johannesburg as soon as possible, or, rather Pretoria really, he thought. In a passing conversation, he had mentioned to Annajie his work in Pretoria and received the baffling reply 'She's a widow now and with two small sons'. Craig had thought the comment odd, but considered it no further, he had Mike Fellows to worry about and update which weighed more on his mind than a random comment.

He phoned C.S.I.R. early the next morning from his flat in Johannesburg to leave Mike a message, heard a vaguely familiar voice on the other end of the line, was told 'Dr. Fellows will be back tomorrow'. He left a brief message from 'Craig' which would be sufficient for Mike to work out from whom it had come and understand the meaning Having done that left Craig almost a full day alone with his regrets, his 'adoption' by the family in Rhodesia in 1972 and the close bonding between him and all members during the 'Chimerenga' was special; he had learned a lot from Mr. Uys and equally recognized the very special debt that he owed too. Rather than mope around, he phoned Moira in the Nationwide George office and told her what had happened. Moira had met Mr. and Mrs.Uys and had connected quickly with them, so she could understand Craig's feelings of loss and sympathise with him. Briefly, she suggested dates that they might get together, but all were so far in the future (or so Craig thought) that their best decision was to leave it until nearer the time before finalising anything.

He was outside Mike Fellows door early the next morning Mike, himself an early riser, had not yet arrived, no-one had yet turned on the coffee machine in the outer office so Craig decided to make himself useful. Before he dare make any coffee, he needed to wash all the mugs and the coffee maker itself. He was up to his elbows in warm soapy water when Mike arrived and shouted in a request for a sweet, white coffee. When the percolator, with a burp, finished its job, Craig poured two mugs, searched the little fridge for milk, found the milk jug with yesterdays' remnants in and took both mugs into the office on a tray. Mike looked somewhat astonished to see Craig with the coffee and asked if his secretary had made the drinks. On being told that this was all Craig's efforts, he grunted, making a comment that his new secretary was normally early (and coffee making was her first task of the day) but that her kids sometimes made her late. 'But you've just got to live with that for good staff' he commented and began outlining Craig's week work programme. As Craig left to the library he heard Mike greet his secretary's arrival with a request for a mug of better coffee and fresh milk!

After spending time in the library mugging up on the various topics that he'd require on the new programme, Craig returned back to Johannesburg and M&R to begin planning their role co-ordinating the practical work. Once more Craig felt that it marked return almost to his Quality Assurance days at Richards Bay, but without the welcome distraction that Moira had provided. He wasn't looking forward to it at all. As he pushed on deeper into the planning, it occurred to him that he could organise himself a more interesting role, so he focussed on doing just that. When all the plans had been made and agreed, Craig made sure that both Mike and his director in M&R were notified and had a full set of plans. Craig was saved the return journey to Pretoria by an M&R messenger who took them over en route to his main delivery at Union Buildings.

When the work programme commenced on Monday of the next week, Craig soon submerged himself in the technicalities so much so that time almost ceased to exist for him. Mike got his regular updates by telephone when he happened to catch Craig in an office and, for almost a month, the programme ran as if on rails. At the end of the first month, a programmed research review had been planned. This meant that Craig had to be fully up to date with the results achieved to date and to present a distillation of his ideas to all parties involved, which included C.S.I.R., M&R and Denel. Such was the paranoia of the times with the security implications of this meeting that it was held in anonymous Army building surrounded by sentries near the Union Buildings in Pretoria. Two days had been reserved for their use, no-one was allowed to leave until the conference ended and everyone received minutes at the end of each day. Secretarial services were provided by the Army and each committee member received his copy at the end of dinner on the first day and was expected to be 'up to speed' before the second day began at 8a.m. Agreement on the matters discussed was duly accomplished and the meeting participants dispersed to their own homes.

Craig had a considerable work load to incorporate the desired modifications into the work-plan and all his changes had to be cleared and agreed by the major participants (M&R, C.S.I.R. and Denel) before they could be acted upon. M&R's drawing section helped by producing things like critical path analysis diagrams once Craig had defined them and their in-house printing unit produced copies of all the documentation for each participant in advance of the dead-line. Couriers personally took copies to each participating company, but Craig was delegated to deliver C.S.I.R.'s and Denel's copy himself. Dutifully, he made appointments in both organisations to hand over the documents to the relevant person and ensured that his schedule was not too tight for time.

Denel were first on the list. In some ways that was logical because he had to pass them on his way to C.S.I.R.; it also meant that the hardest part would be behind him early. Despite Denels' reputation for 'nit-picking', they received the documents gratefully and without fuss. He set off to C.S.I.R. from Denel's considerably earlier than planned, he expected no problems there, but knew that his appointment with Mike Fellows would be inflexibly time-tabled and that he would have to wait once there. Having many friends and acquaintances around meant that his wait would quickly pass, or so he hoped! Looking through the glass panel in Mikes' secretary's door, he could see that the red light was on above Mikes' door which meant 'No Interruptions'. Craig also saw that the door into the small kitchen was ajar and a moving shadow on the floor told him that more fresh coffee was probably being prepared for Mikes' next visitor, i.e. himself!

When the appointed time arrived, Craig walked up to the outer door, looked through the glass, saw no-one, but noted that the red light above Mikes' door was out and reasoned that he was due inside, so he walked confidently inside and rapped on the door. He was admitted by Mike Fellows himself, who showed Craig to a comfortable chair by a low table to the left of the door. Without further ado Mike laid out the new programme papers and got immediately down to business.

"I see that you've defined yourself more of a supervisory role in part 2 than in part 1." was Mikes' first comment. "No real problem with that, but be prepared to ride some of the partners hard. They'll see that move as less supervision over their day-to-day activities and try to slip back into their old ways!"

Suddenly Mike looked over Craig's right shoulder and said "My usual, please, and Craig likes his strong and black. Did you get any rusks?" to his secretary's unspoken question. Craig turned, but the door blocked his view, all he saw of the new secretary was a white hand holding the door and pulling it closed.

"Is that your new permanent secretary?" asked Craig.

"Yes, lovely girl. Already a widow and with two boys to care for. Shame." replied Mike.

"Be good to meet her, I haven't yet." Craig commented.

"Well, here's your chance!" said Mike as he rose from his chair. Craig automatically started to rise and froze halfway up.

"Suzanne!" Craig burst out. "Are you Mikes' secretary?" asked Craig questioningly.

"Do you two know each other?" it was now Mikes turn to be baffled.

Whilst Suzanne remained motionless with the coffee tray in her hands, Craig just remarked "We met in Rhodesia when Suzanne spent a holiday with the Uys girls on their farm and I was on leave."

"Strange world! Now you're both in the Transvaal." commented Mike neutrally.

Suzanne had simply stood still with the tray held before her, then tears started to run from her eyes and she blurted out "I heard about Mr. Uys dying, but couldn't get in touch. I would have liked to have gone to the funeral."

Craig started to answer, but was cut short by Mike who said, quite correctly, "This is not the time or the place for re-unions. Pick it up outside this office, please!"

Craig took the tray from Suzanne's shaking hands, at which point she virtually ran out of the office. Mike was watching Craig's reactions closely and read only puzzlement in his body language.

Nothing further was said about Suzanne; the planned meeting went ahead as normal and working plans were arranged, with Monday being the nominated re-commencement day. Craig would spend the rest of the week within M&R doing the preliminary organisation and then be ready to initiate the new programme from C.S.I.R. on Monday.

Chapter 23

New experiences

In the after programme debriefing meetings, it was obvious that the work had succeeded and that every organisation had gained from their efforts. M&R had gained more customers, but more kudos, its' reputation enhanced throughout the whole land. C.S.I.R., too, had gained; no longer would it be regarded as an ivory tower, out of touch with 'real life and real people'. As facilitator of the work, Craig had gained much very valuable experience, many new contacts and a whole new insight into how to earn money. Despite M&R's repeated assurances that he would soon be promoted in the organisation Craig remained wary. Too often had he met the most competent engineers struggling along, poorly promoted and being paid just sufficient to keep them in their company. He feared becoming one of those that was too good to be promoted within a company and destined to become overworked and under rewarded. Throughout the duration of the project, he had met many people and had slowly convinced himself that he could, and should, establish his own consultancy company. He talked to friends in industry in confidence, sounding each one out for information and ideas. When Dr. van Eick took him to one side one evening 'for a private chat', Craig had no idea that his ideas had leaked out to the people at Wits. Van Eick asked him bluntly what he was considering doing. Craig, straightforwardly, told his old mentor and said that he had made plenty of contacts through all his years of working in M&R and that now was the time to make the change.

Van Eick demurred for a while and then stunned Craig by telling him that he was being recommended for a short duration lectureship at Wits, M&R knew and were supportive of the idea and finally that teaching at Wits would help him get his Professional Engineering registration with fewer problems then if he were a private consultant.

He stunned Craig with his next statement, "You know Wits's commitment to working with Industry, there will be plenty of consultancy work for you and an even greater number of contacts to be made to swell your client list!"

Craig just asked for time to get all the details and to consider his options. All that Dr. van Eick replied was that he should not do anything in haste, think things through completely and call him should he need to discuss anything.

A big month followed, he started a short contract at Wits, which was more consultancy support to the Department than teaching, but he did a bit of that, and he finally became a Professional Engineer. With all of his consultancy earnings through Wits, plus his salary, he was marginally better paid than he had been at M&R and life was feeling good. Craig was still 'doing the miles', travelling between consultancies and Wits., but somehow every mile felt light. Arriving back in the department one afternoon, it was obvious that something big was happening, a South Africa built Cheetah aircraft has managed to get back to base with great difficulty after one of its external air-to-air missiles had broken up in flight. Mike Fellows was leading the investigation at C.S.I.R. and both Doc van Eick and Craig had been seconded to Pretoria to help.

As soon as they arrived at C.S.I.R. both had to be security cleared, Craig was cleared in seconds, even getting a salute from the security officer concerned when he saw Craigs' clearance. Doc. van Eicks' clearance took a little longer to get through, but eventually all was well and he received back all his documents, but without a salute. Basic formalities over and the first hour of the working day fritted away, they went to Mikes' office to find outwhat the problem was. Entering the secretarys' office they heard a furious argument going on. The missile (for that was what awaited them) had been locked in an outside building and every-one had been warned to keep clear as it was still armed. That warning had only been given to keep people from fiddling with the Cutlass, but no-one wanted to go out and fetch the missile into the laboratory! Tempers were getting heated and the matter was moving further and further away from resolution.

Craig knew from his previous Rhodesian experience that once the missile was disconnected that it was 'safe'. Minute by minute the arguments was increasingly more and more furious, yet funnier to Craig who actually knew what the real state of the missile was. Hearing all the fallacies being paraded with increasing anger by both sides, he walked quietly over to a demused Suzanne, enquired where the Cutlass had been stored, was given the store key and walked over to the store. Within 5 minutes he was back in the 'meeting' with the missile cradled in his arms. As he carefully manoeuvred his way through the office and into the laboratory, silence befell the assembled throng.

"Do you know what you're doing?" gasped on spectator.

"Yes! Some-one had to take the sensible line." retorted Craig. "So fags out! The only danger is accidental ignition of the solid rocket fuel. If you want to smoke, go away, far, far away from here. And STAY away!"

He thought that he heard Suzanne giggle and that sounded nice to him, but he remained resolute and impassively faced all the spectators down. Within minutes the source of the problem revealed itself and Craig swiftly detached the offending unit. A brief inspection of the broken flange under a bench magnifier told him all he needed to know, he then walked into Mike's office with the broken part in his hand.

"Who makes these bits?" he asked, tossing the piece onto Mikes' desk. "Whoever it is, they're not to any acceptable code that I know of. There's no way that this bit should ever have left the scrap bin!"

It took only minutes to show and detail the defects to Mike, who was getting increasingly agitated as the explanation continued.

"I'll have to take this up with Denel. All Cutlasses are their responsibility and if something so bad has slipped through their quality system they'll have to be told so they can investigate. In the meantime, can you write me up a brief note saying what you've just said, please? Suzanne will take dictation and type it up. Just tell her I told you to use her!" Mike instructed Craig.

With a brief nod Craig picked up the offending unit and made his way to Suzanne's desk.

He was greeted with a wide, happy smile, Suzanne leaning to one side and patting a seat beside her to indicate where Craig should sit.

"Glad to see you again, it's been so long. What must be five or six years since we last met, hey?" Suzanne said somewhat breathlessly.

"Been a long time, that's for sure, and a lot of water under the bridge, Suzy." Craig answered, before suddenly realising he had made a mistake to call her Suzy.

"You really sorted out those gas-bags who do nothing and spout on about everything all day long. You should have seen their faces!"

"I did! Someone had to cut through all that crap and get something done, otherwise they've still be talking. Doesn't any of them have ANY common sense? After all, they're supposed to be some of the nations' finest minds." commented Craig a little sourly.

They talked on for a few minutes more before Craig had the sudden disconcerting thought of 'Is she flirting with me, or am I flirting with her?' Rapidly pulling the conversation back to work, he dictated his report and waited whilst it was typed, read it, then signed it as suitable for dissemination.

Mike quickly read Craig's report and said it would go to 'the interested parties', before attaching a circulation list and asking Suzanne to copy the report to everybody listed. As he turned to go back into his office he said to Craig the Herman van Eick had gone back to Wits saying that he would see Craig 'in the morning.' Suzanne was standing by the Xerox machine waiting whilst it churned out all the copies needed. Craig asked for his copy only to be told that he wasn't on the circulation list and wasn't entitled to a copy!

"This place is turning into a mad-house" commented Craig as he turned to leave, Suzanne gave him a sympathetic smile which placated him a little. He was sitting in his office at Wits when the phone call came and, although he was loathe to abandon the lecture plan he had worked on, the call was urgent enough to get even the usually placid van Eick moving in a flurry of activity. Both of them were required URGENTLY in the Conference room at CSIR to discuss the 'Cutlass problem'. Craig had rather forgotten the work on the Cutlass, that had gone into stasis over a week before and the whole problem had seemingly vanished into the file. Now, for some reason, it had been resurrected and re-classified as EXTREMELY URGENT. Van Eick and Craig exchanged glances and shrugged as they walked to van Eick's car. En route to Pretoria, they talked about 'the body bureaucratic' and how the priority they assigned to anything often reflected the delay inflicted by the administration.

In the conference room were many much be-medalled officers, each with his own entourage of junior officers and typists. Walking in there alone made Craig felt naked and exposed. Seats had been reserved for both Craig and Doc van Eick alongside Mike's chair, but their chairs faced outwards to the serried rows of senior officers. Craig was seated in third place at the top table, with only Suzanne holding her secretary's note book and a clutch of pencils on his right. Taking his chair, he looked at her giving her a big wink, to be rewarded by a small smile and a comment of 'Be serious for once.' As he sat, Mike called the conference to order and announced that today the topic for discussion was 'the increasing problems arising with the Cutlass missile'. An air-force technical branch General began by saying that a second Cheetah had had problems in flight that could definitely be attributed to the break-up of one of its' Cutlasses breaking up in mid-air. "We have the pilots' report. He survived, but the Cheetah didn't, he had to eject to save his skin." A silence fell over the room which the General himself broke.

"We know that the aero-dynamics must suffer, but just how badly has been a shock to us. Can I ask the CSIR team to tell us about their work on the first failed Cutlass" and after a small delay "Please?"

Mike leaned across van Eick to indicate to Craig that he should describe what he had found. Craig began "From memory . . .", only to be cut short by a red-faced staff officer who shouted "What do you mean, from memory? It's all here in these reports!"

"I don't have any of those reports. I'm not on the circulation list, so all I've got is my own memory to rely on" retorted Craig snappishly. At that it looked as if the red faced officer would explode spectacularly, Craig sat at ease, van Eick had an easy smile on his face whilst Mike Fellows looked decidedly uncomfortable. Suzanne scratched away rapidly, head down, seemingly paying attention only to the floor. Security procedure was questioned by the officers of the audience until the Air-Force General seemingly tired of this debate, sent one of his lackeys to the front table with a sheaf of reports for Craig to read. As he thumbed through them, he was amazed how many there were and at the date on the earliest ones.

"I propose a ten minute coffee break so that the engineer can read the reports. Any security implications will be dealt with by me!" the General informed the meeting. Everyone but Craig rose to leave, his head remained down, reading the reports and making best use of his ten minute gift. He was deep into the paperwork when a cup of coffee slid across the desk top towards him, looking up he saw Suzanne, who smiled and winked at him. As Craig's head went down once more to the reports his face had a happy smile on it. A crashing noise of re-assembling delegates made Craig aware that his reading time was ended, so he neatened up the pile of reports, laying them to his right, immediately accessible. Having composed his appearance, he emptied the now cool coffee in one long drink and turned his attention to the newly re-assembled audience.

"What's your analysis of the problem?" boomed the Air-force General.

"Unbelievably poor manufacturing." replied Craig.

"Do you think that we have any more defective missiles in store?" asked another blue clad officer.

"Almost certainly." answered Craig, "The problem is not do you have any, but how many you have and how do you identify the bad ones? Correction is a simple 'strip and re-build' job using the correctly manufactured part. The difficult task is identifying the defective ones in the stored missiles in the first place!"

That comment caused two Generals to start a private argument: the Maintenance General attacked the Engineering General, trying to place the blame squarely on him. This debate lasted for a couple of minutes before the senior General cut through the squabbling Officers with his booming voice. Craig was asked, as a neutral advisor, how the problem could best be solved in the most expeditious manner. He replied that enough new units to cover all of the potentially defective ones ought to be re-manufactured under much tighter quality controls and then be fitted to existing missiles. After a debate amongst the Air-Force contingent, that was the route that was implemented, but Craig was not off the hook yet. A civilian was needed to act as a neutral observer between Denel and the Air-force to ensure manufacturing compliance, who was better suited than Craig? When it was revealed that Craig was actually employed by Wits, a short contract was hastily agreed with Doc van Eick to retain Craig's involvement, so Craig looked like being back on the travelling circuit once more.

Mike Fellows got hold of Craig and suggested that he use CSIR travel services to organise his itinerary and that Suzanne would be happy to act as his liaison with the travel people. Looking at her, Suzanne gave him a brief nod, but did not look too happy. 'Oh dear' thought Craig, 'I'll have to make my peace with Suzanne, or things could go wrong.'

After every-one else had left the conference room, Craig turned to Suzanne, suggesting that they would have to talk through his travel plans.

"It's late, we need to talk, let me take you for dinner so we can both get away from this place." was Craig's opening gambit.

"Got to look after my boys at home first. So, why don't you come 'round for dinner, too? So long since I've made food for somebody else." She answered smoothly.

"Dinner was supposed to be a bit of a treat and a 'thank you' to you to get you an my side, not to make more work!" was his reply.

"I've got to do the job anyway and making one more portion's no hardship." She added. "I'm still in the same house, so you know where to come, don't you?"

"Six years ago at least since I was there and to get there I'd followed a map some-one had drawn for me! Sorry I don't even know your address anymore!" admitted Craig.

No sooner said than done. Suzanne had sketched a map, written her address and telephone number on a piece of paper, folded it and placed it in his hand.

"The boys will be in bed by seven, why don't you get there before then and meet them? They know a lot about you and would love to meet you." Suzanne innocently said.

"Just got time to get back, change out of working clothes and get back, so I'll be off now. See you later!" called Craig, already walking out of her room.

Fortunately, the traffic between Pretoria and Johannesburg was relatively light and Craig made good time back to his flat. He took the stairs two at a time and almost ran into the bed-room to change; he suddenly realised that he was both happy and excited, feeling light hearted, complete with an expectation of enjoyment. He didn't stop to analyse his feelings, it was too long since he had felt like this, Moira was so far away.

Dressed in more casual clothes, he hurried back to his B.M.W. and drove back to Pretoria, turning off one junction earlier than usual and following Suzanne's sketch map with unusual care. His haste paid off, both boys had finished their food and were slowly playing with toys, but tiring quickly and just about ready for bed. Randolph approached him rather formally, somewhat remote in his manner whilst Carl, his younger brother, clung onto Craig's leg and wouldn't let him go! Both were blond (like their father) and of slim build (also like their father), Craig looked hard at both boys and couldn't see much of Suzanne in either one. Carl and Craig had established an immediate rapport, Carl followed Craig with his eyes everywhere he went and insisted that Craig take him to bed rather than let his mother do the job.

Once the boys were definitely sleeping, and that was only achieved on the third attempt, Suzanne and Craig crept out of the bedroom and into the kitchen. Outside the kitchen hung a mouth watering aroma of roasting meat, an aroma that stopped Craig dead in his tracks whilst he drank in the mix of flavours and scents creeping through the door. Suzanne was sufficiently concerned if Craig had a problem, but he dreamily shook his head with a pacific smile on his face. Throughout the dinner, Craig's taste buds were in overdrive and his appreciation of Suzanne's culinary skills was heightened. After dinner, they washed up together, leaning together over a hot, soapy sink, arm sunk deep in the water finding the last pieces of cutlery. Craig couldn't hide his feeling of happiness and wouldn't have even, if there had been a reason to do so. Suzanne (by this time he was calling her Sue, without hesitation) was obviously happy too. What they talked about, he couldn't remember, it wasn't important, but when Craig rose to go home, Sue told him that he was welcome anytime, she enjoyed having some-one so appreciative to cook for and he was certainly appreciative! Craig, unsure of how long it would be before he would be back on a regular time-table stuttered out that he didn't know when he could, but he would certainly like to return. Sue cut him short by reminding him that she had full knowledge of where he'd be and when he'd be back from his travels and that she would keep in touch with him!

Chapter 24

Life changes

After a brief but intense period of running around between various air-force bases and various Denel sub-contractors, Craig had cured the problem and installed much improved quality systems. He needed a holiday badly before he returned to Wits and the academic grind. His travels had taken him to the Cape and he had managed two days with Moira in between visiting various SAAF bases and lectures to Armourers. Despite being made very welcome by Moira, the interlude had simply been a brief respite. Moira was working hard and had been distracted all the time; Craig had been no better. Neither of them had been thinking of their partner when they were together and afterwards Craig was left feeling curiously empty when he reviewed what should have been a memorable mini-vacation. By the time he got back to his flat, he had a report to write and no time, or inclination, to do so. There was nothing in his 'fridge to eat and no inclination to prepare anything, either. Fortunately, a shopping mall was close by, he had to pick up his mail from the mall, too, so he dug up sufficient energy and enthusiasm from somewhere to go there, pick up his mail and visit a restaurant. Sitting there, he began looking at his mail. Much of it consisted of advertising 'fliers' which got immediately crumpled, but there was one 'real' letter, no stamp on the envelope, so obviously hand delivered to his box. His interest aroused, he tore the envelope open and pulled out a single sheet of paper bearing a simple hand-written message in blue ink saying, quite straightforwardly 'Please keep in touch with me' simply being initialled S.S.

Craig sat back at that point, the letter held in his hand and his eyes fixed on those initials! It couldn't be, it shouldn't be, should it? Why was Sue writing to him like this? True, he had thought about her, but was disconcerted to realise that she had obviously been thinking about him. She would have known in detail his daily travel, she had almost single-handedly arranged the whole time-table for him, so what had prompted this note? He eat the meal he ordered without really tasting it, or even, later, remembering what he had eaten, so distracted was he. Back in his apartment, he vacillated as to whether to call her at home or to leave it until the morning and call her at work. He dithered for about an hour before finally picking up the phone and calling her home number. His reward was that the phone was answered on the second ring, but he still half expected something of a tirade for calling her so late and waking the boys. What he actually got was a very relieved sounding Suzanne, whose tone of voice suggested that he had been missed more than he could ever think.

They talk for a long time that night, all inconsequential nonsense it would have seemed to an observer, but the result was that they agreed to go out to on Thursday night for dinner at a local restaurant and then follow it up with a visit to the Market theatre in Johannesburg. Thinking things over later, Craig could never be sure who had made that suggestion first, but whoever it had been, both had been happy to agree the arrangements. Craig took on the tasks of booking the restaurant and the theatre which, from Wits, involved him in nothing more than a short stroll during his lunch break. Craig couldn't understand it, but he seemed to be feeling a suppressed excitement, mounting as the week went on. Wednesday came and he found a note from the department secretary on his desk which said 'call Mike Fellows office CSIR ASAP', his heart fell, this, he was sure, was an excuse and cancellation of Thursday nights' date. Unwillingly, he picked up the phone, dialled the CSIR number and asked for Dr. Fellows office; that he knew would ensure the call went straight to Suzanne's desk. Sue came on the line using her usual no-nonsense telephone voice, in the back-ground Craig could hear other people talking in her office. As soon as the first words left his lips, she told him that the office was full and she would call him beck in a short while, so he put down the phone, took out some department marking and got started; he refused to worry himself with supposition. Within minutes, his phone rang and he answered, to find an apologetic Suzanne on the other end. First she apologized for being so abrupt with him, her small office had been full and she didn't want to be overheard and then asked why he'd called her. That question rather took the wind out of his sails and he had a passing thought of 'can't she remember WHY I called her?' He commented that it had only been about Thursday evenings' arrangements in a somewhat bored voice, when he heard a squeak of delight come down the line.

"I thought you'd forgotten!" Sue said brightly. "I've heard nothing and wondered if you'd changed your mind."

"No, not a chance! All the arrangements have been made, but I wanted it to be a bit of a surprise." said Craig less brightly than he felt. "What time are you free? I'll come over and pick you up?"

"I've arranged for the boys to be looked after by my brother-in-law Davey and his new wife, so I'll be free at 4. You can pick me up outside the CSIR reception. Can I change somewhere?" Sue blurted out.

"Change in my apartment, it's more or less en route. So, outside CSIR reception at 4 tomorrow evening, then?" asked Craig hurriedly.

"Perfect. See you tomorrow, then."

Craig leaned back in his chair and just thought 'Wow!' and began feeling as if he had just scored a major victory.

Thursday passed in a haze of excitement, nothing troubled Craig, problem came, were solved and went away, the working day passed swiftly. He was getting twitchy as 3.30 approached, he had to leave at that time to make CSIR by 4 and couldn't brook any delay. As 3.30 rose on the department clock, he burst out, completely focussed on getting to his car. His departure intensity was noticed, some-one asked why he leaving so early and so quickly, only to be told by a secretary, 'oh, he's probably got a hot date tonight. You know what these young men are like!' By driving manically, he made it outside CSIR reception minutes before 4. Sitting in his car, waiting for Suzanne to come, he mentally ran through his check-list for tonight, a) car had been cleaned inside and out, b) his apartment should be spotless for this evening (he had paid Mildred (his Tswana maid) an extra R5 to do an especially thorough job.), c) the spare room would have been cleaned to within an inch of its' life (Mildred, knowing he was bringing 'his woman' back, had insisted she do a 'special job' for him.) and d) his best suit, shirt and tie would have been pressed and laid out ready and his shoes would gleam. (Mildred always put on a special show when she knew he was taking a woman out. As Mildred frequently told him:—In her Tswana culture, it was almost an insult for a man like him not to be married with plenty of sons and **HE** wasn't going to insult HER!

So, the apartment should be at its' best and he'd be able to present his best face to Sue, too. As soon as Suzanne exited the Reception door, Craig saw her carrying a small, light case and waved when she saw him. Automatically, Craig was out of the car and opening the passenger side door for her and as she climbed in Sue gave him a quick peck on the cheek ands murmured 'thanks'. On the drive back to Johannesburg, Craig drove as though Sue was a driving test examiner, carefully and correctly, a point which Sue noted with quiet satisfaction. Arriving back at the flat, Mildred had waited with to serve drinks, or so she said; it was obvious that Sue was being checked out for suitability! Craig almost didn't recognize the place, he had never seen it so clean and tidy and when Mildred walked past him, he gave her a big wink and smile. In return, from Mildred, he got an enormous grin and a nod, Sue had met with the highest approval needed! Indeed, Mildred began fussing over Sue and carried her case into the spare room (her approval did not run as far as taking Sue's case into the Masters' room!) Sue went immediately to get changed but before he did the same, Craig slipped Mildred another R5 note and was told 'You keep her, she's a good lady for you.' At that Craig shushed Mildred out through the front door, her dignified bearing showed that she felt proud of him. Showered, shaved and changed, he almost didn't recognize himself when he walked into the lounge and sat looking outside into the communal garden. Evening was some time away still, but the brightness of the day was well past and the garden was looking to be a perfect haven, Craig mused on his good fortune, especially since his departure from Rhodesia and being set up in this flat by the South African government. Certainly, the Government had used his information and skills to their own ends, but he had profited from the transaction of that he was certain.

A noise behind him startled him and he was half out of the seat before he saw that Sue was in the room behind him and trying to catch his attention. She looked gorgeous! A long, slinky red dress, very discreet light make-up served to highlight her flame hair colour. WOW! was all he could think, how did I deserve THIS he asked himself? For the first time, he noticed that Sue was a very sexy woman, not the amorphous office drone as she was treated in the CSIR. Just looking at her, and he admitted it was hard NOT to look at her, made him proud that for this evening, she was his companion. How could this glamorous lady, that was the only word he could honestly use, have had two children?

Shaking his head, he took her arm and led her to the car.

Walking into the restaurant was one more of life's lessons, the *maitre de hotel* pounced on her as soon as they entered and promenaded Sue to their table, making sure that she was noticed as widely as possible. Craig was left to follow in their wake, like some inconsequential afterthought. Throughout their meal, the *maitre de* was attention its' self, Sue's wishes were his greatest desire to fulfil. This evening, Craig was certainly in second place until it came to settling their bill, only then did the *maitre de* deign to acknowledge him! They arrived at the theatre just as the lights were going down and hurriedly found their seats. Momentarily Craig wondered if he should put his arm around her shoulders, but that question soon resolved its' self when Sue reached for his hand and held it against her thigh. Craig was happy enough to accept this position and just relaxed. She only let go of his hand to join in the applause at the end of each act and when they left the theatre was clinging to his right arm almost as if she needed his support, which Craig was only too pleased to provide.

In the car en route home, this time they talked about the future. Suzanne told Craig that the way he had dealt with the Cutlass missile problem had brought his name to prominence with the 'big-wigs' and he was being talked about as a future section leader in the CSIR. At his age, such a position presaged a glittering future almost without any limits. Craig admitted that it was flattering just being thought of that way, but he had his heart set on his own consultancy business, something that all the company contacts that he had made on the Cutlass project had just reinforced.

"If you can make your living that way, why not?" Sue commented "I could always be your company secretary."

Craig just grinned and didn't speak his thoughts, although he had to admit the idea appealed to him. Then they started to talk about Friday evening and the coming week end as though they were naturally and unquestioningly together with no 'ifs, 'buts or maybes'. For Friday evening, Sue decided that they would spend it at her house, Craig would come straight from Wits and Sue would spoil him by cooking a special meal. At that, his mind raced and he wondered to himself how her cooking could get better? Outside her house, Craig walked her to the door with his arm easily and naturally on her waist. At the door, she fumbled for her keys, found them, opened the door, then turned and kissed Craig directly full on the lips. Murmuring 'til tomorrow love', she slid through the open door and left Craig alone and so excited that he had to resist whooping with joy as he walked to his car.

Friday morning found Mildred at work in the kitchen early. By the time Craig emerged showered, shaved and dressed, she had completed a full house survey and determined that Sue hadn't stayed the night (that was all well and proper and accorded with Tswana custom, the next time she WOULD stay and that would agree with custom, too!) All Sues' working clothes were already being washed and Mildred would re-pack them with the unusual care she always reserved for important people in her life. Craig was treated with great benevolence, his food appeared almost instantaneously, as did the coffee and his work jacket was brushed to within an inch of its' life. Mildred couldn't stop beaming for joy. Her master had found himself a woman of whom she fully approved and who obviously made him happy, they were discrete and correct; about the right time for him, she thought and that made her very glad.

Despite a boring and routine day, Craig walked on air, especially when one of the secretaries brought him a note which simple read '6 p.m. at no.32'. Realising that the secretary was still there Craig shook the note and said "Rugby Braai and beer tonight", that satisfied her and she walked away disappointed that she no further gossip to transmit. Friday was historically an early finish, so by 4 o'clock Craig was back at home. Mildred had left at mid-day as was their usual Friday agreement, but food had been prepared and left for him and his best casual clothes had been pressed and laid out on his bed for him. 'Taking care of me again' Craig thought as he surveyed the scene, there, by his cleaned shoes, was Sues' case packed and ready to be taken to her. As usual, he couldn't fault Mildred's choice of clothes for him it had always been much better than his and her choice of colour combinations was more sophisticated than his. He leaned towards the 'loose and comfortable' end of the clothing spectrum, Mildred's was always casual, but with a slightly formal touch which suited him. 'Let's hope it suits Sue tonight' he thought.

He easily made Pretoria by 6p.m., no need to drive madly today, so a minute or two before 6, he drew up outside number 32. Before he could get out of the car the front door opened and Carl run to the garden gate. As Craig opened the gate Carl attached himself to Craig's leg and held on tightly. Carl wasn't a big boy, but Craig found it easier to carry Carl him rather than to try walking with him so tightly attached to his leg. Carl couldn't have been happier, he'd got what he'd wanted! Craig carried him into the house and Carl yelled out "Mummy, look who I've found!" Sue appeared out of the kitchen doorway, Carl squirmed out of Craig's grip and ran, arms forward, to Suzanne, who picked him up and kissed his forehead. Carl quietened immediately and Sue walked to Craig and gave him a long kiss full on the mouth, then muttered 'welcome.' Having done his introductory duties, Carl charged out into the rear garden to continue his game.

"You look good, apart from a dirty little boys hand marks all over your clothes. I should have warned you, but your secretary was getting nosy. What did you tell her?" Sue enquired.

"Rugby braai and beer! Fits the image they have of me, so she didn't think anymore about it." laughed Craig.

"I hope you don't think you're getting beer and braai here!" said Sue anxiously.

"I said the first thing that came into my head, I don't want to feed the department rumour mill any more than you do."

"Good! I've made something special for you tonight." said Sue smilingly.

Once the boys were fed and put to bed (how well trained those boys are, thought Craig) Suzanne returned to the kitchen and pots clattered for a time. Eventually, she said from the kitchen, "Go into the dining room, please and I'll serve the food." He did as he had been bidden and found the dining table laid, complete with sparkling cutlery, candles and crystal wine glasses.

"Who's visiting?" Craig asked taken aback.

"The third most important man in my life!" Sue replied.

"Who's that?" Craig queried.

"You, you fool! And to think I had to tell you what you should know already!" Sue replied patiently. Craig was dumbfounded at that comment, but allowed himself the pleasure of finally accepting what he had secretly hoped to hear. All he could trust himself to do you to hold his arms open to Sue and hug her tightly.

They talked throughout dinner, some very special food Craig had to admit, and continued late into the night. He learned a lot that he should have known or realised and learning these things explained much to him about and other peoples' actions and demeanour over the years.

"I've loved you ever since I met you that first time on the Uys's farm in Rhodesia" Sue told him.

"I thought that you hated me! That's why I kept my distance from you for so long" Craig told her.

"Like all men, you are about as sensitive as a brick wall! Didn't you get the message when you came here on your visits to South Africa?"

"No, I didn't know what to think, but I had so many other things on my mind back then." he replied, shaking his head.

"I knew if I waited you'd come to realize. Now you have, it's just taken longer than I hoped it would. Don't worry about it. We're together now. Come to bed." he was told.

Chapter 25

After a good night's sleep, a time of changes!

E ven before they went to bed together that Friday night, they had permanently and irreversibly bonded to each other. On Saturday morning, Carl walked into the bed-room and didn't seem phased by Craig being in bed with his mother; instead, he scrambled onto the bed and wriggled himself between Craig and Sue and seemed perfectly comfortable. A few moments later Randolph came in, looked around, read the situation quickly and asked his mother why was she still in bed? Craig's presence was not ignored and he was treated, once more, to the wary look that Randolph seemed to reserve especially for him.

When finally they had got the boys out of the bed-room, they showered together, taking delight in drying each other afterwards and then had a lazy breakfast apparently in the middle of one of Carl's games. They spent Saturday and Sunday together as any normal family would, the only jarring note was when Craig left on Sunday night to get back to his Johannesburg apartment. As he left, Randolph remained quiet and a little aloof, whilst Carl was heartbroken and it took a lot to re-assure him that Craig would be back again soon. As a working arrangement they had decided that Craig would remain in his apartment whilst ever he was at Wits, but whenever he could, he would be over with Sue in her Pretoria house. Weekends and holidays were times when they would all be together, doing things that 'normal' families did. Craig was left, as he thought, with only one outstanding problem, Moira, but fate was to decree differently.

One Wednesday afternoon as he sat marking student essays, there came a knock on his door and the door opened a little hesitantly. A face appeared around the door and then the person walked into the centre of the office. Craig had to do a double take, whilst trying not to look too surprised. Liz stood there, looking as if the past few years had not touched her!

"I heard that you came back here." Liz pouted. "Liza's in her last year now and I'm keeping an eye on her!"

"Nice to see you again, Liz, surprised to see you, actually." Craig answered.

"I'm going to be around all the rest of the week and then I have the week end free, I thought you ought to know!" replied Liz in her best seductive voice. "Maybe we can spend the weekends in your flat together?"

"Don't get your hopes up. You told me what you thought of me when you walked out on me the last time!" Craig replied tartly.

"Ah, but this time'll be different! I'll be in the car park, bag packed and ready by four on Friday! Too-daloo, sexy!"

As she left the office, Craig just wanted her to go away, far away and plague someone else, anyone but him! He was saved by a phone call from Eskom 'Could he book Friday to go to Megawatt Park and look at some work for students?' Of COURSE, he could and the best part was that as the link with Eskom and Megawatt Park was part of his brief, he could always go there without notifying any-one at the University. That freedom was a discretionary allowed by the job! Immediately, he phoned Sue and asked her to organize something that they could all go to for the weekend. He didn't tell her that a predatory Liz had re-appeared from nowhere and he didn't want to risk being at home if Liz came looking for him over the weekend!

On Monday morning there was almost an inquest within the typing pool, Craig was scrutinised as were the two reports from Megawatt Park that he gave in for filing. He was immune to the looks and glances he received whenever he approached the typists. Nothing definite was said, but the unspoken attitudes he experienced told him that he was not exactly the flavour of the month! He hadn't wasted his day at Megawatt Park, using it constructively making more business contacts for his forthcoming consultancy company. He was now certain that there was a viable professional opening for the type of business he envisaged. Taking full advantage of his knowledge of the Wits academic staff, he had made a friend of one of the business lecturers who had specialised knowledge of small, start-up companies. Over a few coffees, the odd lunch and an occasional game of squash both knew what Craig's plans and priorities were. Jonathon, true to his word, had produced as full a file as possible for Craig's attention. Included was even a projected cash flow, admittedly based on Craig's own suggestions, for how the business should move forward financially. Jonathon was rightly proud of this study and wasted no time in telling Craig that those projected figures should impress any bank manager and help him get a bank loan. Jonathon said that he would keep an eye on Craig's company and help if needed. What was unsaid between them, but acknowledged by both, was that Jonathon was viewing Craig's company as an experiment to help him establish his own company successfully.

Eventually Craig's short term contract at Wits came to an end. Well warned, he had spent the last few months preparing by sorting out business premises (once more Jonathon's help had been invaluable) and establishing a client list with guaranteed contracts, so that on that first Monday about his only problem was where to buy his milk and coffee. Telkom, true to form, hadn't met their promise of having his phone connected before he moved into the office, but did come and sort things out before the end of the first day. There was something unsettling about one of Telkom's black technicians', at first Craig couldn't identify it, but he knew that he knew THAT smell from somewhere!

As he closed the outer door to lock the office that first night, THAT smell wafted towards him again, but this time instinctively he knew it. It was a Terr! Craig fell to the floor and began searching around, he was sweating and his heart was racing, he was ready to fight again. Carefully, Craig moved and searched the premises, the TERR smell was strongest near the entrance and that area was searched thoroughly to no result. Cautiously, he toured the remaining rooms of his office suite and in each the smell was fainter and fainter, all of which lead him back to the entrance. As he carefully entered the reception area he noted the Terr odour had almost left, the hall way lights had come on brightening up the dark institutional green painted corridor walls. He remained still cautious as he locked his office door and continued that same care all the way to his car. He remembered that, before the corridor lights were on, how oppressive, almost claustrophobic, he had felt that corridor to be. First thing tomorrow, he would paint the walls some lighter, more relaxing colour.

By this time, he, Suzanne and her boys were living together in her Pretoria home. This had been the subject of long discussions, Sue was very concerned about her image with the neighbours. Faerie Glen was mainly an Afrikaans suburb and Afrikaaner morals ruled that living with a man to whom you were not married was strictly unacceptable! Craig was more relaxed about the whole episode, as it was known widely that once his business was established and profitable 'he would do the 'right thing' by Suzanne and make an honest woman of her'. That attitude mollified the local NG church attendees somewhat, some of the older 'tannies' still tut-tutted, but the Dominee knew and respected Craig reasons for the move. Craig's overwhelming argument for moving into Suzanne's house was that the boys would be able to remain in their school without the trauma of changing school and teaching system. This approach was more for Randolph's benefit, as he was nearer his Matriculation year; these next few years would be vital to maintaining his development at the level to go to University. Carl, being younger, would have been less affected by any move, except that he had established himself in the school cricket team and both Craig and Suzanne were loath to compromise his chances of winning a school district representative award. Meanwhile, Suzanne continued working as a secretary at CSIR and Craig rented out his apartment to visiting staff members at Wits. Money wasn't tight, but it, equally, wasn't free!

Arriving back home that night to a celebratory meal, Craig could do no other than tell Sue what had happened and how the smell had triggered an adrenaline rush and taken him back to the bush war. Sue could do little but sympathise and console, her natural caring nature caressed Craig to ease his worries. Apart from telling him to relax and have a drink, she was too concerned with the meal to pamper him. Craig was becoming less worried about the episode, like many ex-combatants, he had 'flash-backs' of battle scenarios, but his were very infrequent and minor.

As it was a special night, the boys had been allowed to stay up a little later than usual and join in the special meal. Both boys had a small gift for Craig, Randolph had bought him a small leather covered note book and Carl had bought a pen. Both presents had been personally wrapped with a varying amount of success, but Craig was touched all the same.

After Suzanne 'shushed' the boys off to sleep, she and Craig could relax for a while and talk over the days 'doings'. CSIR was still going in every direction as always and initial business in the new consultancy seemed to bode well for the future.

As time progressed, prospects blossomed, Sue got a permanent promotion within the CSIR organisation and became the permanent secretary to a head of department, having proven her ability as a temporary with Mike Fellowes. That meant more pay and some more perks, as she was now required occasionally to meet politicians and visiting dignitaries, there was a small clothing and make-up allowance, too. Craig, too, increased his income as his business thrived and he took on staff and extended the scope of his business, but the downside was that Craig's hours could sometimes be long. He had taken to entertaining clients at the office and to do so, meant buying in food that was eaten in the small attached dining room, with the food, there was also a small bar for use of the guests. Sue, only attended these 'in-office' business meetings occasionally, to many prospective customers seemed to think Sue was part of the business deal. Whenever Craig suspected that the client expected her to be part of the business deal, the meeting was closed and all business ceased forthwith. At first, his approach cost him some jobs, many prospective customers expected deals to include 'something extra' (i.e. Suzanne); as was the prevailing business ethos of the era in certain circles.

With his business thriving, it was time for Craig to live up to his promise and take Sue as his wife. It was an undertaking that he was very happy to comply with! They had often discussed their situation and Sue whilst not too unhappy with the status quo still had to contend with the local gossips. Craig, as a successful Buurman, was treated more respectfully but knew that he was still not regarded as a full member of the local community. What they organised was a civil ceremony which legally joined them and a church blessing. Sue was happy with that arrangement, Craig knew that by getting the local church and Dominee involved, their *VERKRAMPTE* neighbours would be silenced and Sue become a respected woman once more. Randolph and Carl enjoyed the day, too, especially the small house party that ended a memorable day. The overdue formalities having been completed, life for the family subsided into a comfortable round of work and leisure.

It became custom for Craig to end the day with a brandy before heading off home, those moments became important to think through the day's activities, but were never prolonged because Craig still found Sue more stimulating than any drink. When work was connected to a 24 hour-a-day site operation, rather than travel there (which was always Craig's last option) he stayed over in the office. He used the all purpose dining room as his bed-room at those times and Sue often passing by to bring him food and clean clothes. However business was progressing, Craig's first priority was to go to Sue and the boys each evening, but when he couldn't deputise one of his staff he reluctantly took to the roads.

His reputation grew rapidly, even in a 'can do' society like South Africa, Craig was exceptional in the breadth of work that went through his company. He had no qualms about 'buying in' the requisite knowledge on a short term basis. Everyone who worked or sub-contracted to his consultancy knew a good job was valued, earning their contributions respect, which ensured further work would come their way. Working with, and controlling, a diverse range of Engineering skills meant hard-work for Craig in keeping a tight grip on each project his consultancy undertook. Never one to be afraid of delegating both power and responsibility to others once they had proven their ability soon made his consultancy a hot-bed of talent. Some didn't stay too long, learning sufficient to begin their own practices, but others did generating reputations for themselves. In the meantime, the reputation of both Craig and his consultancy bureau grew a-pace.

As the 1990's dawned and out-side political pressure grew on the country to reform it's political system sanctions were biting, but the future for specialist consortia, such as Craig's was evolving into, was good. He maintained his consultancy at a reasonably small size by working with selected other organisations always with Craigs' consultancy leading, and taking overall control of the work programme. His was a specialist consultancy bureau, but the range of projects with which they were associated was vast.

Free time for Craig had almost ceased to exist, Randolph had matriculated and gone off to study journalism at Rhodes, Carl was still deep into his cricket and, frustratingly for Craig, showing no inclination to higher education. Suzanne was still a head-turner wherever they went and remained his ideal companion. As his work demands increased his stress level, the number of disturbed nights he experienced grew. Suzanne was always caring and calming, but began to worry as the night-mares got more frequent. Craig at first tried to pass the dreams off as unimportant, but the effect that they were wreaking on his life style became too apparent to ignore.

Never a drinker and never short tempered with Sue or the boys, the situation began to change subtly. Suzanne noticed that now-a-days he always had a stiff brandy nightcap to help him sleep, not that it was always effective. Craig, never forgiving of faults at the best of times, had become much more rigid and unforgiving of what he considered mistakes. Suzanne, meanwhile, completely unbeknown to Craig, had been asking advice of her network of female friends, most of whom were the wives or daughters of soldiers who had fought in the ongoing 'Border War' against SWAPO in South-West Africa. Their compounded advice was to take him away from his high stress job and to get him in touch with ex soldiers who had experienced similar horrors. 'Let the boys talk it out between them and give 'em plenty of cold blikkies' was a sage bit of advice that seemed, to Suzanne, inherently correct.

Suzanne had her own private disappointment hidden away, but there were times when it came to the fore. Craig knew all about Sue's frustration; during Carl's birth, which had unexpectedly happened whilst in a rural Transvaal dorpie, the attending doctor somehow damaged Sue. On their return to Pretoria, Sue had suddenly haemorrhaged and an emergency hospital admission lead to a hysterectomy to save her life, so Suzanne's child bearing days were over. That loss rankled frequently with her, especially as she had wanted Craig's child, but that could never happen. Her maternal instinct frustrated she had switched it to all 'her boys', Craig included; she had become a home maker and the centre of their family life. So, when Craig's nightmares got more frequent, Suzanne's maternal feelings switched fully on to him. Carl had moved away from home, he was following his sporting dream as a professional cricketer, a contract which also provided him an 'out-of-season' job.

Craigs' physcological well being became her only important task and she worked at it as assiduously as always.

One point had been emphasised by her friends, a complete change of background into a no-stress environment and time to equilibrate. She wracked her brains to decide where a 'no-stress' place might be. Craig's consultancy bureau was earning him a very good income and they had amassed a very good savings account, so she thought of them going overseas, maybe even visiting Britain from where had started his African journey. A brief moments' thought was enough to dispel that idea; when

Craig had left to try his luck in Rhodesia, he had left without regrets and had had virtually no contact with his family since stepping on the plane in 1972! An obvious second destination was an obvious one, Rhodesia, Zimbabwe as it now is, but Craig's wartime association with the Special Forces would make it dangerous to return. On further thought, Suzanne also didn't want any risk of Craig's memories being triggered by something or someone there. Much of the world outside the borders of South Africa was not particularly welcoming to South African visitors, the anti-apartheid movement had seen to that! Almost in desperation, Suzanne suddenly decided on a holiday in the 'Cape. For all his travels around the country, she knew that Craig had literally spent only a day or two in the Cape and that was when he was working on the Cutlass missile problem. From Craig's comments, she knew that he had been driven around inside an air-force van after landing at each base and had not been allowed to see outside. So, the 'Cape would be a completely new experience for him and a welcome re-acquaintance with its' scenery for her. Without further ado, she got on the phone and organised a months' vacation throughout Cape Province.

Within his bureau, Craig's temper was getting shorter than usual and even people who had known him for some time were falling foul of his tongue. In short, he was haemorrhaging friends and trusty colleagues at an alarming rate. Suzanne's vacation couldn't come too early, Craig still had trusted people to whom he could entrust the running of his company, although he also organised to phone in daily to enable instant contact should it become necessary. Unbeknown to Craig, every-one had been briefed by Suzanne and all played their parts perfectly and Craig fully believed that he would be involved all through his vacation.

Chapter 26

Re-unions with Rhodies

To start the vacation in the spirit which Suzanne wished to imbue the month, they flew down to Cape Town and had a rented car waiting for them at their hotel. They were met by a courtesy coach and soon found themselves in the Mount Nelson hotel in time for lunch. Craig began fretting about the cost of their room and how many working hours it must have cost. Sue very firmly put that matter to bed by contrasting the cost against the school and University fees that they had happily paid out for Randolph. Over lunch, Sue really made the point that 'this was for them!' Craig had over worked since leaving Wits to establish both his consulting bureau and a secure financial foundation for the family, NOW was the time to re-balance his life, and by extension their life together.

After lunch, they sat out by the pool, Craig in his trunks, Sue in a summer dress and large hat. Around the pool, they heard many languages spoken. Predominantly it was English, but German and French too and one loud Texan made everyone sure of his origins. In his trunks, Craigs 'Boere tan' really showed up his milk white legs and abdomen. A little swimming and lazing in the sun helped develop some colour on his skin. Dinner was booked and an excellent bottle of Pinotage was suggested and drunk; sitting back replete after all the food, Craig began making notes on the back of the menu. As soon as Sue saw what he was doing she angrily snatched the paper from him and instructed very firmly 'No Work, you're relaxing!' Craig felt an initial spurt of anger, which rapidly faded away to be replaced by an odd feeling of minor panic that he was losing control of his company.

For the first week Craig attempted to call his company, but was mainly frustrated by Suzanne being devious. Travelling the length of the Garden Route ensured the evaporation of the need to find a telephone because few existed. Initially despondent, Craig very soon began enjoying both himself and his wife once again. Life was getting better every day! He was getting a light tan on his chest and legs and, altogether, he was looking better than he had for the previous year. Suddenly, he realised that his iron grip on his bureau was not necessary; he wasn't yet relaxed enough to admit to himself that his iron control was probably counter productive, but he was moving that way. As relaxing as life in the Mount Nelly proved, the steady journey along the Garden Route was further balm to his soul. Suzanne surprised him with her knowledge of East London; eventually she admitted that Hans, her first husband, had worked there in Volkswagen' car components division before being transferred to the main plant in Pretoria. As always, Craig felt a pang of jealousy about Hans, but there was no hint of dislike there. Hans had died of cancer, that was his bad luck, but that, equally, was Craig's good fortune and Craig realised that he had best acknowledge Hans' passing gratefully.

All the sounds of bush warfare engulfed him, his rifle was help at high port across his chest and he flicked off the safety as he exited the Allouette. His troop had followed his lead and were spreading out behind, placing him at point and principal tracker of the terrorist gang. Instinctively, Craig searched for spoor, his right hand reaching to the floor to turn over a broken twig or a displaced stone. It was really annoying, the more he caught hold of that twig, the harder it was to move it! Three times already he had had 'hands on', three times had twisted from his grip; this time he would pick it up and examine it. Before he could get a close look at it there was incoming fire raining down on his back. He lost interest in the twig immediately and curled up into a foetal ball, hands over head, just waiting until it stopped. In the meantime, things were falling on his back with great rapidity, but not wounding him or drawing blood; THEN he heard Suzanne calling to him from very far away. A sudden flash of concern, wondering what she was doing here and then his whole world illuminated as Sue turned on the bed-side light.

"You were back there again, weren't you?" she asked him with grave concern.

"Getting incoming and never saw the bastards!" he replied shakily.

"Craig, Craig, my darling! You were dreaming again and this time you were thrashing around, too! I thought that I was in danger."

Slowly, his adrenaline level fell back to normal and whilst they did so he held her tightly to him. It was hard to tell who had been the more shaken of the pair, they were both unable to sleep, too alert to any minor thing that the other might do.

In the cold light of morning they discussed their options, both knew that they really had none if they were to remain as a pair. In one telephone call to Groote Schuur, an appointment with a consultant psychiatrist was arranged for later in the day and both counted off the minutes to then. Craig didn't think he was off his head, Sue was sure that he wasn't, but concerned about these occasional night time lapses back to Craigs' jungle war. When they got to see the psychiatrist, he looked exactly as they had pictured that he would, a cap of floating white woolly hair and a small goatee beard. Rather than ask Craig directly Dr Erasmus interrogated Suzanne, going right back to the origins of their relationship. He said very little, but nodded enthusiastically throughout Sue recitation. Finally he asked Craig a few very pointed questions, nodded at the answers and said 'Hmm' in a very judicial way.

When he finally spoke to the, he began with the phrase 'A text-book case of Post Traumatic Stress Disorder" and went on to explain more about Craig's problem. Dr. Erasmus was certain that Craig's business success was due to his repression of his residual trauma and fear from the jungle war. Starting and developing the bureau had been the perfect sublimation for this repressed fear and uncertainty. Now that he was established and with full control over his situation, uncertainty in business sometimes allowed his residual fears to get loose and produce these nightmares.

"There is no definitive cure for P.T.S.D., even though there are so many damaged servicemen out there. We know that soldiers frequently have to do inhuman things and to do those things have to lose their humanity. Few can do that without permanent mental scarring. All we can do is help alleviate the major damage and trust to nature to help with the rest. In most cases 'talking therapy' works well, so go join an ex-serviceman's organisation, have a few beers and talk to fellow sufferers." Then talking directly to Suzanne Dr. Erasmus added "Craig will have done things, grievous things, of which he is now ashamed, consciously or unconsciously, and he has to make his own peace with those actions. What is laudable in war-time could be criminal in peace-time; those memories he has in his mind and he is the only one that can ever square the circle."

With that said, both Suzanne and Dr. Erasmus turned to look at Craig, only to find him silently weeping and slowly shaking his head.

"Here's an address for ex-servicemen in Simonstown, my advice is to go there and meet up with that group tonight and begin your therapy immediately." Dr Erasmus said, his blue eyes twinkling under his wild, snowy cap of bobbing hair.

Driving from central Cape Town on the new highway took them towards Muizenberg and then the coastal road continued onwards, eventually to Cape Point, but passing through Simonstown *en route.* Cape Point was one of their holiday destinations and they were taking that direction earlier than they had planned, but the road, on the edge of False bay, produced it's stunning vistas, calming Craig as he looked around. Suzanne had insisted on driving, thinking Craig too distraught to drive safely, giving him a wonderful opportunity to imbibe the fresh air and the scenery in equal measure.

They found the ex-servicemen's club easily. Deciding that there was no time like the present, Craig went in whilst Suzanne went to browse the antique shops. He was introduced to established members by the door-man, himself an ex-Royal Navy stocker who had chosen to stay on in South Africa when the Wilson Government handed Simonstown to the S.A. Government. What surprised Craig was the number of former Rhodesian service men in the club. He was soon introduced to a group of 'pongos' and then left to cope. Introductions and brief histories were rapidly exchanged accompanied by the odd comment like 'that one was a bad show', 'I was there then!' and already Craig was beginning to feel at home and part of the crowd. As the evening progressed, Suzanne appeared briefly, summed up the situation quickly, spoke a few words to Harry, the ex-stocker, organised something and left. Harry sauntered up to the bar and caught hold of Craigs' arm simultaneously pushing a note into his breast pocket, leaning towards him Harry whispered directly into Craig's ear "That's where she's got you both a room for the night.'

Craig hardly broke the flow of his tale, briefly nodding an acknowledgement to Harry as he picked up thread of his story seamlessly and continued without hesitation. Although Craig had worked with Rhodesian Special Forces, he didn't know many of the operatives personally and was surprised to know that Simonstown was something of a hot-bed of ex-Selous Scouts. In very short order, he was admitted to their 'club', passing out telephone numbers and business cards amongst themselves. Feeling in his breast pocket, he came across Suzannes' note and read it for the first time and then looked urgently at his watch. It showed him that Thursday had just passed into Friday and he immediately began to make excuses to leave. Before he got out the door, he had agreed to a return to the bar on Friday evening. At the door Harry pointed out the hotel where Suzanne had booked them in and even guided a wobbly Craig to the front door. When he finally found their room Suzanne was in bed, but not asleep and not angry with him. Craig was apologetic, much to Suzannes' amusement whilst she phoned down to room service to order fresh tea. Craig had a well established wobble on, a problem that made his getting ready for bed something comical for her to watch, the more trouble he had doing things, the more he apologized and eventually reduced Sue to a helpless laughing heap. She took charge and managed to get Craig undressed and into bed, well propped up and with a tea-cup in one hand. In truth, Sue couldn't be angry with Craig, it was something that she had wanted for him, to get back amongst his service peers to begin to bury his war-time demons. She giggled to herself, her crude attempt at the 'talking' therapy seemed almost too successful, Craig was obviously happy and relaxed as he had not been before. Sue thought to herself that if it meant that Craig had to have a regular night out with the 'boys', then that was probably a price worth paying if it keep the nightmares away. In some ways, Suzanne's approach turned out to be too successful. Craig came to like the Western Cape area very quickly and was loathe to leave his new friends, but all holidays eventually come to an end and their return to Pretoria was imminent.

On his first day back in his bureau, he couldn't settle and thought the detail of control boring. Whereas previously he had interfered in every decision at every level, now he could hardly bring himself to care. Craigs new attitude was noted, but dismissed by his colleagues simply as 'holiday hangover', something that by the end of the week he would be over and working as hard as ever before. By the end of the month, his attitude was still laid back, true his work output and attention to detail had returned somewhat, but were not running at his previous levels. Monthly financial figures had always allowed Craig tight control over his little empire to ensure its' growing reputation and maintain profitability, this months' figures, however, were a revelation! Profitability has surged at a difficult time and his client list had grown; it was hard to accept, but Craig's previous level of personal care had been made to seem counter productive. Last months' temporary managers were over the moon with their financial results, fully believing that what they had achieved was no accident, but readily achievable throughout the whole year. Craig was actually enjoying his reduced role, he had more time to be with the wife he adored and far less pressure, so he agreed to cede control of his company for a trial year to the current management team.

Once all the details were legally tied up, Craig began to wonder what he should do. Events in Zimbabwe pre-empted his decision. 'War veterans', Mugabe's thugs by any other name, began to seize white owned farms and 'redistribute' them to landless black farmers. This excuse was quickly shown to be threadbare when Mugabe and members of his close entourage began accumulating the most profitable farms. Despite an outward veneer of legality, the Zimbabwean police aided the 'war veterans', many of whom had been born after the end of the war, but were simply ZANU-PF enforcers. Once more, Beit Bridge became a life-line for the displaced people of Zimbabwe. A few years earlier a few survivors of the Matebele genocide of 1988 had crept over that small steel bridge, but now that bridge was threatened with a torrent of dispossessed white families. Mugabe's genocidal and tribal regime had now clearly added racism to it's portfolio by limiting severely the value of possessions that families could take with them. Rapidly, the northern part of Transvaal became almost a refugee camp, with the South African government anxious to re-locate these people. Some families carried on southwards into the plattenlands of South Africa, many more simply stopped at Jan Smuts airport to travel onwards out of the continent to Australia, New Zealand, Britain or Canada in a bid to pick up their lives. Zimbabwean immigration, both legal and illegal, into and around the Transvaal metropolitan areas had now simply become a fact of life. Rumours, too, began to infiltrate the region. One persistent one was that a cadre of ZANU-PF agents had established itself in Johannesburg with the intent of 'removing' those people who, viewed through the distorted lens of Mugabe's 'freedom', were unfriendly to the ZANU cause. It had not taken long for a military intelligence officer to approach Craig and quietly inform him that he was 'on the hot list'.

After independence, the white air-force officer who had betrayed Security force operations to ZANU during the Chimerunga, had gone whole heartedly over to ZANU. His revelations had betrayed many dedicated Rhodesians, both white and black, and now it seemed that Mugabe now considered himself sufficiently ensconced in power as to deal out the retribution. To be sure, there had been rumours of 'tragic accidents' happening to people in conflict with the ZANU ideals, but little credence had been given to rumour. Now it appeared that the rumours had been more than idle rumours, but vaguely factual!

As the end of the three month 'new management' trials approached, Craig had to concede that business was good and readily thriving without his attentions. Without the self imposed business pressure, Craig's nightmares and flash-backs had become rare and life was for both of them was looking better. Never one to ignore the obvious, he appreciated how relatively easy he could now take things. His company had become an established name and the new management ensured that it stayed there. His share of the profits made them very comfortably off with a bank account that readily handled the vagaries of daily life, if he could find some way useful to spend his time, they could then certainly afford to take life easy. Except for the vague threat emanating from north of the Limpopo, life was feeling very good.

Chapter 27

Moving times

As farming in Zimbabwe imploded, more and more black farm labourers lost their employment and rumours of internal strife spread. Mugabe acted in his time honoured way by deploying the Zimbabwean security forces against civilians. Illegal immigration into South Africa started as a trickle. This time people did not use Beit Bridge so openly, that seemed almost reserved for the destituted farmers, not their labourers; instead many trusted to luck, cut through the Border fences and hiked across the Kruger National Park. Stories of missing people and fat lions soon started to circulate, but however valid the rumours were in the desperations to flee Zimbabwe ensured they were widely ignored. Despite Apartheid, South Africa offered more freedom to these immigrants than did their liberated native country. Shanty towns, inhabited by Zimbabwean refugees, sprang up around Johannesburg's' industrial areas as they tried to make a living before the authorities bull-dozed their makeshift homes to move them on. Military intelligence, once more, had begun to pay attention to what was happening around their country's' financial heartland. Craig was brought into the Intelligence fold where his previous expertise was, once more, deemed necessary.

Running his engineering bureau, Craig Burgoyne Projects, had always required Craig to meet many people in very different places an attribute that now proved a positive virtue as he re-entered the clandestine world. As he learned more of the hidden backgrounds of the known illegal

Zimbabweans, some once familiar names resurfaced. To most, he could not attach a face, but could a war record; all had been noted leaders in ZANU's version of Special Forces. As far as Craig could remember (and that ran a long way back!) each name he recognized was deeply politicised, all having been insurgency trained in China or Korea. He was sure that Military Intelligence H.Q. in Pretoria had informers in the shanties monitoring any ANC contact with the Zimbabweans, but he suspected deeper, darker actions were afoot. Explaining his worries to his local contact, he was taken seriously, a little to his surprise, before it was revealed that other sources had made a similar suggestion. Initial Intelligence fears were that the country's power sources would be attacked, so guards around the fuel tank farms and SASOL sites was increased disproportionately. When the feared onslaught did not materialise, cooler heads in the Intelligence community began to speculate on the real reason for Mugabe to dispatch his ZANU Special Force cadres to South Africa.

There had been rumours, of course, but precious little evidence to back rumour up, but there had been a number of inexplicable 'incidents' where both black and white 'dissidents' had been involved in some form of violence. Hit and run car accidents had, at one time, been the main thing, but robberies and muggings were becoming more frequent. To date, no-one had yet been killed but that was just a matter of time. Of course the S.A. Police took an interest in these matters, but violence within a black shanty town was never deeply investigated. It was only when white areas were exposed to lawlessness that Police interest awoke and, up to then, car accidents and minor street crime hardly raised a ripple of interest. Each police station proudly showed the government produced plastic wall-chart of communist mines, bombs and guns to enable the public to identify insurgency weapons. ZANU Special Forces soldiers didn't appear on those wall-charts and so the general S.A. Police perception was that they presented no threat. It was against this complacent background that Military Intelligence, aided by Special Branch officers, laboured. Like Hercules, their task seemed never ending whilst the threat seemed a mere chimera.

Craig didn't take that view, knowing the war-time reputations of some of the ZANU cadre involved, he viewed it as both a real and realistic threat. Military Intelligence had found that his name had come up twice, first because of his links with Rhodesian Special Forces activities and secondly due to his anti-ANC stance whilst at University. Either would have made him a marked man, but it was the attentions of the ZANU people that most worried him, unlike the ANC they had nothing to lose by violence. About the only valid response was to take a watching brief, keeping a close watch on the situation in the hopes of a warning before any situation spiralled out of his control.

Suzanne was immediately aware of his changed situation because his nightmares, when they returned, were close to the earlier level of threat and not the simply unpleasant dreams of recent months. There had never been secrets between them and there was none now. Craig had informed her that he was helping Military Intelligence in a small way and what he had done for them. It was when he recounted what he had learned about the new situation that Suzanne began to get agitated. Increasingly throughout the late 1980's, as the Nationalist Party's power waned, the cry of 'Swartz Gefahr' was increasingly heard as an anti ANC rallying cry. In common with most white women, Suzanne was not immune to the message implicit in those clarion calls and was naturally concerned about dangers real or imagined. She was of Afrikaans stock and couldn't envisage leaving her country, neither would she countenance leaving Craig; those were the two pillars of her life. Both Randolph and Carl had flown the nest and had lives of their own. Randolph had an American girl-friend and was being drawn to a life in the 'States whilst Carl was still enjoying his cricket, but very close to a young woman in Bloemfontein. Both boys were getting themselves established and, although Sue could not stop worrying about them, she knew that both were independent and capable of making their own way in the world independent of her. That left only them, Craig and Suzanne and it was to solve that problem that she applied her thoughts to. Craig had not seen his U.K. family for nearly twenty years and showed no desire to do so; he had so fully converted into a 'White African' that no where else on earth appealed to him. Suzanne acknowledged her own roots, deep in the south of the black continent, knowing that she couldn't leave Africa and, indeed, would wither should she emigrate. Suzanne's solution was to remain in South Africa, but to head south! During their recent long vacation Craig had really fallen for the Western Cape. There was sufficient industry there to allow him to earn a living, not that he needed to, his share of the profits coming regularly from the design bureau more than covered costs. 'No' she thought 'give him something to do and stop him getting bored!' Holding onto her solution, very surreptitiously she began to look at the property market in the 'Cape with the intention of persuading Craig to move down there. Women's wiles would produce the result she wanted, that she knew, to get Craig to follow her plans. All she had to do was make him think that he had had the idea and come up with the solution. 'Ah, no problem there then!' Suzanne thought and began plotting her clandestine campaign in earnest.

Craig was happy at Sue's suggestion that they take their autumn vacation back down in the Western Cape, his intelligence buddies were on the look-out for the ZANU 'illegals, but so little was being found out that it was worrying. Little did Craig know that Suzanne's itinerary was so organised that they would spend most of their time visiting friends and acquaintances living in Cape Towns' Northern suburbs, a freshly expanding, mainly Afrikaans speaking conurbation. Her plans were not harmed by the presence of a number of ex-Rhodesians living there.

It turned into a very jolly time for them both, putting both of them in mind of their earliest experiences in Rhodesia. Craig also was taken by business possibilities, he had ever regarded the Transvaal region as the industrial heart of South Africa. In that, he was right, but, to him, there was a surprising amount of industry around Cape Town and the type of industry into which his organisation could easily move. That discovery quietly excited him, although he struggled not to demonstrate how keen he was or felt. Sue, of course, noted the suppressed interest; Craigs' temperament had suddenly changed up a gear and he was back to his most vibrant and interesting self. Quietly, she was delighted, even should nothing come of this holiday in the short term, she knew that the seed of the idea was well and truly planted in Craig's thoughts. All Sue could hope for was for that seed to germinate and her plan would grow until it couldn't be denied or rejected.

In due time, of course, Craig began looking at business possibilities close to Cape Town. For some-one who had originally immigrated to Rhodesia from Britain, Craig demonstrated a remarkable resistance even to consider moving into Cape Town proper. Of all the localities just outside the Cape Town metropole, he was more keen on the growing area just to the north, as more engineering concerns were located there.

Before any serious move from the Transvaal could be contemplated, the situation of his company had to be regularised. His personal reputation and work ethic had established the reputation of Craig Burgoyne Projects (Tvl), maintained and improved it. True, much of the time now he was no longer involved, more of a remote figure head, but he still had a personal, almost visceral, interest in maintaining the companys' reputation. Somehow, this almost maternal care and concern for 'his' company had to be reasonably sated to clear the way for any long distance move.

Suzanne came to rescue once more. She referred to her knowledge of the organisation of C.S.I.R. Noteably prickly scientists would happily accept transfers to distant places IF they were offered 'associate' positions with the original organisation. Behind his back, Suzy negotiated such a deal for Craig and much to her surprise Craig accepted the deal hook, line and sinker!

Money was hardly a problem for them. Craig had invested wisely and still received an income from his consultancy organisation although he now had little other than a nominal role. Still, a new geographical area offered new chances and it was not as if he positively HAD to make any new company work! They de-camped south, taking their time to drive the 1600 kilometres or so in small, daily packets and staying over each evening in the best hotel in whatever dorpjie they found themselves. Nearing the end of the drive, the route took them through the glorious Hex river valley, through the Hugenoet toll tunnel. As they left the tunnel, the view of Paarl stunned them, but the continued on the motorway, through the historic wine lands to pass the newly invigorated and growing regions of Durbanville, Brakenfells, Kraaifontein and Parow before ending their journey at Bloubergstrand. His previous checking had indicated that those areas were the ones where newer engineering companies would be sited. Durbanville was obviously the most pre-possessing suburb being the largest and most established, even with its' own horse racing track and being an 'Afrikaans' area had only a small population of native English speakers. Big Industry was on, or near, the coast, sufficient close by for business purposes, but far enough away for domestic comfort. Craig and Sue decided to establish their home search centre in Durbanville.

Under no particular pressure, they got to know the dorpjie, now suburb, very well, but there were few properties that caught their eye. Being in no particular hurry and pressure to find a house, they considered themselves on holiday. Each day, either Sue or Craig phoned people back on the high veld, but they were under pressure to do so. Daily they were appraised of the local news; daily it seemed that the roads from Beit bridge into the republic were filling with émigrés from Mugabe's Zimbabwe, always a few whites, but increasing numbers of black Zimbabweans.

Times were changing rapidly in South Africa. In Cape Town, the tri-cameral parliament had been in operation for a few years and a general air of liberation abounded. When news broke that Mandela had had discussions with De Klerk no-one seemed surprised, a general softening of official attitudes to the ANC tripartite alliance permeated politics. As the iron grip of the National Party relaxed a little, crime rates in the (now mainly) white suburbs increased. Some was spill-over from Black townships, but the rest was driven by an increasingly violent 'have-nots' against the 'haves.' This avarice frequently took the form of violent car high-jackings. China and its' communist ally, the Soviet Union, had poured armaments into Zimbabwe and all the 'liberation' movements, with the result that the whole of Southern Africa was awash with illegal fire-arms. Most common weapon in this tide of violence was the AK47 assault rifle and it was widely known that Zimbabwean refugees would sell one for a loaf of bread.

Much of the problems remained in Transvaal, but it was obvious that with increasing numbers of jobless illegal Zimbabwean immigrants that the crime wave would spread steadily throughout the whole country. Remote farmers and their families had suffered, in much the same way as their Rhodesian counterparts had done some years before. Both Craig and Sue knew this and saw how some of their neighbours had strengthened the fences around their property. In the wealthier suburbs of Johannesburg, the use of anti-personnel electric fences around private houses was becoming commonplace. Neither of them saw anything so offensive in Durbanville and crime levels were not a conversation topic in the area. Craig's thoughts returned to their previous visit to Simons Town and the relaxed atmosphere they both noted there: that atmosphere persisted and seemed so normal here! With only a minimum of discussion they decided to stay for a month at least more fully to learn the area. To do that and keep costs within reason, they decided to rent a local house and use their time to search out their dream property. Before the rental period had completed, they were in agreement that there were no existing houses that they both could agree on; however they had seen a building plot, right at the top of the Durbanville hills which offered both room and views. Craig cast an engineers' eye on the plot and unilaterally decided to buy the neighbouring plot too. At first, Sue was horrified. Her nature rebelled at the thought of the cost of building there. Craig was more sanguine. He knew that he could call in a few favours that would offset costs and guarantee good work. Before they left back to Pretoria, Craig had an option on both plots and had spoken with the municipal planning chief.

Events were rushing onwards; the National Party seemed to be crumbling from the inside out. Every day brought news of more un-bannings, more newly accepted political parties, more power leaching away from the broederbond to the citizens.

Concomitant with these changes came an increase in personal crime. Mamaloedi had always been a hotbed of sedition and was now expanding like a balloon as immigrants, from both Natal and Zimbabwe followed the job trail into Transvaal and criminals came with them. True, the crime levels in the townships had always been high, but when crime began to spill over into the white suburbs fear followed as did security measures.

Arriving back in Faerie Glen both Craig and Sue were amazed at the visible changes that the previous month had wrought. Gated communities had been established, electric fences were sprouting around residential dwellings like weeds after rain and more people carried personal fire-arms. Those changes had been evolving, but at a slower rate previously, but recent events had generated a monster in reply to the perceived threat to the White population. Every-one knew that the first open election was coming, faced with the imminent loss of power and privilege white emigration burgeoned. Both Craig ands Suzanne were shocked by the depth to which White confidence had fallen in so short a time.

What probably finally clinched Craig's decision was one Saturday whilst he was in the garden, an unknown black man said to him, 'After the elections, when we win, this house is mine!' Too dumbfounded to reply immediately, Craig could only think of the lot of the white farmers in Zimbabwe and their treatment by ZANU PF. From that time onwards, Craig threw all his energy into establishing their Durbanville home.

As the elections approached, a new wave hit South Africa when cell phones went on the market. Their immediate success in the rest of the world ensured that very soon a cell phone would become a necessity rather than a luxury. Still being connected, however faintly, to the intelligence community, Craig's first thoughts revolved around the potential security implications that they posed. There were still militant political parties operating covertly and an increasing number of armed gangs who could only profit from a secure and mobile communications system. His unease at the Transvaal situation only grew the more. If Suzanne noted his change in priorities, she never commented, but was ever eager to get involved in planning the new house. As Craig commented, this was going to be an expandable house! Sitting squarely on a double plot there was no shortage of space and no need to cramp the accommodation and plenty of room to expand.

Dallas was the most influential TV programme on the newly available S.A.B.C. and certainly influenced the style of home that they had built in Durbanville. Everything was large and spacious, walk-in cupboards, even a walk-in refrigerator in the kitchen. One thing was not immediately included was any advanced security system; Craig felt happy and secure, using only simple garden fences to demarcate his boundaries. For many years those fences were all that was needed, the Western Cape seemingly remote from the crime levels experienced in the Johannesburg/Pretoria metropolitan region.

Chapter 28

Mugabe interferes in Craigs' settled life once more!

After the move to the Western Cape, Craig and Suzanne enjoyed a great life style for some years, fully appreciating the much more relaxed approach to things in the 'Cape. Whilst they knew that all the major towns had problems with unemployed immigrants from the rural areas, generally little was seen in their part of the country. Of course they were aware that Wallacedene, the closest township to them was expanding as was also Kyamandi, close to nearby Stellenbosch, but until that expansion had a direct influence on their lives, it remained in the background of their consciousness. Casual labour was easy to find, but then it always had been and the slow increase generally passed un-noticed and un-remarked upon.

Craig noted that he was getting more Zimbabweans both seeking employment at his house and via his business. He sympathised with them, knowing that work for any non ZANU-PF supporter was a very rare thing, but felt a little sympathy for them. In 1995, Mandelas' 'Rainbow nation' dream was severely tested when the township of Alexandria near Johannesburg exploded in xenophobic violence when Zimbabwean, Mozambiquean and Malawian immigrants were targeted. Officially, the root cause of this violence was never ascertained, but unofficially the immigrants were thought to be undercutting local labour rates and keeping locals out of work. There were some mutterings about 'third party' involvement initiating the violence, but these accusations never progressed further. Down in the 'Cape these problems were noted and 'tutted' over, the feeling being that the problem derived from the 'Jo'burg attitude'.

After the Alexandria riot, tensions remained and were palpable, but seemed almost bearable. Over the years, it was noted, even in the 'Cape, that casual labour was increasingly easy to find. In many cases, the workers were well educated and well spoken black Zimbabweans with more Eastern Cape Xhosas incomers being pushed to the margins of society. Crime was becoming noticeable, although much of it was still confined to the townships, but car crime was a particular concern. Although still not at the levels found around Johannesburg violent, car-jacking incidents where fire-arms had been used, had sporadically occurred in the Cape Town metropolis. Craig had a semi-professional interest in such crimes, he used to be intimately concerned with some of the details, and that previous involvement was hard to suppress. Some reports told that the handguns used were rusty and dirty; Craig believed that such weapons would be more danger to the shooter than the target. Increasingly reports talked about AK 47's being waved about during the hi-jack; Craig knew that the 'banana gun' was dangerous even if dirty and not well maintained. To Craig this development suggested that hidden ZANU arms caches had been breached, hinting at covert ZANU-PF involvement, but to what intent he could not discern. He made this comment to an Intelligence operative he met in a rather off handed manner and was rather surprised to find that the agent agreed with him. Craig was told of the latest Intelligence position and how it might apply to him. Apparently, there was strong evidence that Mugabe's regime was attempting to silence critics both at home and covertly within the borders of South Africa. This warning extended to Craig who was advised to take care because that regime had a long memory for opponents. Any possible threat was so remote that Craig almost immediately gave it no further thought and carried on as he previous had done.

Life continued at a settled pace for a further five years and any problems brewing in the townships never impacted on the Whites' consciousness. An irregular series of 'taxi wars' erupted from time to time, mainly centred around Kayalishia although other townships were affected. Most white commuters had long ago begun believing that the black minibus taxi industry was out of control and a law only unto itself, so taxi strikes only impacted on White affairs when their black staff or domestics arrived late. What few, if any White employers realised, was that these strikes were the pressure relief valve for township tensions. Apartheid levels of segregation existed in most townships with every different nationality and tribal group severely separated. Ethnic violence was a fact of life and, as so, unremarkable. Minor ethnic clashes erupted regularly and were generally reported, if at all they were Reported, aas being due to employment practices. Throughout the ANC's campaign against the minority White government, their slogan had been 'revolution before education'. It had been closely obeyed with the post 1994 result that, when compared with immigrant labour, many black South Africans were functionally illiterate. Employers obviously noted the differences and employed people accordingly. Throughout the Mandela presidency and well into Mbeki's first term ANC control within the townships was effective, if brutal.

In 2000, the Cape Flats erupted in violence, this time lead by the Cape Coloured community, who had been subjected to increased discrimination by the black population since the collapse of the tri-cameral parliament. Violence was fairly generally spread around, the main targets being Xhosas, other blacks were unlucky to be attacked. Police actions were targeted, mainly against known and violent PAGAD members. Peace reigned for only a further year until Zandspruit exploded when the minority Zimbabwean community was given a dead-line of only 10 days to move out of the township by the majority Xhosa community. This targeting of Zimbabweans was deliberate and accurate, initial reports once more stated the preferential employability of Zimbabweans over South Africans. A minority suggestion was that a 'third force' of paramilitary Zimbabweans was taking over, but that idea was quickly rejected. At the end of 2005 and into 2006, once more trouble flared up involving the Zimbabwean community in Olievehoutbosch. A local Black man had been killed, his death being blamed on Zimbabwean paramilitaries enforcing their will on the community.

Peace never really established itself again as Xhosa communities, first in the Eastern Cape and then in Dunoon in the Western Cape, attacked the minority Zimbabwean community. By May 2008, the insensitively named 'Harmony Park' settler camp blew apart. Zimbabweans once more being the preferred target of Xhosa hatred, but this time there was a serious report of an active Zimbabwean third force deeply involved in the confusion at 'Harmony Park'. As far as the rumours went, the Zimbabwean involvement was laid at the door of the C.I.O. Thanks to the theoretically covert support received from C 10 or 'Charlie Tens' (as they were called by the immigrants) groups of 'war-vets' were trying to assert the right of Zimbabweans to be illegal immigrants in South Africa!

Craig, as most people had, had paid scant regard to the township trouble, but now they were forced into his conscious. The troubles had arrived almost on their door step! Reading the reports in both 'De Burger' and 'Cape Times', he noted the reference to the 'war-vets', C 10 and immediately his interest re-kindled. Where 'war-vets' were, the malign hand of ZANU-PF was, acting as Mugabes' shock troops to enforce his policies. Thabo Mbeki as 'front line leader' and the worlds' mouth piece for condemnation of ZANU-PF's open racialism and tribalist policies, had always played a 'gentle touch' game with Mugabe which, quite obviously, had only encouraged the old tyrant. Where the malign involvement of C.I.O. was felt, the desires of the old tyrant were made real, to every-ones' loss.

It was plain to see that there were many more black Zimbabweans around even down in the 'Cape area. Some picked through rubbish bins in White suburbs, having displaced the usual Xhosas, but some had got very good jobs because of their better levels of education. This employability was an un-conscious, but real, tribute to Garfield Todds' 1960's education reforms in Rhodesia, which produced a generation of well educated black Zimbabweans eminently more employable than their semi-literate black South African brothers. This difference increased township tensions. In some townships there was a definite Zimbabwean power hierarchy (probably C 10 inspired), which even the township ANC leadership couldn't or weren't able to control.

Even up in the higher reaches of Durbanville, where Craig and Suzannes' ranch style house sat it was common to find itinerant Zimbabweans, some of whom appeared to have been on the scene since Durbanville expanded in the 1980's. There was never any problem in finding casual labour, most of which spoke very good English, were both hard working and intelligent and Zimbabwean. Along the road onto which their house fronted, a number of Zimbabwean men seemed permanently engaged on various tasks. Craig knew most of them, either by name or by face, and acknowledged them when he passed them. At times, he would stand and converse freely with them and from the talks he knew that many of the longer serving 'residents' had had to quit Zimbabwe early because they had fought alongside the whites during the Chimerenga. They formed a small, but tight, coterie of workers that Craig always tried to use for casual labour and kept themselves very much to themselves. Craig had been surprised to learn that Kraaifontein, a nearby dorpjie slowly being absorbed by the spreading Durbanville, was home to many white ex-Rhodesians. Such were the bonds of loyalty that a number of Black ex-Rhodesians were housed in small units on their comrades' housing plots. Even in South Africa, townships were not safe places for Blacks who had not supported the 'liberation' struggle.

In the townships live the later Zimbabwean immigrants, almost all refugees from Mugabe's genocidal regime, but not all were true refugees. Passing through the townships were a constant flux of 'war vets' and C 10 operatives. These were the regular trouble makers, trained and supported from Zimbabwe to nullify any opposition to ZANU-PF's regime. Craig tried to keep clear of this later group, he didn't know how long the compound ZANU-PF memory lasted, but feared the worse.

Chapter 29

Like an Elephant, Mugabe NEVER forgets!

M'beki was no more! Deposed by the Zuma faction, acolytes of the man that he had tried to destroy with corruption allegations. South Africa almost seemed to exhale a communal sigh now that the personality challenged 'Technocrat' had been removed peaceably by 'a man of the people'.

In very swift order, many of the M'beki governments' doctrinaire beliefs were consigned to the waste-bin of history. HIV/AIDS began to be taken seriously with anti-retrovirals rapidly becoming available to all citizens of the Republic, not just ANC members of Parliament. Overnight, the mumbo-jumbo spouted by M'beki and his alcoholic health minister vanished and action plans instituted. Not that the Zuma presidency appeared overly concerned with the causes of HIV. Indeed Zuma himself appeared positively ignorant and uncaring about the causes; he did not modify his approach to life at all!

ANC divisions were becoming visible in the townships with factionalism running rife until preparations for the 2010 world soccer cup dominated the Economy. Xenophobia reduced in the long build up to the World Cup. Facilities were planned and built without much regard for cost. Most of these plans had been formulated in M'beki's rule and were well underway when Zuma and his entourage came into power. Enough money was made by the ANC cognoscenti for some to trickle down to the lower levels and for the great mass of township dwellers to envisage their lot improving.

A major part of the Zuma faction who worked hard to undermine M'beki came from the ANC Youth League. Sharing jointly their interests in, and appreciation of, the levels of corruption attainable under Zuma's stewardship, they differed widely from Zuma's populist stance. Senior Youth leaders shared M'beki's feeling towards Mugabe and his racist actions which steadily destroyed Zimbabwe's economy.

Once more, Zimbabweans of all races took the route south over Beit Bridge and into the republic of South Africa, many as illegal immigrants. C.I.O., with a memory like an elephant and a burning desire finally to consolidate their 'victory over reactionary white forces', were presented with an unbelievable opportunity. Amongst the thousands of genuine refugees it was no problem to include C.I.O. operatives and ZANU-PF 'wovits' cadres in the southern exodus.

Border and internal controls, in many cases very understrength, were relaxed further, which eased C.I.O. infiltration. Zimbabwean workers were soon to be found in large numbers in all provinces and whilst the work and money continued to flow, the flood of refugees continued, increasing when the DRC adding vast numbers to the Zimbabwean flood. One common, but tenuous, thread existed between those two disparate groups. Blood diamonds fuelled both governments' attempts to exert their political influence throughout the whole of the south of the continent.

In the case of Zimbabwe, their C.I.O and ZANU-PF were well found. In the 'blood diamond' flood Mugabe's acolytes saw a means of achieving their aims without diminishing the inward cash flow from their illegitimate gains. Revenge against ZANU-PF's perceived enemies moved into top gear. To be sure, things did not go at all smoothly, but move forward all their plans and ambitions did. Townships, never very stable at the best of times, were seriously unbalanced by the influx of foreigners, when the barely concealed Xhosa majority's natural tribalism erupted, being directed by local ANC low level leadership. During these times of disruption, C.I.O. cadres spread further a field to achieve their leaderships' perverted aims.

Well founded, these cadres blended with the established flux of traders travelling un-noticed throughout all provinces of South Africa. Since the early days of Mugabe's era of misrule itinerant Zimbabwean traders have travelled all the roads and nations of the Southern Africa sub-continent.

Street traders consequently became virtually invisible; an invaluable asset for covert operation and one that C.I.O. couldn't resist playing.

Political sympathy with ZANU-PF, although officially denied was widely practiced on an unofficial, but non-the-less effective, basis. Cynically, ZANU-PF and C.I.O. exploited the inherent distrust of foreigners in the townships, with the result that many hard-working and innocent Zimbabweans bore the brunt of the xenophobic attacks. Meanwhile the executive C.I.O. and ZANU-PF cadre, hiding well below the detection threshold, simply got on with the planning of their tasks.

Rhodesian Special Forces and their support staff had never been forgiven, even after thirty years. Over those years nature had reduced the numbers of targets for Mugabe's reprisals, but the venomous hatred and desire for retaliation still burned within him. Craig knew that he was on the reprisal list, but the years and the apparent safety within South Africa had diminished any visible threat perception. He still maintained his links with the ex-service mans' organisation and the even more intermittent with their Intelligence contacts which had faded away, quite naturally, as the years progressed. Not having been seen in the ex-services club for a while caused Craig to receive a phone call one day, along the lines of a low-key situation update.

Their Intelligence service was not supported by the SANDF, how could it be? Its' very existence ran counter to the Governments' stated approach to security; one service for the whole country. That laudable aim was severely compromised in practice by the Governments' attitude:—i) contrary to their publicly voiced opinions Mugabe was regarded as a liberation hero and ii) Zimbabwean actions affected only renegade whites and an odd few black lackeys of white imperialism; so few in reality that the government could afford to ignore them. Fortunately for this group, their unofficial ex-military Intelligence service was well founded, whose wide ranging antennae were highly sensitized and aware. At meeting, selected members were taken aside and appraised of their status and any problem likely to face them.

Craig had certainly had a 'briefing'. His notoriety stemmed from the newspaper reports of the trans-border Zambian raids when those papers' credited him as the intelligence mastermind of the operation. At the time, he had submerged his personal worries with the belief that, by shining the spot-light on him, the serious Intelligence operators were hidden in his shadow. After independence, the dark side of that publicity began to become apparent. He became a hate target to ZANU-PF and came under renewed threat. Much of his combat awareness had been subsumed into avoiding trouble in South Africa and he wore his caution like an overcoat. He was not overtly concerned and cautious, but calmly aware. He continued working much as he always had, although he did begin to employ basic security arrangements such as varying his routes and times travelling to and from work. Suzanne had been told, as so often been before, so they were both attuned to changes in local circumstances. Nearly thirty years after the Chimurenga ended, he was unconcerned about introducing himself by his name, never using his old service rank (he didn't consider himself that 'sad', although a number of his ex-services friends happily did!) Should any-one react to his name, that he always paused to review why in the circumstances.

Over the past two weeks, one of Durbanvilles' indigenous black Zimbabweans had taken to saluting him when ever he passed; he always received a very proper, British military salute. Those snapped salutes screamed Rhodesian Army to Craig, his suspicion being that the Zimbabwean had been in the R.A.R. or a similar unit. An old comrade-in-arms! Whenever he saw Monday (as the Zimbabwean ex-soldier claimed to be called), Craig tried to make time for some acknowledgement, however perfunctory. They had spoken a couple of times, too, and Craig feeling only that he was talking to an RAR veteran He decided that he would look out and deliberately find some well paid work for Monday to do at home, that decision making him feel better. Of course, he didn't tell Monday, he was aware of the African tendency to pre-spend their earnings on alcohol. THAT indignity, Craig thought to himself, was one that he wouldn't subject an old comrade-in-arms to!

By the very nature of his work, Craig needed to travel to and from various sites at unpredictable intervals and for widely varying times, although he minimized the nights he spent away from home. Casual black labour, never difficult to find, had got, if anything, easier to obtain and many of them were Zimbabweans or Congolese. Migrants from these two groups tended to be favoured above South African casual labour because of their better work ethic and higher literacy levels.

In Durbanville, each season had specific migrants associated with it, many of them 'hang-overs' from the farms that used to occupy the land, whilst others seemed happy with a peripatetic life style. So a constant flux of black labour was no surprise, indeed it was normal. Extra vigilance was unrewarded, almost counter productive because it introduced another barrier, simply making both sides warier of the other than previously.

Neither close to home, or close to his office, were any serious changes noted; nothing extra-ordinary had happened to alert Craig's senses. Life was good, life was normal. Typical of his behaviour, Craig acknowledged the people he saw regularly: either by talking to them or by some action, he noted the local people. Over the years he had learned that simple conversations could be valuable; it was often the indigent locals who were first aware of negative changes. Officially sanctioned changes in attitude to homeless would not be felt by the homed, but had the potential to destroy indigenous communities and their work.

Craigs' fame from the Chimerunga, as the instigator of the economic attacks against Zambia., had remained around him. To be sure, at this remove, the fame still enveloped him like a very faint miasma. Faint, but still tenacious! Many of the 'old Rhodesia' hands in the ex-serviceman's club knew his name and his detestation of the 'role' that publicity said that he had played. Close friends knew the truth and didn't refer to the stories. Like most ex-servicemen Craig enjoyed swopping stories with other veterans; all groups found the experience positively therapeutic. This was, truly, the 'talking cure' to post-traumatic stress that many still suffered. To be lionised by people who had neither been involved, nor affected by the nastier aspects of that conflagration, was too much for Craig to bear. If he was approached to talk about his experiences by an outsider, he would simply put down his drink and walk away, that was much simpler. It was at those times that his 'fame' began to feel more a stigma.

Craig was working hard, as usual, although he had had no need to work at that intensity for years. He was bringing a special consultancy job to completion, plus he was looking at moving his office bureaux into a newly built suite overlooking the Tyger Valley Waterfront. This new office accommodation was really impressive, Craig had always appreciated the influence that smart offices had on clients.

Tonight, he would be later home than he liked, but a therapeutic brandy would help even if he did leave a pile of work waiting on the morrow. Having decided, he open the bottom drawer and took out the bottle of 'Oude Meester' and examined his rather dirty, well finger printed tumbler, he sat back at his desk, exhaled once more then decided to finish his brandy, then head off home immediately. Washing the glass was the least of his worries and could happily wait until tomorrow.

Chapter 30

Chidudu

By the time he was at his car, his thoughts were again with his family. Suzy, he knew, was loosing patience with his recent behaviour, but he was trying the best he could. He was not getting enough sleep, not nearly enough, the memory flashbacks still came and saw to that! He wasn't relaxed enough, getting so tightly wound that the smallest thing caused him anger. It wasn't her fault, none of it was her fault, but how could he tell her that he couldn't help himself?

Driving home to Durbanville through Brakenfells, he was aware of how the area, though wealthy, was acquiring something of a less cared for, 'down at heel' air. There, just across the street, was old Monday with his supermarket trolley, busy picking through bins searching for something of value. Monday had appeared weeks earlier pushing his trolley, containing all his worldly possession, just another refugee from Zims' continuing implosion. Monday, he knew, spoke Shona first and English a poorer second language, typical of some-one from a rural Zimbabwe village? Monday was proud and didn't want his bin rummaging acknowledged, even though it was his survival route.

Turning into the drive of his house, he could see house lights and knew Suzy would be waiting inside for him. Slowly the drive gate opened, silently as far as he could hear, but he added the job of greasing the gate track to his week-end jobs. When the car was fully on the drive, he thumbed the electronic garage door opener and awaited for the door to open fully. Each evening, he dutifully followed the same routine, drive gates closed first, then garage door, believing that that system gave no chance for *skellums* to infiltrate his private space. He did this dutifully, driven by the warnings from his ex-Military Intelligence buddies, the actions now so automatic that he no longer noticed.

Once the door was three quarters open and high enough to admit the car he started forward, his mind already at home, so he didn't notice the movement in the deep shadows at the corner of the drive. It was only when he opened the car door and was dragged out of the driving seat ands thrown roughly to the concrete floor that he began to realise that his life had taken a considerable turn for the worse. He was wedged tightly between the car and wall, lying almost face down with his right arm trapped under him. When he turned his head to see what was happening, he saw, at uncomfortably close quarters, the business end of an AK 47. He froze. At least two muggers were there, they shouted to each other and in all the confusion, he caught the Shona word '*maningi*' (white man) and he was immediately back to his Rhodesian war days.

They were excited and high on adrenaline and dagga, loud and victorious. That was their down fall. Suzy had seen his car lights sweep onto their drive and was waiting for him to walk into the house through the garage door. When she heard the shouting coming from the garage her first reaction was to hit the panic button and set off the external siren, which she did.

Suddenly, the whole area was drenched in an ear-piercing blast of sound so painful that the muggers automatically covered their ears and forgot about him and his car. They turned and ran up the drive, running through the pools of darkness to get away, but not before one let off a burst of fire aimed at silencing the siren. Green tracer bullets were sprayed around, none going near the siren, whilst two slammed into the rear garage wall, dropping, hot and burning, onto the bare neck of the man on the floor.

At that time, garage door muggings were unusual in Durbanville, but the trend had arrived in the 'Cape from Johannesburg as the ADT investigator told him when he responded to the emergency. A small, well organised armed ADT team were soon at the house before going off to check the locality for the muggers. Although shaken and with an evil red burn on his neck from a spent bullet, he could tell them very little. They soon established that the muggers were almost certainly newly arrived illegal immigrants, who had lighted on this usually safe part of Durbanville as a 'soft touch', ripe for robbery.

When they eventually arrived, the SAP said much the same thing and seemed happy to let ADT deal with things. Once back in the house, he had to concentrate on stopping his hands shaking. 'Stupid', he thought to himself, 'I ought to be used to confrontations with AK's after my time in the bush', but no matter how he tried to rationalise that nights' events, he knew that he had been scared. Badly scared! Mortally scared in fact, more scared than he ever had been during the entire bush war! Sue was calm, much calmer than he was, but what he couldn't overcome was the sheer bloody terror and helplessness that had gripped him there in the garage, his feeling of total helplessness. Even his worst times during the war had not been as bad as that, he had had been armed, prepared, able and capable of defending himself.

Eventually the evening had returned to normal, the police had gone, the neighbours departed and the ADT crew officially 'off premises', he tried to relax. Even after the second whisky he felt tense, certainly, less tense than earlier, but still 'tight'. Once the bedroom lights were off, he felt his body begin to tense again. Suzy, next to him in bed, was warm and soft and soon asleep, but he found himself listening to every sound, unable to sleep. Every time he closed his eyes, the first image projected on his eye lids was that of the black eye of the AK barrel staring straight down into his eyes.

Eventually he fell asleep, a disturbed sleep full of gun flashes, Rhodesian smells and battle noises. He was restless all night tossing and turning, frequently breaking into a sweat. Suzy slept better, but she was still disturbed and woken regularly by his sudden jumpy awakenings. In the morning both were still tired and irritable. He was reluctant to leave home go to work, but eventually he forced himself out. Just driving his car away from home felt to him like leaving his security behind and that he was entering a world far less safe than it had been yesterday.

On his way to work, there was Monday scavenging in the bins again, he noticed but paid no attention. Walking into his office he found it unchanged from the previous night, the work still waiting for him in the order in which he left it. He sat down at his desk pulled some files towards him, but he couldn't concentrate on them. Instead he spent time checking and re-checking his physical security.

'Why am I so edgy?', he thought to himself. It was after lunch that he really began to pay attention to his work, he had been distracted the whole day long. It was only as he left for home that evening that the fear began to return. As he got closer home his a level of worry increased until it was taking all his time simply to drive. Tonight, he had left work early, deliberately to get home before dark.

He didn't drive straight onto his drive, but drove around the area looking for people out of place, strange faces that he did not know. He saw only Monday, but he was part of the scenery, so he drove back to his drive, opened the gate and drove into his garage. He realised that his hands were sweaty, gripping the steering wheel hard and his heart beating fast. Once a garage door locked down and he was home again did he began to relax, his pulse rate come down and a feeling of safety began to wash over him. He was still edgy, however, and Suzy was aware of it.

"I've never known you like this before, what happened to the big, brave soldier boy that I knew and loved?" Susie asked him.

"Don't worry, I'll get over it." he said. "Worse things happen at sea, it will pass!"

"It seems to be you who has the problem, your 'talking therapy' seems to have failed, just when you needed it most!"

"I've got worries . . . ." he began, but that was as far as he got.

"You astonish me" she replied, "You are supposed to protect us, not us protect you! We are your family, you are cracking up, so how can we be safe?"

"This has been on my mind all day, I think we have to move to a safer area."

"No! You move somewhere else until you've got everything together, then I'll decided when it's safe for you come home. You are not the man I married, you're becoming a brandy swilling whimp. If you want us back you will have to get your head together! You were difficult before, but now you are impossible!" Suzy told him in no uncertain terms.

Within a day, he had moved into the back room at his office. His Johannesburg office worked as normal, his associates could run that part, but they were not to know that he had taken up residence in the office This frantic burst of activity did not reduce the nightmares or the paranoia, but l at least, it took his mind off his current position. He phoned Suzy every night and told her what he had achieved it during the day, she was sympathetic, but wouldn't move to invite him back home until she was sure that he wasn't totally cracking up. The new situation calmed him and he began to sleep more regularly and with more sleep came a reduction in stress; his life was improving. His drinking, only ever a safety valve, eased off, he no longer needed to be three quarters drunk to go to sleep. He was working better and even accepted an invitation to a night out with some of his ex-Intelligence pals.

The evening was going well, with copious quantities of 'Castle' being poured down parched throats, when he felt a tap on the shoulder,. Looking around, he saw a small group of ex-Special Branch colleagues standing nearby and the ex-Inspector inclined his head to ask him to join them. Standing with this serious, quiet group in the midst of the barely contained mayhem of a military re-union was like walking into a commercial freezer. The atmosphere around the group was icy and deadly serious, so distinct from the rest of the room that every-one read the atmosphere and avoided them. As he joined the icy atmosphere his ex-CO looked at him with those sharp eyes he remembered so well and told him simply, 'Mugabe's up to his tricks again and he appears set on paying off old debts! You know, of course, that ZANU-PF are seizing all the illegally mined Zim diamonds that they can get? Quite simply, that is how they are funding these attacks. Blood diamonds or not, there are enough people who will take diamonds at the right price without asking questions. Business, as you know, says that it is amoral, *'business is business'*, but actually it is quite immoral in the way profits are all that matter!'

Craig could only nod his head in resigned agreement, wondering just how many times had he unhesitatingly 'gone for the throat' to seal a business deal, so he could only accept the generality and quiet reproach of that statement.

"Look, old chap", what happened to you is so far out of the normal run of things that we think that you should be worried. Very worried!"

By the end of the evening Craig had been fully briefed on everything that the Intelligence service veterans had learned and how the illegally mined diamonds had given the regime a new lease of heart.

"We have good intelligence that tells us of a Canadian that has smuggled out US$ 100 millions' worth of diamonds out to buy a mining house in Canada. How much ZANU-PF are making from those same diamond fields is anyones guess! Just like the old days again!"

In the aftermath of the soccer world cup Xhosa xenophobia had once again reasserted itself. Zimbabwean refugees who had been welcomed into South Africa to escape the devastation and persecution home had suddenly become *persona non grata*. Their new homes suddenly turned against them when the ANC's pro-Mugabe faction instituted their version of *chidudu* (the Terror) against the immigrants. Divisions between the ANC in government and the local township ANC structures meant that immigrants were blamed for all social ills. Officially, the ANC gave sanctuary to refugees from Zimbabwe, although personally supporting Mugabe's anti-white policies, turning many blind eyes to ZANU-PF's abuses of South African hospitality. That thirty year old scores were being settled meant nothing to the ANC, just that their African revolutionary hero was asserting his authority in true communist style.

Car-jackings, which is how the attack on Craig had been classified, were vaguely blamed on 'criminals and illegal immigrants', although no formal government action ever seemed to happen. Through his contacts with the Intelligence community veterans Craig knew that he had been fortunate. Until more control of the streets fell into the SA polices hands, ZANU-PF would continue to enjoy some level of covert security.

Private security companies and neighbourhood groups were beginning to gel together to offer increased domestic safety, but how long would it take? That, in a nut-shell, was Craigs' dilemma. Until that crucial question was answered by government action, the initiative would remain firmly with the criminal classes.

Chapter 31

Cruising around.

Zuma, so recently the S.A. Communist Partys' choice as 'mouldable' president had suddenly shown a surprising resistance to the democratic deformation expected of him by his communist allies. His occasional bursts of pragmatism surprised many and enraged the Communist apparatchiks, who seemed to expect total loyalty and deference to their party line. Formally, Zuma was still in the pocket of the communists, but his independence had come increasingly to the fore with the increase in illegal Zimbabwean immigration and the formal refusal to give the illegals any formal amnesty. Zuma, himself, was threatened both directly and indirectly by his one time accolytes, but at times like those, he seemed to draw closer to his mass of supporters in the townships throughout the land. After all their years of misrule and self enrichment, some of the ANC bigwigs remained close enough to their roots to read the waves of distrust that had begun rising from the townships like a miasma of foul air.

Labour troubles, as always, began the problem. Illiterate South Africans loosing out in the township struggle for what few jobs there were looked for a target to blame for their problems and the presence of better educated foreigners was the obvious one. Of all the immigrants, illegal or otherwise, the Zimbabweans formed a large majority and thus they became the principle recipients of hatred. Being English speakers simply added to the Zimbabweans' worries, it became yet another division between them and their often unwilling South African hosts.

Problem started in a small way, with the shop-keepers being driven away and their food stocks stolen by the mob, but problems escalated. Higher literacy rates amongst the Zimbabweans meant that they could better press their cases with what authorities there were. Inevitably, the trades unions got involved and faced a severe dichotomy. Locally, their support for the militants under the creed of South African jobs for South Africans ran counter to the anti-discrimination stance held by their nation authorities, so attempts were made to smooth out all the troubles. Anger was such that they couldn't be smoothed over, so now the government found its' self on the horns of a dilemma. From the ANC's arrogant opinion that it would never be unpopular or out of power, the very real spectre that the tri-partite alliance would split apart suddenly reared its head.

As in all dictatorships, efforts were put into identifying those who could bear the blame and the Zimbabwean immigrants just happened to be in the wrong place at the time. In contrast with the long time ANC tacit support of Mugabe, as expounded by Mbeki, his regime and its foibles, the growing discontent in the townships was growing too big to ignore, so something had to be done.

As a populist measure, governmental focus shifted onto the plight of the Zimbabwean refugees, especially the illegal ones, living and working in South Africa. Visa restrictions were demanded and granted by a panicking Government, but how was this to help? Many of the illegals didn't have a passport, most had no paperwork what so ever. Many worked for a daily wage, cash in hand, and were unknown to the formal system, so the visa requirement was just a face saving sop to the trouble-makers. Despite his attempts to smooth over problems, Zuma's rule was challenged. The very people, who during the presidential selection process, had sworn 'to kill for Zuma' rapidly turned into his most severe critrics. Direct challenges to his rule as President and threats of 'No second term' started simultaneously with those one time supporters pressing their potential candidacy. In all this, the fate of the Zimbabwean immigrants wandered out of the publics' conscious, so that when the announcement came that Zimbabweans would be repatriated despite the problems in Zimbabwe, many were happy.

Craig was not unhappy about the proposed crack-down, but he had made his own contingency plans, plans for Suzy and himself only. He found himself, once more, thinking like a military intelligence officer. Planning was everything, that he knew! That his home was known was now his greatest weakness and although they both loved their large, somewhat rambling home it was obvious that they would have to leave it behind and move away. Back, unwillingly, in military thinking mode, he decided to consult his most trusted veteran friends. All of them were acutely aware of how one rotten apple in the senior officer corps had betrayed not only them, the military, but the whole country to ZANLA. Despite all the young men on both sides sacrificed to the ego of uncompromising politicians of all hues, one white senior officer sold them all out for personal priority. Still smarting from that betrayal, although thirty years ago, meant that Craigs' select group was a very tight and close group to whom secrecy meant something. He arrived at one meeting to find his host with tears in his eyes, when asked what was wrong, all that happened was for the volume on the music player to be turned up and the instruction to listen given.

"The song is Brothers in Arms", he was told, "written about the brotherhood of the troops fighting in Vietnam and Cambodia, it appeared in 1981, but I find it more applicable to my time in the Central Highlands and the Monomatopas. I'm sorry but whenever that song comes up, I'm back in the bush war and what worries me is that I really enjoyed the comradeship! I admit to feeling shit scared some of the time and bored most of the rest, but, in retrospect, I'm glad for it!" As he listened, Craig heard words reflecting the close bonds between combat soldiers and then thought "If you haven't been there, you'll never know." Taking the CD from the player, snapping it back in the case, it was tossed into Craigs' hands with the instruction to play it when he needed to be reminded of their Great Days.

"We know that Mugabe is becoming to be a puppet of the ZANU-PF ruling group, but a useful puppet and the diamond money is giving them new heart. Morgan Tshangeri and the MDC will begin to feel the full weight of ZANU-PF's hatred as the elections get closer. And so will all other 'enemies'! Get away and vanish for a time for both your and Suzannes' protection!"

There were no permanent ties that bound Craig and Sue to the town & that they had to sever, the boys had long since gone their own way, so just their friends from various phases of life remained. Their plan was simple, but they knew the management of it would be crucial, put simply, they both had to vanish and leave the country. Through close and trusted contacts their Durbanville house was sold. Sue, who had put so much of her love into their home over so long a time, was naturally heartbroken and wept all through the packing. Those same trusted contacts had organised things well. All the funds from the house sale were transferred to a UK bank account to reinforce the impression that Craig and Susan had 'taken the high road' to Europe and that Craig had finally turned his back on Africa.

They took a cruise liner, notionally to the UK, but trans-shipped in Walvis Bay, holidayed in Namibia for a month before driving south, back to the Western Cape, where they moved into a house in Mostertdrift in Stellenbosch. His Durbanville consultancy business, Craig Burgoyne Projects (Cape), went as a going concern to the group running his earlier operation in Johannesburg; to maintain the fiction of their emigration, all his income from the consultancy was sent to the same UK bank, from which they could both access the money electronically.

Whilst these changes in Craig and Susans' life were in progress, the status of Zimbabweans in South Africa altered radically. Even Mugabes minions were negatively affected. CIO had previously taken the chance of open borders to send ZANU-PF killer squads into the republic to 'sort out' Zimbabwes' enemies. Their work started, as the attempt on Craig demonstrated, but was cut short by the potential township uprisings which threatened the very stability of the A.N.C. tri-partite alliance.

A quite unintended outcome of Zumas' struggle to retain power within the ruling party was to expose many of the CIO 'illegals', most of whom were deported back to their ravished homeland with no further chance of completing their mission. During this unintentional spell of reduced Zimbabwean influence, Craig and Sue bought the Mostertdrift house, using money drawn from the U.K. account, which accidentally, but providentially, marked them as UK retirees, emigrating to a warmer climate. Their history having been lost to immediate, simple perception, all they had to do was to begin acting as retired people and remain out of public knowledge. The Zimbabwe threat had not gone away, but weakened so far as to be of no realistic concern.

The area in which they settled was Mostertdrift, full of retired senior academics who enjoyed a generally relaxed life style. They had found an older house on Reygerstraat, a quiet street. Their house was bought from the estate of the (now dead) previous owner and had become a little run down because the previous owner had aged too comfortably within his house. Over time, Craigs' P.T.S.D. faded away to allow them both to enjoy the life style that they had for so long wanted. Sue continued as the home builder, cooking and baking as she wanted. Furnishing their 'new' old house took time and meant that both developed an interest in, and knowledge of, antique furniture, their circle of friends widening both smoothly and steadily over time.

No sooner had they settled into their new abode in Stellenbosch than events within Mugabes' inner circle rendered their covert move an excessive reaction. Spread throughout the news papers on three continents was the story that Grace Mugabe was having an affair with Gideon Gomo, one of 'uncle Bob's' most loyal followers. With elections due within two years and international attention beginning to re-focus on southern Africa and Zimbabwe in particular, the ZANU-PF regime decided to hunker down and brazen out the forthcoming storm. Confusion was further stirred when an unofficial news report announced Mugabes' death. Simultaneously, celebrations prematurely began outside Zimbabwe's borders whilst within their borders, high level party bosses shuffled around, beginning the power struggle to fill Bobs shoes. All to prematurely! The old tyrant was still alive and still attached to Grace and still whielding the rod of power within his personal fiefdom, which most certainly included the Marange eastern diamond fields; the income from which financed Grace Mugabes international shopping sprees!

Where most of the diamonds had been smuggled out of Marange through Mozambique, netting the illegal miners some money, ZANU-PF's forced nationalisation deprived the miners of their income overnight, their freedom and in many cases, their lives. It was conservatively estimated that the income generated from the Marange diamond field fattened ZANU-PF's coffers by about one billion U.S. dollars per year. Fortunately 'blood diamonds' mined in the battle-fields in the D.R.C. had alerted the world to the exploitation of 'Conflict Diamonds'. Any hint of 'conflict diamond' status ensured that any conversion into hard currency was exceedingly difficult, slow and closely scrutinised.

All expectations that ZANU-PF would immediately re-fund offensive operations proved unfounded. Too much money would be needed to restabilise the economy ravaged by two decades of flagrant misrule; pragmatic decisions had to be made. Things went ominously quiet. Official news was not released, but unofficially the pressure eased a little off the democracy movement and all previously identified 'enemies of the state', whilst Mugabe, once again, violently validated his reign on his personal enemies within the borders of Zimbabwe. Within the southern African region, many people took a deep breath, simply awaiting the unleashing of Mugabe's fury, thankful for this shift of focus. Having bigger fish to fry to maintain his rule, the CIO were redeployed internally to stifle all the current internal dissention and historical problems were consigned to the dusty recesses of unachievable practicalities and forgotten.

This, of course, was never formally announced; How could it be? The attacks on the 'enemies of state', as defined by ZANU-PF (i.e. any perceived opposition to ZANU-PF rule) had never FORMALLY been promulgated. Nevertheless, it had happened as the ruminations of a despot. Now the despot was facing his most severe challenge on his home turf and nothing else mattered! Only over the years would the reduced pressure that Craig and people like him had endured since the establishment of Mugabes cursed misrule become noticeable.

In retrospect, the change happened when the worlds' interest re-focussed on the forthcoming election, which ZANU-PF had to steal once more, to continue their great tradition of complete Zimbabwean control. Stealing from the cynical Western comment about African elections (African Democracy; vote early, vote often!) Mugabe's election machine applied that comment verbatim.

That ZANU-PF were intent on stealing the election was proven when the Zimbabwe voting lists were released. In a nation where the life expectancy has fallen to 38years, Zimbabwe suddenly registered the worlds' largest number of centenarian voters. All had one or other of two birthdates and all were 106 years old, but voting for the first time. It appeared that Mugabes' Zimbabwe had, overnight, become the African geriatric idyll! Such cynical and contemptuous actions lost the sympathy of the world which, in 1980, had been sympathetic and hopeful as Zimbabwe emerged from the colonial era, but by 2011, could only condemn the brutal and criminal regime that now occupied Zimbabwe. Mugabes' shadow continues to fall over all of post colonial Africa, but is weakening in areas. South of the Limpopo, Mugabes' aura hypnotised the black racists within the ruling party. Their admiration was more associated with self-aggrandisement and personal power than the liberation theology aimed to benefit the dispossessed 'masses'. 2011 was a watershed year on the Africa continent. In Arab north Africa, when the street people said 'enough' and revolted against corrupt and oppressive leaders, the established power block fell. Successively each leader tumbled, some more gently than others, the people achieved political freedom and open democracy; a point not lost on sharp eyed observers at the southern tip of the continent. Freedoms' wave may take time to pass through sub-Saharan Africa, but that journey has now begun.